PROMISES
IN THE
DARK

BOOKS BY D.K. HOOD

Don't Tell a Soul
Bring Me Flowers
Follow Me Home
The Crying Season
Where Angels Fear
Whisper in the Night
Break the Silence
Her Broken Wings
Her Shallow Grave

D.K. HOOD

PROMISES IN THE DARK

Bookouture

Published by Bookouture in 2020

An imprint of Storyfire Ltd.
Carmelite House
50 Victoria Embankment
London EC4Y 0DZ

www.bookouture.com

ISBN: 978-1-83888-853-4
eBook ISBN: 978-1-83888-852-7

To my wonderful readers, with thanks and appreciation for your support.

PROLOGUE

"You. Get out here. Now!"

Startled, Sophie Wood dropped her phone and gaped at the man holding a gun to her father's head. She shot up from the bed, alarmed by her father's bruised face and red eyes. "Daddy what's happening?"

"Do what the man says, Sophie." He didn't meet her gaze and his hands shook.

"Yeah, do what the nice man says, Sophie." Dark brown eyes peered through the skull-like holes of a balaclava. The man dressed in black slid his attention to her little sister. "You too. Go down to the kitchen and wait with your mom. Better run before I spray the wall with Daddy's brains."

Sophie's heart raced in terror but one look at Jody's wide eyes and trembling bottom lip gave her courage. She needed to protect her sister. Taking a firm hold of Jody's hand, she hurried into the hallway. The man shoved her dad and they followed close behind but her dad was stumbling as if deliberately slowing him down. Maybe he wanted to give them time to escape? She scanned the family room as they descended the stairs, but the closed front door had the deadbolts in place. How had the man gotten inside the house? Her dad was so careful about locking up at night. Beside her Jody sobbed out a wail and broke away from her. The little girl ran ahead and then stopped dead at the kitchen door.

"Mommy?" Jody took a step back and looked up at Sophie, her eyes wet with tears. "Is Mommy okay?"

Fear gripped her stomach as she peered around the door. Sitting at the table tied to a chair, her mother didn't respond to Jody's cries. Her head hung on her chest and a constant stream of blood dripped from her nose to her ripped dress. Heart thumping like a big bass drum, Sophie swallowed hard and then towing Jody behind her, ran for the backdoor. Frantically, she fumbled with the lock but then the man's voice came from behind her. He was calm and in control and gave orders with no emotion as if he was ordering takeout.

"I'll shoot your daddy and then your mama if you don't come and sit down. I'm leaving as soon as y'all behave yourselves." The man thrust her father into a chair and aimed at the back of his head. "I won't stay to keep you company but I'd like to." He pressed the muzzle of the gun hard into her father's head. "Ain't that right, Daddy?"

"You have what you came for, now leave us alone." Her father's eyes flashed with anger. "If you touch my girls, I'll—"

As if in slow motion, Sophie stared as the man raised the weapon and brought it down in a sickening crack across the back of her father's skull. Finding it hard to breathe, she pushed Jody behind her. "Leave him alone."

"Or you'll do what? There isn't a darn thing you can do, princess. Best you do as you're told." The man used the gun to beckon her. "Come here and tie your daddy to the chair. Use the zip-ties your mama kindly supplied for me." He waited for her to comply. "Good, now do the same to your sister." He leaned against the counter and folded his arms across his chest but he still had a hold of the gun. "That was easy and see, no one got hurt."

Sophie stared at him trying to remember everything about him, how tall, his build and eye color. She kept running the description through her mind to tell the sheriff. *White, as tall as Daddy, strong, brown eyes.* She started when he banged on the table and lifted her gaze to him. "What else do you want me to do?"

"Set the table." He aimed the pistol at her. "Do it nice like when someone is coming to dinner."

Sophie cast her eyes over her unconscious parents and then glanced at her sister, who sobbed gently. She eyed the carving knives and wanted to grab one but then he'd shoot her father. In silence, she collected plates and set the table. She rested a hand on her sister's shoulder. "Hush now, Jody, it will be okay. He'll be going soon."

"She's telling you the truth. I'm leaving." The man bent close to Sophie and sniffed her. "You smell all fresh from the shower. Now turn around and I'll tie your hands." He thrust the pistol into the waistband of his jeans, pushed her hard against the wall, and dragged her arms behind her.

She struggled against him. "No!"

"Do you want me to hurt you?" His breath brushed her cheek. "Was that a 'yes'?"

Pain seared into her back just below the ribs taking her breath away. White spots danced before her eyes from the shock of the blow, her knees buckled and she gasped in air. "Don't hit me. I won't fight you."

"Good." He tied her ankles together and then covered her mouth with duct tape. "Sit there and don't move." He went to the backdoor and returned with a bag and a can of gas.

Too scared to breathe, she watched him as he shoved the bag into the family room, opened the gas can, sniffed it, and then placed it on the floor and kicked it over. Fumes filled the room as the gas ran over the tiles. She stared at her sister's crumpled face, wanting to tell her it was okay. She'd do whatever he wanted and he'd leave them alone.

"Stand up." He grabbed her arm. "Be good and I'll walk out of here."

In one swift movement, he had her over his shoulder. Air rushed out of her nose as his bones pressed into her stomach. She wriggled to no avail. He had her in a vice-like grip. *Where is he taking me?* Her stomach ached and she tried to scream as he ran outside but couldn't suck in enough air. The next moment he'd dumped her face down on the dusty back seat of a car. The vehicle sagged as he climbed in and the next moment they sped away. She could hear him counting as they bounced along the uneven dirt road.

Terror rushed over her and with her face pressed into the smelly fabric of the back seat, she fought against the zip-ties binding her hand and foot. Tears streamed down her face but she had to stay calm. The tape covering her mouth made it difficult to breathe and if her nose blocked, she'd suffocate. As the car sped into the night, she pushed onto her knees and peered at the house getting smaller by the second. An almighty explosion ripped through the night and a mushroom of orange flames engulfed her home. Behind the gag, she screamed in horror. He'd killed them all.

CHAPTER ONE

Black Rock Falls

Wednesday

Deputy Dave Kane stared out the windshield of his truck to watch the vehicles go by on Stanton Road, and wondered how he'd become a traffic cop. His previous employment as a bodyguard to POTUS had ended after he'd been involved in a terrorist's car bomb attack resulting in the death of his wife, Annie. He'd had a good career in special forces. As a sniper and one-man killing machine, he'd been perfect to protect POTUS but to guard him from terrorists, intent on revenge, the powers that be informed the world he'd died and even buried an empty coffin beside his wife. He'd arrived in Black Rock Falls with a metal plate in his head, a new face and identity, and with the position of Deputy to Sheriff Jenna Alton, an ex-DEA Agent with a secret past. That was some years ago now and he had to admit, he usually enjoyed his work. The murders in Black Rock Falls since his arrival had been horrendous but they'd caught all the perpetrators. However, the last action he'd seen had been before Christmas and now it was June. Tourists had started to flock to the many attractions in the county and everyone was behaving themselves. It seemed the mountains had given a huge sigh of relief as the warm rush of summer had arrived without a psychopath in sight.

He stared into the forest. In June it changed once more from dark and foreboding to light and inviting. Beams of sunshine pierced the darkness to reveal flowers sprinkling the trails with color. The cool wind blowing from the mountains had the familiar pine scent he'd grown to enjoy. Riding the trails in summer, fishing, and just taking it easy was his recipe for a long life. His thoughts of a weekend in the forest shattered as the radio crackled. It was Deputy Jake Rowley, who was parked a half mile or so along Stanton.

"Older style, blue Ford sedan, heading your way doing ninety."

Kane pressed his mic. "Copy." He flicked on his flashers and pulled out of the trees.

As the sedan flashed by, he gave chase and in no time the driver pulled over. Sliding out of his truck, Kane walked slowly to the vehicle, one hand resting on his Glock. He made out the reflection of the driver in the side mirror. He estimated the young man with messy blond hair was around eighteen. He made a winding down signal with his fingers and the window buzzed down. "License and registration. Do you know we clocked you doing ninety? Once you hit the 'Welcome to Black Rock Falls' sign it clearly states the speed limit is sixty."

"I must have missed it." The young man leaned over to take something from the glovebox.

Cautious, Kane slid out his weapon—being shot in the face wasn't in his schedule for today. When the young man handed him the paperwork, he stared at the image of an elderly woman with white hair. "Keep your hands where I can see them and get out of the vehicle."

When the young man climbed out, Kane took his arm and walked him to the back of the sedan. He pressed his mic. "I need you to run a plate for me." He gave the details.

"No need. I put a BOLO out on that vehicle, it went missing on Sunday. Owned by Mrs. Dotty Grace, an elderly woman. She lives in that

old place beside the Triple Z Bar." Rowley cleared his throat. *"I filed it just before we left this morning. I'm sorry I didn't bring you up to date."*

"Copy." Kane sighed. "I've apprehended a suspect in charge of the stolen vehicle. Come and get him and throw him in the cells. I'll deal with him when I get there. I need to arrange a tow truck for the vehicle." He turned to the guy and read him his rights. "What's your name?"

"Dotty Grace." The young man sneered. "What, can't you read?"

Kane cuffed him and patted him down. "Well unless you've changed sex and time traveled, you'd better come up with a name. I'm arresting you for theft of a motor vehicle."

"Dotty Grace, man. Are you deaf or something?" The young man looked at him over one shoulder.

Kane smiled. "Well, Dotty, maybe you'll change your mind when you meet our sheriff."

After dispatching his prisoner and waiting for the tow truck, Kane followed it to the Black Rock Falls impound yard. He arrived back at the office at noon and after filing a report, strolled into Sheriff Jenna Alton's office. "I'm back from another inspiring morning. Are there any exciting cases for us to solve today?"

"Nope, it's as quiet as the library here today." Jenna rubbed her temples. "Just me and the books."

Kane dropped into a chair. His bloodhound, Duke came into the room, his claws tapping on the tile. He climbed into the basket beside Jenna's desk, did three circles, and sat down with a sigh of contentment. Kane turned his attention back to Jenna. "I booked five people speeding and I want to charge a man for theft of a motor vehicle. Problem is, he won't give his name, which makes filing the paperwork difficult."

"Has he lawyered up?" Jenna lifted her gaze from a stack of files and pushed her raven hair behind one ear.

"Nope. He insists he is a seventy-five-year-old woman by the name of Dotty Grace." Kane smiled at her. "That's all he said apart from insulting my intelligence."

"I'll go speak to him later." Jenna stretched and yawned. "I'll ask Rowley to run his prints. We'll leave him to cool his heels in the cells until after lunch. Maybe then he'll be more cooperative."

Kane removed his black Stetson and ran his fingers over the rim. "You know, I don't have the patience to be a traffic cop." He chuckled. "The problem is they all pull over when I hit the siren and I don't get to chase them down. It's no fun at all. Can't we hire a few rookies to do the grunt work?"

"I'll swap you. I'd prefer sitting outside than dealing with the mayor's office any day." Jenna waved at the paperwork on her desk. "This is the inventory of everything here, for our insurance. I have to get builders in to increase the size of our evidence room because of the amount of work we've had over the last few years." She pushed a set of plans across the table to him. "This is what the architect suggests. It's a two-story extension, which will mean a bigger office for me and then you and Rowley will get this room. The evidence lock-up will be moved upstairs in a secured area along with our locker rooms. If we get the rookies I've requested, they can work out in the main office."

Kane scanned the files. "Apart from Rowley's wedding, it's the most thrilling thing that's happened here in the last six months."

"Now that was a day or should I say a week to remember." Jenna laughed. "I couldn't believe it when the bride arrived in the cabin of a snowplow. Sandy wasn't going to allow anything to spoil her day."

"Yeah, of course, a blizzard had to hit that afternoon." Kane met her gaze. "Thanks to your wedding planner skills, you had everyone except the bride holed up at the Cattleman's Hotel and our horses boarded in town. I'm still not sure why she insisted on remaining at home with her parents."

"It was because she lived close by but nothing would've happened if you hadn't arrived in the Beast with Father Derry." Jenna beamed at him. "It must have been a terrifying trip."

Kane chuckled. "Nah, we were fine. Mind you, I don't figure Rowley or Sandy really wanted us and their folks around for the first three days of their honeymoon."

"Well, you sure didn't get bored, playing cards and pool with the other guys." Jenna rolled her eyes.

"As best man, I had to keep them occupied." He grinned at her. "They all enjoyed themselves."

"They sure did." Jenna smiled. "When the blizzard was over, no one wanted to leave." She sighed. "If you're bored, you can help me take inventory in the evidence room."

"That's non-essential and everything is listed as it arrives." Kane linked his fingers behind his head and stared at the ceiling. "So, this is what we've come to? From special agents to desk jockeys. This is what Maggie usually handles and you have a couple of interns helping her in the office. Why are you doing this, Jenna?"

"Oh, well I did hand out a fine to a man who allowed his dog to foul the footpath this morning. That was the highlight of my day." She collected the papers, tapped them into neat piles, and placed them inside folders. "Maybe a foot patrol would be more interesting."

"Oh, there was something." Kane's attention followed her across the room as she filed the folders. "The fire chief went by, lights and sirens about ten minutes ago. I gave the forest warden a call to ask if he knew about any fires. He said they'd seen smoke out toward Louan."

"Hmm." Jenna leaned against the filing cabinet and folded her arms. "They have volunteer fire fighters in Louan. It must have been a housefire and they needed him to verify the cause for insurance. If it's anything to do with us, I'm sure he'll let us know." She straightened.

"I need a break and something to eat. We could stop by Aunt Betty's Café. Are you hungry?"

Kane stood. His stomach had been complaining for an hour or so. "I thought you'd never ask." He pushed his hat on his head. "I'm sure the town won't be invaded with Hell Hounds while we're out of the office."

"There you go again, tempting fate." Jenna took her weapon out of the desk drawer and holstered it.

"Oh, come on, Jenna." Kane grinned at her. "I don't want a psychopath murdering people any more than you do but you have to admit, a nice drug bust, cattle rustling, or a bank hold up would break the monotony."

"I figure an invasion by aliens would be more interesting." Jenna chuckled and headed for the door. "Can you imagine what Wolfe would do with alien technology?"

Kane whistled Duke and followed her. "Oh, yeah. He'd be reverse engineering everything." He laughed. "But with our luck the aliens won't be little green men, they'll be ax wielding psychopaths."

CHAPTER TWO

Snakeskin Gully

FBI Special Agent and behavioral analyst Jo Wells picked up the phone in her office. "Agent Wells."

"Agent Wells, this is Tom Crenshaw. I'm the sheriff out of Louan, we had ourselves an explosion last night. The fire department was first on scene and found a mess of bodies. I notified the ME out of Black Rock Falls, Shane Wolfe. He arrived with his team and has ruled the explosion as homicide. He mentioned you have an explosives expert and I should bring you in on the case. We need someone to search for secondary devices before we can enter the premises."

Jo made a few notes. "Yes, we have an explosives expert on our team. Give me the coordinates and names of the victims."

"I can give you the name of the person who owns the property but the ME hasn't identified anyone. No one has been allowed to step foot inside the house."

"Okay, that's good. Give me the property owner's name." Jo took down the details and then ran a list of things to ask the man through her head. "Is there a place to set down a chopper close by?"

"Yes, ma'am. There's grassland adjacent to the ranch house. I'll lay down some flares close to your ETA."

"That's great, can you hold for one minute, Sheriff?" Jo muted the call and turned to ex-navy seal and one of the best crime scene investigators she'd ever known, Agent Ty Carter. "We have a case.

Explosion, multiple victims, out of Louan. That's north of Black Rock Falls, in a little place called Aspen Grove. What's our ETA?"

"I refueled yesterday and she's ready to go." Ty ran his hand through his shaggy blond hair, dropped his cowboy boots to the floor, and smiled around a toothpick. "How long will it take for you to be ready? I'll need time for a preflight check and packing our gear." He gave her a slow smile and indicated to a Doberman with a coat like silk, ears pricked and waiting for orders. "The bomb squad is always ready."

Exasperated by his casual approach to everything, Jo sighed and met his amused green gaze with as much tolerance as possible. "I have a bag packed. I can leave in ten minutes. I just need to call home and inform Clara I'll be away for a couple of days. I'll call Jaime after school." She jotted down the info again and handed it to Bobby Kalo, the FBI's computer whizz kid. "I want everything you can find on this man and if he lives at the property. If he rents it, I want to know the name of the tenant."

"You got it." Kalo went to work.

"Okay, we're set." Carter closed his computer. He stood and stretched his lean body before ambling over to a locker. "ETA eleven hundred hours."

Jo unmuted the phone. "Thank you for holding, Sheriff." She glanced at the clock. "We'll be there by eleven."

"Thank you kindly, ma'am. The ME wants to speak to you." There was a rustling as the phone changed hands.

"Hi, Jo, it's Shane."

The image of Shane Wolfe, a six-three blond-haired man built like a Viking marauder, drifted into Jo's mind. In his early forties, Shane worked as the ME for most of the local counties around Black Rock Falls, Montana. He was a good friend, who'd raised his three girls after nursing his late wife through her battle with cancer. Not only a great ME, Shane was also an IT specialist and spent most of his time assisting Sheriff Jenna Alton and Deputy Dave Kane with murder cases at his base in Black Rock Falls. "Hi Shane, what have we got?"

"I thought maybe a gas explosion but I'm not sure. It smells like C-4 and we need a bomb squad to clear the area before we remove the bodies. I don't have time to wait for someone from Helena. I called out the fire chief from Black Rock Falls and he's standing by to examine the area once it's cleared for explosives." Wolfe paused a beat. *"It's a homicide. I can see the remains of zip-ties on one of the victims. Can you handle the case?"*

"That's what we're here for, our field office is available to all who need us." Jo pushed to her feet and headed for her locker. "We'll be there by eleven. Kalo is doing a background check on the property owner. We're leaving now."

"Okay, catch you later." Wolfe disconnected.

After making a call to Clara, her daughter Jaime's nanny, Jo picked up her duffle and headed out the door. She took the elevator to the roof and handed Carter her bag. He'd packed everything they needed in the chopper, including their crime scene kits, Kevlar vests, extra weapons, and a forty-pound bag of dog food. His dog, Zorro—their bomb squad—sat on a back seat in his harness. "Is that everything we need?"

"Yeah, I can refuel in Black Rock Falls." Carter moved his toothpick from one side of his mouth to the other and pulled down the rim of his Stetson. "We'll be able to go by and see Jenna and Kane, maybe grab a meal when we're done?"

Jo smiled. "That would be nice. Let's hope we get this case wrapped up fast. I have no idea what experience the Louan sheriff has in arson cases. We might end up completing the entire investigation alone." She slid on her sunglasses. "At least we're coming into summer. I'm over freezing my butt off in the mountains."

CHAPTER THREE

Although the sobering fact of visiting another crime scene was ever constant in Jo's mind, as Carter lifted the bird high into the air and they headed on their journey, her heart leapt at the sight of Montana's wild and magnificent west. The mountains, standing proud against a clear blue sky, shimmered in the sunshine like a fortress. The vast and lush forests, pristine waterfalls and lakes mixed with the endless color palate and subtle textures of the lowlands. As they flew high above the towns and ranches spreading out across glorious vistas, she wondered how man had dared to taint this beauty with murder.

She glanced at Carter. He was in full professional mode and handled the chopper with skill. His appearance and happy-go-lucky manner fooled many people and lured criminals into a false sense of security. One thing she could say about Carter is he'd never be called one of the boys. He preferred to be alone, just a man with his dog. He'd sure fooled her but underneath his facade, was a complicated man who hid his emotions. Trained as a deadly force with abilities too many to comprehend, he had a way of looking at things from every angle at the same time. He drove her crazy sometimes, but she had to admit, she admired him.

"You okay?" Carter frowned at her. "Worried about leaving Jaime?"

Jo shook her head. "I'm fine, just admiring the view and Jaime is used to me being away on cases. Now she's settled in to life in Snakeskin Gully, she is a happy little girl. It's a great place to raise kids."

"There's no substitute to small-town values and close friendships that last a lifetime." He turned his concentration back to flying the chopper. "The community sure helped me when I went off the grid." He chuckled. "They acted like they were leaving me alone, but the mailman would sound his horn until he saw me heading to the gate to collect my mail. I'd find care packages from the local church, my prescription filled by the pharmacy, food for Zorro. I was being left alone to recover but I was really never alone."

This was the first time Carter had discussed the PTSD he'd suffered after leading a mission resulting in the death of three children. He'd chosen two years of isolation, unable to cope with the flashbacks. Jo understood the condition well, the triggers that plunged a person back into a recurring nightmare would always be lurking in their subconscious. She kept her gaze ahead. Confiding in her about his condition was a breakthrough. He'd grown to trust her. "Do you figure your handler arranged to make sure you had supplies?"

"The meds and dog food would have come from him for sure but the local minister often came by to visit." Carter cleared his throat. "I was rude and intimidating back then but he kept on coming back. The man is a saint. He never gave me the 'it's God's will,' crap. We spoke about baseball mainly and he helped me turn my cabin into a home. He ended the chaos with simple logic and friendship. I owe him bigtime." He lifted his chin scanning ahead. "I see flares, we're close to the coordinates. We made it ahead of time."

They set down in a field of wheatgrass surrounded by trees, the wind from the chopper giving the impression they were landing in a turbulent green sea. When the door slid open the smell of fire filled the air in a choking stench. All fires had their own signature. A housefire carried the smell of burning wood and textiles, the sharp toxic aftertaste of molten plastic fumes and worst of all, the stench of burning hair and flesh. Jo reached into her pocket for a mask as a blast of ash-filled air hit her face, her senses picking up the awful devastation awaiting them. Moments later, a sheriff's cruiser sped out to meet them. Jo climbed from the chopper and shook the man's hand and introduced Carter. "Nice to meet you. Walk us through the crime scene."

"I'll leave that to the ME. He's pulled rank on us, ma'am. Keeping us right away outside the tape. He said he doesn't want anyone tripping a wire. I hope you clear the area soon. The smell is getting so bad my deputies are getting sick to their stomachs."

"Maybe it's time to get real men to take their place." Carter peered at the sheriff over his sunglasses. "How did Wolfe determine it was homicide if he didn't examine the victims?"

"The explosion blew out the front of the house. The townsfolks said they seen an orange mushroom. There's no gas here, so the firefighters turned off the power and doused the flames. They kept their distance in case it blew again. There wasn't too much they could do. It was well ablaze when they arrived." The sheriff helped load equipment and their bags into the trunk of his cruiser. "The ME used binoculars to view the scene and then told me to call you. He's been on scene since we called him. He'll be glad to see you."

"We'll need a list of witnesses and names of the people who called it in." Carter frowned. "Who was first responder?"

"That would be me." The sheriff tipped back his hat to look up at Carter. "I called the fire department and the ME and we've been on scene since."

"Were there any bystanders?" Carter scanned the area.

"A few and we moved them on." The sheriff's cheeks pinked. "I did think to take down their names but I didn't record the vehicles that passed by."

Jo rolled her eyes at Carter and climbed into the cruiser. "Have you gotten experience in arson before, or bombings at all, Sheriff?"

"Can't say that I have." The sheriff drove over the uneven ground and through the trees toward a still smoking ranch house. "We've had fires, car wrecks, and bar fights mostly. All the action happens in Black Rock Falls but that county is huge. Our population is ten thousand give or take, theirs is over a hundred thousand, maybe more with them off the grid in Stanton Forest. I guess that's why the ME called in their fire chief."

"So, the answer is 'no'?" Carter stared at the man. "If we're taking the lead in this case, we'll need accommodation in town and transport. Will our chopper be secure?"

"It can't be seen from the road, and I figure with FBI written all over it, most people would be too scared to go near it." Crenshaw shrugged. "I'm not sure about your other needs, best you go into Black Rock Falls and bunk down there. They have an airport to stow your chopper and car rentals."

"What do you say, Jo?" Carter looked over his shoulder at her.

Jo met his gaze. "I guess we speak to Shane and see what he needs from us first." As they neared the building and parked between a fire department vehicle and the ME's white van, Jo slid out of the seat and went to the trunk. She grabbed a crime scene kit and opened Carter's duffle. "Here." She handed him his explosives gear and mask. "I don't want to sound like your mother but be careful."

"I'm always careful, Jo, but thanks for caring." Carter pulled on his protective gear and grinned at her. "Just keep everyone back. Flying body parts are deadly."

"I sure will." Jo made her way to Wolfe who was in deep conversation with a firefighter in his late forties. The men turned as she walked toward them with Carter close behind. "Nice to see you again, Shane."

"Hey, Jo, Carter. Thanks for coming by so fast." Wolfe indicated to the firefighter. "This is Chief Matt Thompson, the fire chief out of Black Rock Falls. Once you've cleared the area, he'll do a structural safety assessment before we go inside. Matt, this is Agent Jo Wells, Agent Ty Carter, and Zorro."

They shook hands and exchanged pleasantries. Jo looked past them to the two deputies, who both looked green, and turned to Carter. "Okay. What do you need, Carter?"

"Nothing unless Zorro finds an explosive device." Carter unclipped Zorro's harness and the dog quivered in anticipation. His big brown eyes fixed on Carter. "He'll tell me if he finds anything and then, I'll defuse it and we'll do another sweep to clear the area." He gave the dog a command by flicking his fingers.

The Doberman ran toward the smoldering house, sneezed once, and then slowed to a cautious hesitant walk, nose to the ground. Jo watched in awe as the dog moved meticulously from one area to the other. When he sat down and barked once, she noticed Carter tense beside her and then walk to Zorro. He pulled on gloves and bent down and examined a small piece of debris.

Jo's heart pounded. "What is it?"

"Part of a secondary device. Stay back until I give the all-clear." Carter repeated the signal to the dog and bagged the evidence. "He's trained to recognize many types of explosives, which I'm told is unusual for a Doberman but he was top of his class and so was I. We're a perfect match." His eyes flashed in amusement and he headed toward his dog.

"Maybe you can teach him to cook and clean as well?" Jo ignored his snigger and turned her attention back to Zorro. She noticed the smile on Matt Thompson's face and put distance between them. One arrogant man per day was enough to cope with, two, no way.

Taking on a case meant she had to make sure everything was considered, even the victim's animals. She made her way to a corral. No livestock roamed anywhere and she found no signs of any close by.

"How are things working out?" Wolfe moved to her side.

Jo looked at him and shrugged. "Fine, I guess but we've only had one case of cattle rustling and another of a possible methamphetamine lab in six months, so we spend a great deal of time, working out and using the rifle range. I haven't employed a receptionist yet as the phone isn't exactly ringing off the hook." She glanced at him. "The FBI should have given us a field office closer to Black Rock Falls. The cattle rustling, we handed over to the rangers and after investigating, found the meth lab was making hand sanitizer."

"I meant with Ty." Wolfe had dropped his voice. "All good?"

Jo pushed a hand through her hair and flicked her gaze back to Carter. He was following close behind Zorro and then when the dog barked, he bent and fiddled with something on the ground. "He's arrogant, annoying, and he drives me insane but I figure that's a wall he's built around himself to hide behind. I know he's damaged goods but I can handle him."

"Just don't regard him as a case." Wolfe narrowed his gray eyes and looked at her. "He's an asset and needs to learn how to get close to people again."

Jo nodded. "This I know." She gave him a bright smile. "Tell me about the girls."

"Emily is at the office preparing for the victims' bodies to arrive. She passed all her exams and is top of her class. She'll be through her degree in no time flat. My other intern, Colt Webber, came a close second and he is in the van organizing body bags and the gurney." A softness came over Wolfe's face. "Julie is doing well, she's pursuing a career in pediatrics and she loves art, so has a diversion. My little Anna is the light of our lives, smart, funny… She is horse mad and spends so much time with Dave and Jenna riding, I'm seriously thinking of buying a ranch house with stables. All the girls love horses but then I wouldn't be close to town where I'm needed most."

"There's more to life than work." Jo leaned back on the corral fence, one boot resting on the bottom rail. "There must be places close to town with grazing land?" She had an idea. "Maybe stable Anna's pony and hire rides for the others, if or when they want to ride."

"That's an idea." Wolfe smiled at her. "Although when I'm busy, having Jenna to babysit for me is a Godsend. My girls have become very attached to their Aunty Jenna."

"All clear." Carter gave them a wave.

Jo turned to Wolfe. "Okay, it's your crime scene, how do you want to play it?"

"If you don't have full body suits, I have some in the van. You'll need them in there and I don't want anyone contaminating the scene. It's better if Webber films the entire scene before we enter. Fire conceals evidence. We'll take shots of the scene and then I'll go in and examine the bodies. From what I could see, there are three bodies, one I figure is a child. They're seated around a table and their hands are tied. It looks like it's staged for a reason. I'd suggest allowing Thompson to do his assessment with Carter as they're both experts in their fields."

Jo nodded. "Okay, I'll come with you. The scene is very important, if someone planted a bomb and the scene was staged as you suggested. I want to discover the mindset of the person behind this crime and his motive for killing an entire family."

CHAPTER FOUR

The smell of burning eased a little when Jo pulled on the hood of her protective suit and secured the facemask. She was just about to speak to Wolfe when her phone buzzed. She dragged off her hood and pressed the phone to her ear. "Agent Wells."

"Hi, Jo it's Bobby." Kalo sounded like a kid on the phone. *"I have the information on the family who owns the ranch, Isaac and Connie Wood. Both are social workers out of Louan. Not as much as a parking ticket between them and Isaac inherited the ranch from his pa and moved there from Blackwater recently."* He sighed. *"You know, depending on where people work, there might be a small amount of people who have an ax to grind with social workers. I had a few on my case, and many don't always tell the truth."* He cleared his throat. *"No, I'm gonna tell it like it is, Jo, some of them downright lied about me and to a judge and all."*

Jo stared at the smoldering house and at the small wisps of smoke still escaping from the ruins. "Well, it's just as well we found you, isn't it? I'm on scene now, so I'll have to go. Thanks for the info. I'll talk to you soon, bye." She disconnected and pushed her phone into her pocket. As she secured her hood and mask again, she walked to Wolfe's side. "Both husband and wife were social workers, no rap sheets."

"Good to know but it doesn't explain why someone would want to blow them up." Wolfe pulled on gloves.

After Colt Webber, Wolfe's intern, had filmed what was left of the house and taken photographs, Jo waited for Wolfe's go-ahead to enter the ruins. Dressed in what could only be described as hazmat suits, Carter and Matt Thompson, climbed over the rubble at the front of the house. They would evaluate the explosion, as well as the position and composition of the bomb, and then collect samples from the crater for forensics testing. With Carter's expertise in explosives and the fire chief's input, Jo would receive a comprehensive report. Her expertise leaned more to the profile of the bomber and the victims. She prepared herself for a gruesome scene and followed Wolfe and Webber round the back of the house. She slowed as they reached the open backdoor and waited for Wolfe to issue orders. She peered inside the ruins of a once beautiful ranch house. The green paint had bubbled on the door and carried a thick coating of soot. Fire had licked the wall above and dirty rivulets of water from the firehoses dripped down to form black ash-laden puddles underfoot. Jo sensed Wolfe's reluctance to take her inside to view the blackened remains and she met his gaze. "Let's do this, I have seen fire victims before, Shane."

"Two adults and there's a child." His eyes filled with deep sorrow. "It's harder with kids."

Kalo hadn't mentioned the Woods' children. Stomach flip flopping, Jo nodded. "Yeah, I know."

Many victims lived in her memories but her thoughts went immediately to Carter. She had no idea how he'd handle the sight of a child's burned corpse and hoped it wouldn't trigger a PTSD episode. A warning of what to expect might soften the blow. She pressed her mic. "Carter."

"Miss me already?" Carter's voice came through her earpiece.

"Can you be serious for once in your life, Carter?" Jo picked her way through the soaked floor and into the kitchen. The horrific sight before her made her legs weak. "We have three vics. Two adults and a young child. It's about the worst I've ever seen."

*"You never saw combat, huh? Crispy critters are all in a day's work.
I'll be there to hold your hand soon. Carter out."*

His false bravado didn't fool Jo, or his sudden lack of compassion.
He'd adopted a typical self-protection mode. She snorted. If that's what
it took to get him through, she'd just have to deal with it. Jo stood in
the doorway and surveyed the scene, avoiding the charred remains of
the three people sitting around a kitchen table. She needed to take in
the entire picture, to get a feel for the killer. He could've killed them in
any of the rooms. Why sit them around the kitchen table and not use
the dining room? A stack of dishes and pans sat beside the sink waiting
to be rinsed before being stacked into the dishwasher and yet under
the thick layer of ash, she made out the precisely set table complete
with glasses. It was as if they'd just sat down to dinner. She'd counted
three people but the table was set for four. Had the killer included
himself in the family gathering? She scanned the room taking note
of the melted microwave, electric kettle and toaster blackened and
misshapen. The refrigerator door hung open and the seal around the
door had dripped molten plastic onto the tiled floor. One side of the
curtains over the kitchen sink had burned and the other side remained
untouched. The sight of a singed calendar, with birthdays circled,
made her stomach cramp. She heard Wolfe speaking and moved to
his side. Clamping her lips shut to stop them trembling, she surveyed
the pathetic remains of a family. "What did you say, Shane?"

"The killer restrained the family as I suspected. He left nothing to
chance, there's an open gas can over there." Wolfe glanced at Webber.
"Anything left to indicate a robbery?"

"No, the front of the house is destroyed, the stairs are impassable,
but the car is still in the garage." Webber frowned. "Who'd do this to
a family?"

"Just a minute." Jo pressed her mic. "Carter, if the intention
was to kill the family, how come the front of the house is the main

point of the explosion? The kitchen has mainly fire damage, can you explain?"

She heard him walk through the door, his boots crushing glass and debris underfoot and turned to watch his expression. His gaze flicked around the room and then rested on her.

"He used C-4 and an electronic detonator. Zorro found part of it outside." Carter held up an evidence bag with a burned piece of metal inside. "The direction of the blast depends on the shape of the explosive. He wanted to blow out the front of the house. I figure he wanted the family alive for as long as possible, so they'd burn to death." He glanced around and spotted the overturned gas can. "He made sure by pouring gas onto the floor."

"I agree." Matt Thompson walked in behind him, squatted down, and took samples from the kitchen floor. He straightened and made notes on a clipboard. "I've completed my preliminary report on the cause of the fire." He signed the bottom of the sheet of paper, peeled a copy from underneath, and handed it to Wolfe. "Arson, caused by a C-4 explosion and he used gasoline as an accelerant. I've collected samples for analysis and will forward the final report in due course." He tapped the top of the paperwork with his pen. "If necessary, you can contact me on that number."

"Okay, thanks for coming out." Wolfe handed the document to Webber.

"Any time." Thompson shot a glance at Jo. "It's not often I get to work alongside the FBI." He gave her a wave and then picked his way out through the backdoor.

Jo stared after him and then looked at Wolfe. "Why exactly did you call him out here from Black Rock Falls?"

"I needed an expert and there's none with his qualifications in any other town." Wolfe met her gaze over his facemask. "Louan, like most of the towns, has a volunteer fire department and as lives were lost here, it comes down to the local fire chief to file a report. I'll file one as well, it prevents any unfounded negligence lawsuits and is essential for insurance claims."

"I can see remnants of zip-ties around this victim's ankles." Carter bent to examine the corpse. "Is it the same for all of them?"

"Yeah." Wolfe frowned. "He tied them and made it look like they're all sitting down to a family meal."

"What do you see, Jo?" Carter moved to her side.

Jo swallowed the bad taste in her mouth. "The killer hates the family unit and wants to destroy it. I'd say someone took his family away from him. He wants to inflict as much suffering as possible and wants to make them pay for his pain." She glanced at Carter. "We'll need a complete rundown on the members of this family, what they did for a living, their friends, everything. I want to know why he picked them. This isn't random, it's been planned and executed with precision."

"I'd be interested to know if the killer injured them." Carter's eyes narrowed over his mask. "I don't believe a man would allow his wife and kid to be tied up without a fight."

Jo's attention had moved to the refrigerator. On the shelf sat two lunchboxes. Two pink lunchboxes. She walked around the table and stared at them. "Webber, did you get shots of the lunchboxes?"

"Yes, ma'am." Webber nodded at her. "I captured everything in here including the open drawer and the knife block. If someone broke into their home, they had knives here so why didn't they fight back? I found a gun locker under the stairs. It's fireproof and untouched. No one had a chance to go for their weapons."

"Maybe they knew him." Carter shrugged. "We'll check all the locks and see if any show signs of forced entry but it will be difficult to prove after the explosion."

An overpowering feeling of dread slid over Jo as she turned to Carter. "Two pink lunchboxes. Only one child. Where's the sheriff?" She turned and ran out the backdoor.

She found the sheriff leaning up against his cruiser. "How many people lived here?"

"Four. Mr. and Mrs. Wood and two daughters, Jody and Sophie." The sheriff wiped a handkerchief over his sweaty brow.

Chills ran down Jo's neck. "How old are the girls?"

"Let me see. Jody would be about five and Sophie maybe fourteen, I guess." The sheriff frowned. "Why?"

Jo stared at him through the Perspex shield covering her face. "We have one missing."

CHAPTER FIVE

The Whispering Caves

Sophie wanted to die. Trapped deep inside the catacombs, there was no escape. The dark tunnels dripped water, and wind rushed through them like a thousand souls screaming for redemption. The catacombs breathed, moving air back and forth in waves, bringing with it the touch of unseen hands over her flesh. The sensation terrified her. Cold crawled from the rock and all she had was a filthy blanket for protection. He'd taken everything, her family, her decency, and left her curled in the dirt like a filthy naked worm. A living, breathing shell remained, devoid of hope. The filthy mattress under her reeked of urine and everywhere she turned, the stink from the animal scat covering the hard ground accosted her. Rats skittered by and if the lamp went out, they'd eat her alive. She wanted to block out the horror but the moment she closed her eyes, the image of her family tied to the chairs and the explosion spun through her mind in relentless torment.

She'd cried until her head threatened to split open in agony but the man who'd taken her didn't care. He'd make it clear it was his decision if she lived or died and slapped her face so hard her teeth ached. She moved her dry tongue over the cut on her lip and a metallic taste filled her mouth. The thought of him touching her again made her retch. He'd left her after adjusting a trail cam and told her he'd be watching her every move. If she screamed, or tried to escape, he'd know. Her cries would bring the bears roaming the caves and he'd enjoy watching them eat her alive. He'd left her nothing, no food or water, and tethered her by linked zip-ties to a metal loop hammered into solid rock. The tie around her ankle cut deep into her flesh but she'd become dead inside. She had no room to move and lay back staring at the dancing bugs surrounding a small pool of light from the lamp hanging above her.

Cobwebs fluttered in the breeze and a fat spider weaved a cocoon around a struggling moth. She'd die here just like the moth. There was no hope of escape. She was deep in the Whispering Caves, a place closed to the public. Nobody came here and people told tales of ghosts haunting the tunnels in hushed voices. Everyone who'd cared for her had perished in the fire. Not a soul knew what had happened to her.

A beam of a flashlight followed by the crunch of footsteps had alerted a colony of bats and they dashed past her, shrieking in a cloud of black flapping wings. The light blinded her but she recognized the voice of her tormentor and pulled the blanket around her and looked away. The sight of his dark eyes peering at her through the holes in the balaclava terrified her. When he stopped in front of her, she wet her lips. "Why are you keeping me here?"

"Do you feel like a puppy?" The man grasped her chin forcing her to look at him. "Taken from your mommy to be owned by someone?"

Unable to control a sob, Sophie trembled. "You can't own people. You don't own me."

"Oh, but I do. I can do whatever I want with you." He chuckled. "I can cut you into little pieces if I want. You can't stop me but if you cooperate, I'm willing to trade."

Sophie stared at him in disbelief. "I have nothing to trade. You've taken everything I own."

"Oh, but you do." His gloved fingers stroked her cheek. He pulled a small bottle of water from his pocket and one half of a peanut butter and jelly sandwich. "What will you trade me for this?"

CHAPTER SIX

Black Rock Falls

Jenna leaned back in the seat of the Beast, Kane's unmarked vehicle, and considered the afternoon. She'd spoken to the car thief and made it quite clear she didn't intend to play games with him. Sometimes young guys figured her as an easy sell until they met her face to face. After dealing with serial killers, interviewing a smart-mouthed car thief was a walk in the park. She'd discovered his name was Harvey Haralson. His story was, he'd found the vehicle abandoned not far from the Triple Z Bar north of town and rather than wait for the bus, had decided to drive into town and then dump the sedan on Main. She'd appointed him a lawyer, and as he'd admitted to stealing the vehicle, she'd charged him and arranged a ride to county for him to await a court hearing. The rest of the afternoon had dragged and by five, she couldn't leave the office fast enough. She'd been looking forward to going out to dinner with Kane for weeks.

It turned out to be a beautiful evening. The rain of the previous week had left everything fresh and clean. The grasslands and people's gardens seemed to have suddenly come alive with color. She stared out the window as they turned into Main. A crowd of people, dressed for a night out, were making their way to the opening of Antlers, the new western bar. The town had needed a place where regular people could eat a meal, cut a rug, and have some hometown fun any day of the week. She glanced at Kane and grinned. "I'm sure glad we made reservations for a table a week ago."

"Not everyone in town can afford the Cattleman's Hotel prices, and with all the tourists dropping by, we needed something better in town than the Triple Z Bar." He chuckled and joined the line into the parking lot. "It was pure genius to insist they gave the sheriff's department reserved parking. I can still see the owner's face, when you insisted it was in his best interest if we had a place to park in times of trouble."

Jenna grinned. "Yeah, well all bars have fights and this place being smack in the middle of Main, we needed a place to park."

"It's going to be good to have somewhere to let our hair down in town." Kane slid into the reserved parking space and turned off the engine. "I'd forgotten how much I missed dancing until Jake's wedding. We had a ball that night and in truth, we needed a few days snowed in to get over it." His lips curled into a smile. "This place will be perfect."

"Of course, the twenty-two-ounce prime ribeye they have on the menu has nothing to do with it?" Jenna laughed. "Oh, look, Jake and Sandy are right behind us."

"Hey, big turn out." Rowley gave them a wave as he climbed out of his truck. "I hope we don't have to wait too long to be served, I'm starving." He held out his hand to his wife, Sandy, and they headed toward the bar.

Black Rock Falls was a great place to live. Everyone they met greeted them and the townsfolk were in high spirits as they made their way in a procession to the tavern. As sheriff it meant a lot to Jenna that the townsfolk accepted her and her deputies as normal people when they were off- duty. Once seated, they chatted while waiting for Wolfe and Emily to arrive. Jenna leaned back to absorb the atmosphere of the new establishment. Tables were surrounded by a large polished wood dancefloor and on a small stage, instruments were set out for the band. For now, music drifted through the speakers, hardly recognizable above the chatter inside. The crowded bar ran down one wall and was surrounded by people jostling to order. Her gaze scanned the walls. Framed rodeo posters and elk heads adorned the wood paneling. The place had incorporated the old west flavor of a saloon, with swinging doors leading to the restrooms. She'd planned to wait before ordering, so they could all enjoy their meal together but before the server arrived to take their order, her phone buzzed. It was Shane Wolfe. "Hi Shane, we're already seated. How long are you behind us?"

"We can't make it tonight. There was a fire out of Louan, three victims. I'm going to be working on them tonight."

"Oh, that's terrible, is there anything we can do to help?" Jenna stuck one finger in her ear to make out what he was saying. "We can stop by after we've eaten."

"No, it's fine, we have it covered. Have a good night. We'll talk later." He disconnected.

Bewildered by his coldness toward her, Jenna stared at the screen. She turned to Kane. "Wolfe and Em can't make it. He's working on victims of the fire out of Louan. He's doing autopsies tonight." She frowned. "He didn't say too much."

"He must be busy." Kane shrugged and then indicated to the two people being led to their table. "Ah, Jenna. We have company."

The smile on Jenna's face froze at the business-like expressions of FBI Agents Wells and Carter. She waved them to the two empty seats. "What brings you to Black Rock Falls?"

"We have a case out of Louan." Jo looked exhausted. "I'll explain everything once we order. We haven't eaten since breakfast."

"We also came begging for a bed for the night." Carter dropped into a seat beside Jenna, bringing with him the distinct smell of smoke. "We left the chopper at the airport, I managed to get a hangar but we had to cab it into town. No hire cars and it seems all the rooms in town are booked for the summer." He rolled his eyes. "Even the cabins up at the ski lodge are occupied. What's happened to this sleepy town?"

Jenna chuckled. "We've become the trendy place to stay since the town was featured in a series of crime novels. I'm not sure why people want to risk being murdered but you must admit, if you enjoy all the thrills we offer here and wide-open spaces, this is the place to be. The mayor went all out to cash in on the tourist industry." She glanced at Kane, who gave her a slight nod. "You're welcome to stay with us again."

"Thank you." Carter tipped up his Stetson and grinned. "Maggie offered us a cell each if we lucked out. She said she'd clear it with you later."

"Where's Zorro?" Kane leaned on the table. "I thought you and that dog were inseparable."

"We dropped him at Maggie's. He doesn't like crowds." Carter frowned. "He wasn't too happy and refused to eat his dinner. He's stubborn."

Concerned for Maggie's safety, Jenna frowned. "He won't bite her or her husband, will he?"

"Nah." Carter waved a server over to take their order. "He'll ignore them completely and just sit like a statue until I go get him." He turned to Jenna. "If I die before he does, you'll have to show him my body or he'll starve to death."

Seeing he was deadly serious, she nodded. "I'll remember."

The server came to the table and they ordered. Hungry for information on why the FBI was brought in for a housefire, she swiveled in her seat to look at Jo. "So, the case at Louan. Is it anything to do with the fire last night?"

"Yeah but let's not talk about this now." Jo straightened in her seat. "The imagery doesn't sit well with eating." Her lips quivered into a smile. "The local sheriff is handling the situation and should have some information for us by morning. We'll discuss the details after dinner and away from this noise, okay?"

"Sure." Jenna sipped from a glass of water. "It's been so quiet around here of late, we've had time to redecorate the house, well, the house and cottage. My office will be getting an upgrade as well." She couldn't help noticing Jo's usual bright personality was flat. She hoped her young daughter was doing okay. After a messy divorce, the kids were often traumatized. "How's Jaime?"

"She is doing fine, well, better than fine." Jo's smile was genuine and reached her eyes. "I figure not listening to her folks arguing is a good thing and the puppy has made a difference."

Jenna leaned closer to hear her over the noise. "What did you buy?"

"A Boston Terrier by the name of Beau." Jo chuckled. "He is the sweetest thing and even Zorro likes him."

The food arrived and the conversation died as everyone became involved in the meal. Carter and Jo seemed to be more interested in asking Rowley and Sandy about their wedding and recent purchase of a ranch than discussing work. Jenna finished her wine and turned to look at the dancefloor as the band struck up. Under her feet the floorboards vibrated with the stomp of cowboy boots and the next thing, Kane was pulling her onto the dancefloor.

"What's going on with them?" Kane moved her around the floor. "They seem evasive."

After some years of trying, Jenna wasn't very good at the Texas two-step and trod all over Kane's polished boots. "Oops, sorry. I don't know but it must be a complicated case if they've been called in by Sheriff Tom Crenshaw."

"Him and his boys couldn't find a lost dog." Kane frowned. "A sheriff who only deputizes his sons, isn't using his brains. It's an easy paycheck for no work. I mean why does a town like Louan need a sheriff and four deputies? We have you and two, it doesn't make sense."

Jenna sighed as the music went into a slower dance. "It's the smallest county in Montana but the sapphire mine means they have cash to burn. Most of the townsfolks are Crenshaw's relatives so he gets voted in at every election."

"May I cut in?" Carter's voice came from behind Jenna.

"Jenna?" Kane looked at her and raised one eyebrow.

Not wanting to be rude, Jenna nodded. "Okay." She reluctantly let go of Kane's hand and found herself in Carter's arms. "It seems strange you'd take time off in the middle of a case to go dancing."

"We arrived too late to do anything." Carter twirled her around the dancefloor. "The sheriff is the best person to hunt down the missing girl. She could be with friends or a boyfriend. If we show at people's houses they'll clam up for sure. The FBI have a strange effect on some country folks, they don't trust us." He sighed. "I might look and sound like a local but it will be all around town by now that I'm not."

Shocked, Jenna stopped dancing and stared at him. "Missing girl, what missing girl?"

"Oh, I thought Jo had walked you through the case? The bombing out of Aspen Grove, Louan." He leaned closer and whispered in her ear. "We need your help this time."

"A bombing? Good Lord, Carter are you telling me there's a girl missing and we're out dancing? Have you lost your mind?" Jenna spun on her heel and pushed her way through the crowd. She could see Kane standing beside their table watching her.

"Hey." Carter grabbed her arm and spun her toward him. "Like I said, there's nothing we can do right now."

In a surge of outrage, Jenna narrowed her gaze at him. "Do you have any feelings at all or did the military drain every last drop of humanity from you?" It took some effort to control her emotions because he just stood there and smiled at her. "Leaving Sheriff Crenshaw in charge of anything is as responsible as leaving a two-year-old with a Zippo and an open can of gas."

"There's nothing you can do, Jenna." Carter pulled a toothpick from his top pocket and slid it into his mouth. "You don't have jurisdiction. He's the local law enforcement and even a fool can hunt down the friends of a missing girl. It's been almost twenty-four hours and if she was taken by the killer the chances of her being alive are negligible."

Fuming at his cold detached attitude, Jenna pulled away from the hand restraining her. "I would've called Crenshaw and offered my services, if anyone had told me." She snorted. "Why did he call you?"

"Maybe because the town doesn't have to pay us for assistance." Carter met her gaze. "You're jumping to conclusions about the girl, Jenna. She could be safe in town with friends. That's the first place we check, same as you do and Crenshaw is doing that as we speak. He was first responder. His men are chasing down next of kin and the names of witnesses. Wolfe and his team have documented the scene, we've even had the Black Rock Falls fire chief to do a report. Everything is being handled." He sighed. "Apart from the missing girl, this case has turned up an anomaly we can't ignore and is the reason we came here chasing you down. We want you and Kane to consult on the case. You'll be working with us under the FBI umbrella, so no uniform. The freedom to move around would be like a dream come true for you guys, right?"

"What's going on here?" Kane pushed to her side. "You have half the town gawking at you."

Jenna looked up at him. Carter's suggestion brought back nightmares she'd put to rest years ago. "Oh, nothing." She rolled her eyes. "Carter just wants us to join the FBI as consultants."

CHAPTER SEVEN

Louan

The first sweet smell of fire excited him. He loved watching flames lick the side of a building, the crackling of burning wood. He could stand forever watching the way fire waved its magic wand and changed everything it touched. Wood, converted to charcoal, misshapen and blackened, would never be the same. He craved the sound fire made as it roared and leapt to reach out in orange and yellow fingers to capture and consume everything in its path. The explosions of glass, scattering like a shower of diamonds to the ground and the pops and whines as flames gorged on furniture and prized possessions. The fleeting smell of hair followed by burning flesh never lasted long enough, and he wished he could be inside the swirling mass of heat to watch more closely. He'd pored over images of burn victims. In awe of the twisted limbs and gaping mouths of the charred remains. Had they screamed their last breath or was it the magic of the flame?

Fire danced, he'd seen it with his own eyes, and a single flame multiplied from one lowly dancer into many. They joined to thunder their way through buildings and over rooftops. His heartbeat raced as he imagined watching a line of fire dancers streaking across the lowlands toward the trees. In the forest the fire changed again into a massive dragon, spewing fire in all directions and roaring its intent to destroy everything in its sight. Tall pines whined for a second before fire engulfed them in a whoosh of orange, so bright it hurt his eyes, first one and then a thousand in a wall of flames so high it reached the clouds.

Smoke too had its own fascination. First it curled up and away in a white line, innocent and ethereal. Deceptive like a joker, it soon billowed into rolling gray or toxic black clouds. Smoke was as lethal as its brother. It burned lungs and suffocated, filling the air like an afterthought to capture anyone foolish enough to try and extinguish the flames. He enjoyed fire from the very first spark to the steam and hiss from water-soaked flames carrying the distinctive odor that stuck to his clothes. The blackened aftermath called to him. He had to go inside a burned-out shell of a building or walk through a blackened forest. It made him feel alive. Fire made him powerful.

He dragged his thoughts away from his passion and leaned back in the seat of his truck to watch the sheriff and his deputies return to town. Behind them came the medical examiner from Black Rock Falls. They'd been out since dawn, maybe earlier. He'd no idea how much sleep they'd lost, nor did he care. The law had never worked in his favor and he despised every last one of them. The law hadn't protected him as a child and as if fate had caught him in an endless loop of bureaucracy, not one of the goodie-two-shoes, procurers of children for foster homes, had been there to protect his son when he couldn't. He opened his phone and pulled up the trail cam app to check on Sophie. He'd spent a great deal of time setting up the caves. The light ran on a battery but he'd had to run cable from the webcam to a wireless receiver outside the caves to counteract the magnetic force of the mountain. The effort and expense had been worth it. The sight of her helpless and scared made his lips curl into a smile. He'd taken her from her home without a fight. Her father had been weak and done nothing to protect his wife and daughters.

He shook his head. A father should fight to the death for his family, a mother should protect her children. The law should protect children against monsters disguised as foster parents. He snorted. He'd walked right in the house when Sophie had taken out the trash, just like she did every night, and her parents had allowed him to play out his fantasy. Now he had Sophie and they were just charred remains. He stared at her again, curled up under the blanket waiting for him to return and smiled. There was no rush. She wasn't going anywhere and he had all the time in the world. He accessed his blog and added an image of steaks sizzling on a grill. He wrote a post.

Last night, I dropped by a friend's place for a barbecue. His wife made a special effort to make me feel at home. I had a great time. In fact, the night went off with a bang. Everyone had a turn at the grill and I got to take some home to enjoy later.

CHAPTER EIGHT

The mood inside Kane's truck was somber as they waited for Carter to collect Zorro and the assortment of bags and equipment from Maggie's home in town. The knowledge there was a missing girl out there, probably in the hands of a pyromaniac murderer, ate at Jenna but her hands were tied. Without Crenshaw asking for her assistance, she could do nothing. When Maggie's door opened again and Carter spilled onto the sidewalk, the Doberman danced around Carter's legs in an uncharacteristic dance of joy before a click of his fingers had him fall into step beside him. Jenna had watched the affection Kane lavished on his bloodhound, Duke, and wondered if Carter treated his dog the same. Her concerns were answered when the dog jumped into the back seat between him and Jo. She turned to look at Carter. "Is he okay?"

"Yeah." Carter put an arm around Zorro and gave him a rub from ears to tail. "He knows I care about him but he expects orders from me. It's how he's wired. The burst of excitement at seeing me is a left over from when I took a bullet at one time during a tour. They took me away and there was no one left alive in my team to explain, he was part of our bomb squad. I was out of it for almost two days. He didn't eat or drink for all that time. When I explained we worked as a unit and he won't take orders from anyone but me they wanted to shoot him, so I dragged myself out of a field hospital and went to find him. It's been okay working for the FBI in the city, but now we're out west, things happen. Nobody knows us apart from Jo and the two of you."

Jenna stared at him and shrugged. The solution seemed easy enough. "Then add our phone numbers to the one on his collar. We'll come get him if anything ever happens to you."

"I'm not shooting him if you're stupid enough to get killed." Kane turned in his seat to look at him. "No way."

"Once he knows I'm gone, Jo can take over." Carter looked away. "We've been working with her." He sighed. "I figured, since I'm working in your Godforsaken neck of the woods, I need a contingency plan."

Dumbfounded, Jenna swallowed hard and stared at Jo. "What are you two mixed up in, Jo?"

"We'll explain later." Jo frowned. "Carter found something in the fire out of Louan. It's complicated."

After getting their guests and dogs settled, Jenna made a pot of coffee and waited for Carter and Kane to haul in laptops and a couple of evidence boxes from the truck. When they'd finally sat around the kitchen table, Jenna looked from one strained expression to another. "Okay, I know seeing the results of the victims of a fire is harrowing but I'm sure this isn't the reason you two are being so evasive. Why do you need us to assist you? You could call in any number of FBI agents from other field offices."

"Well, unless it's involving the abduction of a child under the age of twelve, we're expected to manage alone. It's not usual to have cases like you have in Black Rock Falls all over the west." Jo flicked a glance at Carter. "We need your help but we've come up with a security issue."

"It goes way up to the top." Carter leaned on the table and stared straight at Kane.

"Here we go." Kane huffed out a snort of contempt and leaned back in his chair staring at the ceiling for a beat before lowering his gaze. "Security issue huh?" He gave Jenna a meaningful stare and then glared at Carter. "Do you figure us backwoods hicks can't keep a secret?"

Jenna held up a hand. Of course, they had no idea, Kane had a higher security clearance than anyone in the room. What had a fire in Louan to do with national security? "Okay calm down, Dave." She glared at Carter. "If you can't trust us why come here in the first place? Did you just want a bed for the night?"

"No, Jenna." Carter looked at her and smiled. "We'd sleep in the cells before we pulled a stunt like that." He glanced at Jo. "Let's cut to the chase. We trust Shane Wolfe. I gather you know he is ex-military and still has contacts. He insisted that we can trust you implicitly but what I'm about to tell you, never leaves this room."

Biting back the need to tell Jo and Carter the truth about her and Kane, she nodded. "That's a given in any case we investigate. Every member of my team is fully aware of keeping the details of a crime secret. Nothing ever leaves my office or here without my permission."

"Okay." Carter went to a sealed plastic box and pulled out an evidence bag. "When I did a search of the scene with Zorro, he found these fragments of the device used to detonate the C-4." He placed the plastic bag on the table and Kane took it and examined it closely. "Do you know about explosives?"

"Yeah, it just happens that I do." Kane lifted his gaze to Carter. "This isn't from the primary explosive charge, it's from a secondary charge."

"Well, lookee here, a deputy with skills in explosives. A little knowledge can be a dangerous thing." Carter grinned at him. "Worked in the mines before you became a deputy, huh?"

"Nah, marines." Kane narrowed his eyes. "I just chose an easier life after my tour of duty. I'd had enough killing."

Jenna looked from one to the other waiting for someone to throw the first punch. "Okay, can we get on with it? It will be midnight before Carter explains why this device is so darn important."

"Yes, get on with it, Carter." Jo raised her eyebrows at Jenna. "I'll pull up the files, so he can explain." She went to work on her laptop.

"Sure." Carter took the evidence bag from Kane. "This is what you'd typically find in a cellphone used to detonate plastic explosives. When the phone rings, it closes a circuit and boom." He pointed to the blackened remains of a cellphone. "The wiring in this phone is the same as we found in three explosions that occurred in DC some years ago. See the three dots of solder with the strikethrough, it's unique, and a trademark of the creator. Two resulted in explosions and housefires. He hit the residences of a lawyer and a social worker, but the last one was different. He used the same type of device in a car bomb and the explosion resulted in the death of a high-ranking federal agent and his wife. We found nothing to link the crimes apart from the detonator." He waved a hand at Jo. "This was the aftermath. I've just forwarded the crime scene files to both of you. They are classified as top-secret and the names of the victims are withheld but you'll need the files for background on the bomber. The explosion in the vehicle was set to specifically kill the occupants, not to ignite the car—there was a small fire but it was extinguished immediately by a passerby. This type of explosive device takes skill and opportunity. It was set inside the vehicle and the agent survived the blast but unfortunately, died on the way to the hospital."

An ice-cold chill sped down Jenna's spine as Jo turned around the screen to display images of a wrecked car with a close-up shot of the body of a beautiful blonde-haired woman, her eyes open and staring in death. She lifted her gaze to Kane. His face had drained of color as his attention fixed on the screen. Panic gripped Jenna and her stomach threatened to empty. The image had to be of Annie; Kane had just been confronted with images of his dead wife. She grasped the laptop and turned it around to face her but Kane had turned to stone, his eyes locked on the space where the laptop had been.

"Okay enough of the gory details." Jenna closed the lid. "You mean to tell me the FBI haven't caught this guy in how many years?"

At that moment, Duke, who'd been sitting with his head on Kane's lap, howled and bolted to the front door. Jenna stared at Kane. He didn't meet her gaze and stood, scraping back his chair, and then headed for the door without a word. Smothering the need to run after him, she cleared her throat. "I think Duke needs to pee."

"Ah, getting back to the case." Jo glanced at Kane's retreating back and then to Jenna. "We thought we'd caught the bomber, he claimed responsibility on his media pages and said he was with a terrorist cell."

Jenna frowned. "So where is he now? Could he be training others to make similar devices?"

"No." Jo reached for her coffee and sipped. "We pinned him down in a shopping mall and he went down in a hail of bullets after threatening to detonate the vest he was wearing." She sighed. "Nothing has happened since and then this device shows up in a small town hundreds of miles from its origin." She looked over the rim of her cup at Jenna. "This means we overlooked a possible accomplice and a serious threat is still out there."

"We have the basic information but there has to be something that sets these victims apart. Something made the bomber hit them, on paper they're as clean as freshly laundered sheets." Carter tucked the device back inside the evidence box. "What if the vic was in witness protection? We have a ton of people out there, who need to stay dead. If there's been a leak and this vigilante is hunting down key people or witnesses, we need to stop him."

With her mind set on Kane's carved in stone expression, Jenna gave herself a mental shake. Being in witness protection, herself, after bringing down a drug cartel, she could be on his list. She swallowed the bad taste in her throat. "And you expect the four of us to hunt this animal down, alone?" She stared from one to the other. "You're crazy."

"No, we're not, Jenna." Jo refilled Jenna's cup and pushed it toward her. "We've given this a lot of thought. This person is very sure of himself and he is either covering up his acts of terror by trying to make us believe he is not who he seems, or doesn't know we found his signature on the previous explosive devices and is enacting out a vendetta or worse still a fantasy."

Jenna looked from one to the other. "You're banking on him underestimating us as a team, right?" She glanced at the door and wondered what was going through Kane's mind right now. Her heart ached for him. It must have been a terrible shock, to see the photographs. She stared at Carter. "As we're talking about underestimating people... Jo is aware of Kane's profiling skills but he has a box of tricks up his sleeve."

"For instance?" Carter looked amused.

"Too many to count, Carter." Jenna stared at him. "But if you need to take out a target, Kane never misses. He was a sniper and is an asset."

"Then it will be true justice if he takes down this guy." Carter reached for a chocolate chip cookie, broke it in half, and gave a piece of it to Zorro. "The agent he killed in the car bomb was one of the top snipers in the business."

CHAPTER NINE

Blinded with ice-cold rage, Kane lifted Duke into his truck and climbed behind the wheel. Moments later he headed out the gate and accelerated toward town. He needed answers and with Jo and Carter close by, his only option was to speak to Wolfe and what he had to say couldn't be said over the phone. He flicked on lights and sirens and the lowlands and hills flashed by in a sea of dark and light gray under the waning moon. The beautiful clear night did nothing to curb the nightmare of seeing Annie's death mask. He'd tried long and hard to remove his last glimpse of her from his mind and replace it with a happy memory but without as much as a single photograph of her, the same lifeless staring image remained fixed in his head along with the metal plate. After slowing to drive through town, he turned off the lights and sirens and took a few deep breaths. He pulled up outside the ME's office and moments later was flashing his card to gain access. With Duke at his heels, he headed for Wolfe's office. As he opened the door and pushed the hound inside, he heard Emily, Wolfe's daughter, calling his name. He straightened and looked at her. "I need to speak to your dad."

"Did you want to watch the autopsy?" Emily frowned over the top of her mask. "I wasn't aware this was your case."

Kane shook his head. "No, I'll wait until he's finished."

"We're done with one victim and the others are on the list for tomorrow." Emily's gray eyes met his with concern. "Is something wrong? Is Jenna—"

"Jenna's fine, everyone is fine." Kane stared at the floor. "I just need to speak to Shane—alone."

"Okay, I'll go get him." Emily pushed open the doors to the examination room and went inside.

Kane paced the spotless white tiled floor, ignoring the smell of antiseptic and burning flesh. It was cold and at least ten degrees lower than outside but Kane welcomed the chill on his boiling flesh. His mind was in turmoil. He'd been told the man responsible for Annie's death had been killed but had that just been a ploy to keep him in Black Rock Falls? He recalled the shock on Jenna's face. She had seen what haunted his every waking moment. Now he understood why he could find no peace. The man responsible still walked the earth. Had Annie been reaching out from beyond the grave to tell him so?

The door to the examination room opened in a whoosh. Kane stopped pacing as Wolfe appeared and peeled off his scrubs and tossed them into a bin. He walked slowly toward him. "You know why I'm here, don't you?"

"Nope." Wolfe stood hands balled on his hips and stared at him. "Is there a problem?"

Kane swallowed the grief blocking his throat. "It's private."

"Okay, we'll speak in my office." Wolfe led the way and once inside, went straight to the coffee machine and brewed two cups. "You're wound up as tight as a drum, pace up and down or do whatever you need to do while you explain, but I've been working for eight hours without a break and I'm making coffee."

The coffee machine hummed and hissed before spilling out two cups. Trying not to pick up the machine and toss it against the wall, Kane took a few deep breaths and dropped into his state of calm. There were two sides to this state. One, he could withstand an incredible amount of pain or suffering and the other, he could kill without conscience. He'd never used it to keep calm when his mind was screaming for revenge and not when dealing with a friend. He hadn't fooled Wolfe and he noticed the change in his expression. Even Duke eyed him with suspicion. He sat down and waited.

"Drink the coffee." Wolfe piled a cup with sugar and cream and slid it over to Kane. "You look like you're going into shock. What the hell is happening to you? Is it flashbacks?"

Ignoring the coffee, Kane rolled his head from side to side, he'd been clamping his jaw so tight his neck ached. "Why didn't you tell me Carter was the lead investigator on my case?"

"I didn't want to drag up unpleasant memories for you." Wolfe frowned. "It's not as if you can thank him."

"Thank him? I don't think so." Kane stared at Wolfe's confused expression. "You informed me the FBI took care of the terrorist group that killed Annie. Was that true or just a way to keep me here?"

"It was the information I received from the top, why?" Wolfe pulled out a box of cookies and placed them on the table. "Eat something. You look like shit."

Remaining in his calm state, Kane took out his phone and accessed the images of the car bombing and slid them across the table to Wolfe. "Carter has these and discovered the device used to murder Annie was made by the same person who made the bomb in the Louan case."

"Oh Lord." Wolfe's face went sheet-white. "He didn't mention anything to me about the device. He asked if I could trust you both to keep a state secret, so of course I said yes. He doesn't know anything about you or Jenna."

Kane gathered his thoughts before he attempted to speak. "I was led to believe the case files were sealed. I want to know how much Carter knows about me and why he is spreading the files around. Does he know I'm alive—or my name?"

"No, not a chance. Carter doesn't have the clearance. He's a specialist in his field and a darn good investigator. He risked his life to take out the bomber. This is why he has access to the files, and recognized the match in the devices." Wolfe frowned. "You can trust him."

"Can I? He killed the wrong man. A terrorist maybe but I'd bet my last dime, the guy wasn't involved in my wife's murder." Kane slammed his fist on the table, making the coffee wash over the sides of the cups. "Now I know why Annie won't allow me to get on with my life. The man who killed her is still out there and now he's killing again. This time he's turned up his game. You know as well as I do, Shane, if there's a girl missing from the house, he has her. He's a pyrotechnic psychopath hell bent on teaching someone a lesson but I have the upper hand this time. When I'm given a target, I never give up and he doesn't know I'm alive."

CHAPTER TEN

Thursday

After a restless night worrying about the missing girl and Kane's sudden departure, Jenna woke at five to the sound of his voice outside her bedroom door. It wasn't unusual for him to let himself in after he'd finished tending the horses but as he hadn't returned the previous evening to discuss the case, she was anxious to know if he was doing okay. She'd fended off questions about Kane's sudden departure with Duke, telling white lies about Kane being concerned about Duke's health and perhaps he'd gone to visit the vet. Albeit at ten at night. With Kane missing and everyone exhausted, she'd opened the door to the cottage for Carter and after making sure Jo was settled in her spare room had lain awake for hours. She scrambled from the bed and went to the door. She noticed Carter lingering in the hallway and looked at Kane. "Did you want to speak to me?"

"Nah, just letting you know, we're heading to the gym." Kane gave her a look that gave no clue to his absence and waved Carter away. "Go ahead, I'll be right behind you." He turned back to her. "You planning on a quick workout? You'll have two partners this morning."

"Forget that. What happened to you last night?" Jenna looked up at him. "I had to make out Duke was sick and you'd gone to see the vet."

"I knew you'd think of something." Kane narrowed his gaze. "I needed to speak to Wolfe."

Bolstering her courage, Jenna dropped her voice to a whisper. "That was Annie in the photos, wasn't it?"

"Yeah." Kane stared at his boots as if unable to face her. "That's all I remember before I passed out. It was the last time I saw her." He looked back up and she could see the torment in his eyes. "She was my soulmate, Jenna. It tore out my heart when she died." He rubbed a hand down his face. "Wolfe told me they'd taken the bomber down and now I discover he's still breathing."

Feeling his pain, Jenna squeezed his rock-hard arm. "He won't get away this time with the four of us chasing his tail. I want to get into the office as early as possible. I'll need to make arrangements for Rowley to take over the day-to-day running of the place if we're going to be helping Jo." She stared at him. "Maybe you should skip your workout this morning?"

"I need to hit something, Jenna, and Carter won't hold back." Kane leaned one hand on the doorframe and lowered his voice to a whisper. "I hope you don't try and play the conflict of interest card and pull me off the investigation."

The thought had plagued Jenna all night. She sucked in a breath. "It's the right thing to do. We have two main problems as I see it. The fire bomber and a missing girl. Perhaps you can take the lead in the missing girl case? The idea it's been left to Sheriff Crenshaw is eating me up inside."

Jenna took a few steps back at the expression on Kane's face. His eyes flashed with anger so intense it startled her. When he stepped inside her room and closed the door behind him, she swallowed hard. "So that's a 'no'?"

"Jenna, I respect you but do you honestly think I'd trust Carter to find the man who murdered my wife?" Kane clenched and unclenched his fists. "I'm sorry but if you insist, I'll disappear, and go so deep no one will ever find me but I can guarantee Annie's killer will end up dead."

Shocked by his threat to leave, Jenna blinked. "So, it was Carter who investigated your case?"

"Yeah, I couldn't figure out how he had access to the case files when they're sealed. I went to see Wolfe and he confirmed it last night, but Carter doesn't have names or know anything about me apart from the fact I was an agent. His main focus was on the DC bombings." Kane paced up and down her room. "Obviously, from the new evidence, Carter took down an innocent man, although I'd have no problem killing a terrorist hell bent on blowing himself and others to kingdom come either." He stopped pacing and took her by the shoulders. "This one is complicated. What was behind the first three attacks? Why the time lapse before starting again and why did he change his MO and take the girl? He has her for sure, she symbolizes something to him."

Jenna looked into his eyes and nodded. "Yes, I've been worrying about her all night. There must be a connection between the cases apart from the detonator?"

"So, am I in?" Kane gave her a determined stare.

She sighed. "Okay, but we do this by the book."

"Sure." Kane's expression hardened. "I'll give him the same consideration he gave Annie."

Jenna shook her head. He was like a timebomb waiting to explode. "You'll have to curb that temper, if you're planning on working with me, Dave. I understand your anger but you can't allow it to overshadow your professionalism. You're the ice-man and you need to fall back on your training or you'll be no good to anyone, least of all me." She lifted her chin. "One mistake in front of Jo or Carter and they'll recognize an agent of your caliber. Think, Dave. If we catch him and it comes out you have a connection to Annie, it will never make it to court and he'll walk."

"I'm dead." Kane dropped his hands from her shoulders. "Ghosts can't investigate crimes, Jenna." He turned and walked out the door.

After heading down to the gym and watching Kane and Carter fighting like two men trying to prove a point, Jenna decided against a morning workout and went to the kitchen to put on the coffee. The aroma of a brewing pot reached her from the hallway. She found Jo at the kitchen table, pouring over files. "Morning."

"I couldn't sleep." Jo looked up from the laptop. "I contacted the Louan sheriff for an update. He wasn't too happy being called at five but I needed answers. There's no sign of the girl but they'll be out searching again at first light. Nothing from the BOLO or the media release. It looks like she didn't escape or she'd have shown up by now. I'm convinced the bomber has her. She is now our priority. Find her and I figure we find the bomber."

"Maybe but why take her? What's his motive?"

"I'll need more information, Jenna. I'm guessing right now." Jo scrolled through the statements on her screen. "The autopsy results will give me a better idea. I need to know what happened before he set the bomb. Its family orientated at first sight."

Jenna peered over Jo's shoulder at the open files the Louan sheriff had sent. "If you think its family orientated, we'll need to look closer at family members."

She scanned the statements from witnesses to the explosion and from the three people who called it in. "We have more resources in my office and will be able to work better from there. I'll start breakfast. If you can go and haul the guys from the gym, they'll have time to shower." She glanced at the clock. "I figure we'll have some long days and nights ahead of us."

"Sure." Jo stood and stretched. "I'll go and speak to the guys but you go and get dressed. I'll start on breakfast and then we'll all be ready to leave once we've eaten." She met Jenna's gaze. "Is everything okay with Kane?"

Jenna forced a laugh as she headed for her bedroom. "Yeah, nothing bothers him unless Duke is sick. He spoils him."

Once they arrived at the office, Jenna delegated tasks to everyone. The large communications room they set up to view CCTV surveillance of the town was rearranged. Kane and Carter moved the screens to one wall and organized the long conference table to supply work areas for the four of them. Both of Jenna's coffee makers were installed and by the time Rowley and Maggie arrived at eight, Jenna and Jo had entered every scrap of available information on the whiteboard and the team had a rough timeline.

Jenna took Rowley into her office. "How do you feel about running the office for a week, maybe two?"

"You planning on a vacation?" Rowley smiled at her. "About time. Sure, I can manage with Deputy Walters, he's getting bored sitting around home, retirement isn't his style and I can go to Wolfe if there's a problem I can't solve."

Jenna nodded. "Oh, I'll be here but not here. If you need me or Kane, we'll be in the communications room, now the temporary FBI office until further notice. You'll be working in my office. We're consulting with the FBI on a case out of Louan, so we can't run the office as well. The FBI room is off-limits for everyone."

"Oh, sure." Rowley touched his hat. "I'll go and call Walters." He turned to leave looking very pleased with himself.

Jenna hustled back to the others. "Okay, now we have this set up, what's first on the list?"

"We should head out to Louan and I'll walk you through the crime scene." Carter moved his toothpick across his lips. "We need to find a clue to where this guy has taken the girl. Right now, the local sheriff is chasing his tail."

Taking a seat at the table, Jenna stared at him. "What makes you think he's left a clue?"

"There's always a clue." Carter leaned back in his chair and stretched like a cat. "We just have to find it. Are you going to partner with me on this case?"

Although she would value Carter's insight, she worked with Kane and they were supposed to be consultants, which left her in limbo without any powers at all. Jenna glanced over the files and tried to be diplomatic. "As I have a small team, I usually delegate the work to the people with the most experience. As we're all experienced in the field, I can't see any reason to split up. It's counterproductive at this stage of the investigation." She looked at Jo and wondered why she'd left Bobby Kalo, their black hat hacker, behind at the field office. He was very useful at hunting down information. "What about Kalo? Is he available if we need him?"

"Yeah." Jo nodded. "He works better from our office. He has everything he needs there."

"You're the highest-ranking officer, Jo, how do *you* want to play this?" Kane leaned back in his chair. "One of you has to take the lead or we'll be running around bumping heads."

"We'll work together and pool resources. I'm happy to take charge of the office but I'm not a detective. What about you, Carter?" Jo glanced at Carter.

"I'd rather Jenna takes the lead." Carter looked at Kane. "No offense but she is your boss. Jenna is known throughout the local counties and people trust her. I figure if the victims have any skeletons in their closets, the locals are more likely to open up to her than us.

Her record for solving crimes is impressive." He shrugged. "As far as I'm concerned, we're all equals here. Let's do as Jenna suggested and go with the most experienced in solving murder crimes."

Jenna exchanged a look of bewilderment with Kane. "But you're FBI Agents—we don't have the power to arrest anyone outside Black Rock Falls."

"When the time comes, Jo or I will make the collar." Carter smiled. "So, it's nice and legal but who we use as consultants to get to that point is at our discretion."

"At this point we're all working under the FBI umbrella." Jo went into her briefcase and pulled out two cred packs and handed them to Jenna and Kane. "We have jackets for you as well, for in the field if there's a situation." She smiled at Jenna. "Take charge, Jenna. There's a ton of information to sort through before we start a list of possible suspects. I'll work on a profile and I'd appreciate Kane's input but I agree with Carter, we'll need to walk you through the crime scene. You'll see things we might have missed."

Confused no one seemed to be worried about the missing girl, Jenna drummed her fingers on the table. "Okay, I'll take the lead because right now we're running around in circles. We'll visit the crime scene later, right now we need more boots on the ground to find the girl. What's happening now, Carter? Do you know if Crenshaw organized a search of the Woods' farm and surrounds?"

"Yeah, I called him just before and they're searching the area now, along with some volunteers from town. There's no sign of her, Jenna. I also called Kalo and told him to hunt down any firebugs in the area."

Glad that the Louan sheriff had the search covered, she glanced at the statements on her screen. "We'll start with the witnesses' statements. Once we have an idea what happened prior, during, and after the explosion, we'll head out to the crime scene."

They all worked in silence for some time. Jenna made notes on a few points. The people who called in a crime, especially in a fire, were often involved. A firebug enjoyed watching the firetrucks as well as the blaze.

"Now this is interesting." Carter scrolled through the statements. "I've found a report of an older model blue Ford sedan seen in the vicinity of the Woods' ranch before the explosion." He frowned. "They didn't take down the plate number but the vehicle was parked alongside the road just before nightfall and then drove into the Woods' ranch. The neighbor, Joe Ranger, noticed it as he was feeding his horses." He continued scrolling through the information on his screen. "Ranger headed into town soon after and didn't see the fire."

The memory of yesterday morning's conversation with Kane flashed through Jenna's mind. "Kane picked up a stolen vehicle fitting that description on Stanton Road the day after the fire. It's in the impound lot in town." She scanned her files. "The driver, Harvey Haralson, is in custody. We have his statement. I'll add it to the files."

"I'll call Wolfe." Kane pulled out his phone. "That car may hold the clue you're after."

"As firebugs like to watch the fire—" Jo's attention moved to Kane "—did you smell smoke on him? It would've been hard to miss if he'd been close."

"No." Kane's brow furrowed. "The vehicle went missing on Tuesday, was used in a crime that night, and found abandoned in the forest opposite the Triple Z Bar, the following morning, so I doubt the eighteen-year-old I pulled out the car was the bomber. I'd like to know why he was at the Triple Z, he's too young to drink. How did he get there and where was he coming from? We could stop by county and let Carter flash his creds to put the fear of death into him by threatening to charge him with murder one?"

"Yeah, good idea." Carter smiled and pushed his toothpick to one side of his mouth. "But he seems a mite young to be our bomber, unless his daddy taught him." He looked at Jenna. "It might be an idea to find out if the kid was related to the DC bomber?" He accessed a database and they all waited expectantly. "No, Harvey Haralson is not related and has lived here in town all his life."

"I don't think he's involved but we shouldn't discount him completely. These days, men of his age are volatile and some are easily led into crime." Jo looked from one to the other. "I'll contact county and inform them he's a person of interest in the bombing. They'll be able to hold him until we can get to interview him."

"But why would he risk being caught in a stolen vehicle after the bombing?" Carter frowned.

Jenna nodded. "I agree. No one is that stupid. He'd have known someone could've seen him by the ranch. He was out there before dark in plain sight."

"Yeah but remember, if we're dealing with a psychopath, they never believe they can be caught." Kane crossed his legs at the ankles. "The arrogance I witnessed is typical behavior."

Jenna stood and added Harvey Haralson and the vehicle to the whiteboard. A thought grabbed her. "Has the Triple Z recently installed a CCTV in the parking lot?"

"Now that would be a first." Carter snorted and grinned at her. "Trust me, none of the clientele in that place want a record of their comings and goings. This one is going to be tough."

"No one said solving crimes was easy." Jenna pushed both hands through her hair. "Kane, call the impound yard and make sure no one goes near the car before Wolfe collects it. Carter, get out another media statement asking for any information on the vehicle. Someone might have seen it after the explosion. If the fire had people out sightseeing someone might have passed it on the highway." She frowned. "Let's get to work, we have a missing girl out there and someone has to have seen that car."

CHAPTER ELEVEN

The Whispering Caves

Deep inside the Whispering Caves, water trickled just out of Sophie's reach. Trying to ignore the tantalizing drip into the small pool of crystal-clear water, she swiped her parched tongue over her cracked lips and picked up the small rock. Trying to concentrate as she dehydrated had become harder by the minute but determined to cut herself free, she used the sharp rock to keep up a relentless sawing across the zip-tie binding her ankle to the ring in the ground. Blood trickled from her palm making the stone slip and slide. She'd dropped it so many times and suffered waves of frustration when it blended into the rock bottom of the cave. Acutely aware of any sounds in the catacombs, she stopped to listen but the skitter scatter wasn't the man returning, it was the critters that shared her hellhole. Right now, he couldn't see what she was doing and she knew exactly what turned on the trail cam. If she moved, the red light came on, so she turned her back, covered herself with the blanket and waited. Once the whir of the camera stopped, she moved one hand carefully to avoid triggering the motion sensor. The camera had come on at other times as well, so she figured he must have a way of watching her at any time.

Time was non-existent inside the cave. It had become one endless night and she'd gone from her stomach reminding her she hadn't eaten, to rolling in waves of pain. Her body ached and her brutal captor reminded her each time he visited how nobody missed her or cared if she lived or died. He'd described in detail how her family would have looked after the fire. The sound of his laughter at her suffering filled her head in an endless tormenting earwig. He wanted to watch her starve to death and no doubt would find the rats consuming her dead flesh entertainment. She had to get away.

In desperation, she tugged at the fraying zip tie and suddenly it snapped. Lunging on unsteady legs, she crawled to the pool of water. It tasted metallic but she didn't care and scooped it up in her hands to quench her thirst. Her stomach rolled as the freezing water slid down her throat making her nauseas. Slowing her pace, she sipped slowly. Sharp rocks dug into her bare flesh but she didn't care and splashed water over her face. Breathing heavily, she didn't hear the footsteps at first but the cough was unmistakably human. Frozen with fear, she turned and stared into the lens of a camera. The echo of footsteps rumbled toward her. The unmistakable rhythm of his walk was imprinted in her mind. He'd decided to torture her again.

Panic gripped her as she scampered back to the filthy mattress and snatched up the blanket. She fashioned it around her for warmth. Trembling, she glanced at the lantern. Indecisions clutched at her. If she took it, he'd find her in seconds but her fear of the dark made the pitch-black tunnels leading away in all directions terrifying. A cool wind blew against her cheek and she moved closer to the forbidding abyss. There had to be a way out. And the draft was coming from outside. She glanced behind her down the main tunnel as a slither of light bounced off the walls from his flashlight. His footsteps had gotten closer and now she could hear him whistling. Whatever the darkness held for her it had to be better than suffering a moment longer. She gathered her courage and ducking under cobwebs, ran into the darkness.

CHAPTER TWELVE

Jo climbed into Jenna's sheriff department's SUV and glanced at Carter. They'd decided to take both vehicles, mainly to carry all their gear and two dogs. "What possessed you to give the lead to Jenna? You're one of the top people in your field."

"Like I said, she has a reputation in the local counties, many of the deputies have worked under her before. It was the right move and leaves my hands free to investigate. If Kane has the knowledge he claims to have in explosives, then we'll be working on identifying the bomber using our expertise. Jenna is great at finding potential suspects and with you profiling, we have everything covered." He glanced at her and his green eyes flashed with amusement. "They can't arrest anyone unless the killer walks into their county but we have that covered. Don't worry, Jo, everything will work out just fine."

"Oh, I don't have a problem with Jenna, I just don't want you and Kane butting heads." Jo sighed. "It doesn't take a behavioral analyst to recognize something isn't sitting too well with Kane. His reaction to the images of the car bombing surprised me." She shook her head slowly. "I was expecting this case to freak you out, not Kane, he seems so laid back."

"Did you know, he has a metal plate in his head?" Carter flicked her a glance. "I read up about him: after the marines he joined the force and took a bullet in the head during a gunfight. I'm guessing he suffered PTSD and maybe the images triggered an episode. He took a deputy's job in a backwoods town for some peace and quiet." He snorted. "He's not having too much luck to date, is he?"

They soon arrived at the crime scene and Jo climbed out and waited for Jenna and Kane. She had questions but would ask them later, when she and Jenna were alone. She waited for them all to pull on protective suits and gloves. "Okay, it's best if Carter explains the technical side of the explosion. We have the report from the Black Rock Falls Fire Chief as well."

"That's good and with Kane's input we should get a very clear picture of what occurred here." Jenna turned toward the gutted remains of the large ranch house and then looked at Carter. "I can see the perimeter is marked. Have entry and exit points been established?"

"It's good to know you follow procedure." Carter smiled around his toothpick and tipped back his Stetson. "Yeah, we enter around the detonation crater and exit by the backdoor."

"As we haven't reevaluated the crime scene yet…" Jenna waved a hand in the direction of the ruins. "Why isn't there a deputy on duty around the clock to preserve the evidence?" She scanned through the files on her screen. "Anyone could've been inside since the ME left."

Jo walked to Jenna's side. "Webber took a video and hundreds of pictures. Wolfe and the fire chief both took samples of the crater and the accelerant. They found a can of gas upturned on the kitchen floor."

"Okay." Jenna looked up. "Who collected evidence from the second floor?" She looked puzzled. "I see from the preliminary report, the fire destroyed the stairs."

Jo frowned. "No one went upstairs to collect evidence as far as I'm aware, Jenna."

"Really? We'll need to get someone up there to collect evidence and take some shots. I'd say the youngest victim would have been in her bed around the time the bomber broke into the house. How old did you say she was?"

A vivid flash of the charred body crossed Jo's mind as she opened her iPad and scrolled the information on the family. "Jody Wood was five. The explosion occurred a little after nine."

"Kane, can you hunt down a ladder and gain entrance to the second floor?" Jenna looked at the images on her tablet. "The bottom of the stairs are toast but the structure looks okay."

"Are you suggesting the fire department didn't clear the upper floor for survivors or bodies?" Kane shot a look at Carter. "Surely once the area had been cleared of explosives, the fire chief would've checked?"

"Not that I'm aware." Carter frowned. "I assumed it had been cleared before we arrived. Everything was out and the firefighters had left by the time we arrived."

"You assumed?" Jenna rolled her eyes. "You're an expert in your field and you didn't ask if the upper floors had been cleared?"

"I was called in to hunt down a secondary device." Carter shrugged. "I did my job and cleared the crime scene of explosives."

"And yet you didn't clear the upper levels?" Jenna glared at him. "Why was that?"

"The stairs were gutted." Carter met her gaze unperturbed. "It's highly unlikely a bomber would bother to place another explosive on the second floor. He wanted a big bang and backed it up with a secondary device and used gas as an accelerant. Trust me, there is no bomb upstairs."

"You should have cleared the area anyway." Jenna lifted her chin. "It is normal procedure. You couldn't hunt down a ladder?"

"Oh, the boss has claws." Carter straightened, removed his hat, and ran a hand through his shaggy blond hair and stared down his nose at her. "Don't let the promotion go to your head, honey."

"Pull your head in, Carter." Jenna stared at him, unmoving. "You chose me to lead the case, and if you don't like to follow procedure, too bad because I do, so quit the sexist remarks and suck it up."

"Fine, but you should be blaming the fire chief or Wolfe, not me." Carter was holding his ground. "We cleared the area and Zorro would have alerted me if there'd been another explosive device close by. I did a thorough search of the ground floor. Zorro doesn't make mistakes and neither do I. It wasn't my job to search for bodies. I collected evidence in the bombing, which led to the connection between this case and the ones in DC." He creased his hat down the center and slammed it back on his head. "Since when did calling a woman 'honey' become sexist? It is an endearment, not a slight."

"It's rude and demeaning. I know you've been living alone for a couple of years but you're representing the FBI now and need to get your filter back in place. We're not living in the 1970s." Jenna's eyes flashed with anger when his mouth twitched at the edges. "Forget it. I'm not standing here arguing with you all day. We have a case to solve."

"I'm not arguing, Jenna." Carter's infuriating smile was back in place. "You're so easy to rile. Loosen up a bit and we'll get on just fine." He indicated to Jo with his thumb. "Look at Jo here, she doesn't take offense to every word I say but if my being friendly makes your hackles rise, I'll do my best to think before I speak, okay?" He glanced at Kane. "Man, is she this hostile with you?"

"Don't drag me into this." Kane held up both hands.

Concerned by the friction Carter's attitude was causing, Jo moved between them to face Jenna. "This is why there was a delay in searching for Sophie Wood." She met Jenna's annoyed gaze. "There was the chance of a secondary explosive device and Wolfe refused entry until we arrived to clear the scene. It was hours after the explosion by the time we arrived. It wasn't until we counted the bodies that I discovered Sophie was missing."

"But how do you *know* she's missing?" Agitated, Kane rubbed the back of his neck. "She might have been trapped upstairs. Dammit,

Carter, you sayin' the fire chief sent out a finalized report without checking the entire building?" He stormed off toward the barn muttering under his breath.

CHAPTER THIRTEEN

During her time as a DEA agent, Jenna had often attended the aftermath of a meth lab explosion and taken the lead in investigations far more complex and dangerous than this one. Mistakes and miscommunication happened when cases moved between agencies but this one was becoming a nightmare. She looked at Jo's apologetic expression and sighed. "I told you Sheriff Crenshaw was a jerk." Jenna shook her head. "Although, Wolfe is usually on his game. I've no idea why he didn't question the sheriff or the firefighters about clearing the second floor." She tried to ignore the acrid smell that hung around a housefire and clung to anyone passing close by. She tucked her tablet under one arm and pulled out her phone. "I'll call Wolfe and find out what the hell happened here. I'll put it on speaker." She made the call.

"Dad is in the middle of an autopsy and he hasn't gotten out to look at the car yet. He's rushed off his feet, Jenna, is it urgent?" Emily Wolfe's voice came through the speaker.

Jenna bit back a sigh of frustration. "Yeah, it is. We're out at the Louan fire scene and I need clarification. Can you disturb him. It won't take long."

"Okay."

The familiar swish of the examination room doors opening at the morgue came through the speaker and then Wolfe's voice.

"Shane here. Is this sensitive? I have Emily and Colt with me"

"No." Jenna flicked a glance at Carter. "I'm at the Louan fire scene. Did anyone clear the upper floor for bodies? It's not in the report from the fire chief."

"From what I understand, the firetruck was able to extend a ladder to the upper front window, and extinguished the blaze. Crenshaw informed me the upstairs was empty. So, one of the firefighters must have done a walk through." Wolfe sighed. *"I pulled everyone away from the building and called Jo and the fire chief in case there was a secondary explosive device on the ground floor, which there was and Carter cleared it. I didn't go upstairs personally as the stairs were consumed by the fire but I will, once I've discovered the cause of death of the victims. The crime scene is being protected, isn't it? I did leave instructions with Crenshaw to leave a deputy out there."*

Jenna exchanged an exasperated look with Jo. "No deputies here and Kane is heading up a ladder to look inside now. I figure the youngest girl would've been in bed when the bomber arrived. He must have used inducement to make them come downstairs. Most kids would hide if they thought they were in danger." She sighed. "We have no proof anyone went inside. What if the missing girl is still up there?"

"I hope not." Shane sucked air through his teeth in an agitated whistle. *"I'm used to working with professionals. I don't usually have to question anyone on their reports, especially the fire chief. He should've been on the ball."*

"I guess it depends if he took the word of Sheriff Crenshaw and the local firefighters. In my opinion, as it was his responsibility to clear the building, he should have gone up there himself or at least make mention of not being able to inspect the second floor in his report."

"I agree and I'll be talking to him about his report as soon as I'm through here. He needs to up his game if he wants to keep his job. Do

you want me to come out and do another forensics sweep today?" Wolfe cleared his throat. *"I'm almost done here. Thanks to the Blackwater dentist, I have positive IDs on Isaac, Connie, and Jody Wood. It was fortunate Bobby Kalo traced the family to Blackwater, the Louan dentist had zip. You can go ahead and notify next-of-kin. Something you should know, Mrs. Wood was raped and suffered head trauma before the fire. Her nose was broken and she had teeth missing. I'll give you more details after the autopsy but this is the most staged and brutal explosion I've seen."*

Jo stepped closer and her mouth turned down. "Jo here. Yes, this changes everything about his profile. The girl, Jody Wood, did he hurt her?"

"From the toxicology tests I did on the gasses in her lungs, she died before the fire got to her and from the X-rays, I couldn't find any major signs of trauma. She wasn't raped. I believe the blast wave from the explosion rendered her unconscious, so that's a small mercy." Wolfe paused a beat. *"I haven't completed the examination of Mr. Wood but he has a skull fracture, consistent with blunt force trauma. We need to meet up and discuss my findings. This is one twisted SOB."*

Jenna nodded and her gaze drifted to Carter climbing the ladder after Kane. "Okay, we'll leave it until all the autopsies are complete. We have a ton of things to do here yet."

"Okay, I'll call you when I'm through here and I've gone over the vehicle at the impound yard." Wolfe disconnected.

Jenna pushed her phone inside her pocket and stared up at the house. The sodden blackened mess before her had once been a family home, filled with happiness and laughter. From the lovingly tended garden and the ashes of a climbing rose bush hanging from what was left of a trellis, the occupants had enjoyed gardening. "I wouldn't like to be in the fire chief's shoes. I figure he's never seen Wolfe angry before." She glanced at Jo and caught the tiny twitch of a smile. "What?"

"Matt Thompson is his name and he's good-looking and uses his firefighter allure for all it's worth." Jo rolled her eyes. "He might as well have 'Player' tattooed on his forehead."

"Good to know." Concerned for Kane and Carter's safety, Jenna kept her attention on the second-floor window. When Kane stuck his head out and waved to her, she hurried forward. "Did you find her?"

"Nah. It's pretty much untouched up here." Kane pulled down his facemask. "I found a smear of blood on the doorframe of the girls' bedroom and along one wall in the hallway. I took a few swabs. The room has smoke damage but that's all. All the rooms look undisturbed. No sign of a struggle but I've bagged the sheets from all the rooms, emptied the laundry basket in case we need the girl's scent, and Carter's taken photographs. I'll throw the evidence bags down."

After Kane and Carter had finished, Jenna pulled up the files. She examined the diagrams of the crime scene from Carter's comprehensive documentation. She had to admit it was faultless. He'd recorded the time of inspection, the approximate time of the explosion, weather conditions, odors, and structural damage along with his observations. There was so much more but she wanted to hear it from him. She waved a hand toward the house. "Carter, give us the tour."

"Okay." Carter led the way and skirted a crater in what used to be the family room. "The method of bomb delivery was C-4, in a primary and secondary explosion set a few seconds apart. The blast effects as you can see are projected out and not toward the victims. In fact, they would have been protected to some degree by being in the kitchen. The crater and burn pattern suggest the bomber used an accelerant. The thermal effects, the bend in the metal furniture frames, and melting of the kitchen utensils show the fire reached a higher temperature than I'd have thought normal for a housefire." He looked at Jenna. "I've sent a report to all the appropriate agencies to hunt down any other cases or incident reports." He walked through a gap in the wall and into the kitchen. "The can of gas was found in here and Wolfe took samples as did the fire chief but from the smell it was gasoline. The victims were placed around the kitchen table, all secured to chairs. The chairs were knocked over due to the blast wave but the victim closest to the open doorway would have taken the force of the blaze. As you can see from the burn pattern over the ceiling and stairs there was a flashover, the fire went over the victims like a wave and down the walls."

Dismayed at the complete destruction before her, Jenna allowed her gaze to settle on the distinct outline of a small figure on the charred wooden floor. An overwhelming sadness engulfed her. The person who did this had taken the older girl and she could only imagine what horrific torture he could inflict on her. After no sightings of Sophie Wood, the chances of her surviving a monster like this killer were minimal. She looked at Jo. "We need to move faster on this case, someone like this is going to strike again, isn't he?"

"That's very likely, if he's acting out a vendetta." Jo shook her head. "It's well planned. From what I'm seeing here, we have a serial killer on our hands."

Jenna dragged her gaze away from the floor, scanned the room, and then walked out to the destroyed stairs. It was tragic and oppressive being inside so much destruction, she could almost feel the hate from the man who'd caused it. Ahead, the way to the backdoor was clear. "They would have been able to exit by the backdoor if they hadn't been restrained."

"The explosion would've knocked them unconscious." Kane moved to her side. "Do you remember how far we were thrown during the explosion at the old school house?"

Remembering only too clearly how it felt to be picked up and thrown across the ground, she nodded. "But they were behind the blast. It wouldn't have been as bad as what we went through and we survived."

"These people were on top of it, Jenna." Kane turned her around to face him. "It would've been quick. Unconscious and then they probably died from inhaling the fumes before the fire engulfed the room."

Jenna nodded and straightened. "Okay, I've seen enough. We'll stop by the search command center and chase down the witnesses while the incident is fresh in their minds." She looked at Carter. "Anyone here, watching the show when you arrived?"

"Nope." Carter peered at her over his facemask. "The sheriff had cleared the spectators but he gave me a list of everyone who came by." He pointed to her tablet. "It's all in the case files."

"Thanks. We'll head into town now and find out if anyone took videos of the fire, it might show people or vehicles in the area at the time." Jenna turned to Carter and walked with him out of earshot of the others. "I owe you an apology. The recording and observations of the scene are some of the best I've read."

"Well thank you, ma'am." Carter smiled at her and then his expression changed to serious. "I'm real sorry for riling you before, it wasn't intentional. I respect women but admit I'm a little rusty being alone for so long but I promise not to step out of line again. I just want us to get along, Jenna. Can we be friends?"

Astonished by his sincerity, Jenna blinked. "So, no more smartass remarks and sexist comments?"

"Cross my heart." Carter's green gaze searched her face.

Jenna smiled. "I'd like that, thank you."

"Good. Now I can get my mind back on the job." Carter gave her a salute and headed out the backdoor.

CHAPTER FOURTEEN

The Whispering Caves

Gasping for breath, Sophie flattened herself against the wall of the cave. She could hear the man coming, his steady footsteps crunching through the never-ending gravel under her feet. She couldn't tell if he'd entered her tunnel or was walking close by. Sound became distorted inside the caves. A tumbling rock was amplified into a rockfall and the sound of her heavy breathing seemed to bounce back at her as if mocking her attempts to escape him. Blackness hung over her, obscuring everything, so she couldn't see her hand in front of her face. Terrified of taking another step into oblivion, she slid her fingers along the damp rock walls and gripped the blanket covering her shoulders.

"Come out, come out wherever you are." His voice echoed toward her in a rush of sound.

She wanted to scream and run away but the gloom held her prisoner in her fear of the unknown. She edged forward, step by step. Something touched her face, and the unmistakable tickle of a spider's web clung to her. Critters brushed past her in a rush to get away and underfoot, the hard cave floor had become smoother and angled downward. A sticky substance squelched through her toes and she slipped and slid, losing her blanket. With no time to stop to find it she pushed on, but each forward movement brought with it another horror. The air moved, sending another blast of coolness over her sweat-soaked brow. She could hear him now, and a beam of light lit the rock above her head, sending bats flying in all directions. The panicked beasts caught in her hair and she screamed in terror, swiping them away with her hands.

"I can hear you." The man's voice rumbled up the tunnel. "I won't be leaving a lantern for you next time, Sophie. It will be you and the rats and I get to watch them eat you alive in night vision. How sweet is that?" He chuckled deep in his chest. "Maybe if you come to me on hands and knees and beg a little, I'll go easy on you."

Frantic, Sophie scrambled on, feeling her way along the cave walls into the void. The air coming toward her had gone from a slight breeze to pushing the hair from her face. Under her fingers the unforgiving rock walls had turned to ice. In the distance she could make out a rushing sound. Could it be the wind that made the tunnels whisper or was it the rush of water? Images of ghouls and monsters ran in chaos through her mind but she'd rather face them than spend one more second with her tormentor. Swallowing her fear, she kept moving. Behind her the man's footsteps grew louder. The way ahead bent to the right and underfoot became slippery and she tumbled, falling with a splash into ice-cold water. Teeth chattering, she grabbed at the slippery walls and pushed to her feet. The rumbling sound had gotten louder. She recognized the sound of a waterfall and almost whooped with joy. She'd visited Black Rock Falls with her family and heard stories about the catacombs. The tunnel must lead out to somewhere near the falls. Determined to find a way out she hastened her step and waded on blindly. Without warning, the ground dropped away and fast flowing water picked her up and dragged her along like a cork. She bounced off the walls as it headed downward in a rush into the murky darkness.

"Sophie... Sophie, I'm right behind you." The man's voice seemed closer now and the beam of his flashlight was bouncing off the water.

In blind terror she struck out swimming with the current. The thundering noise was getting louder by the second and an unforgiving sheet of water pounded her from above. She couldn't stop now, and kicked her legs hard. She had to keep her head above the water. Suddenly a current swirled her around and tugged her under, spinning her like a top. Trapped in the inky water, she couldn't breathe. Her heart pounded in her ears and her lungs screamed for one precious mouthful of air. Blindly, she fought to the surface and sucked in a breath as the fast-flowing torrent swept her along.

The ice-cold stream surrounded her, numbing her legs but she kicked her leaden feet and fought to find the rock wall. Hands flailing, she found nothing but air. Sophie cried out in horror as the torrent increased speed. Pain shuddered through aching bones as it hurled her without mercy against the walls on its way through the weaving passage. Water filled her nose and mouth, cutting off any chance to breathe. Dizzy from colliding with the rocks, she gathered her last ounce of strength and fighting for a single breath, she tumbled onward like a stick in the rapids. All around her, the deafening roar of water filled the cave.

In the distance a beam of light peeked through long strands of green undergrowth. Daylight bounced off droplets of water in rainbows and the noise was so loud, it filled her head. She had to slow down or the water would carry her over the edge of the falls. Gasping for air, she grabbed at outcrops of rock, anything to slow her progress but the mossy rocks slid against her palms. Sheer terror gripped her as she burst into the blinding sunlight and caught one glimpse of a cloudless blue sky before the waterfall claimed her for its own.

CHAPTER FIFTEEN

Getting involved in other people's arguments was a recipe for disaster but Kane had to say something. They needed to work as a team and the friction between Jenna and Carter was getting out of hand. "Do you mind if I say something?" Kane turned the Beast onto the highway and headed into the town of Louan.

It was a glorious day, sunshine, blue skies and away from the smell of fire, the air was sweet. Jenna loved days like these and her hostility disturbed him. He'd rarely seen Jenna in a mood. Determined maybe, but when she was on the job, she was professional all the time. After flicking her a glance, he waited for her to close her tablet and look at him.

"Since when do you need my permission, Dave?" Jenna's brow furrowed. "What's up?"

"These arguments with Carter." Kane cleared his throat. "He likes you. I figure he riles you up to get attention. I've seen it before; you know the love-hate relationship."

"Oh, Lord, Kane." Jenna grinned at him. "Don't you think I know when a guy is hitting on me, however subtly? Trust me, he's not. Carter isn't the relationship kind. Being an arrogant ass is all part of his game. He likes to see how far he can push me." She looked away to give the air-con controls her full attention. "He's not interested in me, or anyone else. In any case, we have a truce. I praised his work and we're cool. Don't worry." She tossed her bangs out of her eyes. "I shouldn't have risen to the bait in the first place.

I've noticed how Jo just ignores his stupid comments completely and it seems to work."

"Does she?" Kane kept his eye on the road. "Maybe he doesn't act like an ass with her because she's his superior?"

"Ha." Jenna shook her head. "He pushes her buttons too but she worked him out way before I did. I doubt it will happen again but if it does, I'm either going to ignore his sexist remarks or punch him on the nose." She chuckled. "I'm all for equality, and if a guy made a sexist remark to you, you'd do the same, right?"

Not sure if she was joking, Kane shrugged. "Maybe he thinks he's being funny?"

"Oh no, he knows exactly how to get under my skin." Jenna stared out the window. "It just took me a while to understand his angle. I thought at first it was because he'd been off the grid for a couple of years, but I see right through him now. He doesn't know how to act around women and how old is he? Thirty or something and he still acts like a kid."

Kane had his own ideas about Carter, if she'd listen. "More like he's trying to cover up any lapses into PTSD episodes by trying to be funny. He was leading a team where kids were killed and it knocked him sideways for a time." He scratched his cheek, thinking. "He is arrogant, but I think he means well." He shot her a look. "As a Seal, he was a team player, and it won't take him too long to fall back into the way of things. It's a way of life for them and he's been alone far too long."

"Maybe." Jenna snorted. "You don't need to make excuses for him, Dave."

"Then what can I do to help?" Kane headed down the main street of Louan. "I figure you'd like to keep some distance between you and Carter for the next couple of hours?"

"Yeah, I sure would. Get him out of my hair for a while and go and hunt down the people who came out to look at the fire. See if they have any footage, and if they noticed anyone else hanging around that's not on the sheriff's list." She chewed on her bottom lip. "I'll take Jo and we'll hunt down the victims' friends and family. Although, I figure everyone in town knows about the explosion by now." She checked her tablet. "I want to find out who had it in for the Wood family."

Kane glanced at her. "So where are you going first? The sheriff's department?"

"Yeah, I want to know why there's no one out at the scene." Jenna lifted her chin. "He'll be surprised to see me. I'm sure he won't be too happy the FBI chose us as consultants. You don't have to wait. I'll update the sheriff and we'll meet up at the diner at one." She glanced behind them. "Carter and Jo are right behind us, pull up here and I'll bring them up to speed."

"Sure." Kane pulled into a space outside the Louan Sheriff's Department and Jenna slid from the seat. "Catch you later."

He took out his phone to access the files and pulled up the list of people who'd watched the fire. A tap came on his window and he looked up to see Carter and Zorro. He buzzed down the window. "It looks like we're working together today."

"Yeah, that bit I know." Carter removed his toothpick and tossed it into a trash can. "What's on our list?" He settled Zorro beside Duke and climbed into the passenger seat.

Kane explained and entered the first of the witnesses' addresses into the GPS. "Going on the theory that if this is a firebug, it's likely this isn't his first dance, I figure we dig a little deeper into the witnesses before we speak to them. How fast is Bobby Kalo at hunting down jackets?"

"Fast." Carter smiled. "I'll send him the file now." He pulled out his phone and then chuckled. "Do you know your truck smells like honeysuckle?" He grinned. "Jenna leaves a little ray of sunshine wherever she goes, huh?"

Kane backed out onto Main and headed out of town. He slowed as a group of townsfolk spilled onto the blacktop grappling a banner for an upcoming rodeo that was flapping in a sudden gust of wind, and turned to Carter. "Jenna had to fight for her position as sheriff. She's a respected member of the community and doesn't need you smart-mouthing her every time we meet."

"I was just joshing with her." Carter tipped up his Stetson and whistled through his teeth. "Okay, who do we have first?" He peered at his phone, just as it buzzed with a message. "It's Kalo. He's updated the files already, man that guy is fast. Three of the witnesses to the fire have priors. Two had fines for lighting fires and one of the guys, John Cleaves, who called it in was also fined for stealing C-4 from his workplace. The others are clean but an Audrey Johnstone, has already posted the explosion on social media. She caught the footage on her dashcam driving by, same with John Cleaves, both have dashcam video."

Kane pulled up to the curb. "Does Kalo have a link?"

"Yeah, he sent the files to you already." Carter peered at his phone. "I need to see this on a bigger screen."

"Sure." Kane went to the mobile digital terminal "I'll feed it through the MDT."

They stared as the screen lit up with a huge red mushroom. Against the dark sky it blossomed red, then seconds later another explosion shook the camera and the red cloud shot up again falling in a canopy of destruction. Flames leapt into the air in a rush of bright orange and blue, illuminating the ranch house and all around in a yellow glow. Smoke billowed like an afterthought and as the flames cut electricity wires, sparks danced through the black mass like lightning through storm clouds. Kane reversed and replayed the explosion over and over, going from one recording and then the other. "Two blasts as we thought, seconds apart and then the whoosh as the gas caught fire."

"Yeah, you got it." Carter leaned into the screen. "He aimed the main force away from the family as I figured but why if he wanted them dead?"

With his focus on the two vehicles in the video, Kane thought for a beat. "I guess he wanted them to suffer. Revenge maybe." He pointed to the screen. "I believe that's the blue Ford I pulled over for speeding and the license plate of the truck is caught in the headlights of the driver with the dashcam. He's some ways off but Wolfe has a way of enhancing the film."

"Nah, he's busy doing forensics and we have Kalo twiddling his thumbs." Carter called Bobby Kalo. "Great work on the background checks and video. Can you enhance the other vehicles? We need a positive on the license plate of the truck and who was driving the Ford sedan leaving the scene." He smiled at Kane and nodded. "As soon as you're able, we'll be speaking to witnesses so message me with the details. Thanks man." He disconnected.

Kane pulled back onto Main and followed the directions on the GPS and pulled into the curb ten yards from a neat redbrick with a garden overflowing with flowers. "Okay this is the home of John Cleaves, forty-eight, shift worker with a mine supply plant. He's the guy with the first dashcam video. He called in the explosion. Let's hope he's home." He climbed out the truck and opened the door for the dogs to stretch their legs.

When Carter joined him, and they walked toward the house, Kane looked at him. "Will Zorro pick up if this guy has been using C-4 lately?"

"That would depend on how fastidious the man is about his personal hygiene." Carter shrugged. "I'll give him the command and we'll see." He turned to Kane. "If we have any indication from Zorro, we should obtain a search warrant for the girl as well. Do you have the girl's garment you took from the laundry basket at the fire scene?"

"Sure have." Kane tapped his pocket. "I took out everything in the basket and bagged it. I don't think it has been damaged by the smell of the fire. Duke may still be able to track the scent." He smiled at Carter. "How fast can you obtain a search warrant?" He opened the white iron gate and their boots crunched on the gravel walkway winding its way between fragrant flower gardens to the house.

"A man with priors in explosives and a positive reaction from Zorro? I'd say as long as it takes to fill out the form." Carter tossed a toothpick into his mouth.

Kane frowned. "Are you trying to give up smoking?"

"Me, nah." Carter chuckled. "Gum. I was eating so much I was getting an ulcer." He banged on the front door of the house.

"Can I help you?" An elderly woman peered around the door.

"Mornin', ma'am. I'm Special Agent Carter and this is Dave Kane, we are looking for John, is he home?"

"He's asleep. He worked last night." The woman frowned. "What is this about?"

Kane smiled to calm the old woman. "He posted a video clip of an explosion on social media. We'd like to know what time the explosion happened and if he saw anyone leaving the area." He met her watery blue eyes. "A young girl went missing after the explosion and we need as much information as possible to find her."

"Oh, I see." She stared at Kane for a beat as if trying to make up her mind what to do. "He gets a mite angry when I wake him but I guess he'll understand. You being the FBI and all." She shut the door in their faces and through the side window Kane could see her shuffling away.

"Is that his mom?" Carter raised his eyebrows. "She looks way into her nineties."

Kane shrugged. "Grandma maybe." He flicked through the files Kalo had updated. "He's not married and lives with his grandma."

Raised voices and footsteps came from inside and the door flew open. A tall rugged man, his dark hair tussled and eyes bleary from sleep, glared at them. "What do you want?" He took a holster carrying a pistol from a hook by the door and strapped it on. "I know my rights. You can't just walk into a man's yard and demand to see him."

"The FBI has many rights and one of them is walking onto an unposted property to speak to the occupier." Carter held up his cred pack. "Are you impeding an investigation, Mr. Cleaves?"

"I guess not." Cleaves' eyes flashed with simmering anger.

Kane was keeping one eye on the man's hands. He straightened. "Remove your weapon, sir. We wouldn't like any misunderstandings, now would we?"

"Give up my weapon?" Cleaves shook his head. "No way." His fingers twitched.

Kane drew fast and aimed at Cleaves. "You see how easily things get out of hand? Now remove the weapon from the holster and hand it to me grip first."

When the man complied, Kane smiled and holstered his weapon. "See that wasn't so bad, was it?" He removed the clip and pocketed the weapon.

"Ask them to come inside." The old woman was standing in the hallway. "You'll have the neighbors' tongues wagging again with all this arguing."

"They have dogs with them, Gran." Cleaves looked belligerently at Kane. "They can stay outside."

"No, they're coming in too." Carter moved his toothpick over his lips. "They are FBI, same as us. Where we go, they go. Don't worry they won't mess on your floor." He pushed past the man and followed the old lady into the family room.

Kane followed, keeping the man between them but when Zorro stopped and sat down at the door to what resembled a broom closet, he hung back. The Doberman had given a positive sign for explosives. He waited for everyone to move inside the room and then pulled the plastic evidence bag from his pocket and waved the contents under Duke's nose. He dropped his voice to a whisper. "Seek."

Duke would alert him if he found anything. Kane walked into the room and stood with his back to the fireplace. The house had a strange odor, like boiled soup bones and lavender. As Cleaves sat down beside his grandmother, he waved Carter into an overstuffed chair. The fact both dogs had suddenly gone missing hadn't been noticed by Cleaves. When Carter pulled out his notepad, it was obvious he'd decided to take the lead in the questioning. Kane had some questions of his own. He'd noticed a pair of muddy boots outside the front door, which seemed unusual when the gardens were pristine, but he recalled seeing recently turned soil in a garden bed adjacent to the backdoor of the Woods' house. He'd made a note of it in the case file but as the firefighters had washed away any evidence of footprints, until now it hadn't been relevant.

"We noticed your video of the recent explosion out at Aspen Grove last Tuesday. You called it in and we need to know all the details you can remember." Carter looked at Cleaves expectantly. "First oblige me with a timeline. Where were you coming from at nine-forty at night?"

"From home." Cleaves frowned. "I was heading to work in Black Rock Falls when the explosion happened slap bang in front of me. I called 911 and then called my boss and explained why I'd be late, helping the sheriff and all. They told me to take the night off, so after waiting for the sheriff and his boys to arrive, I came home and uploaded the video to my page. I called the local news channel but they didn't want my footage, they'd already taken another from some woman." He snorted. "I missed out on some fast cash."

"In the footage we noticed an older model blue Ford sedan." Carter looked at him. "Did you notice where it came from or where it went?"

"That wasn't a blue Ford, it was gray and belongs to Simon Dexter. He lives here in town." Cleaves stared into space. "Yeah, he went by and then stopped to watch the fire. He walked down to speak to me."

"How was he acting? Ah… just a second." Carter glanced at Kane. "Is Dexter on our list of witnesses?"

Kane recalled Dexter was also a firebug. He nodded. "Yeah, and he's on Kalo's list as well."

"How was he acting?" Cleaves frowned. "Excited, I guess. He couldn't stand still and once he'd given his name to the sheriff, he headed out toward Black Rock Falls." He thought for a beat. "He asked me for a copy of the footage. I emailed him one when I'd gotten home."

"Did you see anyone else in his vehicle?" Carter made a few notes.

Kane watched the man's eyes flick from side to side and his posture stiffened. What could he be hiding? He caught sight of Duke peering through the door and patted his leg. No sign of the girl in the house but Zorro hadn't moved from his position outside the closet door.

"I didn't see anyone in the vehicle. He went by so fast." Cleaves looked at Duke and then up at Kane. "Where's the other one?"

Kane noticed a bead of sweat trickle down the man's forehead. "Just outside the door."

"Okay, did you notice any of your neighbors watching the blaze or anyone coming through the fields?" Carter lifted his chin. "Anything at all you can remember will help. Did you see a girl?"

"No, I don't remember seeing a girl. There were other vehicles pulling up to look but it was dark." Cleaves scrubbed both hands down his face and lifted his gaze to Carter. "Is that all?"

"Just a few more questions." Carter stood and waved a hand to the hallway. "Do you have explosives in the house?"

"Explosives?" Cleaves shot to his feet. "No!"

"Then why is my dog sitting outside your hall closet?" Carter folded his notebook and pushed the pen into his pocket. "He's trained to sniff out explosives and he's never wrong. How about you open that closet door and give me a look see? It will save us getting a search warrant and as a man with priors concerning C-4, we'd get one within the hour, maybe less."

"Okay, okay." Cleaves walked into the hallway and stopped dead when Zorro lifted his lips to expose his canines. "That dog's dangerous."

"He sure is." Carter flicked his fingers and Zorro dropped to his haunches. "What do you have inside?"

"A little C-4." Cleaves looked chagrined. "It was left behind when the sheriff raided the place and charged me with stealing. That was five years ago."

"If you open the door, I'll take a look." Carter stood back and waited for Cleaves to open the closet door and flick on a light. "I'll send Zorro in to check it out."

When the dog barked, Carter went inside. Kane turned to Cleaves. "Where have you been to get mud on your boots?"

"I… um, I think that was at the fire." Cleaves frowned as if stalling. "I went to take a pee in the bushes. It was muddy there if I recall."

Kane nodded. "Mind if I take a sample?"

"I guess." Cleaves flicked his gaze to the closet and shuffled his feet.

Kane pulled out his notebook and made a note of Cleaves' agreement to the sample and search of his closet. "Print and then sign your name and add the date, just for the record." He handed him the notebook and pen.

"Then will you leave?" Cleaves signed his name and thrust the articles back at him.

Kane smiled. "Sure thing, Mr. Cleaves; we'll be out of here before you know it." He waited a beat wondering if he was looking at the man who'd murdered Annie. The notes said he'd lived in Louan for a time but as it was his grandmother's house, maybe he'd moved around some during a vacation. "We're almost through now, Mr. Cleaves, just a few more questions. When were you in DC last?"

"DC?" Cleaves looked taken aback. "My old girlfriend worked there for a few years and I visited her. Why?"

The hair on the back of Kane's neck prickled but he kept his expression passive. "It came up in a report is all. Can you be more specific?"

"She moved back last year, so from about five years ago I visited her during my vacations in June most times and any time I could get there. We've broken up now so all that traveling was a waste of time." Cleaves rubbed the back of his neck and stared at the floor. "I'm not sure why all this has to do with the video I took of an explosion."

Kane gripped his pen so tight he could feel it crunch under his fingers. "I'm tying up loose ends is all."

He forced himself into a state of calm but Annie's face danced across his mind. His instinct to shake the truth out of the man slid away as he took control over his emotions. Nothing would be gained by aggression and might only trigger another episode of killing in an already unstable man. He dragged in a deep breath of the rancid-smelling air and let it out slowly through his nose. "Oh, and another thing. How well did you know the Wood family?"

"He was okay but his wife liked to cause trouble." Cleaves eyes flashed with anger.

Kane kept his face neutral. "How so?"

"Aw, I was just being friendly." Cleaves snorted. "I was chatting to their daughter, Sophie, in the local store and her ma became riled up, saying her daughter wasn't available to anyone in our church."

"That was a strange thing to say." Kane shook his head. "And how did that make you feel?"

"Angry." Cleaves shook his head. "Now look at her, she's dead and someone has one of her daughters."

Puzzled by the man's reply, Kane made a few notes.

When Carter came out the closet with an evidence bag and held up a small amount of C-4, Kane turned back to Cleaves. "As the explosives are part of a previous investigation, we're confiscating it as evidence. We won't be charging you." He added a note about the explosives to the statement and handed it over to Cleaves. "Sign where I've added the explosives and we'll be on our way."

When Cleaves agreed without complaint, Kane followed Carter to the door. He dropped the man's pistol on the side table with the clip and headed outside, glad to be in the fresh air again. As they walked to the Beast, he fell in step beside him. "He was in DC around the time of the bombings. I wonder if the C-4 is from the same batch used in the bombing?"

"Hmm, Wolfe has the equipment to find out." Carter removed his hat and scratched his head making his hair stick up in all directions. "No sign of the girl?"

Kane shook his head. "Nope but he's been walking through mud and there was a freshly dug garden bed right outside the Woods' backdoor. He had a problem with Mrs. Wood and I figure a crush on Sophie." He smiled. "I do believe we have a suspect."

CHAPTER SIXTEEN

The FBI and the Black Rock Falls sheriff were using the divide and conquer routine to speak to everyone even remotely involved in the explosion. They could hound him as much as they liked but he wasn't worried at all. There was no evidence against him, he'd been too careful. The way to grease the wheels was to be as cooperative as possible and carry on life as normal. He'd be heading into work soon but had something to do before he left. He backed his truck out of the garage and picked up the hose. He liked to keep his truck clean, and people didn't take too much notice of him as he washed and polished his pride and joy. There was something therapeutic about hosing down and washing his truck, he liked to watch the mud from his wheels wash away in a gray swirl into the gutter and down the drain. He bit back a grin. Kind of like watching Sophie bobbing along in the water and then plunging over the falls. He'd heard her scream disappearing in the distance before the falls swallowed her up. Now the urge to go look for her was driving him insane. He wanted to be there when they dragged her broken and battered body from the river. Or would anyone find her before the wildlife? So many people walked into Stanton Forest and never returned. The dense mass of tall pines, mountain peaks, and caves held their own danger, not to mention the dangerous ravines cut from glaciers millions of years ago that claimed many lives. Once the forest had taken a person, they vanished forever.

Her escaping had been fortunate. It had saved him the trouble of getting rid of her and he'd have had to sooner or later, because as much fun as it would have been leaving her to the rats, he needed to use the cave again. He had to admit, she'd been no fun at all. She'd refused to play his game and sulked most of the time and he'd tired of her. Now the falls would cover his involvement in her disappearance and wash away any evidence. Many had fallen to their deaths over the waterfalls in the forest and after the pummeling of millions of tons of water on flesh, the result wasn't pretty. He sighed, he had better things to do than think about Sophie Wood—in fact he'd visit his cabin soon and make plans. He'd lain awake at night planning just like before.

He took a cloth and wiped down the paintwork. He'd followed the media coverage on his last acts of revenge. They'd murdered an innocent man to atone for his crimes but he'd never believed his actions were wrongdoings. He'd never killed anyone who didn't deserve it. He hadn't killed Sophie, had he? She had made her own fate. The others, the families, and kids, well they were what the government called "collateral damage"—those killed during a mission to remove someone who'd become a danger to others. He'd read that somewhere and it rang true. Everyone he'd blown up or burned had been a danger to others and what kind of man would he be if he'd left the kids alive to be shoved into the system? He understood the system only too well. He looked at his reflection in the window as he wiped away the water droplets. People would call him a psychopath, a man devoid of emotions, who held no value to life. This was the problem—he cared too much. He accessed his blog. Writing his cryptic posts made it real and reading them gave him a sense of achievement but only he would know their true meaning. He smiled as the words formed in his mind.

I'm alone again, my visitor left today; we'd had fun playing games together. It was surreal, sharing my time with her but we all know that life ebbs and flows like a river. My friend decided to join the stream back to reality.

ت

CHAPTER SEVENTEEN

It was going to be one of those days when an investigation was as slow as walking in quicksand. Jenna climbed behind the wheel of her vehicle, turned on the engine and cranked up the aircon. It was a beautiful day, not at all hot but inside her SUV the temperature had become uncomfortable. She waited for Jo to slip into the passenger seat. They'd covered a lot of ground in the last few hours. After dropping by the command center set up to find Sophie Wood, she'd been disappointed the widespread search had yielded no sightings of the girl and nothing positive had come in on the hotline. They'd gone on to visit the family and friends of the Woods. It had been an exhausting task even though the town of Louan wasn't large, it was compact and their visits had entailed disturbing people at their workplaces to gain information. She turned to Jo. "It seems the Woods were angels according to their family and friends but I've never met anyone working in social services who hasn't upset someone."

"Me either." Jo pulled a bottle of water from a cooler on the back seat and opened it before handing it to Jenna. "I figure we go and speak to the people in their office. There's always gossips and knowing what cases they are currently involved in might give us a lead." She grabbed another bottle and turned to face her. "Although we'll have to come in heavy. You know how difficult it is to get people to talk. Someone obviously had it in for the family and someone has to know who it is."

Jenna sipped the water and then started the engine. "The Child and Family Services Department should be on Main. Kane tried to get some information from a social worker about a suspect on a case we were working on, multiple murders or known pedophiles and got nowhere, so I'm not holding my breath."

"Sometimes, flashing my creds helps loosen their tongues." Jo fastened her seatbelt. "The fact that the people we're asking about are deceased will help too." She shrugged. "We really don't have any other avenues to explore. If we don't find any clues, I'll be hoping Kane and Carter have gotten something."

After dropping her sunglasses over her eyes from their position on the top of her head, Jenna headed down Main and pulled into a space near the CFSD. She slid out and glanced up and down the street. The townsfolk bustled along in their daily routines but it wasn't like Black Rock Falls. Her town was a working town and dusty battered pickups and men with the heels worn down on their cowboy boots was a normal sight. In Louan, clean and sparkling late model vehicles moved through town, or had parked at the curb. The local stores also showed a marked opulence compared to her town and the prices of shoes alone seemed exorbitant. She doubted the Louan homeless shelter was overflowing like out at Black Rock Falls because the Louan noticeboard had tons of employment opportunities. She decided to snap a few photographs of the board and send them to Father Derry, the local priest who ran the soup kitchen and shelters in Black Rock Falls.

"Looking for a new job?" Jo smiled at her. "If you're ever planning on leaving Black Rock Falls, I'd love to have you join me in Snakeskin Gully. We work well together and I don't figure my boss would complain about me having a permanent consultant or two on the payroll."

Laughing, Jenna pushed her phone back into her pocket. "Thanks, but I think I'm needed in Black Rock Falls. I was sending the details of the jobs to our local priest, so he can spread the word."

"That's a great idea." Jo indicated toward a redbrick office building. "Let's hope we get some cooperation and then we can head for the diner. I'm starving and in need of caffeine."

They entered the cool, quiet building and Jenna stood back to allow Jo to flash her creds and speak to the receptionist.

"We're here investigating the deaths of Isaac and Connie Wood and their daughter Jody in a housefire." Jo leaned on the counter. "I realize how difficult it is for social workers these days and wonder if you recall any one of the Woods' clients making complaints or causing trouble?"

"They're dead?" The woman looked aghast. "It is not my place to talk about their cases."

"Okay then, are there any of their fellow social workers we could speak to, who might be able to help?" Jo gave her a stiff smile.

"I'm sure I don't know." The receptionist went back to her computer screen.

More than a little annoyed at the woman's complete lack of empathy, Jenna stepped up to the counter. "We'd like to see the person in charge. Can you at least give me their name?"

"That would be Mr. Phelps and you'd need an appointment if you're planning on speaking to him." The woman with tight brown curls and an expression as if she had a permanent bad smell under her nose looked at Jenna with a triumphant expression.

"As this is an FBI matter, call him and tell him we're here." Jo rolled her eyes at Jenna.

"Then take a seat and wait." The receptionist didn't pick up the phone and just went back to her computer.

Anger seeped under Jenna's mask of professionalism and she leaned on the desk. "We're in the middle of a murder investigation and have a missing girl to locate. We don't have time to sit and wait. Get on your phone and call him now."

"He doesn't like to be disturbed during his break." The receptionist glanced at the clock. "I'll tell him you're here after one."

Jenna looked at the small foyer behind her and the shingle on the door, *John A Phelps, Director.* She nodded to the woman and turned to Jo. "He's through that door, come on."

"But you can't—" The receptionist shot up from her seat.

"Oh, but we can." Jo followed Jenna into the foyer.

Having been raised to be polite, Jenna knocked on the door before walking inside the dim office. The blinds had been closed and a tall slim man lay stretched out on a sofa with one arm flung over his eyes. Soft snoring filled the room. She moved close and raised her voice. "Mr. Phelps, wakey, wakey. The FBI are here to speak to you."

"W-what!" Phelps sat up and glared at them. "How did you get in here?"

"FBI, Mr. Phelps." Jo went over to the blinds and twisted the rod to allow the sunshine to filter into the room. "I'm Special Agent Jo Wells and this is Jenna Alton."

"FBI?" Phelps dropped his feet to the floor and stared at them as if they were apparitions. "What could you possibly want with me?"

Jenna dropped into a chair in front of his desk. "Answers, Mr. Phelps. Please join us, we don't have all day."

"Okay." Phelps pushed both hands through a head of thick black hair and stood. "What is this all about?"

Jenna pulled out her notebook and pen. "What can you tell me about Isaac and Connie Wood?"

"In what respect?" Phelps looked from one to the other.

"What were they working on?" Jo sat beside Jenna and smiled. "Any cases that could've had repercussions, made enemies, bad blood or whatever?"

"No, not that I recall." Phelps went to his computer and tapped away at the keyboard. "No, in fact, Connie's on leave to complete her studies. I thought it best for her to get away for a time. She worked in child safety for some years and became very upset when one of the children she placed in foster care was killed."

Jenna blinked. She hadn't been made aware of any child murders lately. "Murdered?"

"Oh heavens, no." Phelps looked shocked. "An accident."

"And Mr. Wood, anyone on his case files who might have had an ax to grind?" Jo crossed her legs. "I am fully aware the job of a social worker can be very difficult but if one of his clients was responsible for murdering the Woods family, we need to know."

"The Woods are dead—murdered?" The color had drained from Phelps' face. He gripped the sides of his chair and swayed. "Dear God, I can't believe it."

Jenna exchanged a meaningful look with Jo. This man was either distraught or a very good actor. "Well, do you recall anyone who might have had a beef against Mr. Wood?"

"I don't usually divulge the names of people who come to this center for our help but I do remember two individuals who, as you say, had a beef with Isaac. I'll get you their details." He scanned his screen and after a few minutes, his printer burst into life and spat out a page. "Here you go."

Jenna scanned the document and then looked at him. "What exactly caused a problem between these men and Mr. Wood? They obviously lodged a complaint or you wouldn't have it on file."

"Roger Suffolk is out of Buffalo Ridge. He came here with his wife for counseling and when things didn't work out, his wife left him. Soon after, he came to Wood's office and made threats. Our sheriff let him off with a warning but Wood was convinced the man was following him."

"Was he violent toward Mr. Wood?" Jo leaned forward in her chair. "And did he ever hit his wife?"

"He yelled some and threatened to complain to the board about Wood's unsound advice and yes, according to Wood's case notes, Suffolk disciplined his wife on numerous occasions but to no avail." Phelps continued to scroll through documents. "After his wife left him, he went through a period of violent behavior but settled after the sheriff gave him a few days in the cells to straighten himself out."

Shocked by Phelps' attitude toward women, Jenna raised a brow. "He wasn't charged for spousal abuse?"

"There's no need to ruin a man's life for a domestic, Agent Alton." Phelps gave her a slow smile. "Some women step over the line with their husbands and it's the husband's duty to show them the error of their ways." He met her eyes. "She did after all promise to obey when they made their vows. It is a contract only broken by a court."

Outraged by his comments, Jenna leaned forward to give him a piece of her mind, when Jo touched her arm. After seeing firsthand, the damage spousal abuse caused to families and the amount of deaths of both men and women due to their partner's aggressive behavior, she had a no-tolerance rule in her town. She had founded the Her Broken Wings Foundation with Kane to support battered women and had made consideration for men caught in similar circumstances. She cleared her throat. "I assume Sheriff Crenshaw agrees with your decisions on this matter?"

"He does indeed." Phelps looked pleased with himself. "He is very supportive of the CFSD."

"This man on your list, Peter Huntley, what problems did he cause the Woods?" Jo sat up straight and gave him a direct stare, her face emotionless.

"That was some time ago. Connie took the children away from them because they were dependent on welfare." Phelps towered his fingers and leaned back in his chair. "There is no excuse not to work in Louan, Agent Wells, we have work for everyone here. The children were placed in care and offered up for adoption. Connie arranged it all and found them caring homes but Huntley went over to Black Rock Falls and spoke to a lawyer over there. He represented Huntley in court and took the case not to the local magistrate but insisted on a judge presiding over the case. The children were returned to the parents. I do believe they moved to Black Rock Falls."

Jenna wanted to smile but swallowed the urge. There was one Black Rock Falls lawyer she'd butted horns with many a time. He was the best defense lawyer she'd met. "Ah, I see. Would the lawyer have been Sam Cross by any chance?"

"Why, yes, that's his name." Phelps gave her a long considering stare. "They are the only complaints we have on record and anything else would be hearsay."

Jenna pushed to her feet. "Okay, thank you for your assistance, we'll let you get back to your nap."

Outside the office, Jenna turned to Jo. "I don't think we have to worry about Peter Huntley. His name hasn't come up since I've been in Black Rock Falls. If he'd neglected his kids or caused a problem, I'd be the first to know. Since we busted a pedophile ring some time ago, the schools and social workers don't take any chances when it comes to kids' welfare. We'll need to concentrate on Roger Suffolk. His place of employment is listed as the local blacksmith at the Crazy Iron Forge."

"From the description of him, he fits the profile. Although he's forty-five, that's a bit older than I'd imagined." Jo frowned. "Maybe we need to wait for Kane and Carter before we go see him. He might be dangerous."

Jenna smiled. "Don't worry. Nothing can possibly happen at his place of business. We'll be fine." She headed for her vehicle.

CHAPTER EIGHTEEN

The Crazy Iron Forge lay on the outskirts of town at the end of a circular driveway wide enough to take an eighteen-wheeler and then some. Situated some ways from a ranch house, set back on sizable acreage, the forge was housed in a redbrick building with a massive chimney stack, billowing a heat haze into the summer sky. To one side of the building, horses' heads peered over gates in a stable block. Jenna pulled up alongside the stables to keep her sheriff's marked SUV out of sight; she didn't plan on spooking Roger Suffolk. As they walked toward the forge, she could hear hammering on metal and then the hiss as the hot object was plunged into the barrel of water to cool. From the lineup of labeled farm machinery and implements leaning against a wall, Roger Suffolk was a busy man. A large white truck was parked outside emblazoned with the Crazy Iron Forge logo but no other vehicles were in sight. She turned to Jo. "I wonder if he works alone?"

"I guess we'll find out soon enough." Jo pushed open the door.

Jenna followed and stepped inside the huge building. Walls lined with tools met her gaze, and benches with a variety of machines. The place had a strange smell of fire, ash, and sweat hanging in humidity she could cut through. Mechanical bellows hit a raging fire making it roar and bright orange flames danced in the red glowing forge. As they stepped inside, a wave of heat hit her like a wall. In front of the fire a man with broad shoulders, wearing a blue T-shirt with a sweat stain down the middle of his back, turned a metal rod in the fire. As he lifted the glowing red rod he turned slightly and Jenna made out his thick leather apron, protective gloves, and mask. His glossy sweat-coated muscles bulged as he lifted a hammer from a bench and, after placing the red-hot metal on an anvil, struck it several times. She watched, mesmerized, as the metal appeared to curve and bend with each strike.

Keeping her distance from the man working with deep concentration, she raised her voice. "Mr. Suffolk?"

As he turned and regarded them with narrowed eyes, Jenna suppressed a shiver. It was an instinct danger was close by. This huge three-hundred-pound man beat on his wife and from the size of his hands, a slap would be like being hit by a truck. The thought lingered in her mind, that she should have taken Kane's advice and loaded her weapon with hollow points. If this giant of a man came at her she'd like to take him down with one shot. She waited as Suffolk dropped the hot rod into a barrel of water. He was momentarily hidden by the steam as the water bubbled and hissed. Her heart skipped a beat as he emerged from the cloud, metal rod in hand, and started toward them. "Mr. Suffolk? May we have a moment of your time?"

"Are you selling something?" His voice was deep and rumbling. "If you are, get the hell off my property."

"No, I'm Jenna Alton and this is Special Agent Wells, FBI." Jenna stood her ground. "We'd like to speak to you."

"Sure." Suffolk tossed the metal rod on a bench, and removed his gloves and protective facemask. He looked from one to the other and shook his head slowly. "I can't imagine why they allow women in the FBI to bring down criminals. You should be at home caring for your menfolk."

Hackles on full alert, Jenna held his gaze. "We don't have any menfolk to worry about, but that's none of your concern."

"I might have guessed." Suffolk snorted and then seemed to gather himself. "What can I do for you, Agents?"

"You had a few problems with Isaac Wood after a counseling session and put in a complaint against him. We're just following that up." Jo flipped through her notebook as if she wasn't interested in what he had to say.

"Isaac Wood?" Suffolk pinched the bridge of his nose. "He didn't understand the way of things. Most of the families who live in Louan had the same upbringing as me. We have our own way of doing things. Not like some of the newcomers." He leveled his gaze on them. "He told my wife she should leave me and was an equal partner in our marriage. I objected and gave him my opinion, is all. For that I was hauled into the sheriff's department for questioning and by the time I'd gotten home, she'd gone. So yeah, I was pissed." He swiped sweat from his brow. "It's too hot here to talk. Come up to the house. Dawn will have my lunch ready."

Jenna opened her mouth to decline but Suffolk just removed his apron, brushed passed them, and headed up a pathway to the house. She looked at Jo. "I think we've been ordered to follow."

"What is it with him and the director of the CFSD? Do they belong to a cult or something similar?" Jo stared after the man with a concerned expression. "They treat their women like objects."

Jenna shrugged. "I have no idea but I plan to find out. Problem is most times our hands are tied. We can assist any woman who needs our help but we can't interfere with people's choice of religious practices. If he comes from a sect that believes women should be beholden to men, we can't get involved."

"I don't like this at all." Jo stared after Suffolk. "He's confident but there's an underlying aggression. We're walking into an unknown situation here."

"Okay." Jenna pulled out her phone and called Kane. "Hi, we're at the Crazy Iron Forge out at Buffalo Ridge and heading into Roger Suffolk's house and he's a strange one. I thought I'd call it in just in case there's a problem."

"Send me the coordinates. We're almost through here and I'll head that way but if you get into a situation, call me or activate your tracker ring." Kane sounded concerned. *"What's worrying you about him? Do you want us to come by anyway? We're not far from your position."*

Jenna sighed. "Good to know. Yes, come by and I'll explain later."

"Any news on the search for Sophie Wood?"

"No sign of her." Jenna chewed on her bottom lip. "Sheriff Crenshaw said he'd call if they found any trace of her. I gotta go. We'll talk later. Bye." She disconnected and looked at Jo's worried expression. "The guys are close by and heading this way if we need backup." She smiled. "And we're armed. He might not realize we have shoulder holsters under our jackets. Come on let's go, I don't think he'll enjoy us being tardy."

The ranch house was about fifty years old and had a wide porch with a swing. Such a romantic thing for a man who didn't appear to have one romantic bone in his body. An ancient gnarly pink rose bush, its trunk thick and woody, climbed over the wooden railing. The scent gave Jenna memories of her gran's house. The front door stood open and through the fly screen, she could see straight down a hallway to the kitchen, and to the doors running off each side. The floor shone from layers of polish and the side table held a bronze statue of a cowboy.

"Don't just stand there, wipe your feet and come in." Suffolk waved them inside from the kitchen door.

Jenna wiped her feet on the mat and stepped into the house. It smelled like polish and fresh coffee. She led the way into the kitchen scanning the rooms each side of the hallway. A big family room, an office with a desk, and walls lined with books all as neat as a pin, not one speck of dust anywhere. The older style kitchen had a scrubbed wooden table and benches that sparkled. It was as if nobody lived there, no personal items, no photographs, or even the usual notes on the refrigerator or beside the phone. Her attention moved to the two women standing to one side. They were covered from neck to knee, with caps covering their hair, and wearing huge aprons. An older woman in her sixties maybe and a young woman, perhaps sixteen or a little older, looked at her as if she'd grown two heads. She smiled at them. "Hello, I'm Jenna and this is Jo."

"They don't speak to outsiders and no doubt they're wondering why I've welcomed you into my home. You see we don't approve of women wearing pants or taking men's jobs." Suffolk went to the kitchen sink to wash up. He looked at the women. "This is my ma and Dawn. Ma is here to teach Dawn the way of things, so we can marry. I'm not making another mistake, so I chose a young one this time."

"Did you divorce your wife?" Jo's lips flattened as she regarded the young woman.

"Nah, she died." Suffolk shrugged. "Without a man's protection bad things happen." He turned his hard glare to Dawn. "Don't they, Dawn?"

The girl kept her gaze on the floor and that warning prickle crawled up Jenna's neck again. "May I ask how she died?"

"Her brakes failed and she wrecked her ride, out near Blackwater." Suffolk dried his hands on a towel Dawn supplied. "Take a seat. Coffee and cake or would you prefer lemonade? My ma makes it fresh every day." He sat down at the table and looked at Dawn. "I'm sitting and you're still dithering. Time's money and I need to be back at work." He swung his gaze back to Jenna.

"Coffee is fine for us, thanks, no cake." Jenna sat at the table as Suffolk drummed his fingers on the table clearly agitated.

"You DC types are always watching your figures." His gaze moved over them. "It's an obsession we don't allow."

I wonder when he was in DC. Jenna shrugged. "I see. I haven't been to DC for years, when where you there?"

"A few years ago, I guess." He narrowed his gaze at her. "I'm not giving you a reason for being there if that's what you're fishing for, a man has a right to go where he pleases during his vacation."

Jenna raised a brow at his attitude and smiled. "I couldn't agree more."

The coffee and fixings arrived in seconds and Suffolk's huge plate of sandwiches. The next moment the women scuttled out the door like frightened rabbits. Jenna added cream and sugar to her cup. A worry crept over her about the young vulnerable woman and she had to ask. "So does your mother live with you?"

"No, she has Pa to care for but she comes by to watch Dawn when I'm working." He looked from one to the other. "Dawn isn't from around here. She came recommended by one of my colleagues. If she shapes up, I'll marry her." He waved a hand around the house. "So far she is working out just fine. She doesn't say much and that's fine by me."

"How old is Dawn?" Jo stirred her coffee. "She seems a mite inexperienced for a man of your age."

"Coming up sixteen." He ate slowly. "Enough of snooping into my private life. What is it you need to know about Isaac Wood?"

Trying not to change her facial expression, Jenna sipped the coffee but inside her mind was reeling. Suffolk had just added another reason for her to be suspicious of him. He had an underage girl living with him and if she made an issue out of it, she might place them all in danger. Having no idea what this huge man was capable of, she'd have to act nonchalant and wait for backup. She tried to focus on the questions but inside, she wondered if the timid girl was the missing

Sophie Wood. "Just the details of the complaint. You mentioned he gave you bad advice about your wife?"

"Not to me, to her." Suffolk bit into a sandwich and chewed thoughtfully. "You need to understand the way of things here. We look at marriage a little differently from some folks. Our church started here in Louan fifty years ago. Our womenfolk accept that we are the providers and they are chattels. They promise to obey and we enforce the contract. Any females born into our church are the chattels of their father and do as they say, marry who they say. Understand?" He sighed. "He told my wife she had the right to complain and go against my wishes. He said she could leave at any time and wear what she decided. That's not our way."

"What did you expect a marriage counselor to say to you?" Jo frowned. "That's how most of the people in this country show respect to each other."

"That is not how we measure respect. I wanted to go and speak to an elder of our church and ask him to enforce our teachings but she refused and insisted we go to speak to a social worker. How Phelps ever put us with Wood I don't know, he has our own people working there." He huffed an annoyed sigh. "I figure that receptionist of his had a hand in it. She is an old busybody. I spoke to Phelps and he knew nothing about it."

"I see." Jenna watched him eat and tried to understand how a woman could be treated as property. "Wasn't your wife from your church?"

"Of course, she was." He gave her an exasperated stare. "But she went to the hospital on a few occasions and some of the nurses there brainwashed her." He snorted. "This is why I wanted her to speak to an elder but then she refused to do my bidding. I had no choice but to haul her down to speak to a marriage counselor. My word nor the back of my hand made any difference, and after the meeting with Wood she was past redemption."

"So, you put in a complaint and the next thing Wood's entire family dies in a housefire."

"You don't say?" Suffolk's gaze was cold and expressionless. "Now some would say that was divine intervention, same as the car wreck that freed me from my wife and allowed me to start fresh."

"It was homicide." Jo was watching him closely. "Someone planted an explosive device in their home and kidnapped their daughter."

"And you're telling me this why?" Suffolk sipped his coffee, eyeing Jo suspiciously.

"Because of the complaint, we're hunting down anyone who might have had a problem with Mr. Wood." Jo placed her cup into the saucer. "When did you last see Isaac Wood?"

"The day we had the counseling session." Suffolk snorted. "Why would I need to see him again? The man is a fool."

"And where were you around nine on Tuesday evening?" Jo lifted her chin. "Just for the record."

"I was in Black Rock Falls." He leaned back in his chair making it creak under his weight. "I had an urgent delivery for Miller's Garage. I spoke to George and then had a meal at Aunt Betty's Café. I dropped by the Triple Z Bar for a few beers and I'm not sure when I arrived home." His mouth formed a thin line. "Why?"

Jenna noticed Dawn hovering near the doorway trying to get her attention. She gave her a very slight nod and stood, collected the coffee cups, and then took them to the sink. As she passed the kitchen door, Dawn thrust a note toward her and Jenna slipped it into her pocket. Without missing a stride, she retook her seat. "I'm sure you understand, Mr. Suffolk, when we chase down leads, we like to have a timeline of where everyone was at the time of the incident. It's nothing personal."

"I didn't have anything to do with the explosion. I made a complaint against Wood, which is my right." Suffolk leaned back in his chair again and eyed her critically. "I could've taken him out back and had it out man to man but he was a puny guy and I'd have gained no satisfaction out of it. They say the pen is mightier than the sword and bruises fade but a black mark on a man's work record stays forever." He pushed to his feet. "Time's up. I have work to do. People rely on me being punctual with their repairs."

Jenna stood. "Thank you for the coffee." She hurried out the door with Jo on her heels.

Aware of Suffolk crunching down the pathway behind them, they dashed to the safety of Jenna's SUV. Taking a glance behind her, Jenna's heart quickened as she stared into Suffolk's eyes as he stood watching them, huge hands balled at his waist. He'd been in DC around the time of the bombings but so had thousands of people—but not all of them had conveniently lost their wives in a car wreck. Her gut was telling her there was more to Roger Suffolk than met the eye. She needed to find out what had happened to his wife and why she required frequent hospital visits. The accident seemed way too convenient. Had Suffolk tampered with the brakes on his wife's vehicle?

When they reached the SUV, Jenna took off and once safely away from the property pulled into the curb. She searched her pocket for the scrap of paper Dawn had given her and stared at it. Panic for the girl's safety shivered down her spine. She swallowed the lump in her throat and handed the note to Jo. On the edge of the newsprint was scrawled:

Help me.

CHAPTER NINETEEN

It was unusual for Jenna to be concerned about interviewing a suspect. In fact, Kane found her to be confident and professional at all times. She'd spoken to dangerous men before and he wondered what she'd discovered about Roger Suffolk that had spooked her. He pushed his phone into his pocket and returned to Carter's side. They'd spoken to two men with priors and both had solid alibies for the time of the explosion. The third, Simon Dexter out of Prairie View, was the driver of the gray car captured on scene by Cleaves' dashcam and a known firebug.

"How was it you were out near the Woods' ranch?" Carter inclined his head, and looked at Dexter, his pen hovering over his notepad.

"I was heading home after picking up six peach pies from Aunt Betty's Café in Black Rock Falls. I freeze them and take them to work in my lunch pail. I live alone and don't have a wife to fix my meals." Dexter shrugged. "The ranch went up like a bomb and I stopped alongside the highway with some of the other drivers to watch the show."

"You didn't call it in or go to offer the residence assistance?" Carter looked down his nose at him, his green eyes flashing in annoyance. "A family died in that blaze, you may have been able to save them but you chose to stand by and watch 'the show' as you called it."

"Well, yeah but I wasn't the only one." Dexter's face had drained of color and his hands shook as he pushed a slick of greasy hair from his eyes. "And that's not fair to say I don't care about the Wood family.

I had a hankering after Sophie, and asked her father if he'd put me on his list of men interested in taking her for their wife."

"His what?" Carter leaned forward, looking incredulous. "Wood had a list of prospective husbands for his fifteen-year-old daughter?"

"Well, yeah, I guess." Dexter frowned. "Although, when I asked him, he told me to get off his property." His mouth turned down. "I had a right to ask."

"Did you now?" Kane observed him closely. "Getting back to the night of the explosion, what did you hear and what did you see?"

"A boom or maybe two booms and then a scream." Dexter stared into the distance as if thinking. "It could've been an echo and the scream could've been from the explosion. The fire burst out of the mushroom of dust."

"Did you see anyone leave the ranch, or did any vehicles pass you?" Carter made notes.

"I don't recall. I parked my car to watch the blaze, and then walked down to speak to John... John Cleaves. He has dashcam footage and sent me a copy. I have it here if you want to see it?" He reached for his phone.

Kane shook his head. "We've seen it. Thanks, and if you think of anything else, give me a call." He handed Dexter his card and with a look indicated to Carter their need to leave.

"What's the rush?" Carter fell into step beside him. "I wanted to lean on him a little harder. He could have set the explosion and set if off by remote as he drove by. We have no idea when the bomb was set, only when it was detonated. I'm keeping him on our persons of interest list."

Kane lifted Duke into the back of his truck and then climbed behind the wheel. In seconds, Carter had Zorro settled and was in the passenger seat. He turned to him. "Jenna called and she's concerned about a suspect they're interviewing by the name of Roger Suffolk.

She said he was acting strange. They're heading into his house and I figure we should hightail it over to the Crazy Iron Forge and make sure they're okay." He tossed him his phone, started the engine and the Beast roared up the blacktop. "She just sent me his details."

"I'll enter the coordinates into the GPS." Carter scanned the messages. "Got it. It's on the outskirts of town. Head west."

Kane accelerated but had only traveled a mile before he caught sight of Jenna's SUV heading toward them. He flashed his lights and the SUV slowed and pulled onto the grass. He stopped opposite and Jenna climbed out and ran across the road toward him. He buzzed down his window. "Does this mean it's time to head out to the diner?"

"No." Jenna thrust a piece of paper toward him. "Suffolk is part of a sect or something that has peculiar ideas about women's rights." She pushed the hair from her eyes. "Long story but he has a fifteen-year-old living with him training to be his wife."

Kane stared at the scrawled message and opened his mouth to say something but she glared at him.

"Let me finish." Jenna pointed to the note. "She slipped me the note. This is a cry for help, we have FBI Agents with us so there's no reason we can't take her under our protection. I wanted to get her out of there without a fight and trust me, taking her from a three-hundred-pound blacksmith wasn't going to be easy."

Astonished by her reluctance to just take the girl, Kane nodded. "Okay, so two FBI agents drawing down on him didn't faze him?" He couldn't help grinning at her annoyed expression and just had to tease her. "Or did he pull an AK47 on you and tell you to leave?"

"Dave, it's not funny. He could be the bomber and we don't know where the girl came from, do we? They call her Dawn but what if she's the missing girl? They look similar but it was difficult to tell with the cap the girl was wearing." Jenna met his gaze. "If she isn't Sophie Wood, I didn't want to bring in Sheriff Crenshaw and compromise the investigation by tying him up with a case of underage dealing." She snorted. "Not that it would stick. Crenshaw is a member of his church and already allowed Suffolk to walk after threatening Wood."

Bemused, Kane scratched his cheek. "Hmm okay, follow us back to the forge, we'll keep him busy and you go get the girl. He'll never know who took her."

"Yeah he will, his mother is there." Jenna frowned. "There must be some way of getting her out unnoticed."

"Send Jo to the front door and make up some excuse about dropping an earring or something." Kane smiled at her. "You go round back and get the girl."

"I knew you'd figure it out." Jenna squeezed his arm. "Forget eating here, we'll head straight to Black Rock Falls and I'll get her into the Her Broken Wings shelter."

"Great we'll get to eat at Aunt Betty's Café." Kane waved her away. "We'll go in first and you hide your ride somewhere." His stomach growled and he caught her pained expression. "I hope this doesn't take too long, I'm about ready to eat Duke's doggy snacks."

"That desperate huh?" Jenna shook her head. "I can tell time by your stomach. It rumbles every few hours." She gave him a wave and headed back to her SUV.

He waited for Jenna to turn her vehicle around and then headed back along the highway.

"Here." Carter handed him an energy bar. "One thing I've discovered working with Jo is eating is the last thing on her agenda. I keep a good supply of these in my pockets."

"Thanks." Kane grinned at him. "I figure Jenna gives me time to eat because my stomach growls so loud it makes Duke whine." He unwrapped the energy bar. "But she'll be discussing the case all through lunch. She never slows down during the day."

"Are we going in as FBI?" Carter looked at him. "It might make him suspicious."

Kane shook his head. "Nah, I'll ask him about gates. I do need some for the corral I've been building, and maybe a new fancy door for the cottage." He headed to the front of the forge and slid out the door leaving the dogs inside, with the windows open.

"I'll hang at the door while you talk to him." Carter met him stride for stride. "I'll remove my hat when Jenna has the girl."

Kane nodded. "Copy that."

CHAPTER TWENTY

Heart thumping with exhilaration, Jenna crept her SUV along the Crazy Iron Forge driveway. Ahead, Kane had parked the Beast to obscure the entrance to the forge. She smiled to herself; this way if Suffolk popped his head outside, he wouldn't see her approach or departure. She backed her SUV in behind the stables again nose out ready for a fast getaway, and then turned to Jo. "There's a path going around the back of the forge to the house, if we go that way we'll avoid being seen. How are you going to play this?"

"The lost earring ploy." She pulled out the stud in her ear and slipped it into her pocket. "I'll find it at the appropriate time. Just make it fast."

Jenna slipped from behind the wheel. "Try to keep her talking. If Dawn is in the kitchen, I'll grab her and run but if I head upstairs, you'll need to shut the kitchen door so I can leave by the front."

They made their way along an overgrown walkway behind the stables walking in single file and keeping in the cover of the bushes. As they passed the end of the forge, Jenna waved Jo in the direction of the front porch of the ranch house and headed around back. A small gate in a very old fence led into the backyard and Jenna scanned the neat vegetable bed with not a weed in sight. Close to the back of the house, a line with white sheets swung in the breeze. The closed frosted kitchen widows would hide her approach. Adrenalin pumped through her veins as she headed for the open backdoor. At the foot of the steps a small flower garden, lovingly tended, exploded with color and gave her a lump in her throat. Dawn was obviously trying to make this house a home and she wondered how she'd become involved with Roger Suffolk.

Pressed against the wall of the house, Jenna listened. She heard Jo knocking on the front door and slow footsteps along the polished wooden floors. Moving with stealth, she crept up the steps and found herself in a mudroom off the kitchen. She was in full view of the kitchen and was just in time to see Dawn head down the hallway.

"Go to your room." Mrs. Suffolk's stern voice seem to echo through the quiet house.

Jenna waited for voices and slipped from the mudroom and headed toward the stairs. She could see the back of Mrs. Suffolk not five yards away from her. If she turned now, and caught her inside the house, all hell would break lose. The next moment, she heard Jo asking about the rose bush and drawing Mrs. Suffolk outside onto the porch. Not wasting a second, Jenna bolted up the stairs, her gaze flicking right to left searching for Dawn. She found her sitting on her bed staring at the wall. She lowered her voice to a whisper not wanting to startle her. "Dawn, if you want to leave, I can help you but we have to go now."

"Oh, it's you." Dawn stood and smiled at her. "I knew you'd come back. I've packed a bag but how are we going to get past Ma?" She bent and pulled a backpack from under the bed.

"Don't worry about her, my friend will keep her occupied in the kitchen but we have to move fast and silently." Jenna held one finger to her lips. "No talking. We're going down the stairs and out the front door."

Pulse thumping in her ears, Jenna listened at the door. She heard voices and footsteps heading for the kitchen. She eased out onto the steps and started as the kitchen door opened. *Shit!* Ducking back inside the room, she looked around frantically for a hiding place.

"Dawn, get down here and help us search for an earring." Mrs. Suffolk's loud voice seemed to fill the room.

"I need to use the bathroom and then I'll be right down." Dawn poked her head around the door. "I can't wait."

"Don't be long." Mrs. Suffolk's footsteps shuffled back along the hallway. "Now, where do you figure you lost your earring?"

"Is that it down there behind the door?" Jo's voice sounded strained. "Let me look."

The kitchen door closed and Jenna grabbed Dawn's arm and they moved down the steps. Each creak of the floorboards sounded like a gunshot but they only had seconds to get to the door and out to freedom. She pushed the girl ahead of her and as Dawn brushed past the statue of the cowboy the hanging strap of her backpack snagged it. The statue rocked and toppled. As if she still played on the high school softball team, Jenna scooped it up and extricated it from the backpack. After setting the statue in the middle of the table, she followed Dawn out the door and closed it silently behind her.

Jenna waved Dawn on. "Take the path behind the forge. I'm parked beside the stables. Run!"

CHAPTER TWENTY-ONE

Kane had his story straight by the time he paused at the entrance to the Crazy Iron Forge and scanned the building. His attention settled on the blacksmith repairing what looked like a piece of a tractor. Jenna hadn't been exaggerating about the size of Roger Suffolk, although her estimate of three hundred pounds was light. He walked inside and caught the man's attention. "Afternoon, I'm looking for a corral gate and a wrought-iron door and frame for my house. I live out of Black Rock Falls and hear tell you're the best around."

"You'll have to be more specific." Suffolk plunged the ironwork he'd been working on, into the water and waved a hand toward a bench against the wall. "There are different types of gates and even more designs for doors." He led the way to the bench and pushed a binder toward Kane. "What gauge do you want the door for the cottage? Is it to look pretty or for security?"

Kane peered at the designs. "Both. The cottage is old, over a hundred years, I'd guess, so something suitable."

"Then something like this?" Suffolk flicked through the designs. "This is old style."

Kane nodded. "Yeah I like that one."

They went on to discuss gates and timeframes, with Kane drawing out the conversation for as long as possible. He noticed the way Suffolk kept flicking his attention to Carter, but Carter played his part well, leaning against the doorframe looking suitably bored. After some purposeful dithering, he could see Suffolk getting agitated and pointed to one design that would suit his cottage. "That one will look real good. I'll go with the basic corral gate. This one here will do. I'll make a note of the design numbers and call you with the measurements." He pulled out his notebook and wrote the information down.

"I'll make a note as well, so I know what you're talking about when you call." Suffolk added notes to a large dirty fingerprint marked book and lifted his gaze. "Name?"

"Dave Kane." He handed him his card and noticed Suffolk's eyebrows raise when he read it.

"So, you're the deputy sheriff out of Black Rock Falls?" Suffolk stared at the card. He straightened and his eyes flashed with something close to anger.

Kane ignored the hostility and smiled. "Guilty as charged." He pushed the notebook into his pocket. "But I still need to order the gates or do you have a problem selling to members of the sheriff's department?"

"Nope." Suffolk closed his book. "A sale is a sale and I deliver to Black Rock Falls. In fact, I'll be heading that way as soon as you leave." He pulled the machinery part he'd been working on from the water and dumped it on the bench. "I had a rush job." He removed his apron. "So, are we done here?"

"Ah... Boss." Carter removed his hat and pulled out the toothpick from the corner of his mouth. "The dogs are getting restless."

Kane nodded. In his faded jeans, cowboy boots, and untidy blond hair hanging over his collar, Carter slipped into the role of ranch hand without a problem. "Be right there." He held out his hand to Suffolk, fully aware he may be shaking the hand of the man who killed Annie. The guy was big, sure, but looking into his eyes, a rage like no other threatened to overtake him. He could take him down in seconds and revenge would be sweet but allowing that side of him to take control would make him no better than the psychopaths he hunted. Deep inside, he could hear Annie's voice pushing him to find justice for her. It had become painful, relentless, and it took an effort to keep his professional mask firmly in place. He ground his teeth and had the urgent need to wash the man's touch from his hands. "Thanks for your time, I'll be in touch."

"Sure." Suffolk followed Kane to the door and stared at his truck.

Kane gave him a wave, climbed behind the wheel, and headed down the driveway. In the distance, he could hear a woman's voice calling out. He glanced in his mirror at Suffolk's annoyed expression as he turned to stomp toward the house. "Time to go." He accelerated along the trail sending up a great cloud of dust. "They've noticed the girl missing already. Are Jenna and Jo clear?"

"Oh yeah, Jenna hightailed it out of here like her cruiser was on fire." Carter grinned at him. "They work well together. Jenna is a natural leader. Why the hell is she wasting her time in Black Rock Falls?"

Kane flicked him a glance. "Catching a ton of serial killers isn't what I'd call 'wasting her time.'"

"So, did you use your profiling magic and read anything about Suffolk?" Carter tossed another toothpick into his mouth. "He doesn't suffer fools too well and you having a hard time making up your mind was riling him." He sighed. "If he's like that at home, it's not too difficult to understand why the girl needed help. Do you figure he's mistreating her?"

"He's training her to be his wife... *training* her." Kane shook his head. "What is happening in the world? If he's the bomber, and I discover he's been abusing that girl, I'll have more than one reason to take him down. I can't abide men who raise a hand to a woman and pedophiles, well, they're the scum of the earth."

"Amen to that." Carter smiled as they turned onto the straight highway and headed for home. "That would be Jenna up ahead breaking the land speed record, lights flashing and pedal to the metal."

Kane looked at the clear highway ahead and accelerated. As the lowlands flashed by in a sea of green, dotted with ranches set back from the road, he allowed the impressions of Roger Suffolk to settle in his mind. He glanced at Carter. "I don't have too much to go on with Suffolk yet to create a profile. After we get an update from Jo and Jenna it will be easier. A couple of things come to mind. He's big enough to overpower most men and Wood was only a small guy. The other thing is, he likes fifteen-year-old girls."

"Hmm and a blacksmith knows about fire." Carter reached for the radio at the sound of Jo's voice and Kane's call number. "Carter here. Is the package secure?"

"Yeah, we'll be taking her straight to Black Rock Falls General for the usual tests."

"Keep her out of sight, Suffolk is heading your way." Carter flicked a glance at Kane.

"Copy that." Jo sounded calm but there was an unmistakable edge to her voice. *"Jenna tells me they have a secure ward there and we'll get a statement. The girl isn't Sophie Wood, her name is Dawn Richardson and she doesn't want to be returned to her family. She said they'll just send her back. Her father entered into some type of agreement with Suffolk."* She huffed out an exasperated sigh. *"It's what they do. I've placed her in protective custody and Jenna will have her settled in Her Broken Wings shelter until we can find her a place to live."*

"I hear they have suitable foster families in Black Rock Falls." Carter shot a glance at Kane.

Kane nodded. "Yeah, there's not many but what we have are solid."

"*No, it's too close to home. I'll find her a place in Snakeskin Gully. I know a couple of families there who would give her a good home. They're in the foster home system and ended up adopting their kids. Nice folks.*" She cleared her throat. "*Ah this may take a while, Jenna said you should head straight to Aunt Betty's, we'll catch up with you later.*"

"Okay, sure. Carter out." Carter looked at Kane. "Good, it will give us time to upload our notes. Jo will have her case files updated by now, she works in the truck between interviews."

Kane smiled. "Jenna is the same. It looks like we're going to be taking a long lunchbreak."

"Now that sounds like a plan." Carter chuckled.

CHAPTER TWENTY-TWO

Rowley leaned back in his chair and read through the report that Matt Thompson, the fire chief, had delivered to the office. Curious why he hadn't emailed the file straight to Jenna, he glanced over to the man sitting across the desk and cleared his throat. "I'm not sure why you brought this to me. This is an FBI investigation."

"Yeah, I'm fully aware of the FBI throwing accusations at my department." Thompson leaned forward and dug his index finger into the desk. "I wanted to speak to Sheriff Alton personally. She took it upon herself to blame me for not inspecting the upstairs of the Woods' ranch."

"Well—" Rowley opened his hands wide "—you can see she's not here." His hackles rose at the unwarranted complaints against Jenna. "I haven't heard her complaining about you and I'm sure she would've taken into account the report you gave her was only the preliminary, after all you wouldn't have had time to speak to the firefighters at Louan when you examined the scene." He gave him a long stare. "Really, you need to talk to the sheriff. This isn't my case."

"Just make sure she reads the complete report." Thompson snorted. "The Louan chief did send men to the second floor. His verbal report to me was it was clear and only smoke damaged. I had no need to go up there, my concern was on the bombing and subsequent fire. I also had to report on the structural integrity of the building." He pushed his finger into the table again. "She shouldn't jump to conclusions and make like I'm not doing my job."

"Okay." Although annoyed, Rowley kept his voice calm. "I'll see that she gets the report."

He needed to get Thompson out of the office before Jenna returned. She had enough to worry about without Thompson chewing her out. He opened his mouth to say something when Deputy Walters knocked on the open door. The old man's face was grim. "What's up?"

"A body has washed up, out on one of the lakes that's fed by Black Rock Falls." Walters let out a wheezing sigh. "The forest warden called it in. The corpse is caught in the rocks, you'll need help to retrieve it."

Rowley made a few notes. "Where exactly did he find the body?"

"He said some of the fishermen call the area 'Dead Man's Drop'." Walters shrugged. "I'm not familiar with that part of the river but Atohi Blackhawk is in town, he came by before with something for Maggie. He'll know where to find it for sure. Want me to call him?"

"Yeah, and he'll know the quickest way to get there." Rowley swallowed the acid crawling up his throat. "Did the warden say anything else, is it a male or female?"

"Didn't say. He gave me the coordinates. You'll be able to drive most of the way if you take the firebreaks. He's staying there until you arrive. I'll give you his number and you can talk to him yourself." Walters rubbed the end of his nose. "Want me to call Jenna?"

Annoyed, Rowley stood. "No way. I'll give Wolfe the heads up and we'll go there as a team." He reached for the phone.

"I'll come with you." Thompson cleared his throat. "I know my way around the forest too and have everything you need in my truck to pull a body out of the river." He pushed to his feet. "I can call in the local squad if needs be?"

Rowley looked at him and nodded. "Yeah, come with us but I figure five of us will be enough, thanks." He made the call to Wolfe.

*

Rowley drove through town. He planned to rendezvous with his team at the firebreak cut into the forest alongside Stanton Road. His fingers itched to call Jenna and apprise her of the situation but she'd given him the chance to prove he could run for sheriff one day. As a married man with plans to fill his home with kids, he needed to plan for his future. He'd show he could handle serious cases by following the procedure she'd drummed into him since he started working as a deputy, and by getting the job done. As he drove, he ran the mental list of things to do through his mind. He had everything covered and once they'd fished the body out of the lake, he could go to work hunting down missing people in the area. Often people didn't report missing persons immediately but someone usually came forward before too long.

The drive along Stanton took him to the edge of the forest, a dense mass of pine trees that covered over a million acres and extended up to the black mountain range. The smell of fresh pine and mountain air filled the cabin of his truck. There was always something special about the beginning of summer and in the mountains, everything was bursting into color. Long walks in the forest with his wife, Sandy, had opened a whole new world to him. She reveled in the abundance of wildflowers in the forest and he found himself appreciating nature's changes in Black Rock Falls each season. He pulled into the fire road and stopped beside a patch of mountain harebells, a splash of blue waving in a shaft of sunshine. Alongside the track, glacier lilies had created explosion of yellow and he wished he could be strolling hand in hand with Sandy along the forest trails instead of heading out to recover some poor soul's decomposing body.

He sighed with relief as Atohi Blackhawk pulled his truck in behind him. His Native American friend was one of the best trackers around and knew the forest like the back of his hand. He valued his friend's opinion and it was nice to have him along. Before he climbed out of his truck, he called the forest warden, Bob Chandler, to give him an update of their ETA. "Hey Bob, this is Deputy Rowley, we've arrived at the fire road on Stanton. I have the ME with me and the fire chief has offered to assist. What information can you give me on the body?"

"From what I can see, female. She's naked and has long dark hair." Bob sounded shaken. *"It isn't pretty. She was stuck between two rocks at first but the current washed her into a pool. Some of the people here assisted in damming up the edge of the pool. I haven't attempted to haul her out the water, I was concerned about destroying evidence."*

Rowley slid from behind the wheel and after giving Blackhawk a wave, headed over to Wolfe's ME's van. "Okay that's fine. We're on our way." He disconnected as Blackhawk jogged to his side.

"The fishing hole is not too far from here. Good fishing if you know where to find it. I can get you there in about ten minutes." Blackhawk frowned at him. "The falls break up into many fingers, it is unusual for a body to have fallen into the water and end up there, unless she fell from the Whispering Caves. They come out halfway down Black Rock Falls. Water spills in from above and rushes out to join the falls. In time gone by, people who wandered inside the caves, thinking they'd found a way out, ended up in Dead Man's Drop."

Rowley slapped him on the back. "That's good to know."

The window buzzed down on Wolfe's van and Rowley gave him an update.

"Have you called Jenna?" Wolfe raised one blond eyebrow. "They are chasing down a missing girl out of Louan."

Rowley shook his head. "Nope, not yet. I figure we need eyes on the body first. I'll get some images and send them to her." He nodded to Colt Webber and Emily Wolfe inside the van.

"If it's Sophie Wood I can do a visual ID based on photographs on file." Wolfe frowned. "I'll run a DNA profile when I get her back to the lab. I have her parents and sister on ice, they're victims of the bombing Jenna and Kane are investigating with Jo and Carter."

"Copy that." Rowley indicated with his chin toward the fire chief's truck. "He volunteered to help and Atohi will guide us to Dead Man's Drop."

"We'll follow you." Wolfe started his engine.

Rowley hurried back to his truck and turned to Blackhawk. "Do you want to lead the way or ride shotgun with me?

"You drive." Blackhawk headed back to his truck, grabbed his rifle, and climbed into the cab beside Rowley. "Follow the fire road."

After following a grid of firebreaks, they parked in a fire engine turnaround. The place was more popular than he'd been led to believe. At least six other trucks had parked alongside the track, their noses pushed into the forest. Rowley climbed out and scanned the area. Droplets of water formed from the damp air like tears on the snowberry bushes as the falls roared close by. Black Rock Falls had a spectacular beauty but a tragic past. He'd watched a close friend commit suicide by jumping into the falls and his stomach twisted at the memory. He grabbed a few essentials from his truck and stuffed them in his duffle and then waited for the others to collect their gear. Walking in pairs they followed Blackhawk along a well-used path through the forest. Behind him, Wolfe carried a stretcher with Colt Webber, and Emily, blonde hair tied up in a ponytail, wearing a plaid shirt, blue jeans, and rubber boots, walked beside Webber with a forensics kit. Matt Thompson strolled beside Wolfe chatting about the weather.

They found a crowd of people on the edge of the lake when they'd arrived. For an unknown fishing spot, it hadn't taken long for the news to get out and people's morbid curiosity had gotten the better of them. Amazed that the public had made it there before him and the forensics team, he glared at the curious faces. The forest warden had kept everyone back using his horse to block the line of vision. Rowley moved beside Wolfe as they all stared into the rockpool. His stomach lurched; the river hadn't been kind to the young woman and her battered body bobbed on the water arms outstretched.

"We'll get her out." Wolfe turned to Webber. "Come with me."

"I'll help." Matt Thompson stepped forward. "Between the three of us if we step over the boulders, we'll be able to lift her clear and carry her back to shore."

"Okay." Wolfe gave him a curt nod. "I'll meet you over there but just you and me." He turned to Emily as Thompson walked toward the water. "Spread out the plastic on the shore over there and open a body bag. I want her on ice as soon as possible." He turned to Colt and lowered his voice. "Get the images and then video the extraction. Make sure to zoom in on any ligature marks. If this girl is Sophie Wood, it's likely she was restrained with zip-ties like the others." He looked at Emily. "If this is the case get her covered up immediately, we don't need that information getting out to the public."

"Gotcha." Webber nodded and extracted the camera out of a bag over his shoulder.

"Maybe get a few shots of the crowd as well." Emily peered toward the bank. "Jenna will want to know who was watching."

Rowley pulled out his phone. "I'll do that, they'll be so involved in what you're doing they won't notice me." He turned to Blackhawk. "Could you help the forest warden keep the crowd back?" He pulled a roll of crime scene tape from his duffle and handed it to him. "I'll head over to speak to him as soon as I'm through here."

"Don't fall in the rockpool." Blackhawk's mouth turned down as he scanned the dark water. "There are many disturbed souls in there and they want revenge. The lake is angry. Be careful." He turned away and headed toward the man on horseback.

Unease rolled over Rowley and a cool breeze seeped through his shirt, raising goosebumps as he stared after him. Atohi Blackhawk had knowledge way beyond his years. He understood the forest and all that lay within. There was a calmness about him that Rowley appreciated. He was glad to call him his friend. He moved his attention to the water. The lakes all through Stanton Forest reflected the deep blue sky. The water was known for being crystal clear and pristine, running straight from the mountains but here, with the trees closed in around the rockpool and with the excessive turbulence, it looked dark and foreboding.

As the team went to work, Rowley shook off the gloomy feeling stalking him and decided to get his own shots of the area. He photographed the crowd from all angles before turning his camera to the scene. He moved in close to capture the retrieval. If this girl was remotely involved in Jenna's case, she would want to get eyes on the images as soon as possible. His gaze moved over the body of a young woman. Her skin was so pale it was as if all the color had been washed away. Her eyes were closed and long eyelashes brushed a bruised cheek. Her full lips held a distinct blueish hue and she had a dimpled chin.

She'd been pretty and he tried without luck to pull on the mask of professionalism, something both Jenna and Kane had in spades. They'd all witnessed gruesome scenes but somehow managed to put themselves outside the now. He'd seen it in Kane. One minute he was normal, the next his eyes would change to granite as if he held not one ounce of compassion but that couldn't be further from the truth. Rowley bit down on his cheek to push the sadness away and clicked his camera phone as Wolfe and Thompson lifted her from the water with gloved hands. The girl's head dropped forward, her soaked hair falling over her face. The cold water had likely delayed rigor mortis. When her feet broke the water every hair on his body stood to attention. Around one ankle was a zip-tie.

CHAPTER TWENTY-THREE

Exhilaration thrummed through him as the ME's team wrapped Sophie's body in a black body bag and zipped it up. He'd enjoyed every delicious second as they'd photographed and prepared her for her journey to the morgue. Avoiding the deputy's camera had been easy enough, and by moving this way or that, he'd kept well out of any shots. A glow of satisfaction washed over him. He'd planned it just right to be there when her body was fished out of the lake. He'd known she'd end up here. The moment she fell into the swirling water in the Whispering Caves there could be no turning back for her. The crowd whispered suicide, but the truth was his alone to know. He'd enjoyed his time with Sophie, it had been rewarding. The thrill from a fire or bombing never lasted long enough and taking her had stretched out the experience.

He'd held his breath as she emerged from the water, her face untouched by her fall, and then he'd smothered a grin. It would have been inappropriate to smile at her battered remains with so many people looking on but being there and seeing her face again made his heart race. She was the opposite to her family, they'd burned to a crisp, becoming black and distorted—and she resembled an ice queen. Her skin so smooth as if carved in white marble but he could still make out the marks he'd inflicted to make her obey him. She'd soon learned to cooperate. Even the river couldn't wash them away and she wore them like his signature. He'd owned her.

CHAPTER TWENTY-FOUR

Duke had started to whine by the time Kane and Carter had finished filing their reports. They'd spent the last hour or so eating and working on their laptops in Aunt Betty's Café. It was a soothing place to work, not too noisy but the constant flow of hot coffee and the delicious aromas of the daily special made it cozy. There was something about Aunt Betty's Café that soothed even the roughest day, like sitting in your grandma's kitchen and waiting for the cookies to come out the oven. Kane let out a contented sigh and caught Carter looking at him. "What?"

"This place, it's special." Carter rubbed his belly and sighed. "If I could bottle the smell and atmosphere, I'd make millions." He glanced around the room. "I wish we had a place like it in Snakeskin Gully or Jo had set up shop here."

"It reminds me of visits to my grandma, which were few and far between." Kane smiled. "I'd eat all my meals here if I could and I figure by the flow of people through the door, many townsfolk feel the same way." He sighed. "I'll order some pies and have them delivered to the office, in case Jenna and Jo haven't eaten yet."

"Any excuse huh?" Carter chuckled. "I figure we go and walk the dogs; they're getting restless."

Kane finished his coffee and nodded. "Sure."

Jenna hadn't called to give them an update but Kane assumed she was insisting on a rape kit examination on Dawn and it would take time to organize a place for her to stay. He closed his laptop and looked at Carter. "There's a dog friendly area in the park we can use and then we'll head back to the office. I'm done waiting here for them. I'll send her a message."

"Good thinking. It will be crazy when Jo and Jenna arrive. They must be swamped. They haven't added any reports to the files." Carter collected his things and stood. Beside him Zorro snapped to attention, ears pricked and ready for action. "I guess it's gonna be a long night."

After ordering a takeout delivery, they stashed their laptops in his truck and Kane led the way across Main and into the park. One end of the park had an enclosure with swings and slides for young kids to enjoy but they headed in the opposite direction and let themselves into a fenced area reserved for dogs. Here the dogs could run unrestrained and had access to the perimeter of a wooded area through an open gate. The trees backed onto a line of houses set behind a high fence on Maple Drive. The local council had created a safe environment for dog lovers.

Kane closed the gate, grabbed a plastic bag from the dispenser, and pushed it into his pocket. He patted Duke on the head. "Off you go and have some fun."

Beside him, Carter surveyed the area. "Is it safe? Zorro goes kinda ballistic when I give him the order to let loose."

"Very." Kane looked at Zorro. The dog's entire body was trembling with excitement and his teeth clicked together making him look as if he was smiling. "I've never seen him so excited. Maybe he can encourage Duke to walk around some?"

"Playtime." Carter flicked his fingers and Zorro bounced into the air.

Amused, Kane watched what could only be described as a doggy happy dance. The Doberman jumped and wiggled and then dropped down on his front legs before leaping away again. He rolled in the grass with his legs running in midair. The next moment he sped off like a greyhound out of the starting gates and flashed toward the woods. Within seconds, he came shooting back with a stick in his mouth. He dropped it neatly at Carter's feet and barked.

"Okay." Carter picked up the stick and hurled it.

Zorro took off and skidded to a halt, throwing up dirt as he retrieved the stick and dashed back to Carter. Kane soaked up the sunshine and watched Carter play with his dog for some time. All the while Duke sat by his feet his head following the action. He rubbed Duke's ears. "I guess you prefer to watch, huh?"

To his surprise, Duke wandered off toward the woods. He shrugged and turned to Carter. "I think I hurt his feelings."

"Nah." Carter threw the stick again. "He's just doing his own thing. Bloodhounds are motivated by different things. They like to rest for the time they'll need their energy but Zorro here has pent-up energy he must let out. Sitting around all day isn't his style." He indicated with his chin toward the open gate. "What's Duke picked up?"

Kane jogged over to the gate and grinned at Duke. His dog was attempting to negotiate a two-yard-long tree branch through a yard-wide gate. After repeated attempts, Duke dropped the branch and barked at him. Trying not to laugh, Kane walked through the gate, picked up the branch and tossed it over the fence. "There you go. What are you planning on doing with it?"

Duke followed him, picked up the branch and carried it to where Carter was standing. Bemused, Kane followed. He raised an eyebrow at Carter. "Maybe he wants you to throw it, javelin style?"

"You don't know much about your dog, do you?" Carter shook his head slowly. "I guess you haven't raised him from a pup, huh?"

Kane frowned. "Nope, he was a rescue. I found out later, from Atohi, that his cousin trained him as a tracker out on the res." He shrugged. "I'm getting to know what he doesn't like but he's never collected tree branches before."

"Ah, that makes sense." Carter bent and rubbed Duke's head and sides. "He's saying, Zorro might be fast but he only brought back a tiny stick and I found the whole branch." He took the stick Zorro had found and it fit neatly against a missing part of the tree branch. "That is one smart dog. Don't underestimate him."

"Never have."

A whistle came from behind them and Duke did his happy dance and took off bounding toward the gate. Kane turned to see Atohi Blackhawk heading in their direction. He raised his hand in a wave. "Now there's a man who understands Duke." He frowned. "I wonder what's happened, he doesn't look too happy."

He heard a growl and beside Carter, Zorro was baring his teeth. "You've met Atohi before, haven't you?"

"Yeah, sure. Nice guy." Carter flicked his fingers and Zorro sat beside him not making a sound. "Zorro senses people's emotions. I figure Atohi is here to deliver some bad news. It looks like playtime is over."

Kane walked toward his friend. "Problem?"

"You could say that." Atohi fell in step beside them as they headed back to the gate. "I went with Rowley to Dead Man's Drop, a fishing hole out at the bottom of the falls. They pulled a young woman's body from the rockpool and Wolfe figures she's the missing girl you've been hunting down in Louan. He's taken the body back to the morgue and is running a DNA comparison against the bodies from the explosion."

"Why didn't he call one of us?" Carter went over to a tap and rinsed his hands. "If it's Sophie Wood it's an FBI matter and Rowley shouldn't have been involved. Did they process the scene?"

"Trust me, Rowley is a by the book guy." Blackhawk stopped walking and balled his fists on his hips. "He and Wolfe have worked together many a time and Wolfe's team doesn't miss anything." He snorted, clearly agitated by the slight on his friends. "The call came in from the forest warden, the information Rowley received was he found a body floating in the lake is all."

Kane slapped him on the back. "I appreciate you letting us know. Wolfe wouldn't bother us unless he has a positive ID and that will be an hour or so away. We'll head back to the office and wait for his call." He smiled. "I'll give Jenna and Jo the heads up."

"See that you do." Blackhawk grinned at him. "I'm heading to Aunt Betty's to grab some takeout and then I'm heading home. You know where to find me if you need me for anything." He turned to Carter. "Nice seeing you again, Agent Carter." He gave them a wave and hurried across Main.

"I figure we head straight for the ME's office. We have those mud samples from Cleaves' shoes to give him and I don't plan on waiting for information on the girl." Carter wiped his wet hands on his jeans. "If she is Sophie Wood, how the hell did she end up dead in Black Rock Falls?"

CHAPTER TWENTY-FIVE

It was getting late in the day by the time Wolfe had the body of the young woman safely inside the refrigerated drawer in the morgue. He'd set up the DNA machine and processed the samples from the body, before he removed his gloves and called Jenna. "Hey Jenna. Where are you?"

"At the hospital. We had to rescue a young woman from an abusive situation." Jenna sounded exhausted. *"We'd hardly headed off when Kane called to inform us that the guy that had her in his house was heading our way. We're holed up at the secure ward at the hospital. The girl is still undergoing tests. She's been abused, Shane, and sent to this monster by her father to be trained as his next wife."*

Hearing the anger in Jenna's voice, Wolfe frowned. "How old is she?"

"Fifteen but naïve. She gave me a note asking for help when we dropped by to interview Roger Suffolk." Jenna gave a long sigh. *"I was going to place her in the Her Broken Wings women's shelter but with Suffolk making trips into Black Rock Falls, Jo thinks she'd be safer in Snakeskin Gully. They have foster homes available and it's far enough away no one will find her."*

"That sounds like a good idea. I guess Jo will sort out the legality of removing her without a court order." Wolfe leaned against the counter. "The reason I called is we pulled a body out of a fishing hole in one of the smaller lakes in Stanton Forest, this afternoon. She resembles Sophie Wood. I'm running a DNA profile to see if she's a match with the Woods. If she is, I strongly suggest you all come by for the autopsies."

"You found her in a lake in Black Rock Falls?" Jenna sounded incredulous. *"What makes you believe it's our missing girl?"*

"There's a close resemblance to the image we have on file." Wolfe cleared his throat. "The other reason I've withheld from everyone but our team and Rowley, is she has a zip-tie around her ankle. Same type and color as the ones we found on the bodies of the Wood family."

"Has she been in the water long?"

"I don't think so." Wolfe's attention moved to the stainless-steel drawers set into one wall. An entire murdered family were lying within a few feet of him. The idea chilled him to the bone. He forced his mind back on track. "The body temperature taken on scene was inconclusive. The water was very cold but the skin didn't appear to have been submerged for long. Maybe two or three hours. I haven't completed a preliminary yet, I haven't had the time. I'll get the results of the DNA test and schedule the autopsy for first thing in the morning. I'll call you when I have the results."

"Sure, we should be through here soon and heading back to the office." Jenna yawned. *"I have to go over the case with Kane and Carter. We split up to cover more ground."*

Wolfe frowned. "Any suspects?"

"Yeah, a few but we don't have enough evidence to charge anyone." Jenna covered the mouthpiece and Wolfe could hear a muffled conversation. *"I've gotta go, the doctor wants to speak to us. Talk soon."* She disconnected.

Wolfe glanced at the clock. He'd promised to take Anna, his youngest daughter, to her ballet class and stay to watch. He had absolutely no interest in ballet but if Anna enjoyed the classes, well he would too. He pushed a hand through his hair. He needed a haircut but hadn't had time. In between working with Emily on all aspects of forensics, he'd had the task of teaching Julie to drive. She'd passed her driving test yesterday and he'd given her a slightly battered SUV to drive. Anna was comparatively easy, she loved to ride which meant most weekends and school holidays revolved around Jenna and Kane's workload. He could drop her at their ranch for a couple of hours and collect her later, overloaded with sugar and smelling of horses. The ballet was a new passion for his little girl, and if it made her happy that was fine by him, although he had to admit becoming one of the stage "moms" was slightly uncomfortable at times, with four divorced mother hens clucking around him batting their eyelashes and squeezing his muscles. He rolled his eyes just thinking about it but as usual Kane had come up with a plan. If the women harassed him too much, he'd bore them with gruesome facts about forensics. The body farm story had become a favorite.

He contemplated making coffee and headed into the hallway. The sight of Kane and Carter heading toward him stopped him in his tracks. "If you're here for results, I won't have my report on the Woods' autopsies until tomorrow. I've been flat out all day and I'm busy tonight."

"We have samples of mud from a suspect's boots." Kane held out an evidence bag. "And a sample of C-4 taken from his house."

Wolfe looked over the evidence bags to check the labels were filled out correctly. "I'll run tests on these first thing in the morning. Did you have a search warrant?"

"Nah." Kane smiled at him. "I have a signed statement. Thanks, man, we'll stop by in the morning."

Wolfe nodded but he could see there was something else troubling Carter. He opened the door to the lab and dropped the bags into a container. "If you're planning on dropping by for the results of the autopsies on the Wood family tomorrow, you'll need to be here no later than ten." He frowned. "Anything else on your mind, Carter?"

"The body you pulled out the lake, we want to see it." Carter removed a toothpick from between his teeth. "We ran into Blackhawk downtown, he mentioned being there."

Wolfe looked at Kane. "At this moment, this isn't your case. Rowley was the lead investigator. Did he call in the FBI for assistance because I didn't?"

"Come on, Shane, we know you figure it could be Sophie Wood." Kane removed his black Stetson and slapped it against his thigh. "We're all part of the same team."

Wolfe looked from one to the other. "You'll have to wait for the DNA result for a positive ID. If she's Sophie Wood then I'll do a preliminary examination but I'm leaving here at six. I have an appointment at seven and I haven't eaten since breakfast." He glanced down at the dogs. "We'll wait in my office and you'll have to leave the dogs in there. I'm not having dogs in my examination rooms."

"Is everything okay at home?" Kane searched his face. "Girls okay?"

Wolfe smiled at his friend. "The girls are fine, more work than I had ever imagined, even with a live-in housekeeper. They all deserve my time but so does my work. There are only so many hours in the day. I'll be glad when Em is qualified to take some of the load. Being the ME for four counties now is time consuming."

"How much longer until Em does her finals?" Kane walked beside him toward the office.

Wolfe sighed. "December. Colt finishes this semester; he only required an associate degree to work here but Em wants to become a certified medical examiner." He scratched his cheek. "It's been four years come December since she started college. Time has gone by so fast."

"Did they assist at the lake?" Carter followed them inside Wolfe's office.

Wolfe went to the coffee machine, popped in two pods and placed cups under the dispenser. "I love this machine. No wait, no delay." He waited for the cups to fill and handed them to Kane and Carter before repeating the process.

"Thanks." Carter removed his hat and dropped it on the desk before taking a seat. "If this is Sophie, how did she get into a lake out of Black Rock Falls?"

Wolfe took his cup from under the machine and sank into his office chair. "I don't know. It's too far to walk and she was naked. Even if she'd made it to the falls there are forest wardens and tourists all over the forest, she could've asked for assistance." He sipped his drink and allowed the rich taste to spill over his tongue. "The fishing hole is part of a small lake deep in the forest, it's called Dead Man's Drop. From what I understand, people who explored the Whispering Caves and got turned around, headed toward a light source believing it was a way out. According to Atohi, the falls run in to the caves there from a fissure in the rocks causing a whirlpool effect. Once someone is in the water they're washed out and over the falls. Before entry to the caves was prohibited, some twenty years or so ago, deaths frequently occurred there."

"So, I guess it's not a particularly popular fishing hole?" Kane looked at him over the rim of his cup. "You'd never know what you might haul out of there."

Wolfe leaned back in his seat. Oh, Kane was good, in fact they both were exceptional detectives, and the way they were extracting information from him was very subtle but he wasn't planning on giving up any vital information just yet. After all, Jenna had taken the lead in the case and would be pissed with him if he gave the information to Carter before her. He smiled at Kane and heard a buzzer sounding from the laboratory. "Exactly. Wait here, I need to check on something." He emptied his cup and hurried out the door.

He collected the data from the DNA sequencer machine and ran a comparison on his computer to all three of the Wood family. There was no doubt, the young woman in his morgue was Sophie Wood. He pulled out his phone and called Jenna. She picked up after a few rings. "Hi Jenna, it's Shane. I have a match for Sophie Wood. Kane and Carter are waiting in my office. Carter wants to see the body. I haven't given them the result yet."

"Yeah, show them the body. We'll stop by soon." Jenna cleared her throat. *"Did you get a chance to look at the blue Ford yet?"*

Bone weary, Wolfe rubbed the back of his neck. "Not yet. The vehicle is locked up out back of the morgue. I'll get to it tomorrow." He leaned against the counter. "I know you need the information yesterday but I'm going as fast as humanly possible. I'll do the sweep and have answers late tomorrow afternoon."

"That's fine. I do understand your workload, Shane." Jenna sounded sincere. *"We shouldn't be too long. Jo is sorting out the legal side of keeping a minor in a secure ward. She's already organized around the clock security."* She laughed. *"I'd forgotten how fast the FBI moved. I'm hanging around here doing nothing but waiting. I'll call Rowley and give him the results. He'll probably be glad to hand over the case to us."*

Wolfe scratched the stubble on his chin and made a mental note to shave before taking Anna to ballet classes. "That will save me the trouble. If you're planning on dropping by to see the body, I must be out of here by six. I'm taking Anna to ballet this evening and I promised to stay back and watch."

"Sure. Ah. It looks like Jo is ready to leave. We'll see you soon." She disconnected.

Wolfe stood and pushed his phone back inside his pocket. He walked out the lab and grabbed scrubs, facemasks, and gloves for the three of them. When he walked into his office, he dropped them on the desk. "Suit up. The DNA is a match."

CHAPTER TWENTY-SIX

Jenna pulled her SUV into an empty space beside Kane's truck. She turned to Jo. "I hate this part of an investigation."

"Really?" Jo unclipped her seatbelt. "I find the forensics fascinating. The tiniest discovery can link a criminal to a crime and solve murders." She sighed. "Although, I have to admit since I've had Jaime, detaching myself emotionally from child victims during an autopsy has been difficult."

Understanding, Jenna nodded. "Yeah, kids are difficult but I have a different response and it's probably unhealthy." She collected her things and stared at Jo. "Seeing a murdered child makes me angry. I should be feeling sad but it's never sadness. I feel this welling up of anger and feel like screaming." She looked away. "I'm not normal, am I?"

"You're a sheriff and you're responsible for the lives of the people in your town." Jo squeezed her arm. "Of course, you feel angry. You want to bring the criminal to justice. I figure Kane feels angry too. He doesn't show it but I've seen his combat face. He hides his emotions well but not from me." She waved to the ME's office doors. "I guess we'd better view the body."

Jenna used her card to access the door. The reception area was empty, Emily and Webber had left for the day. They went through the next set of doors and the cold chill of the morgue greeted her with its normal unearthly smells of antiseptic laced with a hint of decaying flesh. She headed for the examination room with the red light glowing and peered through the glass window to see Kane's wide back blocking the view. "They're inside." She grabbed scrubs, facemask, and gloves and suited up.

"Okay, I'm ready." Jo pulled on her gloves. "Let's go."

Jenna flashed her card over the scanner and the doors whooshed open. All the men's eyes turned to her but she was focused on the young woman lying on the metal autopsy table covered with a white sheet. "Okay, what do we have here?"

"I've been X-raying the body and taking samples from under her nails so far." Wolfe turned to examine a slide under a microscope. "No skin or fibers." He looked at Jenna. "From a preliminary examination of her skull, I'd guess she struck her head during the fall and drowned. Of course, as you know, I'll have to do a full autopsy to determine COD but I can't see any other reason for her death. There are no signs of strangulation, ligature marks, or pressure marks around her throat." He pulled back the sheet and examined the girl's body under the light. "Help me turn her over."

"Sure." Kane stepped forward and they rolled the body over.

"No stab wounds." Wolfe narrowed his gaze as he laid Sophie back on the gurney. "These bruises on her face are at least twenty-four hours old." He looked down the body. "Same with her inner thighs."

Jenna stared at the girl's body and felt the anger rising. "He raped her, didn't he?" She pointed to the distinct finger marks on Sophie's thighs. "I've seen that before on rape victims." Her gaze moved to the girl's ankle and the deep welt in the skin around the zip-tie.

"I'll examine her." Wolfe proceeded to a pelvic examination. He straightened and nodded. "Yeah, there's clear evidence of rape. I'll process the swabs in the morning." He took a sample and smeared it on a slide and then went to the microscope. "No evidence of semen. I doubt we'll find anything to tie one of your suspects to the kidnapping and rape. I'd say the waterfall washed away any trace evidence on her skin but I'll check during the autopsy."

Gathering her thoughts, Jenna nodded. "Thanks, we'll get out of your hair. What time tomorrow?"

"Ten." Wolfe covered the body and slid it back into the drawer. "Try and get some rest, Jenna."

Exasperated, Jenna tore off her mask and threw her hands in the air. "We have a psychopathic pyromaniac murderer running loose who likes to kidnap and rape girls. I won't be able to rest until he's behind bars."

CHAPTER TWENTY-SEVEN

Blackwater

Pamela Stuart made a habit of dropping by her grandma's house to take her fresh milk on the way home from school. Her grandpa, Sheriff Buzz Stuart, was always too busy to remember, and grandma was still recovering from hip replacement surgery. She loved Grandma's house because it always smelled of fresh baking. She had a bag of cookies in her school bag for later and her mouth watered to eat them on the way home. It was a long walk to her home if she kept to the sidewalk but if she used the cut-through that went through the woods, it wouldn't take long. It wasn't dark yet and nothing bad ever happened in Blackwater.

She made her way along the path, listening to one of her favorite tunes via her earbuds. She noticed a shadow moving ahead and stopped walking. Her heart pounded. Bears often wandered close to town to raid people's trash cans. She pulled out her earbuds and froze, listening.

"Oh, thank goodness." A man stepped out of the bushes. "Can you help me? I think my arm is broken." He indicated to his arm tucked inside his shirt front.

Unsettled but not stupid, Pamela stared at the man. "Why do you need my help? It's not far to town, you can walk there."

"It's not for me." He indicated into the woods with his chin. "I came here to give my pup a run and someone set a trap. He got caught in it. I opened the trap but it snapped back on my arm. Toby's hurt and I can't leave him out here all alone. If you could carry him for me, my car is just at the end of the trail. I only need one hand to drive him to the vet." He looked at her. "Please. I won't go near you, just help Toby."

"Okay." Pamela peered into the shadows. "Where is he? I'll go get him."

"Through there." The man pointed. "See the snowberry bushes? Just past them on the left."

Pamela pushed her earbuds and phone into her school bag and propped it beside a tree. She moved into the dark damp woods and stepped carefully along an animal track. "I can't see him."

"Just a bit further, see over there." The man came up behind her. "Please hurry."

Unable to see much at all in the dim light, Pamela hustled deeper into the woods. She heard breathing behind her and then pain shot through her head. White spots danced across her vision and she staggered forward. Panic gripped her and she rubbed her head. "Why did you hit me?"

The next moment something slid around her neck and tightened. The man pushed her to her knees and before she could scream, he'd covered her mouth with tape. She tried so hard to stop him but he was so strong. Agony tore through overstretched muscles as he wrenched her arms behind her, binding them with tape. With her face pushed down in the damp leaves left from last fall and her arms secured tightly behind her, she couldn't fight the man tearing at her clothes. He said nothing and by the time he'd finished, tears streamed down her face. Terrified and hurting bad, she rubbed her face in the cool leaves. Maybe he'd go now and leave her alone.

"Can't breathe huh?" He used her panties to wipe her nose. "When I'm sure you won't scream, I'll remove the tape."

She looked over her shoulder at him. Pleading with her eyes and shaking her head. She'd never forget his face and when she told her grandpa what had happened, he'd put him in jail.

"Don't worry, Pamela. I'm not going to kill you." His raspy voice came close to her ear and she could smell cigarettes on his breath. "If you're a good girl and do what I say, I'll let you go. I only need you for a little while. If not—" he tugged at the cord around her neck "—this can get a lot tighter." He dragged her to her feet. "Now walk. We're going for a little ride."

CHAPTER TWENTY-EIGHT

Friday

After returning to the office on Thursday evening and updating the files, exhaustion had overcome Jenna and her suggestion of a steak dinner in town and an early night had been welcomed by all members of the team. She'd spent her evening going over the case files while Jo chatted on the phone with her daughter, Jaime. She'd been interested to receive a report from Rowley on the Louan fire written by the fire chief, Matt Thompson. Rowley had scanned all the pages and sent the file to her by email with a little note explaining Thompson's visit and complaint against her. She'd read the report with interest and found nothing added apart from a positive swab for gasoline as an accelerant in the fire and the assurance the Louan volunteer fire department had searched the bedrooms.

Friday morning arrived with blue skies and a cool breeze blowing from the mountains. It was such a glorious day that Jenna couldn't resist taking her toast and coffee on the porch to enjoy a few moments of peace. Jo and Carter had taken her cruiser and headed into town but she had time before she had to leave with Kane for the office. They arrived before seven and made themselves comfortable in the temporary FBI office. She looked over her laptop at the others. "Okay first of all, Kalo has analyzed the video taken by John Cleaves at the scene of the fire. No one is seen leaving the area and he validated the plate numbers of the vehicles. The Ford does belong to Dexter as we believed. If there's any other information, he'll contact me again. So, if you're ready, we'll go over the main points of the investigation?" She stood, moved around the desk, and plucked the whiteboard pen from its holder. "Okay, we have three people of interest to date. The two most probable are Roger Suffolk and John Cleaves. We'll start with Suffolk." She entered his name on the whiteboard and listed his information. "Motive: Lodged a complaint against Isaac Wood. He claimed Wood encouraged his wife to leave him. He became so violent toward Wood that Sheriff Crenshaw threw him in a cell but laid no charges because Crenshaw is a member of his church and likely believed Suffolk had just cause to be angry."

"His wife died in a car accident, brake failure." Jo flipped through her notebook. "We'll need to look into that as well. He made the comment that it was God's will to set him free of her."

Jenna added that to the notes on the whiteboard. "If Wood was a problem for other church members, maybe it went further than Phelps let on. With the amount of men trying to date Sophie, he would've been making waves. Maybe Suffolk decided to remove the problem and take Sophie. We know he has a hankering for underage girls. I believe Dawn Richardson and we have proof she had sexual relations recently but unfortunately, she refuses to return to Louan to give evidence against him in court." She frowned. "The case won't stick, even if we pushed it, she'd had boyfriends before and we can't prove Suffolk touched her."

"Don't forget, Mrs. Wood was raped. We have proof of that at least." Jo pushed a hand through her hair. "Another violent act. Killing wasn't good enough, he wanted to humiliate and dominate his victims."

"Why didn't you arrest him?" Carter tipped back his Stetson and narrowed his gaze at her. "Even if you can't prove he had sex with a minor. He was living with an underage girl and statutory rape is a criminal offense in this state. I'm sure you could talk her around to testifying."

Not fazed by Carter's annoyance, Jenna turned to look at him. "I have three reasons to let this go for now: the first we were invited by Louan county to investigate the bombing, which leaves Dawn's case under the jurisdiction of Sheriff Crenshaw. Secondly, because most of the town belongs to the same church and have the same beliefs… that is, taking a child and training her to be a wife is okay, so the chances are he won't spend a second in custody. Thirdly, Dawn has been through enough, dragging her through a court case, when we all know she can't win, will traumatize her even more. It's her choice if she decides to go ahead if more women step forward later." She looked at him. "I called my contact in the FBI Child Protection Agency and as she is over the age of twelve and now safe, they don't have time to get involved."

"I had to pull a lot of favors to have Dawn placed in my custody." Jo went to the coffee machine and refilled her cup. "By rights, she should've been placed into the care of the Louan CFSD, but as Phelps, the director, is a member of the church as well, he'd return Dawn to her folks and they'll give her back to Suffolk. They probably have an agreement or even a contract."

"I don't agree." Carter stared at the ceiling for some moments and then lowered his gaze to her. "Because with Dawn's testimony we have more than circumstantial evidence to charge him with the Woods' murder."

"I don't think we can risk the case on one young woman's testimony. The defense will tear her to shreds." Kane joined Jo at the coffee machine. "I'd like to see more evidence or he'll slide. He said that on Tuesday evening he was making a delivery at Miller's Garage here in Black Rock Falls and didn't get back until late. We could waste a whole lot of time hunting down someone who he spoke to, but if the bomb was set off by remote—"

"Dang!" Carter sprang from his chair and started pacing. "The family had the table set for dinner. What if our timeline is corrupted? Say Suffolk was at the Woods' ranch earlier than we suspected. He subdued and restrained the family and set the bomb. He kidnapped Sophie and stashed her somewhere before he drove to Black Rock Falls to set up his alibi. It's only half an hour's drive from Louan to Miller's Garage. He could've set off the bomb with a simple phone call while he was there."

"Exactly." Kane glanced over his shoulder at Carter. "He also admitted being in DC around the time of the earlier bombings, which is another strike against him. Here's where I have a problem, and it suggests reasonable doubt. Suffolk is a big guy and him and his truck would be well known in Louan. How come nobody noticed him or his truck near the Woods' ranch on the night of the bombing?" He filled his cup and returned to his seat. "We also don't know if he has any knowledge of explosives." He sighed. "We'll need more information on Suffolk before we move on him. The underage dealing must be rife in Louan if it's thought to be normal practice. I hate to say it but if Suffolk has been raised to believe that behavior is okay, it doesn't make him a murderer."

"I have to agree." Jo stared at Jenna. "Without a direct link to Suffolk, like for instance, he used his own phone to call the burner to detonate the bomb, and with him establishing an iron-clad alibi, it's not going to fly."

Unconvinced, Jenna chewed on the end of the pen thinking. "What if he didn't use his truck? Remember, we discussed the possibility of the blue Ford stolen by Harvey Haralson being involved in a crime?" She went back to her desk and scanned the files. "Haralson said he found the vehicle abandoned at the edge of the forest opposite The Triple Z Bar. Suffolk admits to being at the Triple Z bar on Tuesday evening. What if he parked his truck in the parking lot, took the Ford from Dotty Grace's yard, and drove back to Louan to commit the crime? When he had Sophie holed up somewhere, he left the Ford in the forest and went back to the Triple Z Bar, collected his truck and went home?"

"Yeah, possible." Kane scanned his notes. "The rancher, Jo Ranger recalls seeing a blue Ford in the vicinity of the Woods' ranch before the explosion."

"Okay." Jenna added Jo Ranger to her to do list. "We'll speak to him."

"Has Wolfe done a forensic sweep of the vehicle?" Carter frowned. "I don't see a report in the files, or a final report on the fire victims."

Jenna shook her head and went back to the whiteboard. "Not yet, he's been snowed under. He'll give us a final report on the Wood family when we go for Sophie's autopsy."

"What else have we got on Suffolk?" Carter sat down and pulled a toothpick from his top pocket. "He's on the top of my suspect list."

Jenna made notes on the whiteboard. "Kane mentioned Suffolk was heading this way yesterday to make a delivery. It would be interesting to see if he is in the footage Rowley captured of the people hanging around the lake."

"Yeah, killers often return to the scene of the crime or want to look at the bodies of the people they murdered." Jo stirred sugar into her cup. "Some return over and over. We should get IDs on everyone watching."

Jenna nodded. "I'll ask Rowley to look into that for us."

"If he doesn't get hits in a few hours, hand it over to Bobby Kalo, he has face recognition software and way more databases to search." Jo looked at her. "Some of the people could be tourists."

"Sure." Jenna smiled. "I keep forgetting about Kalo. I'll send him a copy of the footage to do his magic." She added it to her list. "Okay what do you have on Cleaves?"

"Our interview with him was interesting." Carter placed one cowboy boot on the knee of his other leg. "We found C-4 in his broom closet and he had mud on his shoes. The samples are with Wolfe. He was on scene and took footage of the explosion, was also in DC around the time of the previous bombings."

Jenna rested one hip on the corner of the desk. "Motive?"

"Well, he didn't like Mrs. Wood. Apparently, she objected to him speaking to Sophie. Now we have a clearer understanding of the way of things in Louan, the Woods being outsiders would have upset many of the members of the same sect or whatever." Carter snorted. "With C-4 in his possession, an attraction to Sophie, and being on scene, he is a possible as well."

"Okay." Jenna looked at Kane. "What about Simon Dexter out of Prairie View. Your notes mentioned he was the driver of the gray car captured on scene by Cleaves' dashcam and a known firebug?"

"He has a motive as well, much the same as Cleaves." Kane sipped his coffee and regarded her over the rim of the cup. "If fifteen is the age the girls are let's say 'trialed' by potential husbands, we're dealing with statutory rape. I'm guessing they marry at sixteen. Here that's legal although we don't see it happen very often in Black Rock Falls. Sophie would have become a contender in the eyes of many single men from the same congregation. From what we're hearing, the Woods were getting angry at the local men for pestering them about Sophie. Who knows how many Isaac Wood threatened to shoot? This is a motive and from where I'm sitting, removing Sophie from her family meant she was available." He sighed. "I figure, she escaped her kidnapper and her death was an accident. From what I'm seeing, there's a shortage of fifteen-year-old girls in Louan." He shot a glance at Carter. "I know the FBI can look into this practice. You'll have to do something."

"We've one case." Carter cleared his throat. "No matter how distasteful we believe this practice, we're going to have one hell of a time proving it. How many girls raised to accept this as normal will be willing to come forward?"

Jenna pushed a hand through her hair. "I doubt we'll find one, willing to go against their family and church. It is their first amendment right to practice their beliefs. We'll do what we can to help Dawn and make noise about anyone else needing assistance to come forward. We have the Her Broken Wings hotline and I'll make sure the flyers are worded to let anyone in a similar situation aware we can help them. I'll have them posted in the local schools as well."

"I figure we're getting way off track." Kane straightened in his chair. "We're looking at the Woods' murder as an excuse to kidnap Sophie. Has it slipped your minds this lunatic has the same MO as the one in the DC bombings?" He waved one hand toward the board. "Raping the wife and then kidnapping the girl was the icing on the cake, his reward and an escalation." He looked at Jo. "I'm right, don't you agree?"

"Yeah." Jo rested her chin in her palm and looked at the whiteboard. "Or he's smarter than we think and he's using the girl as a distraction?"

Jenna snorted. "I don't call rape a distraction."

"No, I didn't mean that, Jenna." Jo frowned at her. "It shows a vicious brutality but on top of all the other traits we're seeing in this killer, now we can add narcissist. He thinks only of himself. He has no empathy for anyone or he wouldn't have killed the child, or raped the mother and Sophie. Both these are acts of extreme violence. This man is angry and whatever triggered him in DC has set him off again but this time, it's tenfold."

Jenna nodded and scanned the faces of her team. "I have my own conclusions. Yes, he's been triggered again but this time he's not killing people by remote. In DC, the bombs were set and he walked away nice and clean. It wasn't up close and personal. It was more like revenge for something they did to him. He's nothing like the psychopaths we've dealt with in the past. This time, it's personal, so he needed the connection with his victims. He wanted to see the fear in their eyes and listen to them plead for their lives. He tied them up so they know what is going to happen, he no doubt taunts them before they die and makes it a slow death. The problem is, the explosion and fire just weren't enough, he needed more control. He wants to hurt them as much as someone hurt him, so to twist the knife, he rapes the wife in front of her family and kidnaps their daughter. He kept Sophie alive to torment for as long as possible. This is revenge in spades and I don't believe it's anywhere near over." She took a deep breath. "I think he's just begun and the Woods were only the first on his list."

CHAPTER TWENTY-NINE

He'd taken Pamela Stuart to a cabin in Stanton Forest, Black Rock Falls. It was convenient and not too far to walk from a firebreak road. Although it was coming into summer, this part of the forest wasn't a popular hiking trail and wasn't in a hunting area. The old man who owned the cabin had lived off the grid until he'd died. The cabin remained just as he'd left it. Canned goods on the shelves and the bed neatly made. No one had claimed it and when he came across it, last fall, he'd found the key to the door under a bucket of kindling on the front porch. He'd spent some time nailing the shutters closed, added a *Keep out, trespassers will be shot on sight,* sign to the front porch and taken the key. He didn't intend to leave Pamela in the cabin, he wanted her in the Whispering Caves where he could set up his trail cam again and watch her.

He'd spent some time with her last night before attaching her ankle to a long chain. He couldn't allow Pamela to escape, she'd seen his face and could identify him. He'd set up his trail cam and told her he'd be watching her. She'd become passive and pliable. Having a girl cooperate was surprising because he could see the fear in her eyes. He wanted to frighten her, it put him in control and he liked that.

He walked through the trees and joined a small track that led to the cabin. It was well hidden by the forest and bushes grew right up to the porch. He unlocked the door and stared at her. The room smelled of sweat and the pee in the bucket stunk. She stood up dragging a blanket around her. He glared at her. "Are you trying to make me mad, Pamela?"

She shook her head and the fear came back into her eyes. He'd been generous to her and made a hole in the tape covering her mouth to push a straw through so she could drink water. It thrilled him to see she hadn't attempted to remove the tape. She could have, her hands were free. He walked toward her and ripped off the tape and stared into her eyes. "Sit down. I'll give you something to eat and when you're finished, put this on." He opened his backpack, pulled out a dress he'd taken from the collection bin outside the shelter and tossed it on the bed. He handed her a takeout bag of sandwiches. "We're going for another ride and then a hike." He pulled his Glock out from the holster behind his back and pressed it hard against her temple. "One word, and you die. Understand?"

"Okay." Pamela's fingers trembled as she pulled the dress over her head. "Why are you doing this to me?"

He sat in a chair and studied her for a long while. All the time, he could see the terror building in her eyes. She didn't take her gaze off him but her bottom lip had started to tremble. He didn't care if they cried, Sophie had wailed, sobbed, and fought back but this one was different. Perhaps her grandpa had taught her cooperation was her best chance of survival with a man like him. He smiled and caught the shock in her eyes. "Maybe I wanted to spend some time with a pretty girl."

"You could've asked me. You didn't have to hit me." Pamela tossed the takeout bag of sandwiches from hand to hand. "Now you've had your fun, let me go. I won't tell anyone."

"Uh-huh." He rubbed his chin. "How did I know you'd say that? But I'm not done with you yet." He stood, walked over to her, and cupped her chin lifting her head to face him. "Did your grandpa tell you to cooperate if a man grabbed you off the street?"

When she nodded slowly, he smiled. "That was nice of him but he forgot to mention that trying to reason with a man like me is a waste of time. You see I don't *care* about you. I'm only feeding you because if I don't, you'll probably faint and I don't plan on carrying you through the forest. If you don't cooperate, I'll kill you. You see, to me you are just a means to an end, like the wrapper on a burger. It keeps my fingers clean but when I've eaten my fill, I toss the wrapper away."

"My grandpa will have people looking for me." Pamela lifted her chin. "He'll find me."

He snorted. "Really? You didn't even make the news, sweetheart. Nobody is out looking for you and you're in a different county. No one will look for you here." He looked into her unblinking wide eyes. "Now eat, my time is valuable."

He gathered up her clothes, tossed them into the grate and set them on fire. He watched the flames dance and the smoke curl up the chimney. He added some kindling to make sure not one trace of material remained. He heard her move behind him, a little sob, and a clink of chains. Turning to look at her he narrowed his gaze. "What?"

"Why did you burn my clothes?" Pamela stared into the blackened grate. "That was my favorite jacket."

"Because you no longer exist." He unlocked the chain from the bed, picked up his backpack and waved her to the door. "Pick up the bucket. You can empty it outside. Move."

He ushered her through the door and locked it behind them. After waiting for her to empty the bucket, he pushed her toward the forest. "Don't take the trail, we're walking through the trees."

She said nothing and walked ahead of him, head held high. The dress was too big for her and fell off her shoulders. It looked almost comical. A cool breeze rustled through the forest and he urged her toward the old sedan he'd stolen from Black Rock Falls. People were so trusting considering it was supposed to be serial killer central. He'd had his choice of vehicles and found one in a barn with the keys in the ignition. He'd return it and maybe they wouldn't even notice it had gone missing.

"Come here. Lift your foot." When she complied, he bent to remove the chain from her ankle, straightened to open the trunk, and placed it beside the spare wheel. He grabbed Pamela by the arm and squeezed hard. "Get inside."

"I'll be good and won't scream if you let me ride up front, I promise." Pamela turned wide eyes on him. "Please don't put me in there again. I'm frightened of the dark."

"Then you're gonna love where I'm taking you." He picked her up and tossed her into the trunk. She flopped inside like a rag doll and curled into a fetal position. He stared down at her for a long moment and then showed her his weapon again. "Not a sound." He dropped the lid.

CHAPTER THIRTY

It was a little after nine by the time Jenna's team had devoured the ton of takeout Kane had ordered from Aunt Betty's Café. His excuse that they might be held up all through their break at the Sophie Wood autopsy made her smile but Jenna had little appetite and picked at her food. She'd had a restless night filled with bad dreams about her cat, Pumpkin, drowning in the lake. She'd headed into the kitchen to find Jo at the table sipping hot chocolate, another victim of bad dreams. She had no idea why the Woods' case had made such an impression on her. She'd investigated far more gruesome murders in the past.

"You okay, Jenna?" Kane sat beside her scanning his files.

Jenna snapped back to the present. "Yeah, but I'm starting to believe this case is getting to me. I had nightmares last night and that's unusual."

"Have you ever suffered PTSD?" Carter looked at her from across the desk. "I'm not prying into your private life, Jenna, but I have some experience with the disorder."

Jenna nodded. "Yeah, two guys I thought were friends kidnapped, drugged, and tried to kill me. It messed up my head some is all."

"Well, I stopped having the flashbacks about a year ago and boy they were nasty. The night terrors then were a reenactment too. Sometimes I didn't know if I was asleep or awake." Carter removed his hat and ran a hand through his hair. Troubled green eyes met hers. "After, odd things happened that gave me nightmares but the dreams were unrelated to my situation." He popped a toothpick into his mouth. "The girl being kidnapped and obviously restrained kicked off the nightmare. Don't worry about it. I figure it beats the hell out of a flashback."

Jenna nodded, what he said made sense. "Thanks. I guess we'd better get back to work. The autopsy is at ten and Wolfe doesn't like us to be late."

"Before you start. Did you follow up with Joe Ranger, the rancher who called in about a blue Ford sedan near the Woods' ranch?" Kane scrolled through his notes. "I only have his statement here, taken by Sheriff Crenshaw."

"Yeah we spoke to him." Jenna turned in her seat to look at him. "He gave a verbatim account as in his statement. I asked him if he was one hundred percent sure the vehicle he saw was blue and he replied in the affirmative." She scrolled through her notes. "He didn't take down the plate number because he had no reason to suspect the driver was doing anything wrong but the vehicle was parked alongside the road just before nightfall and then drove into the Woods' driveway around eight." She looked up at Kane. "Ranger headed into town soon after and didn't see the fire." She added a note to her to do list. "Okay this is what we need to cover today if possible. Carter, I want you to contact Bobby Kalo and ask him to hunt down if Suffolk has experience with explosives. I also want him to run a facial recognition scan on the footage taken at the lake. When you've done that, I need you to find out what you can about the car wreck that killed Suffolk's wife."

"Bobby can handle that as well." Carter made notes. "He's been complaining he has nothing to do."

Jenna pushed her hair from her eyes. "Sure, if you figure he can handle it?"

"He can handle it with his eyes shut. What else is on the list?" Jo peered at the board. "We could split the grunt work. I'll go with

Carter and speak to the old lady, Dotty Grace, about her car. She lives near the Triple Z Bar and we could stop by and ask about Suffolk. Like Kane said, he's a big guy and easily noticed. We've had dealings with the barkeeper before, he might cooperate."

"Okay, that sounds like a plan." Jenna made a few notes. "Kane and I will stop by Miller's Garage and Aunt Betty's and see if they recall him being there on Tuesday night."

"I noticed on the file Rowley has added a note about Harvey Haralson—the guy I charged for being in possession of a stolen vehicle—he's out on bail." Kane leaned back in his chair. "I'd like to find out where he was on Tuesday night, and if he comes up clean, we'll need hair and saliva samples for Wolfe to eliminate from the samples he takes from the vehicle. Carter, can you collect the same from Dotty Grace? There's everything you need in the forensics kit in Jenna's vehicle." He looked at Jenna. "It sure looks like the bomber used the blue Ford to kidnap Sophie Wood."

"Damn right." Jenna nodded. "Well, that's settled. I hope Wolfe will find time to do a forensic sweep of the vehicle today. If it is involved, it's one more piece of the puzzle." She glanced at the clock. "Okay, when you've made the calls, Carter, we'll head over to the ME's office." She stood. "I'm going to touch base with Rowley before we leave."

She hurried to her office door. It was open and Rowley was pounding away at the keyboard. She knocked on the door and smiled when he looked up. "Just touching base, anything interesting happening in town today?"

"Another stolen car, strange, it's almost the same as the last one. This one is another sedan, taken from a barn out on Stanton." Rowley frowned. "Apart from that, not much is happening. We've had a few complaints about dogs barking and I've been writing up a report about the body in the river."

Jenna nodded. "Keep me informed about the stolen vehicle and the body is Sophie Wood. We've sent the footage you took on scene to an FBI agent to do a facial recognition scan and see who was there. We're hoping we might find a clue to the bomber."

"I'm glad I was of some help." Rowley leaned on the desk and looked at her. "I'm happy to assist in any way I can."

"You could tell me what exactly Matt Thompson said about me? You didn't give me any details in your note." Jenna frowned. "Did he make a complaint in writing?"

"Nope, he was just mouthing off about you saying he wasn't doing his job is all." Rowley's mouth twitched into a smile. "He's one of those guys who believe all men have a beef about women. I figure he had his nose out of joint about you being thorough." He grinned. "He didn't get too far with me, Sheriff."

Jenna sighed. "That's good to know. Thank you."

"One thing." Rowley looked expectant. "I know you don't want me interfering in the FBI case and all, but Atohi called and suggested we head up to the Whispering Caves and see if anyone has been there. He figures the girl's body could have fallen from there."

Jenna didn't want Rowley or Blackhawk risking their lives in the catacombs. "It's closed for a reason. People go inside and are never seen again. I'm not sure it's safe to go there alone."

"Atohi has a friend willing to come with us and his grandfather who knows the caves. We'll be making chalk marks on the walls as well." Rowley frowned. "What if the guy who kidnapped the girl is using the caves to hole up in? He'd know no one would go near the place."

Jenna nodded. "Okay but have a regular check in with Maggie, say every half-hour. Take a Sat Sleeve for your phone and some communication packs with you." She tapped her chin thinking. "And the helmets. Make sure everyone is suited up."

"Sure, we'll be fine. Don't worry." Rowley pushed to his feet. "Thanks."

"Stay safe." Jenna heard voices in the hallway. "I have to go. We're attending the Sophie Wood autopsy at ten." She headed for the door and then turned to smile at him. "That desk suits you."

CHAPTER THIRTY-ONE

The sun warmed Jenna's face as she followed Kane to his truck. It was a beautiful day, the sky stretched out for miles, blue and cloudless. She took in the view, inhaling the exquisite perfume of summer in Black Rock Falls. The hint of pine and the wealth of wildflowers came on every breeze. After witnessing horrors no person should ever experience, nature was a soothing balm, and a constant beauty in her life. She climbed inside the truck. "I'm glad to be working alongside you today."

"Missed me, did you?" Kane chuckled. "I missed you too, especially our breakfast together. Working out with Carter is okay but all business, whereas we have fun. I'm not sure I could work with him all the time, and living with him makes my brain ache." He shook his head. "He doesn't have an off button. When we're on a case together, we have our quiet times but Carter never stops talking."

Jenna laughed. "I've noticed, although he seems to have stopped teasing me at last."

"Yeah, well you know that selfie you took of us outside the ski lodge?" Kane backed out the parking space and headed down Main toward Wolfe's office.

She nodded. "Yeah, what's that got to do with Carter?"

"I enlarged it and it's in a frame over the fireplace in the cottage." Kane winked at her. "He looked at it and said to me, 'Nice pic.' He was quiet for a while as if processing the fact we'd gone there together for a vacation, I think. Although, I'm sure we mentioned it during the case last winter. Maybe now he'll leave you alone."

Jenna laughed. "He thinks we're a couple? Well if that makes him pull his head in, it's fine by me."

As they took the backroads to Wolfe's office, Jenna admired the riot of color in the front gardens of the houses lining the sidewalk. With her window down, she caught the fragrant mixture of blooms blowing into the cab. Above the forest the sky framed the dark mountain peaks in the distance. The beauty of Black Rock Falls with its diversity and ever-changing landscapes made her heart twist. She had fallen in love with the town and its people. Her work as sheriff gave her life purpose and her friends had become the family she thought she'd never have again. It was hard to fathom how much her life had changed since leaving DC. Murders aside, moving to Black Rock Falls had been the best thing in her life.

Suddenly she realized Kane had parked outside the ME's office and was staring at her. She cleared her throat. "Sorry, did you say something? I was miles away." She buzzed up her window and collected her things.

"Nope, I was enjoying the quiet." Kane slid out the door and waited for her on the sidewalk. He indicated toward the road. "Here they come. Wanna wait for them?"

Jenna tipped her face up to catch the sun and sighed. "They can't get in the door without us. I'd say Emily and Webber are assisting Wolfe. There's no one at the front desk."

"They could ring the bell." Kane raised an eyebrow. "But then, I guess we'd still have to wait for them to suit up."

A few minutes later, Jo and Carter joined them. They moved inside the morgue, suited up and headed for the examination room with the red light glowing outside. Jenna breathed in the menthol salve she'd placed under her nose and stepped inside the cold room. She nodded to Emily and Webber. "Morning."

In front of her, three gurneys covered bulky twisted shapes that had once been people and to one side, white feet stuck out from under a sheet. The normally sterile, antiseptic air was heavy with the acrid smell of burned flesh. The odor seeped through the menthol barrier and crept up her nostrils. Jenna had to push down an awful need to run out the room. She shuffled her feet and caught Kane looking at her over his facemask. By the compassion in his gaze, he could just about read her mind. She straightened and gave him a nod. The next moment Wolfe walked out from a side door and glanced around the room. Stepping forward, Jenna met his gaze. "What's first on the list today?"

"I'll walk you through my findings on the burn victims and then we'll start on Sophie Wood." Wolfe flicked on a screen and images of inside the Woods' house lit up the room. "This is where we found the victims. As you can see the shockwave from the explosion toppled both Mr. Wood and his daughter's chairs over but Mrs. Wood remained in an upright position." He went to the X-rays. "Jody has a slight contusion on the right side of her skull, consistent with hitting the floor during the blast. From the toxicology, I've tested for carbon monoxide and from the amount inhaled, she died before the fire took hold. She wasn't injured or sexually abused." He waived toward the smallest body. "She was secured by zip-ties and was wearing PJs." He glanced up at Jenna. "Questions?"

Glad that Wolfe had left the tiny body covered, Jenna shook her head. "Not at this time."

"You can put Jody back, Em." Wolfe removed the sheet from the next unrecognizable victim. The charred remains curled up in a fetal position. "This is Mr. Wood." He clicked a remote and an X-ray came onto the screen. "He was found on his left side but has blunt force trauma to the back of his skull. I've made a comparison with various implements and have concluded he was hit with a weapon in a downward motion." He formed his hand into a pistol and struck downward. "From the position of the injury, the victim must have been sitting in the chair at the time of impact. The hematoma to the brain, would suggest he survived for at least five to ten minutes after the injury. From the fibers I found embedded in his flesh, he was dressed in casual clothes and secured with zip-ties. His cause of death is complicated by the degree of carbonization." He pointed to the position of the body on the image. "Seated close to the doorway, he took the full force of the shockwave and the gas can was close by. He would have been unconscious due to the head trauma but the fire killed him." He looked at Jenna.

She stared at the charred figure no longer resembling anything human and swallowed hard. "And Mrs. Wood?"

"She was brutalized." As Emily slid Mr. Wood back into the mortuary drawer, Wolfe went to the next victim. He clicked up images on the screen. "Her nose and jaw are broken. She has a cracked eye socket. I conclude this woman suffered a severe beating. Her body isn't as fire damaged as the others and rape is evident. She was alive and burned to death. I found traces of smoke inhalation in her lungs. She was dressed but her underwear was missing." He tossed the sheet back over the body. "All victims had eaten at least one hour prior to their deaths." He looked over his mask at Jenna. "I'm ruling all three deaths as homicide."

"Do you have a time of death?" Carter stared at the gurney.

"No time of death but we know when the explosion took place and these people were alive before the fire, so we can use the documented time of the explosion for the TOD." Wolfe looked toward Jo's raised hand. "Jo?"

"The last meal, was it their dinner or a snack?" Jo adjusted her facemask. "I'm wondering how long the bomber was in the house before the explosion and as the table was set, did he arrive before dinner?"

"It was a typical meat and potatoes dinner." Wolfe pushed the gurney toward Emily. "No snacks. The adults had wine with their meal."

Jenna glanced at Jo. "So why was the table set for dinner?"

"Like I concluded before, it was part of his fantasy." Jo folded her arms across her chest. "He wanted to recreate a scene in his past maybe. He likely incapacitated the husband, raped the wife in front of him and then made them sit around the table as if everything was normal."

"I've seen this before." Kane frowned. "Well, read about something similar. The killer is recreating something he witnessed maybe, or what happened to him."

"Possible." Jo looked at him over her facemask. "Or it may be symbolic. He was restrained and raped as a child perhaps. What happened to him was at dinner time and nobody did anything to help him, they just sat around the table. The raping of the woman in front of the husband is significant. The hatred he had toward her is palpable."

Jenna looked from one to the other. "Are you saying Mrs. Wood was the target of his hate and not Mr. Wood? If so, this changes everything."

"They're just theories at this time, Jenna." Jo moved to her side. "I could also say, he wanted to show his dominance over a weaker man by violating his wife in front of him. Both theories carry weight. The problem is with only this case to go on, we have nothing to compare it with."

"What about the DC bombings?" Kane narrowed his gaze. "Apart from the detonator this is nothing like any of the other crimes."

"Yeah, it is. The method he used is almost a signature." Carter scratched his head. "I still figure it's the same guy but as you would say, he's escalated to rape and brutality."

"Let's not forget, kidnapping." Kane shook his head. "His crimes are becoming quite a list."

CHAPTER THIRTY-TWO

A prickle of discomfort slid down Jenna's back as the body of Mrs. Wood slid into the metallic drawer. The woman had suffered and then died a horrendous death. How could they catch this killer, when he moved around like a ghost? She gathered her professional mask around her and looked at her team. The autopsy on Sophie Wood would be traumatic and she wanted to be through as soon as possible. "Okay, we can discuss the killer's list of crimes later when we have more time."

"Next we have the body of Sophie Wood." Wolfe removed the sheet.

The familiar Y-shaped autopsy stitched wound was evident and Jenna shot Wolfe a look. "You've already completed the autopsy? Why didn't you tell me? We should have been here."

"I'm sorry, Jenna. I made the call." Wolfe indicated to Webber. "I didn't have time to haul you out but Webber lives close by and acted as the law enforcement witness. I dropped by to run some tests last night and the body was deteriorating rapidly so I completed a full autopsy, diagnostic tests, X-rays, and ran a tox screen."

Something inside Jenna was glad she didn't have to watch the dissection of the young woman. "I trust your judgment. What did you discover?"

"As you were here for the preliminary, you know some of the findings. My conclusions are, Sophie Wood was restrained since going missing, she hadn't eaten. I believe she cut herself free using a sharp rock or something similar and escaped. She has incisions to the palm of the right hand consistent with holding a sharp object. The bruising on her face is consistent to a punch or slap and it happened at least twenty-four hours prior to her death. There is evidence of prolonged rape. I found no trace evidence from her attacker anywhere on her body." He looked at Jenna. "She struck her head during the fall. I can prove this by the microscopic fragments of rock in the headwound. This would have rendered her unconscious and as I found lake water in her lungs, she drowned. I can't determine if she fell or someone pushed her over the falls. So, my ruling for cause of death is open. The time of death is estimated about two hours prior to the discovery of her body." He covered the body and slid it inside the drawers.

"No semen?" Carter pushed a hand through his hair.

"Not a trace." Wolfe looked at him.

"Then he must have left a pile of condoms somewhere." Carter's eyes flashed. "Rapists aren't that careful."

"If he had her tied up, he could have taken his time." Kane's eyes narrowed as he looked at Wolfe. "Same as Mrs. Wood. Did you find anything on the bedsheets?"

"I found no trace of foreign DNA." Wolfe met his gaze. "Did anyone check the garbage at the Woods' house?"

Jenna shook her head. "Not that I'm aware." She looked at Carter. "Did you check the bedrooms?"

"Yeah, and I checked the trash in every room but I didn't see a condom." He stared at his boots. "You sayin' this guy breaks into a house, ties up the husband, casually rapes the wife using a condom, and then flushes it down the toilet?" He shook his head. "He wouldn't have had time. There were two kids in the house, the wife would've been screaming. It makes no sense."

"Yeah it does." Jenna looked at him. "An armed man comes into the house, and a mother would do anything to protect her kids. I bet she didn't make a sound. She would have cooperated."

"It didn't look like she cooperated." Emily Wolfe's brow creased into a frown. "If she did, it didn't stop him brutalizing her. Same as with Sophie." Her eyes flashed with contempt. "For heaven's sake, she has muscle deep bruises on her thighs. He wanted to hurt her."

"Emily, you can't get emotionally involved with this case." Wolfe removed his gloves and facemask and then tossed them in the trash. "I know it's difficult but you must see the case from the outside looking in. If you don't, you'll miss vital evidence. You must be compassionate but non-judgmental and only consider the facts that are before you."

"I am, Dad, and I see injuries consistent with a brutal attack over a sustained period on a fifteen-year-old girl." Emily ripped off her gloves and glared at him. "This wasn't a grab, rape, and run type of man. This person played with her like a cat does with a mouse."

"Maybe so but you need to be objective." Wolfe huffed out a long sigh. "Go and take a break. We'll talk later."

"If you insist." Emily tossed her gloves and mask into the trash and in a whoosh of doors had vanished into the hallway.

Sickened by the sight of so much destruction, Jenna turned to Wolfe. "Maybe I should join her because I agree with her findings."

"There are many aspects of a forensics investigation that differ from yours, Jenna." Wolfe crossed his arms across his chest and gray eyes settled on her. "Everything I say to you, every decision I make, whether I like it or not, is backed by forensic evidence." He waved a hand toward the bank of shiny stainless-steel drawers. "Do you figure that I don't care about that family? In fact, the father in me wants to find the man who did this and strangle the life out of him with my bare hands. The medical examiner part of me wants to find absolute proof which man committed this crime and be able to stand up in court to give evidence for his conviction. Trust me, if I allow the father in me to take over, I'd be no use to you or anyone else."

"That's all well and good, Shane, but Emily has made her conclusion on the evidence before her and I happen to agree with her."

"Emily is making a call before all the evidence is presented." Wolfe sighed. "She knows the majority of tox screens haven't come back yet. I want her to make sure she has all the evidence before she makes a conclusion. For instance, do we know if Sophie had a boyfriend? Did they engage in rough sex? Did she take drugs?" He looked at Jenna. "Don't look at me like that, Jenna. These are reasonable doubt questions that could see this man walk."

"Okay, point made." Jo's eyebrows rose. "In my professional opinion, this killer is so evil he would have messed up the wife's face for fun. He likely only slapped Sophie so she didn't bleed on him." Jo leaned against the counter. "You've seen men like this before, haven't you, Kane?"

"Yeah, we've had cases with men like him before." Kane nodded. "They're animals. They can't inflict enough pain and suffering. Rape is used as a punishment and sex has nothing to do with it."

"And they are fully aware of leaving trace evidence." Wolfe turned off the screens. "This is what makes convicting them so difficult, we can leave no stone unturned. He has to make a mistake sooner or later."

"He already made one." Carter rubbed the back of his neck clearly agitated. "He took the girl."

Jenna removed her mask and rubbed both hands down her face. "Carter, trust me. This type of psychopath is very smart. He'd have planned this kill down to the second. He knows everything about leaving trace evidence. He'd have been wearing protective clothing, a balaclava, and gloves for sure. He immobilized the husband and likely after abusing the wife and tying her to the chair, washed up in the downstairs bathroom." She sighed. "These men are arrogant and don't believe anyone can catch them. Sophie was found in Stanton Forest, so disposing of condoms would be the least of his worries and our chances of finding them impossible." She looked at Carter. "One thing we know for sure, this killer wasn't afraid of moving Sophie to Black Rock Falls and I figure he used the blue Ford, the one Wolfe has out back, to do it."

"You may be right." Wolfe looked at her. "The results of my findings will be ready soon. We can wait in my office."

CHAPTER THIRTY-THREE

Excited to be involved in the investigation, Rowley followed Black-hawk along a narrow trail on a trailbike, with its saddlebags crammed with necessities. Once he'd called Atohi, his friend had arrived with two trailbikes strapped to the back of his pickup, helmets, and a box of useful items to take with them. As they weaved their way through the barriers and warning signs, he noticed Blackhawk's friend, Mingan, and his grandfather, Nootau sitting on top of a boulder waiting for them to arrive. As they approached, the men slipped down to the ground.

"You will remember Nootau Blackhawk?" Atohi motioned to a weathered elderly man with greying hair and laughter lines around his eyes, wearing a battered Stetson. "He knows the Whispering Caves. We are in safe hands." He waved to Mingan. "And my friend, Mingan."

Rowley held out his hand. "Yes, it's good to see you again." He shook hands with both men.

"Atohi, tells me he thinks a fool has entered the caves, perhaps kidnapped a young woman and held her inside?" Nootau shook his head. "Maybe he can't read." He waved to the signs, warning of danger. "The girl, you figure, might have fallen from the falls?"

Rowley, hoisted a backpack over one shoulder, nodded and followed him to the entrance. "We imagine she came from here."

"Spirits walk these caves." Nootau glanced at him as they paused at the entrance to turn on their flashlights. "You'll hear them calling. They say they are lonely and call people to their deaths." He grinned and his teeth flashed white in the dim light. "And then there are the bears."

"You'll have him running back to town with those stories, grandfather." Atohi chuckled and grinned at Rowley. "Not too many bears come in here, it's too wet. They prefer dry places."

Straightening and forcing a smile, while he thought up something profound to say, Rowley nodded. "Well as I don't believe in ghosts, there's nothing to worry about."

"You will by the time we leave here." Nootau's expression was serious as he turned and led the way into the darkness.

Unconvinced, Rowley followed and joined the others inside a large cave with a selection of dark, foreboding tunnels heading in different directions. "Which way?"

"Give me time to look." Nootau moved his flashlight over the damp cave walls, disturbing a colony of sleeping bats.

Rowley ducked instinctively at the sound of flapping wings. Blinded by the light the creatures flew around in all directions. He noticed Atohi's grin and straightened. "I don't like bats."

"So I see." Atohi shook his head. "Keep the helmet on or they'll get stuck in your hair but they won't suck your blood. That's a myth."

Chagrined, Rowley straightened. "I know that." A strange moaning sound came on a rush of wind. He turned his light toward the sound and a cool breezed brushed his cheeks. "Hear that?"

"Yeah and we'll hear many more spirts on our journey." Atohi waved him toward him. "Stick close together and don't be seduced by their voices and you'll be safe."

"Maybe this way." Nootau shone his light on a metal anchor hammered onto the rock wall. Hanging from the spike was a broken piece of twine. "This is recent, someone used a cord to find their way back to the entrance. We can do the same." He pulled a ball of twine from his pocket, attached it to the anchor and then moved a few steps town the tunnel and sniffed. "It stinks like man, not bear." He indicated to Rowley's Glock holstered at his waist. "I hope you can use that weapon. If the man you're hunting is down there, he'll hear us coming for sure."

Rowley nodded. "Yeah, I can use it and will if I have to."

"I know this tunnel. It curves and bends then splits into four. One of the tunnels joins three others and lead to the Swirling Cave." Nootau took the ball of twine and let it out as he moved deeper into the tunnel. "If we get close, you'll hear the whispers, like sirens calling a soul to their death."

Rowley shuddered. "I can't wait."

"The Swirling Cave fills with water from the falls." Atohi fell into step beside him. "It comes through fissures in the rocks from many directions and the water spirals like it's going down the drain in a sink."

The memory of Sophie Wood's pale floating body filtered into Rowley's mind and coldness closed around him. "And it sucks a person over the falls."

"Yeah, bears too." Atohi searched the ground below their feet. "The current must be powerful, so you must keep clear of any water. Things change in these caves depending on the weather." He stopped and aimed his flashlight at what looked like a cobweb. "Look here."

Rowley turned his flashlight toward what had caught Atohi's interest. In the beam something glistened. "Is that hair?" He moved closer and dragged a surgical glove from his pocket. "Don't touch. It might be evidence." He snagged the hairs and they broke in his fingers. "No, they're just cobwebs."

"If she was in Dead Man's Drop, she had to have been here." Atohi looked at him. "Maybe she holed up here?"

"I don't think so. It would have been frightening for a young girl alone." Nootau frowned. "Do you believe the man who set the explosive brought her here?"

The bruises on Sophie and the zip-tie around her ankle made sense now. The cruelty she must have endured was coming to light. Rowley nodded. "Yeah, it sure looks that way but somehow she got away from him."

The whispers and strange sounds came at them in a relentless pace. Critters scampered away, red eyes reflecting in the beams from their flashlights and with each step darkness closed in behind them. It was like being trapped in an elevator with strange smells and unrecognizable music. Rowley could almost feel the threat in the caves, it seemed to come in waves of strange breezes and sounded so much like someone whispering it made the hairs stand up on his flesh. He searched the ground and the walls with each step and noticed Atohi doing the same but the solid rock gave no more clues until they moved over a patch of soil. In the damp earth that had spilled down from a gap in the cave roof, he made out indistinct marks. He laid a hand on Nootau's shoulder for him to stop. He bent and took photographs with his phone before they moved on.

Stink filled the air and the foul odor smelled as if a sewerage pipe had burst close by. Something was very wrong. Rowley had lived in Black Rock Falls all his life and he'd smelled blood and death in the forest but this stench was man's doing. Ahead the tunnel bent sharply to the left. They stopped as one and looked at each other. Rowley's heart picked up a beat and he indicated to them to turn off their flashlights and be silent. The non-stop moaning coming on the foul breeze surrounded them like an entity and Nootau's stories suddenly made a whole lot of sense. He drew his weapon and indicated to them he would go first. Atohi, Nootau, and Mingan vanished into the shadows behind him. Holding his flashlight down the barrel of his Glock, he kept close to the wall of the cave and moved forward, step by step, into the darkness. He held his breath as he turned the corner, aware a monster might be waiting in the gloom to kill them all.

CHAPTER THIRTY-FOUR

A somber mood had descended on the team as Kane followed Wolfe into his office for the results of the tests he'd conducted on the blue Ford sedan and the evidence taken from John Cleaves house. As they pulled up chairs around his desk, Emily jumped up from his office chair and set about brewing coffee. Kane pulled out his notebook and flicked through the pages. He looked up at Wolfe, who was accessing files on his computer. "The mud on John Cleaves boots, did you have any luck with getting a location?"

"It's from the local area and we know he was there watching the blaze." Wolfe narrowed his gaze. "The sample of C-4 was much more interesting. It is the same batch used in the explosion and the same used in the DC bombings."

"So, does this prove the bomber is John Cleaves?" Jenna shot a look at Kane. "The one who took the video of the house burning."

"Not necessarily." Wolfe looked from one to the other. "They make a great deal of C-4 and the same batch could be widespread but the batch number on the wrapping tells me it's at least five years old." He leaned back in his chair. "The analysis matches the batch used in the DC bombings."

"This surprises me." Carter moved his toothpick to the corner of his mouth. "I'd have to check on distribution but I can't imagine the same batch appearing in different states and used for a crime. That is way too coincidental."

Kane allowed the interview with Cleaves to run through his mind. "Cleaves was charged for stealing it from his workplace, right?"

"Yeah but what is military C-4 doing at a mine's supply depot?" Carter removed his hat, scratched his head with both hands and looked at him with a bewildered expression. "What is it with this part of the country? I've investigated weird stuff before but nothing that happens here follows the normal course of events. Since I arrived, it's like I've walked into another dimension." He held out a hand to take the coffee Emily offered him with a nod and gave an exasperated grunt. "It's as if we have two separate halves of one man. Cleaves knows explosives, is in possession of C-4, is excited by fires, and then we have Suffolk, who is threatening and has a fondness for underage girls. Put them together and we have a solid suspect."

Kane smiled. "Yeah the cases get a little twisted around here and don't discount Harvey Haralson and Simon Dexter, any of them could be involved."

"We haven't discussed the possibility of two men being involved either." Jenna stared at the ceiling and sighed. "What if Haralson is in it up to his eyes? He might be the follower. We've seen psychopaths with men who admire them and go along just to be involved in something exciting. The bomber could have used him to steal the vehicle and, Haralson was on his way to dump it when Kane pulled him over." She dropped her gaze and looked at him. "We need to look closer at Haralson and Dexter."

"The blue Ford is likely the vehicle used to transport Sophie." Wolfe glanced at his watch. "I'm waiting for the DNA result and it won't take too much longer to confirm." He sipped his coffee and sighed. "The prints in the vehicle belonged to Haralson, so he wasn't taking precautions or didn't have time to wipe the vehicle clean. It was wiped down prior to him returning it because I didn't find the owner's prints anywhere. However, I did find hairs in the back seat and blood. The hairs are the same color as Sophie's and the blood will give us proof one way or the other. The mud on the tires is from Stanton Forest and it contains small amounts of gravel, so I would assume it was driven on a fire road during the time it was missing."

"If Harvey Haralson took it from opposite the Triple Z Bar and drove it into town, he wouldn't have been anywhere near a fire road." Jenna looked at Kane. "The Whispering Caves are deep in the forest but since they cut the new fire roads, he could have gotten closer than before. I bet there's easy access to them by foot now."

Kane smiled at her. "I looked into the area last night. There are trails that hikers have used for years to the area but if he followed one of the fire roads we took to get to the lake, it would be an easy walk to the caves from there. The old trails are signposted as restricted but that wouldn't stop a killer."

"Hmm." Jenna drummed her fingers on the desk. "Rowley was heading up there to take a look this morning. It will be interesting to see what he finds."

A buzzer sounded and Wolfe stood and headed for the door. Kane stared after him. "That must be the results."

"I hope Rowley didn't head up there alone." Jo looked anxious. "This killer is dangerous. One young deputy will be no match for him."

Kane barked a laugh. "He's highly skilled."

"And he has Atohi, his grandfather, and a friend with him, they'll be fine." Jenna sipped her coffee. "He'll check in every half an hour but I'm not sure if he'll get any bars inside the catacombs."

"Okay." Wolfe came back into the room. "The blood in the vehicle is a match for Sophie Wood."

"This, the mud on the tires, and Sophie Wood's body showing up in Dead Man's Drop, is sure making the Whispering Caves look good as the bomber's hideout." Carter moved the toothpick across his lips. "I figure we need to contact Rowley, like yesterday."

"Okay." Jenna pulled out her phone. "I'll put it on speaker." She called Rowley.

Unease crept over Kane as he listened to the unanswered call. He leaned forward in his chair trying to be positive. "He's likely out of range. The mountain is magnetic and there's no signal deep inside there."

"What about the guys that set up trail cams inside caves?" Jenna stared at him. "They seem to get them to work just fine."

Kane shrugged. "They run a cable to an antenna on the outside and we don't have that equipment on hand at the office." He looked at her. "One thing's for sure, the satellite phone won't help him. That needs to be out in the open."

"I'll check with Maggie to see when he checked in last." She made the call, listened, and frowned. "Okay, let me know when you hear from him." She looked at Kane. "Not since he left the office. It's been over an hour. She tried to call us earlier but she couldn't reach us." She glared at Wolfe. "Did you really install dampening fields in the examination rooms? I thought you were joking."

"Yeah, I can't do my job properly with phones going off all the time." Wolfe leaned back in his chair, coffee cup in hand. "If she'd called the front desk, a light flashes in the examination room. She didn't call."

"Can we get back to Rowley's safety, please?" Jenna stood, collected the empty cups, and placed them in the small sink set into the counter beside the coffee machine. "How long do we give him before we hightail it up there? I don't like this situation one bit."

"Rowley is going into the caves with an experienced caver." Carter stared at Jenna. "I've met Blackhawk and he'll have his back. Plus, they have another man along." He flicked his toothpick into the garbage and reached for his cup. "I wouldn't worry just yet."

"Maybe not." Jenna straightened and pushed hair behind her ear. "But the Whispering Caves are coming up clear as the bomber's hideout. I figure we should head up there anyway. It will serve two purposes. We'll be checking out a possible crime scene and Rowley at the same time."

Kane nodded. "That sounds like a plan and we have hiking boots and equipment at the office and Duke would love a run in the forest."

"We don't." Jo wiggled her feet to show her low-heeled sandals. "How about we go and speak to Harvey Haralson? According to the update from the DA he got bail and would be home by now." She turned to Carter. "I'm sure you'll be able to pry out information from him. If he's involved in the kidnapping, we need to know."

"He's got a smart mouth." Kane stood and stretched. "I couldn't get a straight sentence out of him."

"As long as he doesn't lawyer up, I'll give him some outs." Carter grinned. "I'll make sure it's in his best interest to cooperate."

Kane patted his leg and Duke stood slowly and yawned. He looked at Carter. "Do you want us to take Zorro with us?" He noticed the Doberman didn't as much as move a hair at the mention of his name.

"Ha." Carter brushed off his Stetson and pushed it over his shaggy blond hair. "Like I told you once before, you'd have to show him my body before he'd go anywhere with you." He winked. "But you can try."

At the idea of a challenge, Kane looked at Zorro. "Hey Zorro, playtime. Come walkies with Duke, come on boy." He twitched his fingers in the same manner he'd seen Carter do a thousand times.

A tremble went through the dog's muscles but his gaze remained locked on Carter. Kane looked at him. "Would he come with us if you told him to?"

"Nope." Carter glanced at Wolfe. "You know the deal, right?"

"Yeah." Wolfe nodded. "Carter found him in a drain after a tornado destroyed the house where the bitch and her pups lived. He raised him on a bottle and they've only been apart when Carter was wounded." He looked at Kane. "They have a special bond."

"Yeah." Carter patted Zorro on the head. "I kept him alive and found his owners, but by that time I'd become attached to him. I offered to pay them for him but they gave him to me, they said we were meant to be together. He went through training by my side, came on my tour of duty, joined the FBI with me." He looked at Kane. "He's family."

"That's lovely." Jenna looked all dewy eyed. "I've seen a side of you I never expected to see."

"Nope." Carter's green eyes flashed. "That's not a side to me, what you see is what you get, Jenna. Zorro is my Achilles heel is all."

Kane rolled his eyes toward the ceiling. The conversation about dogs was going on far too long and did Jenna realize that Carter was trying to twist her around his little finger? "That's good to know but Rowley might be in trouble. You coming, Jenna?" He headed for the door. "I'll wait for you in the truck."

CHAPTER THIRTY-FIVE

Excitement ran through him as the sedan bumped over the uneven trail. It was a clear day with no rain forecast and a perfect time to be in the forest. He'd found the old trail months ago and after removing a few fallen logs had made it so he could gain access to the Whispering Caves without using more than one of the firebreak roads. He figured the old trail had once been used by tourists, way back in the day before the forest wardens had closed access to them for fear of another person vanishing within their dark depths. He'd dragged tree branches over the entrance and now he could vanish into the forest without a trace. It was only a few hundred yards to the caves and he could leave his vehicle hidden in the forest, not that he ever used his own vehicle. He wasn't that stupid.

The end of the trail loomed up ahead. At once the canopy of tall pines and thick undergrowth made the area dimmer. The darkness of the forest worked well for him, the girls he brought with him could clearly see they had no chance of escape. So deep in the forest, their screams would be unrecognizable from the wide variety of wildlife. Not that they screamed. They learned fast after the first slap, that keeping their mouths shut was the better option. He turned the sedan around just in case he had to make a fast getaway and parked it hard up against the trees where it blended into the bushes. After collecting his backpack, he slid out and went around to the trunk and popped the lid. His gaze slid over Pamela. The dress he'd given her had ridden up to expose her long legs and the curve of her buttocks. He ran one hand over her flesh, waiting for her reaction. Most would pull away or attack him but she looked up at him, blinking with her mouth working but forming no words. Perhaps some exhaust fumes had leaked into the trunk and if he'd left her much longer, he'd have found a corpse. He chuckled and tugged at the cord around her neck. "Get up. I'm taking you for another nice walk in the forest."

"Okay but don't pull the rope so tight, I can't breathe." Pamela coughed and slid her fingers under the rope. "I'm no good to you dead, am I?" She tried unsuccessfully to climb out a few times but then crawled awkwardly out of the trunk and stood on unsteady legs swaying a little. "Why did you kidnap me? A good-looking man like you wouldn't have any difficulty getting a woman." She lifted her chin defiantly and glared at him. "Or are you a pedophile and can't do it with women of your age?"

Rage smashed into him making his hands tremble. She was a smart-mouth just like her grandpa and he wanted to hurt her. "It's not about the sex, sweetheart." He pulled her around and tightened the slipknot on the rope around her neck and stared into her bulging eyes. "It's about the pain."

He shoved her through the trees, as she stumbled on tethered to him like a dog on a leash. The spikey lower branches and under-growth would be cutting into her flesh but she made no complaint. He urged her forward toward the black mountainside rising to the sky. It dominated the edge of the forest for miles in all directions and dropped a shadow over the forest. This close to the Whispering Caves, it was like twilight and held an eerie silence until he heard the voices. Walking ahead of him, Pamela heard them too. He tugged at the leash to prevent her screams and then dragged her into the shadows. He put his mouth close to her ear. "Shut your mouth."

"Noooo." Pamela turned, one hand raised to strike him.

He grabbed her arm and pulled her against him clamping one hand over her mouth. Just in time to silence her before four men, one a deputy he recognized from Black Rock Falls, broke out the forest and headed toward the entrance to the Whispering Caves.

In his grasp, Pamela wriggled and kicked frantically, making grunting sounds. Gripped by the fear of being discovered, he tightened his hold around her chest and slid his gloved hand to cover both nose and mouth. Once unconscious, he'd hide her under the bushes until they left and she'd come around soon enough once he allowed her to breathe again. She fought hard, and he enjoyed her feeble attempts to get free before lack of oxygen stilled her. He leaned back against a tree breathing heavily as the men disappeared into the tunnels. Had his secret place been discovered? He'd removed all trace of his visit from inside the caves. The old mattress was fouled from bears and critters. He'd sprayed it with a very useful agent he'd discovered after dating the owner of a DNA testing laboratory. A handy non-corrosive liquid that removed all trace of DNA. He'd stolen a case of the spray bottles from her storeroom and that night the entire place had exploded due to a gas leak. He grinned into a shaft of sunlight. No one would ever know he had the magic liquid.

He released his grip and Pamela slid to the ground. He couldn't take her there now. He'd take her back to the cabin. She wouldn't be able to escape and she'd be easier to visit until she'd served her purpose. He looked down at her and rolled her over. Wide staring fixed eyes looked back at him but saw nothing. He pressed two fingers to her neck feeling for a pulse. "Dammit. Did I say you could die on me?"

He paced up and down for a few moments to clear his head. He couldn't leave her here. If anyone found her, the local sheriff would know for sure he was using the Whispering Caves as a hideout. Right now, if the deputy found nothing inside, they'd leave and he'd have his special place back again. He lifted Pamela's inert body over one shoulder and headed back to the old sedan. He dropped her in the trunk, stashed the chain under a fallen log, and spent time wiping down the vehicle. He'd been wearing gloves but checked all over for anything incriminating. He went back to Pamela ripped off her dress and pocketed the cheap metal chain with a tiny unicorn attached, she had been wearing. Taking a spray bottle of DNA remover from his backpack, he sprayed her all over. He looked at her; without the fear, she was nothing to him, just another piece of garbage he had to dispose of. He'd left his truck hidden in the forest about two hundred yards away from the barn where he'd taken the sedan. It was a wooded area, easy enough to drive in unnoticed by the backroad and slip away without anyone seeing him. The ranch house was facing the main driveway. He'd return the vehicle and leave her inside, the old folks living at the ranch would never know what had happened.

He climbed into the sedan, pulled on a baseball cap and sunglasses, and then headed back to town. He turned off the fire road and on to Stanton but had not driven half a mile when a woman standing in the middle of the road, flagged him down. He buzzed down his window and looked at her. "Is something wrong, ma'am?"

"Yeah, I have a flat but my spare is at Miller's Garage." She gave him a small smile. "I'd ask my husband to go get it but I can't reach him on the phone right now. Could I get a ride into town with you?"

He cleared his throat. Unbelievable. He had a body in the trunk and now this woman not only wanted a ride but could identify him as the driver of the old sedan. He glanced in his rear vision mirror. Not a soul was on the highway and making an excuse would make her suspicious. He smiled and teased her a little. "Oh, I'm not sure, picking up a beautiful young woman might get me into trouble with my wife." He rubbed his chin. "Why not call out one of Miller's mechanics to help you?"

"I'm sure it will be okay and I'll be happy to explain to her if you want." She looked desperate. "I'm Sandy Rowley, I'm married to Deputy Jake Rowley. With all the serial killers stalking these parts, I really don't want to be out here on a lonely strip of highway all alone." She patted her purse. "Even if I am carrying a weapon."

He grinned so wide his face ached. As if that would stop him. "Well then, I guess you'd better jump inside."

CHAPTER THIRTY-SIX

Concerned, Jenna climbed into Kane's truck and fastened the seatbelt. She turned to look at Kane as he started the engine and backed out. "Do you think something's happened to Rowley?"

"Nope." Kane flashed her a smile. "I'm just sick of hearing about Carter's life. He's trying to make you feel sorry for him. I figure it's a ploy to get women to like him."

Astonished, Jenna stared at him. "He's a good-looking guy and I'm sure women like him just fine." She shook her head. "So why the rush to go find Rowley?"

"I'm starving." Kane headed down Main. "You mentioned Rowley was with Blackhawk, his grandfather, and another friend by the name Mingan?"

Not surprised in the least by his excuse to leave, Jenna nodded. "Yeah."

"Well, Rowley is armed, Atohi can take care of himself, and Mingan, I met at Rowley's dojo. Between them, one of them would get away to call for backup if something went wrong. Nootau knows the caves like the back of his hand and there would be other ways in and out. Don't worry." He pulled up outside Aunt Betty's Café. "Give me five minutes to grab some takeout, we might be stuck out in the forest for hours."

She waved him away. "Sure."

The door slammed behind him as Jenna's phone chimed. She glanced at the caller ID and sighed with relief. "Maggie, any news from Rowley?"

"Not yet but that's not why I called. The Blackwater Sheriff has put out an Amber alert, his granddaughter, Pamela, is missing. She didn't arrive home after visiting her grandma last night. Sheriff Stuart has had everyone out looking for her and they found her school backpack in a wooded area close to town. I thought you should know as she is coming up fifteen, like Sophie Wood."

Jenna put the phone on speaker and pulled out her notepad. "Okay, so she went missing when?"

"She was last seen leaving her grandma's house at about five-thirty last night. She likes to stop by and have a chat on her way home from school. Her folks don't get home from work until six, so I guess it passes the time."

If the girl did the same thing every night, someone could have been watching her movements. Jenna frowned. "No signs of a struggle?"

"The information I have is what I told you. Do you want me to call and ask?"

She leaned back in the seat. Could this be a coincidence or related to the kidnapping of Sophie Wood? As nothing linked the cases, no fire or explosion, she dismissed the notion. "If you could call them and inform them, we had a missing girl the same age out of Louan, they might be prepared to share the information but I doubt the cases are related."

"Okay." Maggie sounded relieved. *"I'll call as soon as Rowley checks in."* She disconnected.

Jenna brought Kane up to speed when he returned. They headed out of town and along Stanton when Jenna noticed a pickup on the side of the road with a flat tire. "Hey, hold up. That's Sandy's vehicle."

"You sure?" Kane backed up, stopping opposite.

"Yeah, she has a pink teddy bear hanging from her mirror and a sticker on the windshield for the school parking lot." Jenna jumped from the truck, dashed across the road, and tried the doors. "It's locked."

"Maybe she got a ride into town or to work?" Kane shrugged. "Get back in the truck and call her."

Jenna slid into the front seat and made the call. The phone went to a message and she left her own. "It's Jenna, we saw your truck on the side of the road. Just checking you're okay."

"Where would she go and turn off her phone?" Kane munched on a sandwich.

"Work or her mom's place. Her mom insists they don't play with their phones when they visit." Jenna sighed. "She must still think she's a kid." She looked at Kane. "Should we be worried?"

"Not yet." Kane headed back down the highway. "We'll find Rowley and he'll be able to hunt her down. I recall him mentioning dropping a tire into Miller's, so maybe she's had two flats in a row?"

Unable to push the concern for her friend from her mind, Jenna chewed on her fingers. "Did Wolfe give her a tracking device?"

"I have no idea, he doesn't keep me in the loop of everything he does, Jenna." Kane turned onto the first firebreak road. "Once we've hunted down Rowley, what's next on the list?"

Jenna opened her iPad and scanned the files. "We go see George at Miller's Garage and see if Suffolk was there on the night of the explosion."

"I already asked in Aunt Betty's Café and the manager, Susie Hartwig, is going to check the CCTV footage for Tuesday evening, she'll get back to us." Kane slowed as Blackhawk's truck came out of the forest and onto the fire road. "That's Blackhawk."

Jenna sighed with relief when she spotted Rowley in the front seat. She climbed out and went to his window. "Look, before you say anything, we spotted Sandy's truck on the side of the road. I can't reach her by phone."

"Yeah, I have a trillion messages, she got a flat and couldn't reach me." Rowley frowned. "She left a message saying she'd hitched a ride into town and would ask the mechanic from Miller's to bring her back and change the tire." He opened his phone. "That was twenty minutes ago. She's probably in town and ignoring me or has walked round to her mother's house to wait for the mechanic, it's not far from Miller's Garage."

"Oh, I see." Jenna looked past him at Atohi's grinning face. "Okay, well then what did you find out at the caves?"

"Apart from the ghosts, bats, and critters?" Rowley shivered. "Nothing but an old mattress that could have been there for years." He sighed. "No sign of the girl ever being there but someone ventured down there recently because we found twine attached to a bolt in the cave wall. It wasn't covered in cobwebs like everything else. Atohi believes the forest wardens go in there sometimes to check no one's been trespassing."

Jenna nodded. "Okay, head back to town and hunt down Sandy. Take the time you need to find her."

"Thanks." Rowley smiled at her. "Appreciate it."

After climbing back into Kane's truck, Jenna leaned back in her seat. "Don't go just yet. This is a great place for a picnic and I'm suddenly famished." She reached for a sandwich. "It's been a long day and we deserve five minutes."

"There's something special about the forest in summer." Kane sipped his coffee. "We sure need to take a day and bring the horses down for a ride. Maybe find a swimming hole and have a picnic."

Jenna sighed. "That would be wonderful but leave it a few more weeks, the water is still freezing cold."

They sat in silence, eating and just enjoying the view before heading back into town to interview George the proprietor of Miller's Garage. The middle-aged man was surprised when they walked into the office. Jenna exchanged a look with Kane and went to the counter. "Afternoon, Mr. Miller."

"Sheriff Alton, has something happened to Deputy Rowley's wife? He was in here before asking about her." George scratched his head. "I don't know where she went, she didn't say."

Relieved, Jenna nodded. "So, she's in town somewhere?"

"I guess, she dropped her keys here, asked us to fix the flat and bring it here for repairs, and she said she'd stop by later to collect her keys." George frowned. "I offered her a ride back to her vehicle but she hasn't called to see if the mechanic I sent out to fix the tire has returned yet."

Jenna pulled out her notepad. "I didn't come by to ask you about Sandy Rowley. Do you recall Mr. Suffolk from the Crazy Iron Forge out of Louan, dropping by before closing on Tuesday night?"

"Yeah, so happens I do." George went to a book on the counter and flicked through the pages. "He repaired a part I needed for a tractor I'm working on and was kind enough to deliver it for me. It was a rush job. I paid him and made a note of the payment and time of the delivery in my invoice book. I know, I'm old school but my daughter uploads everything into the computer for me. One thing, my old invoice book can't catch a virus." He chuckled.

"What time would that have been?" Jenna made notes. "And when did he leave?"

"It was a little after five." He thought for a beat. "We chatted for a while and I helped him load another repair onto his truck."

"Did he have anyone with him?" Kane leaned against the counter. "Anyone waiting in his truck?"

"Nope."

Jenna folded her notebook and pushed it into her pocket. "Okay thanks."

As they walked back to her vehicle Kane's phone buzzed. She leaned against the Beast's door enjoying the sunshine as he answered the call.

"Kane." Kane moved closer and put the phone on speaker. "Yes, Susie. Did you find anything on the CCTV footage?"

"Sure did. Roger Suffolk was here, just before six, he ate his meal and was away by six-thirty. I ran the footage right up to closing and he didn't return. Does that help you?"

"It sure does. Can you download a copy onto the flash drive I gave you?" Kane glanced at Jenna and shrugged.

"I already have." Susie chuckled. *"I'll keep it safe until you stop by."*

"Thanks." Kane disconnected and looked at Jenna. "Hmm, this leaves Suffolk's alibi wide open. I don't like Jo and Carter's chances of finding anyone at the Triple Z Bar willing to stand up in court and testify he was there around the time of the bombing."

Jenna strolled around the hood and rested one hand on the door handle. "My thoughts exactly."

She glanced at her watch. "Jo and Carter should be through speaking to the barkeeper at the Triple Z Bar by now, I'll give them a call." She placed the phone on speaker and waited for Jo to pick up. "Hi, Jo, did you get anything from the Triple Z Bar?"

"Yeah, the barkeeper mentioned he'd seen him around seven but doesn't recall when he left. It was busy but he remembers Suffolk asking him if he needed any repairs at any time, to call him and gave him his card." Jo sounded animated. *"Think about it, Jenna, when we spoke to him, he was snowed under with work, yet he made a point of speaking to the barkeeper, to establish an alibi."*

Jenna exchanged a meaningful look with Kane. "Yeah, it sure sounds suspicious. We have him in Black Rock Falls until around six-thirty." She smiled. "He had plenty of time to drive into Louan and commit the crime."

"Not only that." Carter's voice came through the speaker. *"We've walked from the Triple Z to where the blue Ford was stolen. He had plenty of time to steal the Ford, commit the crime, stash the girl, and*

return the vehicle. He wouldn't have been seen in the dark and the parking lot at the Triple Z has no CCTV cameras. No one would have seen him returning to his truck."

"Then Haralson gets a ride to the Triple Z the following morning and spots the open vehicle, keys in the ignition, and decides to drive it into town." Jenna could picture the entire scenario in her head. "He would have checked out the glovebox, looking for anything else he could steal, read the registration and gave that name when Kane pulled him over for speeding."

"The Ford had been wiped clean and Wolfe only found Haralson's prints." Kane turned to face her. "I don't figure Haralson was involved in the kidnapping."

Jenna agreed and chewed on her bottom lip thinking. "Hmm, I'm inclined to agree. He sounds like a kid who took the opportunity of a free ride. I figure he'd have dumped the Ford in town and walked away."

"Yeah, we felt the same." Jo came back on the line. *"The tires would have already been caked with soil from the forest."*

"Something else, Maggie called." Jenna's stomach gave a squeeze. "I'm sure it's nothing to do with our case but the granddaughter of the sheriff out of Blackwater has gone missing."

"I doubt it's the same man." Jo sighed. *"It's a different MO and Blackwater would likely be out of our guy's comfort zone. If it's the same bomber as in DC, he kept to one area, and they don't usually change."*

After considering what Jo had said, Jenna shook her head. "Not if you consider the three points: Louan, Black Rock Falls, and Blackwater make up a nice triangle, he could be living in the center."

"Or maybe move between the three points in his day to day routine."

All the clues pointed to Suffolk. "Yeah, like Roger Suffolk." She sighed. "Now if Kalo discovers he has some background in explosives, we have a prime suspect."

"Yeah, he sounds like a fit." Kane raised both eyebrows. "But I'm not ready to discount Dexter or Cleaves yet. They fit the profile as well and unlike Suffolk we can put them at the scene."

"I have to agree with Kane." Carter was back. *"What we have is circumstantial at best. Without hard evidence, the judge will never issue an arrest warrant."*

Of course, he was right. Jenna let the case run through her mind. Chasing their tails wasn't an option, with only one possible case to compare with the DC bombings, she'd have to do the grunt work and re-visit the persons of interest. She'd missed something, a small clue to link the cases together other than the detonator. "It's getting late. I figure we return to the office and regroup. We're chasing shadows."

"We could work from the ranch tonight?" Jo sounded tired. *"Then there's no long drive home to fall into bed."*

"Sure." Jenna glanced at Kane who shrugged. "I'll need to head back to the office. I want to make sure Rowley's wife is okay. I'll explain later. We'll update the case files, and then call it a day. I'm guessing you'll want to stop by the steakhouse for a meal before we head home?"

"You're reading my thoughts again." Carter's voice came through the phone. *"We might as well eat before anything else happens. Jo has been insisting all day, if this guy is out for revenge, he isn't done yet."*

A cold shiver ran down Jenna's spine at the thought of more burned bodies. "They never do stop at one, do they?" She sighed. "We can't have eyes on all the suspects, all the time."

"If we set up surveillance it might not help." Carter cleared his throat. *"If it's the same guy as the DC bomber, he'd have everything planned and could have planted the devices by now. He's very smart and finding a way into people's homes isn't that difficult. Disguised as a meter reader, for instance. All he'd have to do is detonate them when he's ready. We*

don't know if he's planning on repeating the same scene as he did for the Woods. My guess is as the FBI is all over the case, he'll be more careful."

Suddenly cold, Jenna rubbed her arms. "There's nothing we can do to stop him, is there? Let's just hope we figure out who he is soon and pray he doesn't hit another innocent family tonight."

CHAPTER THIRTY-SEVEN

The idea of driving around with a body in his trunk gave him a buzz he couldn't explain. A tingle at the base of his spine, the wiggle of butterflies in his stomach, and the way his heart pounded was different from the euphoric rush of pleasure he'd always gotten from watching fires. It had happened the moment he'd given Deputy Rowley's wife a ride into town. The moment she'd slid inside the old sedan, his heart had raced with excitement. He imagined the thrill of driving far and wide to kidnap women in the same beat up old sedan. He'd drive them somewhere secluded, watch their eyes widen with fear as they realized he wasn't the helpful, kind man they'd believed. When he'd finished with them and before they took their last breath, he'd show them the pile of bodies in the trunk. He chuckled and wiped his mouth with the back of his hand. He wanted to start now and gazed at the scattering of women hurrying home along the main street. Such a delicious selection and it would take nothing to encourage one to come close to his vehicle. He sighed. "Not yet but soon."

Collecting women's bodies would be his new hobby. The rush he experienced dominating and killing women was exhilarating. He wasn't like the other men who committed such crimes, in fact, what he'd done in his life, couldn't be called a crime because he hadn't killed anyone who hadn't deserved it. Once his revenge was satisfied why shouldn't he indulge himself in a little fantasy? He'd suffered more than his fair share of injustices in his life. It was way past time for him to break out and enjoy himself.

It was dark by the time he arrived in Blackwater and left the old sedan in a parking lot alongside the general store. He was a creature of the night. Nothing could look better than leaping flames against a dark moonless sky. Fire came to life in the darkness, the still of night enhancing the crackle of burning wood. It reminded him of happier times around a campfire before the strangers came and snatched him away from his home never to return. Now the instant he witnessed a fire, the smell of blackening timbers and the acrid bite from melting plastics lured him. He wished he could stand inside a fire and watch the destruction around him. Fire was after all, a living, breathing entity, controlled sometimes but rarely beaten until it had consumed its fill.

He took his time scanning the parking lot before opening the door. No CCTV cameras facing toward him and enough vehicles for it to blend in unnoticed. He climbed out, locked the door, leaving his drone covered by a blanket, and took his backpack. His plans for Sheriff Buzz Stuart had been sheer genius, with his men all out hunting down his granddaughter and a command center set up in Pamela's house waiting for a ransom call. Once the old sheriff returned home, he and his wife would be all alone and he had the bait to hook the old guy into allowing him inside. He hustled along the sidewalk keeping to the shadows, crossed the main road, and headed down the treelined road leading to the sheriff's home. He grinned into the darkness. The sheriff's cruiser was parked right outside.

Confident, he walked right up to the front door. His fingers closed around the Glock in his pocket as he knocked on the door. The familiar buzzing came in his ears, telling him it was time to get even. Time to kill.

CHAPTER THIRTY-EIGHT

Bone weary and barely able to stand from worry, Sheriff Buzz Stuart dragged himself to the front door. He'd been out searching since his daughter had called to say Pamela hadn't gotten home from school. He'd searched all day and been forced to return home to rest by the mayor. There had to be some news about Pamela soon, the search parties had been out for over twenty-four hours straight. He'd insisted the search and rescue teams set out at once, knowing instinctively something was very wrong. His granddaughter was reliable and sensible, she wouldn't take a ride with anyone or wander off without telling someone but as each hour ticked by, the chances of finding her alive diminished. The search party would be scaled down tonight and a fresh team of volunteers would hit the ground at daybreak. His heart seemed to miss a beat as he reached for the doorknob. He couldn't take bad news and it would as sure as hell kill his wife. Taking a deep breath, he opened the door and stared at the man on his stoop. In the shadows he couldn't make out his face. "Yeah, what can I do for you?"

"I've been with the search party. The deputy there said I should ask you if this belongs to Pamela?" The man held out a bracelet. The base metal chain had a unicorn hanging from it. "I found it alongside the road, near the wooded area at the top of Main."

Stuart recalled seeing Pamela with something on her wrist but couldn't see the item clearly in the dim light. "Come inside, son. My wife is in the kitchen, she'll be able to recognize it."

He led the way inside with the man following close behind. He noticed the man's leather gloves and turned to him. "It's a warm night, why the gloves?"

"Oh, the deputy said to wear gloves if we found anything." The man's lips flattened. "These are all I had with me."

Stuart nodded and waved him into the kitchen where his wife was nursing a cup of coffee. She hadn't stopped crying and her face was red and bloated. "Cathy, this man is one of the people searching for Pamela. He found something. Take a look, does it belong to her?"

"Yes, that's Pamela's, she loved unicorns." Cathy let out a wail like a slaughtered pig and dropped her head onto the table. "She's dead, I know it."

Stuart went to comfort his wife when the shock of a blow to the side of his head, sent him reeling. He stumbled landing heavily in the chair beside his wife. "What in darnation are you doing?"

"Buzz, who is this man?" Cathy stared at him eyes wide with shock.

Blood seeped into his eyes and dropped over the table. Dazed and bleary-eyed, he went to stand but the stranger grabbed his arms, pulled them around the back of the chair, and tied them tight with a zip-tie. "Hey." He tried to stand but the chair moved with him.

"Stay still, old man." The man chuckled close to his ear. "Or I'll mess up your wife real bad."

Tight bands closed around his ankles shackling him to the chair. He wiped his eye on his shoulder trying to get a better look at the intruder, hoping he could recognize him. "Okay, take whatever you want but don't hurt my wife."

"What's going on, Buzz?" Cathy stared at him uncomprehending.

"One word, lady, and he dies." The man grabbed her by the throat. "Understand?"

Terrified for her safety, Stuart, blinked at her through the blood. "Do what he says, Cathy."

"I figure she's a little old for me, so she gets a pass." The man quickly secured Cathy to the chair and then grabbed her hair and turned her face up to his. "Although, Pamela was special. So young and fresh. She enjoyed her time with me. I'll miss her." He calmly wrapped gaffer tape around Cathy's mouth. "Oh, now I see the resemblance. They have the same eyes."

Anger broke through Stuart's fuzzy brain and he glared at him. "If you've touched one hair on her head, I'll—"

"Do what old man?" The man leaned against the kitchen counter, grinning at them. "Bring me to justice? Fight me?" He strolled over and pulled the phone out the wall. The cellphone on the kitchen table, he popped into the microwave and chuckled as it crackled sending sparks flying.

Stuart looked at his wife, who was panting and shaking her head. "I have cash, over there in the cookie jar. Take it and leave. I won't say a thing. Just go and leave us alone."

"Cash, huh?" The intruder sauntered over to the cookie jar, removed the lid, and pocketed the roll of bills. "Thanks, but now I have to go."

Relieved, Stuart leaned back in his chair. It would be over soon. "Before you go, at least tell me where you have my granddaughter."

"Do you really want to know?" The man calmly wrapped the tape around Stuart's mouth. "I killed her. It was an accident; I'd planned to keep her for a while. We were getting on so well together. She was so obedient but I couldn't allow her to scream." He looked deep into Stuart's eyes. "It hurts when someone you love is taken from you, doesn't it? Can you imagine the terror of being burned alive?"

Sheer panic made Stuart's heart race in his chest. He couldn't suck enough oxygen through his nose. He shook his head but the man just smiled at him.

"You're gonna find out real soon." The man walked over to the kitchen windows and threw them open to the night air. "Do you have a flashlight?"

Stuart had only one choice and that was to cooperate. He nodded and tipped his head toward the kitchen drawers. He watched with interest as the man placed the flashlight on the table, the beam shining at the refrigerator. What was his game? Had he just come by to boast about killing his granddaughter, if he had at all? The man was obviously delusional but a nagging doubt pulled at Stuart when his gaze settled on the bracelet.

"I'm leaving now." The stranger walked to the oven, opened the door, and turned on the gas. As he left, he turned off the lights and headed for the front door. "And you're going straight to hell."

The door clicked shut and as gas fumes filled the air, Stuart bucked in the chair to get free but the sturdy chairs held him fast. The zip-ties cut deep into his flesh in his attempt to break free. Why open the window and turn on the gas, it made no sense at all? Behind the gag his wife was screaming and fighting to break the tape, her chair rocking back and forth. Gas fumes filled his lungs, but if he could break the chair, he might get free. He struggled for some minutes before he stopped to listen. A soft humming sound filled the air and a dark shape appeared at the window like a huge insect. In the darkness, he made out the outline of a drone hovering at the kitchen window. The flashlight beam reflected in a lens mounted at the front. What the hell was happening now? The drone made a series of mechanical whines and then shot two projectiles into the room. One of them, a soda can, spun across the table and fell to the floor at his feet. The drone hovered in front of his face for a second or two before lifting into the air and vanishing into the moonless night. A bad feeling crawled up his spine and panic gripped his heart so tight he couldn't breathe. He'd seen similar IEDs placed inside soda cans to kill US troops during his tour of duty many years ago but they were rigged to explode if someone kicked them. These had been dropped, so maybe not an explosive device after all but what?

A flash of light blinded him and then the stove exploded. A blast of hot air and flames smashed into him, throwing him to the floor. He lifted his head just as the second explosion tore a hole through the kitchen cabinets. A wall of flames crawled toward him and thick black smoke filled the air. The curtains caught fire in a whoosh. Through the smoke he made out the body of his wife staring, sightless. Heat seared his clothes in a rush of agony. As flames licked his legs, he screamed behind the tape. He couldn't breathe. A third explosion lifted him into the air. The smell of his flesh burning seared his nostrils. He didn't hit the ground. It was as if someone had extinguished a candle, the pain vanished and he fell into merciful blackness.

CHAPTER THIRTY-NINE

It never ceased to amaze Jenna how differently people acted away from an office environment. Inside their FBI room at the Black Rock Falls Sheriff's Department, the team had a more professional attitude to the case, but sitting around the family room, it felt as if she was losing control. She cleared her throat to get everyone's attention but the conversation carried on as if she'd suddenly become a ghost. Dave and Carter had completely forgotten they were in the middle of a murder investigation and turned the discussion to the merits of different hunting rifles, and Jo was talking to her daughter Jaime, with one finger stuck in her ear to hear over the chatter. At her feet, Duke and Zorro sprawled on the rug in front of the cold fireplace sound asleep. The house smelled of coffee, the chocolate-chip cookies she'd baked and dog. After perusing her notes again, Jenna tapped her pen on the coffee table, piled high with plates of food, a fresh pot of coffee and the fixings, laptops, and phones. "Can we get back to work? It's getting late and we haven't made any headway in the case."

"Sure. Kalo should have updated our files by now." Carter opened his laptop and scanned the page. "Ah-huh, well, he's sent a copy of the accident report from Mrs. Suffolk's car wreck. Give me a second."

Jenna waited impatiently for Carter to read the documents. It would have been faster to email the files to everyone but he had a way of doing things and although annoying at times, he rarely missed evidence. "Okay, what did he find?" She poured everyone another cup of coffee and sat back in her seat staring at him.

"Something interesting." Carter glanced up over the screen and shrugged. "Personally, I'd have fully investigated this accident and had the vehicle inspected by someone who knows what they're doing. The official cause is brake failure due to loss of hydraulic fluid but it doesn't specify if someone tampered with the lines, or the leak was a gasket failure or whatever."

"They'd have been looking for a cut in the line but what if the connection was loosened?" Kane added cream and sugar to his cup and stirred slowly. "The fluid loss would have been gradual, so the brakes would have been fine when she left home but gotten worse the more she used them until they failed." He met Jenna's gaze. "It would be easy to see if someone had loosened the cable. There's a ton of dust on our roads and if the connections were clean, there's a good chance someone tampered with them."

Recalling all the engine parts and other motor connected paraphernalia Jenna had noticed at The Crazy Iron Forge, it was obvious that Suffolk had knowledge of vehicles. "You're saying Suffolk could have tampered with his wife's brakes, say the night before she left to drive to Blackwater, knowing that she'd have an accident?"

"It's possible." Kane sipped his coffee. "It would be very convenient for him if she died. He'd lost control of her and she'd humiliated him in the eyes of his church."

"We know Suffolk was raging mad with Wood. I wouldn't put it past him to kill his wife and the Woods family and then take Sophie out of spite." Jo's brow wrinkled into a frown.

"Yeah but why kill her?" Carter pushed a hand through his blond hair and yawned explosively. "Oh, sorry. I'm beat."

Unsure of where he was going with this line of conversation, Jenna straightened. "Suck it up, Carter, we're all exhausted. Read the file, if you remember the COD for Sophie Wood was drowning. We can't pin her murder on Suffolk, the defense lawyer will laugh us out of court."

"It may have been an accident. If I was a fifteen-year-old girl who'd been raped by that huge guy, I'd run at the first opportunity, which I figure is exactly what she did." Carter loaded his cup with sugar. "She ran for her life and probably fell over the falls. I'm still not convinced she wasn't holed up in the Whispering Caves. It seems too much of a coincidence she was found in Dead Man's Drop."

Conceding he had a point, Jenna nodded. "You may be right about where the bomber was keeping her but he didn't drown her. So far, the only evidence we have on this killer is the detonator—his MO is different to the DC bombings but you say the signature detonator is unique. So why not a copycat?"

"The information on the detonator was never released." Carter took a long drink of his coffee. "The bomber wouldn't know we found evidence linking the cases at the three DC bombings. It was a high-profile case and the FBI don't allow anything to slip."

Jenna looked at him dumbfounded. "You're saying the bomber doesn't know we've linked him to all the bombings?"

"Not that I'm aware." Carter massaged the back of his neck. "I figure, if he had, he would have tried to retrieved the incriminating fragments but he hasn't."

"And there's no other cases you can link him to?" Kane flicked Jenna a concerned look before turning his attention back to Carter.

"Nope and trust me, before we nailed the bomber—or who we thought was the bomber—" Carter gave a nonchalant shrug "—I ran the type of explosive device he used through the databases. Believe it or not, we don't have that many bombings in America, it's not usually the weapon of choice for most killers."

"I have an opinion about the bombings." Jo curled her feet under her on the sofa and her gaze rested on Jenna. "It's not about the explosion, it's about the fire. All apart from the car bombing have resulted in fire. Fire is cleansing." She turned her attention to Carter. "How come the agent's vehicle didn't catch fire?"

"The SUV was built to survive a bomb." Carter shrugged. "The agent was all about safety. POTUS could have ridden inside without a worry. Problem was the agent's wife carried the bomb into the vehicle with her in her purse, so she took the full blast. There was a minor flare up but nothing inside the vehicle was flammable, so the fire was extinguished in seconds. The agent was struck in the head, likely by the Glock we found in the back seat that came from the wife's purse."

"In her purse?" Kane's face had turned sheet-white. "How would he have gotten a bomb into her purse?" He stared at him. "How did a bomb get through the security at the front door?"

"A mobile phone wouldn't be scrutinized and C-4 wouldn't show on an X-ray. The killer could have easily assembled the bomb in the men's bathroom. I'm not sure how he slipped it inside her purse—maybe she left her desk for a moment and he was in the waiting room? Who knows for sure?" Carter looked at him and frowned. "Apparently, the husband picked her up outside her office, she climbed in, and boom. I inspected the scene. I believe she was the target all along but the powers that be insisted the terrorist was hunting down the agent."

"I see." Kane scrubbed both hands down his face and looked at Jenna with disbelief all over his face. "Look at the files, there has to be a link." He reached into his pocket for a bottle of pills and took two swallowing them with coffee.

"Headache?" Jo frowned. "Migraine? You're as white as a ghost."

Needing to cover for Kane, Jenna shook her head. "He's okay. Dave was shot in the head on a case, sometime ago. Smashed his kneecap as well but we caught the serial killer. Since then and a metal plate in his head, he gets the occasional headaches."

"You don't need to make excuses for me, Jenna." Kane seemed to draw down his curtain of professionalism. "I'll be fine." He waved a hand at her. "We need to find a link."

"Let's get to it people." Jenna went through the DC cases and then back to the Louan bombing. "Hmm, a magistrate's secretary, a social worker, and a lawyer." She looked up at Kane. "The only similarity is the social worker."

She scanned the files again, went into the backgrounds of all the people involved. She looked up at Carter and the words fell out before she realized the implications. "What were the names of the car bombing victims? I can't find them in the files."

"The file is closed and opening it goes way above our paygrade." Carter looked at her over the top of his laptop. "They are John and Jane Doe."

Jenna went over the other victims' files, taking her time, and then the similarity slid home. "Oh, I've found something. All the victims are involved in family law in some way or another. A family law lawyer, a social worker and the secretary of a Family Court magistrate." She drew a breath. "Then the Wood family, both husband and wife worked as social workers. The killer has a problem with family law, not FBI agents, unless the agent was involved in arresting him for child abuse or something similar."

"No, he wasn't." Carter narrowed his eyes at her. "So, you figure I'm right, the wife was the target?"

"But why target a secretary?" Jo looked aghast. "She wouldn't have any sway in family court matters."

"If you're correct there's more of a link than we anticipated." Kane leaned forward in his seat, his expression granite. "We need to hunt down any cases they were involved in and cross match the names to see if any of our suspects came in contact with the Wood family." He glanced at his laptop screen. "The Woods moved to Louan recently from Blackwater. Did either of them ever work in DC?"

"I'll get Kalo on it first thing in the morning." Jo observed him closely as if assessing him. "The plate in your head obviously doesn't interfere with your reasoning. Just out of interest, any side effects?"

"Apart from the headaches, no." Kane frowned. "So, you found no evidence at all apart from the detonator in all the cases so far?"

"Nothing, no footprints, nobody saw him, we had zip." Carter popped a toothpick into his mouth. "All remotely detonated, he could have sent them in the mail for all we know."

Although the lack of evidence was daunting, Jenna was determined to find the bomber. "Look at what evidence we do have, not what we don't have. This guy is careful, he's not going to leave any evidence. Heck we've dealt with so many serial killers who do the same thing. They're smart and these days he'd have to be dumb not to know about DNA evidence. People watch TV shows, they're fully aware of forensics, which makes our job harder."

"But nobody is perfect." Kane leaned back in his seat and placed the side of his boot on one knee. "They all make mistakes, maybe very small but we usually find them."

"Oh yeah." Jo smiled. "Trophies being their biggest mistake. They know keeping items from a kill is dangerous but they can't resist it." She looked at Carter. "Has Kalo found anything on Suffolk to do with explosives?"

"Nothing specific but he did purchase some Semtex a year ago to blast a boulder from his property. He was building a shed apparently."

Carter looked at Jenna. "Which is good enough for me, he'd have to know how to detonate it. It's a putty similar to C-4."

Jenna couldn't avoid the eyeroll. "Yeah, I know about Semtex." She thought for a beat about Suffolk. "At least Suffolk hasn't directed his anger toward any of us. That has to be a first."

"Did you have to say that?" Kane winced. "You know what happens when you tempt fate around here."

Jenna laughed. "Moving right along." She glanced at her notes. "I figure we look at Cleaves and Dexter again. It will mean another trip to Louan but after finding Sophie in Black Rock Falls, we need to know if they were over this way on the day we found her body, same with Suffolk." She looked around the table. "We know all three men interacted with Wood they all went to DC at the same time. If we can link one of them to the DC Family Law offices, we have our man. That's enough for tonight. I figure we're real close to closing this case now."

"So do I." Kane looked at her and his eyes softened. "It will be good to lay the ghosts to rest." He looked at Carter. "You ready to leave?"

"Yeah." Carter looked relieved and closed his laptop. "I sure need some sleep." He collected the empty cups from the table and headed for the kitchen.

"One thing before it slips my mind. Did you find out where Sandy Rowley disappeared to today?" Jo stood and picked up the coffee pot and a plate of cookies. "You haven't mentioned her."

Jenna smiled. "She's fine. She was heading into town for an appointment with Doc Brown when she had the flat tire. Rowley said she hurried from Miller's Garage and made it in time. That's why her phone was turned off."

"She's not ill, is she?" Jo frowned.

Jenna shook her head. "Not that I'm aware." She collected the rest of the plates and stared at Kane busy on his laptop. "You told Carter you were leaving and you're working again. You need to get some rest. We've gone as far as we can with this case tonight. Whatever you're doing can wait until morning."

"Oh." Kane gave her an angelic smile. "Sorry, I was just checking tomorrow's specials at Aunt Betty's." He rubbed his stomach. "Mmm ribs. They'll be worth the wait if we're driving to Louan. It will be something to look forward to after a busy day."

The sudden change in his demeanor made her smile. The anger at the man who'd murdered his wife had melted away as fast as it had emerged, or he was better at hiding his emotions than she'd imagined. Whatever the reason, she'd play along. "That's a good idea."

"Did I hear you say ribs?" Carter came back into the room, eyebrows raised in question and one hand rubbing his belly. "I sure hope they'll have some left by the time we get back."

"I've already sent Susie a message, she'll hold back a stack for us." Kane chuckled. "She's never let me down yet."

CHAPTER FORTY

Saturday, 1 a.m.

"Jenna, wake up." Jo's voice broke into a dream. "Jenna."

Jenna slapped at the hand shaking her awake. She had been asleep for what felt like seconds and her head was still in slumber mode. Forcing her eyes open, she made out a shape in the light filtering in from the hallway and blinked at Jo's shadowed face. "What's wrong?"

"You awake?" Now Kane had walked into the room, fully dressed and armed.

Jenna sat up and stared at him. "It seems I'm the last one to the party. What the heck is going on here?"

"Kane will explain, I'll go and get dressed." Jo hurried from the room.

"I called you and then Jo." Kane picked up her phone and stared at it. "Your phone is on silent."

"Yeah." Jenna pushed the hair from her eyes. "I'm not on call for the 911 emergency line, so after working a seventeen-hour day, I didn't want to be disturbed by townsfolk complaining about a dog barking." She glared at him. "What's so important you're in my bedroom in the middle of the night?"

"One of the deputies out of Blackwater called in an explosion at Sheriff Stuart's house." Kane switched on the light beside Jenna's bed and looked down at her. His hair was damp from the shower and Jenna wondered if he'd slept at all. "At first, he figured it was a gas leak but the neighbors heard three explosions. After what happened in Louan, he called the FBI and they contacted Carter. Wolfe is heading out there as soon as he can get his team together. I figured you'd want us on scene too."

A pool of acid formed in Jenna's stomach. It was always difficult when bad things happened to folks she knew. She'd called on Sheriff Stuart many a time for assistance, and respected him. With effort, she pulled on her cloak of professionalism and nodded. "Survivors?"

"Not a hope in hell." Kane shook his head. "It's bad. The place was fully ablaze in seconds. Whoever was inside didn't stand a chance."

The shock of losing a fellow officer jolted her fully awake. She tried to shake off the wave of incredible sadness engulfing her and swallowed hard. In times of great stress and tragedy sticking to procedure lightened the burden. It was as if the way ahead had already been mapped out. No flustering or second thinking. All she had to do was move forward one step at a time down an imaginary list in her mind. "Is the local fire department on scene?" She slipped from the bed and dragged clothes from the closet and threw them on the bed.

"Yeah but they're volunteers, so if there's another unexploded device lying around, we don't want them going inside. The local deputies have sealed the town, no one in or out accept essential services. We'll need to move fast." Kane frowned. "I'm concerned about this, Jenna."

Jenna stood and stared at him. "Okay, so why are you worried? We've dealt with worse cases than this one? How do you know it wasn't three propane tanks exploding? People often have more than one for the house."

"Maybe but think about the surrounding circumstances." Kane stared at the wall as if mulling over the problem. "Sheriff Stuart's granddaughter goes missing and then his house is set on fire. It's as if someone used the girl to clear the way to the sheriff. All his men would be out scouring the countryside for his granddaughter, and if he'd called for backup, it would have taken ages for anyone to respond."

She noticed the tick in his cheek; he was angry, not concerned. "You figure it's the Louan bomber, don't you?"

"Yeah and if this is the bomber, we might be walking into a trap. He'd know for sure we'd be called in again." Kane pulled out his weapon and checked the clip. "It could be three propane tanks exploding but until we're sure, we should take all necessary precautions."

"Yeah, my thoughts exactly." Jenna shrugged off the concern, she had a team of professionals around her. "What about taking the chopper?"

"Yeah, I thought about that too but Carter said it will take longer to prepare the chopper than it will take me to drive, if we all ride in the Beast." Kane met her gaze. "I'll go and make sure we have everything we need packed in the truck. We'll need Zorro, so I'll leave Duke here to save room." He turned and headed for the door.

Jenna glanced around at her team as they all climbed into the Beast. All wore liquid Kevlar vests, helmets, and com packs. Taking the extra precaution against an unknown threat might save a life, although if they tripped an IED they'd be toast. She turned to Carter. "Do you worry about sending Zorro in to look for explosives?"

"Of course, I do." Carter attached his seatbelt and patted Kane on the shoulder. "Go, we need to be there yesterday." He looked back at Jenna as Kane swung the Beast around and headed down the long driveway. "It's not a case of, 'the dog will get blown up first and protect us.'" He snorted. "We're a highly trained team, but he smells what my eyes miss. I've seen him discover IEDs hidden in places many would have overlooked. He's very smart, he won't walk into a situation and he won't allow me to do so either."

Surprised by his passion, Jenna nodded. "Good to know."

They went through the gates and Kane hit the winding blacktop. Once they'd blown through town, he took the on-ramp to the highway and punched the gas, throwing Jenna back in her seat with the force of acceleration. She relaxed the moment she caught sight of Kane's determined grimace. His truck was like another limb and she had complete confidence in his ability to drive at hair-raising speeds. Lights flashing and siren wailing they sped along the highway leaving the tall pines of Stanton Forest far behind them. The Beast passed vehicles so fast, they became indistinguishable shapes with lights. They hit the long curving stretch through the lowlands and groups of industrial buildings loomed up like dark lumps in the distance. The mood inside the vehicle was somber, everyone deep in their own thoughts. It was as if they were all heading out on a combat mission and making plans on how to survive.

As they rounded a long curve in the road, Jenna tried to center her mind on anything else but blackened burned bodies and had a flashback to the night in the middle of winter when she'd first met Kane. He'd appeared out of the freezing cold night to rescue her from an upturned cruiser on this very stretch of highway and she'd stuck her Glock in his face. She grinned into the night at the memory. He could have disarmed her and broken her neck in seconds but he'd called her ma'am, and then been so darn polite, she'd thought him too good to be true. Dealing with an overprotective ex-sniper with more baggage than a freight train had been an experience but she'd never regretted one single day.

As they left Black Rock Falls county, the ranches on the outskirts of Blackwater, some with lights blazing in the windows, came into view. They passed through a small forest and came out on a long straight stretch of highway. In the distance a red glow lit up the sky. "Oh, that doesn't look good."

"I think that's Wolfe up ahead." Kane lifted his chin but his eyes remained fixed on the road. "We've made good time, he left well before us."

"I'm sure glad we caught up with him." Carter leaned forward and peered at the glowing sky. "It's not safe to go near that place. The fire department called out the Black Rock Falls fire chief the moment the explosions went off, so it's possible the Black Rock Falls Fire Department is here as well. They'll know to keep clear."

The idea of her local fire department getting there before Jenna concerned her. "They should have called us first. We needed to be on scene from the get-go."

"You're asking a lot from a deputy who is used to following orders, Jenna." Kane flicked her a glance. "Think about it, his sheriff has just been blown to hell and he wouldn't have the contacts the sheriff had on hand. His first priority would have been to evacuate the neighbors and stop the fire spreading. His volunteer fire department would have panicked. I'm guessing they needed assistance so the fire chief would be the logical person to call. When he arrived, I'm guessing he called the Louan sheriff, as he's just dealt with a similar situation and Crenshaw told him to call the FBI. That's why we had the delay."

"He followed procedure." Carter sighed. "Let's just hope no one has tried to be a hero and ended up spread over half the town."

Huffing out an annoyed sigh, Jenna looked at Kane. "I know the deputy followed procedure; I meant the fire chief. He was fully aware we're involved in a similar case out of Louan and should have called us before he left for Blackwater. He's irresponsible. One mistake I'd overlook, but two? Not a chance in hell."

"You go straight for the jugular, don't you, Jenna?" Carter barked a laugh. "I would too. If he has a problem with you, he could have called me. I gave him my card."

"Well, we can deal with him later." Kane slowed the Beast to the same speed as Wolfe's van.

Jenna snorted. She didn't like the fire chief's attitude toward her. "Oh, I intend to."

CHAPTER FORTY-ONE

The smell of the burning wood filled the cab, and smoke swirled around them rising in great plumes and moving across the blacktop in a slow procession. Ahead flames reached for the sky like red and orange dancers with waving outstretched arms. The trees around the house had burst into flames and firetrucks, set well back from the blaze pounded them with jets of water in what looked like an insurmountable battle. The water boiled and hissed, sending out great clouds of steam but the fire had escaped. It roared like an angry lion determined to tear everything in its path to shreds. The recent dry spell had desiccated the undergrowth to kindling making it a perfect medium to spread the flames. Horrified, Jenna stared in disbelief. Inside the raging inferno that was once a family home, Sheriff Buzz Stuart and his wife Cathy had perished. She turned to Carter. "You can't send Zorro in there."

"I'm not a fool, Jenna." Carter peered over her shoulder at the blaze.

"How close do you need to get?" Kane slowed to a crawl. "It's getting hot in here already."

"Not close at all, keep well back. We'll need to access our equipment and a have a safe place to rest up if necessary." Carter pointed to an open area of plowed land, where Wolfe had just parked his van. "Follow Wolfe. It looks safer, dirt and no trees to catch fire."

"Good choice." Kane headed to the field and drove through the open gate. "The wind is heading in the other direction as well." He turned the truck around and stared out the windshield. "I thought you said the fire chief was on scene?" He indicated toward the road. "That's his truck heading our way now."

Moments later, the fire chief pulled in beside them. Jenna jumped out the truck and was blasted by hot and smoke-filled air, ashes twirled around her falling like snow. Although the middle of the night, the light coming from the fire illuminated the area in a rosy glow. She marched straight up to him. "I thought you were on scene?"

"I *am* on scene." Matt Thompson gave her a quizzical stare. "Did the smoke get in your eyes, Sheriff?"

The air between then sizzled with more than heat from the fire. Jenna waved a hand toward his truck. "You've only just arrived. I saw you coming in behind us."

"Have I?" Thompson rolled his eyes in an exaggerated manner. "In case you haven't noticed the fire is spreading east. I moved my truck to a safer position. I could say: 'What took you so long?' but I really don't give a damn."

Anger threatening to bubble over, Jenna folded her arms across her chest. She had to deal with him, she had no other choice. "Give me the rundown."

"Ah… I know you were brought in on the Louan case but Blackwater isn't in your jurisdiction and I believe you're only under the FBI umbrella as a consultant." Thompson removed his helmet and looked down his nose at her. "I'll give my report to Agent Carter."

"She's leading the investigation, man." Carter walked up beside her.

As Kane and Jo joined her, Jenna stared at him. "If that's a problem for you Chief Thompson, we're all here now so how about bringing us up to speed?"

"Sure. Nice to see you again Agent Wells and you too, Agent Carter." Thompson ignored Kane and waved a hand toward the firetrucks. "The house was well ablaze when I arrived. The local boys could see the house was too far gone to save, so they evacuated the ranch houses either side and then called it in. My crew have been containing the fire since arriving, preventing the spread." He shrugged. "It's all we can do. The fire will burn itself out soon."

"There were three explosions?" Carter looked at him, grim-faced. "All gas bottles?"

"I'm not sure, I didn't see them explode and to make things worse, the sheriff had a ton of ammunition inside the house." Thompson frowned. "If he stored it inside a metal container the heat from the blaze could have caused an explosion. I'll have a better idea of what happened when we get inside the house." He looked at Jenna. "That won't be for hours."

Astonished, Jenna shook her head. "Then call out the Louan Fire Department as well. They can assist with preventing the spread and your crew can get the fire out." She lifted her chin. "For God's sake, there are people in there. We need to know if a crime was committed. Leaving it to burn itself out will destroy evidence."

"And I'll need to get closer and check for unexploded IEDs." Carter stared at the fire. "You have no idea what else is hidden around the perimeter of the building. You're putting lives at risk."

"I am not." Thompson's eyes flashed with anger. "I'm keeping my men well out of harm's way. I gave them strict orders not to move inside the fence."

Jenna stared at him. "I'm ordering you to call in assistance. I want this fire out. Do it now!"

"You can't give me orders." Thompson shook his head in disbelief. "I'm the fire chief but I will call in the Louan crew just to keep the peace." He stomped toward his truck and climbed inside, slamming the door behind him.

"Jenna." Kane moved to her side and handed her a jacket with FBI written front and back. "There are two deputies just south of the firetrucks, maybe we need to have a word with them as well and see if they've found the girl?"

"Yeah." She turned to Carter and Jo. "I'm going to speak to Wolfe and then go talk to the deputies."

"Okay." Jo indicated to a group of sightseers bunched together alongside the road. "We'll see what they have to say." She headed off with Carter and the fluorescent FBI logos on their jackets bounced away into the night.

Jenna hustled over to Wolfe's truck. Inside, she could make out Wolfe, Emily, and Webber staring at the fire. As he buzzed down his window, she moved closer. "The fire chief figures it will be hours before we can get inside. He's calling out another crew to hurry things along."

"Colt's been filming the blaze and we've been scanning social media for any footage." Wolfe's eyes reflected eerily in the fire. "I might not be able to get inside the house but I'm observing the fire. I've seen one hell of a lot of housefires but nothing like this one. How did it get out of control so fast? From the reports of the blasts the local fire department were on scene in ten minutes, which for a volunteer crew is pretty fast." He sighed. "Unless the sheriff had a ton of combustibles inside the house, it shouldn't have flared up so fast."

Jenna nodded. "I thought the same and the fire chief said ammunition was popping and if the sheriff had stored some in a metal box it could have caused an explosion."

"Do you keep your ammo in a metal box?" Wolfe raise an eyebrow.

"No, but it's all over the house, in drawers."

"Sheriff Stuart was a sensible man, no way he'd have stored ammo in a metal box in his home." Wolfe met her gaze. "If the propane gas bottle exploded, it would have blown the house apart but it dissipates fast or burns up. The deputy I spoke to on the phone told me they heard three clear explosions. A whoosh and two loud cracks. I'm seeing debris all around, so a blast of extreme force. It sure sounds like C-4 to me."

"Me too." Kane leaned on the van with one hand and peered inside. "I figure it's the same MO as the explosion at Louan but this time he didn't plan on leaving any evidence."

Jenna looked from one grim expression to the other. "I noticed a couple of cruisers over by the firetrucks. We'll head across this field and speak to the deputies. It will keep us out of harm's way. Maybe they'll have a lead on who did this."

Heat from the blaze warmed Jenna's cheeks as she headed across the uneven ground with Kane at her side. The smoke was getting so thick she could hardly breathe. "Here." She dragged a couple of facemasks from her pocket, handed one to Kane, and removed her helmet to push the other one over her nose.

"Keep your helmet on." Kane adjusted his chin strap and pulled down the visor. "I sure don't like the look of this blaze."

Jenna nodded. "Yeah, something's not right here."

Through the smoke she could make out the flashing lights on the cruisers but underfoot the plowed ground was treacherous. She pulled out her flashlight, glad she'd filled her pockets with everything she might need. The duty belt she usually wore held everything she needed but in plain clothes with a shoulder holster, she needed more pockets. She trained the flashlight beam on the ground and they hurried over the plowed field toward the cruisers. A whizzing sound flashed past her shoulder, and she ducked as an explosion shook the ground. Before she could think, a blast of hot air shot her high into the air. She couldn't breathe, spinning in a ball of smoke and soil. The ground came up fast but instinctively she wrapped her arms around her and tucked in her head, taking the impact on her back, and throwing out her arms to spread out the shock. Although her vest had taken most of the impact, pain shot through her lungs as the air was forced out. Spread-eagled in the moist soil, she sucked in agonizing breaths.

Another loud boom and a flash of light broke through the smoke. The next moment something huge streaked over her head and landed close by with a whine and a thud. She flinched at the sight of a cruiser door embedded in the soft soil, its window intact. *Oh Jesus.* Instinct to survive kicked in and she rolled into a ball as debris rained down on her. The helmet and liquid Kevlar vest Kane had insisted they all wear would protect her from serious injury. Coughing, she rolled to one side to scan the smoke-filled area for Kane. Her flashlight was gone and the smoke was so thick, she couldn't see more than a few yards in any direction. Shredded paper and pieces of cloth fell from the sky in an almost graceful descent, like birds coming into land. Amazingly the facemask had remained in place under her visor. Moving her limbs and wiggling fingers and toes, she appeared to have come through the explosion unscathed. She coughed violently and then lifted her voice above the roaring in her ears. She pressed her mic. "Kane. Can you hear me? Is anyone out there?"

Nothing. It was as if she was the only person on earth.

"Kane... Kane." She coughed and wheezed. "Dave, call out. Carter, Jo... Wolfe?"

Nothing.

Disoriented and nauseous, she crawled around on her hands and knees, hoping not to come across any body parts. The rear vision mirror of the cruiser lay on the dirt still attached to part of the windshield. Trembling and suddenly afraid for everyone on scene, she swallowed the acid crawling up her throat. Could she be the only survivor in a mass bombing attack? *I must get up and search, there must be someone else alive.*

Sitting up slowly, she stared around the smokey field but couldn't make out any movement. Years of training fell into place. First, she must evaluate her condition and supplies. She checked her pockets: apart from the flashlight, everything was in its place. Her clothes had come through intact, although encrusted with dirt. Her bare hands carried a few scratches and her neck was a little sore. Too dizzy to stand, she looked all around praying everyone was alright. She sat staring into the smoke for what seemed like forever before she caught sight of flashlights bobbing in the distance. The next moment, Wolfe burst out of the smoke, with Webber and Emily close behind. From another direction, Zorro dashed toward her his mouth opening but not making a sound, and behind him she could see Carter, his eyes wild as he searched the area. Behind *him*, Colt Webber was running toward the firetrucks. Why would anyone place an IED in a plowed field? Who was the intended target? It made no sense.

She stared up at Wolfe. He crouched beside her and his mouth was moving but no words came out. Emily was there too, rifling through the medical kit but all Jenna could hear was the roar of the fire. She blinked at him and shook her head. "I can't understand a word you're saying. I'm okay, where's Kane?"

She glanced down as Wolfe handed her his phone. He'd written her a message.

Not sure, Carter and Webber searching now. Where does it hurt?

Jenna handed him back the phone. "I'm fine, can't you hear me either?"

When Wolfe smiled at her and nodded. Jenna touched her ears. "Oh, it's the blast, I hear roaring in my ears. It will be okay soon, right?"

Wolfe nodded again and then wrote another message and held out the phone for her.

You have a few scrapes. Em will tend them. I'll go check on Kane, Carter went to find him.

"Okay." A rush of anxiety hit her and she trembled. "I hope he's okay."

Wolfe peered at her and passed her the phone again.

He won't be able to hear us calling him either. Take out your earbud. It will have protected one ear at least.

The next moment, Wolfe threw himself over her and Emily and then pushed them to the ground. He stared at Jenna and mouthed the words: "Shots fired."

On her back, Jenna stared into the strange glowing sky. She cried out in terror as an explosion high above the ground, lit up the night like a starburst. The loud bang came through her already buzzing ears and then Zorro burst through the smoke, behind him Kane and Carter ran toward the explosion. "Let me up. I can see Kane and Carter. Look over there." She gave Wolfe a shove and sat up.

She pressed her com mic. "Kane, please tell me you can hear me. Are you okay?"

"Well, it seems I can hear in one ear. The other is ringing so loud I can't think straight." Kane sounded fine. *"I saw you hit the dirt. You okay?"*

So happy to hear his voice, Jenna's fingers trembled as she pressed her mic. "Yeah, I'm good. Casualties?"

"Just the deputy's cruiser, and a few cuts and bruises from falling wreckage."

Jenna sighed with relief. "Who was shooting?"

"That was me." Kane sucked in a breath and coughed. *"Carter found me. My earbud had fallen out and then Zorro spotted a drone. It turned out to be carrying an explosive device. I must be concussed from the blast."* He sounded bemused. *"It took me two shots to bring it down."*

CHAPTER FORTY-TWO

Slightly off kilter, Kane leaned against the Beast and sipped water beside the open passenger door. His head throbbed but physically he'd survived the explosion with only a bruise caused by his weapon and a sore shoulder. The buzzing in his ears seemed to resolve itself faster than most people but the headache was a problem. His helmet had protected his head just fine but since the second metal plate had been inserted, he'd found a vulnerability he could well do without. He'd chosen not to take the pills he carried for pain, and decided to wait. Wolfe would check him for concussion and he'd be good to go. He glanced at Jenna and chastised himself for not protecting her from the blast. If he'd been following her across the field, he'd have had time to react.

After seeing her tuck and roll as she fell, a move he'd insisted she perfect after the last time someone tried to blow them to kingdom come, and then flex her arms and legs, he'd assumed she hadn't sustained any serious injuries. This time he hadn't been able to protect her. The missile had flown by and she'd dived away out of his reach. As it exploded the shockwave had thrown them in different directions. Being heavier than Jenna, he'd rolled like a pile of autumn leaves across the field and come to rest in time to see her fall out of the smoke. When Carter found him, Zorro had gone ballistic and it didn't take them too long to spot the drone. It had destroyed a cruiser and was coming around for a second attack. He didn't hesitate and aimed to bring down the drone intact, so they could trace the owner. He'd clipped it and taken another shot when it self-destructed, knocking them off their feet in the blast. He sipped his water and shook his head in disbelief. Somehow, they'd all come through two explosions uninjured.

"I refused to give the bomber the satisfaction of scaring us away." After brushing the dirt from her clothes, Jenna climbed into his truck. "When you're good to go, I intend to remain on scene and gather evidence."

Kane leaned into the cab and looked at her closely. "Sure, I'm waiting on Wolfe to check me out but I'm just fine, don't worry." He took in her pale face and the nasty scratch down one side of her neck. He figured her anger outweighed the shock. He could just about see her mind working on how next to proceed.

"Fine huh? You look like shit." Jenna scanned his face. "Don't go all macho on me, Dave. I can see your head is killing you. Dammit your eyes look weird." She stared out the window. "Where the hell is Wolfe?"

Kane straightened; leaning forward was making his eyes blur. "He's checking on the deputies to find out if anyone has laid eyes on the missing girl, and he wants to speak to the local doctor, who I gather has just arrived on scene."

"Kane." Carter placed a hand on his arm to get his attention. "I've collected the remains of the drone. Whoever was controlling it detonated the explosive the moment you shot it. He didn't plan on leaving incriminating evidence behind but the detonator is intact. It has the DC bomber's signature, same as we found at the Louan fire." He scratched his cheek. "I'm seeing something different here. I figure he's upped his game. That wasn't just a C-4 explosion. I figure he added an incendiary device. Did you see the flare up? He's added something else to the mix. He wanted a fire and as much destruction as possible."

The explosion had been on Kane's mind as well. He nodded. "Yeah, seems that way but I'm not sure why he took out an empty cruiser. Just to scare us off maybe?"

"Like that will work." Carter shook his head. "For a guy smart enough to build these devices he sure is acting dumb."

"He has to be close by." Jenna dropped her legs out the door and slid from the seat. "He's here somewhere in town, or in a vehicle close by. He has to be, to control the drone."

Kane moved to one side and closed the truck door behind her. "Not these days, no. Drones can travel miles from the operator. He could be tucked away anywhere within a five-mile radius maybe more. It depends on the drone."

"I'd like to know if any of our suspects are in the local area." Jenna looked around in dismay. "But that will have to wait until we check out the scene. We'll need statements from witnesses before they vanish."

"Jo is working through the witnesses with a couple of deputies. The first responders have a list of everyone on scene and will email it to us." Carter smiled at her. "We have everything covered."

"How come you can hear?" Jenna stared at him. "I'm only hearing in one ear right now."

"I had the earbud in one ear and an ear plug in the other." Carter shrugged. "It's usual to wear them when dealing with explosives." He turned toward the fire. "The fire is under control and I gave the fire chief the go ahead to go into the kitchen via the front. It's too hot for any of us to risk it right now. Wolfe will have an update soon." He grimaced. "Although, nothing is left inside by the look of the house. I figure the bodies have been cremated."

"You know this, how?" Jenna folded her arms across her chest and leaned against the Beast. "Explain."

"When I was over there before, I used my binoculars to see inside. It looks like a crater. There is a clear path from the front to the back of the house. Trip wires couldn't have survived the extreme temperature and detonators would have melted. I'm not so sure about the entire yard. I'll need to clear it before we go in." Carter narrowed his eyes. "Do I have to explain everything to you? Explosions and fire are my world, Jenna. You need to trust my judgment."

"Sure, sorry." Jenna pushed her hair from her eyes and sighed. "I'm used to working on the front line."

Kane handed her a bottle of water from the back of his truck. "We're a team. Jo, Carter, and I are your eyes. You don't need to be everywhere at once. You'll burn out at this rate."

He'd wanted to remind her how an FBI team worked together, all collaborating but using their expertise, but now wasn't the time. His knowledge of IEDs had come from experience in the field but he'd seen enough to understand where Carter was coming from. "If anyone has footage of the fire, it will give us a better idea of what happened. The bomber used a drone and that makes me wonder if it's the same man. It's a different MO."

"Not necessarily." Carter frowned. "Drones have been around for a long time now and it doesn't take too much knowledge to make them shoot missiles. The domestic ones have extended range now but from what I'm seeing in the wreckage, he's using military style."

Kane glanced up as Wolfe came out of the smoke. The visibility was rapidly improving and behind him, the sheriff's department had set up a command center with halogen lights to replace the dying glow of the fire. "Any other casualties?"

"Minor cuts and bruises from flying glass." Wolfe moved to his side. "Em is assisting the local doctor. No one needs the paramedics." He looked at Jenna. "There's no sign of the girl. The trail went cold after they found her backpack. The search and rescue will start over first light. Jo has collected the phone footage of the fire from the onlookers and has a list of everyone on scene."

"Did you get inside the house yet?" Jenna stared into the direction of the smoldering embers.

"No, it will take hours before we'll be able to go inside. The fire chief and one of his men went in to look around before all the evidence is consumed. They have protective clothing and we don't." Wolfe's expression was grim. "I used Carter's binoculars, and from what I could see the tabletop protected the lower section of one of the victims. I asked the firefighter with Thompson to take a few images for me and then lift the tabletop. The remains of one of the victims, the lower legs, are intact and there is evidence of zip-ties around the ankles." He pulled out his phone and scrolled through images before handing it to Jenna. "I've ordered the local deputies to secure the area until we're able to remove the bodies. The fire chief reckons it will be cool by noon."

"Oh, sweet Jesus." Jenna lifted a sorrow filled gaze to Wolfe. "This seals the deal. It has to be the same man." She shook her head. "Why is he here? Blackwater isn't part of his comfort zone."

"Like you said, it forms a triangle." Jo seemed to appear from nowhere. "He's probably living in Black Rock Falls. It's central to the areas he's hit so far."

Kane rubbed his chin considering her theory. "Yeah but nothing could be farther apart than a social worker and a sheriff. What's his motive?"

"A sheriff is involved with the family court to some degree." Jo frowned. "He's the first responder to a call for help or to handle a complaint against anyone. He'd call in social services, so yeah, he'd be involved." She stared at the gutted building. "Which makes his motive close to the DC bombings, apart from the people killed in the car bomb. What do a sniper and a secretary have in relation to members of the family court?"

The hairs on the back of Kane's neck stood to attention. He had the answer and would have to bite his tongue. He recalled his wife, Annie, complaining about a young man insisting on seeing the magistrate about a complaint. It had gone on for a few days before Annie had called security. He recalled her frightened voice on the phone. She'd been scared and he'd hurried to meet her to take her home. That was the day of the bombing. He leaned against the Beast suddenly dizzy. Annie had been targeted because she'd refused to allow the bomber to speak to the magistrate. She'd died for nothing and the knowledge ripped a chasm in his heart. Now he knew the truth, nothing would stop him taking down this monster.

"There is a link but it's top secret. I had to pull a few favors to get this information and it's hearsay at best, so, you didn't hear it from me." Carter moved closer. "The secretary, whose name is suppressed, was the magistrate's secretary. Apparently, the day of the bombing, she had someone removed from the premises. A man had requested an appointment to speak to the magistrate about abusive foster homes. The magistrate instructed his secretary to send the man to the local police to put in a complaint and it would be dealt with through the normal channels." He shrugged. "He called himself 'John Doe' so we found no trace of him."

Kane could feel Jenna's eyes boring into him. She could sense his anger and he valued her company and support. She kept him sane and focused. Right now, if he discussed the bombing a moment longer, he'd explode. He needed an excuse and looked straight at Wolfe. He cleared the lump in his throat. "My head is throbbing. Do I have concussion?"

"Come with me." Wolfe led him to his van. "Take some deep breaths, you know the drill. I know all this is bringing back painful memories and wanting to get revenge is normal but acting on it is not. You know that, right?"

Kane said nothing.

"You owe it to Annie to keep it together." Wolfe's expression was grim. "She wouldn't want you in jail, she'd want you to have a long and happy life. Find the bomber and let the courts deal with him. Find the evidence and make the case. That's what she'd want you to do."

Kane tried to ignore the pain crushing his heart at the mention of her name and nodded, forcing words from his dry throat. "She understood my work and I made her promise to go on with her life if I died, she made me promise the same. At the time, I thought it would be me."

"When her killer is behind bars, you'll have to keep your promise." Wolfe laid a hand on his shoulder. "Start living again, Dave, before it's too late."

After Wolfe examined his eyes and gave him the all clear, he searched his pockets for the pills he carried in an emergency and took a couple. They worked fast restoring his equilibrium and the headaches usually faded away. He noticed Wolfe looking at him. "Did you find anything else?"

"Not yet." Wolfe ran a hand down his face and removed his smoke covered mask. "The local deputies are with Webber. They're photographing the explosion scene and marking evidence. The entire area will need to be cordoned off so we can come back in the morning." His shoulders sagged. "I'll have six people to assist me. I'll work the scene as soon as Carter has cleared around the house for explosives." He turned to Jenna. "There's nothing else you can do here."

"Okay." Jenna looked at Carter. "You go and clear the area around the ranch house if it's safe. I know it's late but I'd really like to stop by and see if our suspects have been tucked up in bed tonight."

CHAPTER FORTY-THREE

Anger had replaced the glow of satisfaction at the direct hit on the deputy's cruiser. He punched the door of his truck. How had anyone survived the explosion? He'd gaped in astonishment when the drone's camera had picked up the two FBI agents through the smoke, one aiming a weapon at his drone. It was as if the gun was pointed directly at him and he'd used every evasive maneuver in the book to avoid being shot down but the man aiming the weapon was good. The first shot had the drone spinning out of control and the second obliterated his camera. Detonating the explosive and destroying his prized possession was his only way to conceal his identity. The explosion had been spectacular, one of his best, and lit up the sky like a firework and spread his drone all over the ground in a thousand pieces. Nothing would remain to trace the drone back to him and if necessary, he could build another.

Seeing the orange flames jump high in the sky had energized him. The danger he'd faced to complete another part of his plan had been worth the risk. Sheriff Buzz Stuart was already a distant memory, as was Pamela. He chuckled. To think, the sheriff's granddaughter had been twenty yards away from his house all the time he'd been inside. The drive to Black Rock Falls to return the old sedan had been necessary, but the fire had called him back to Blackwater. Following the firetrucks into town behind the usual group of sightseers had been exhilarating. The crackle and roar of the fire, the clouds of thick smoke and the smell had thrilled him.

He leaned back in his seat to watch the firefighters soak the last dying embers. The team of firefighters from Black Rock Falls had already headed for home. He glanced toward the group of FBI agents, all huddled around. Shaken but uninjured unfortunately. It would seem even a near death experience wouldn't slow them down.

He took one last look at the smoldering blackened shell of the sheriff's house, catching the image and setting it deep in his mind. He often recalled his memories of destruction, and could call on them at any time, day or night. He wouldn't forget the satisfaction of telling the sheriff and his wife he'd killed their granddaughter. Sending the explosives inside the house and then watching the couple burn had triggered an emotion in him, he'd thought long gone. He'd found pleasure in destroying the happy families on his list and making them suffer mental and physical pain. It had been a long time since he'd experienced any emotion other than anger but now, he understood how to turn his anger into an actual feeling. He craved more, needed more and deep down inside he'd come to realize his craving would never be satisfied.

He opened his social media page and thought for a time about what to say. He smiled into the darkness.

I enjoyed an eventful night with old acquaintances. There's nothing better than sitting around a kitchen table and chatting about family.

With reluctance, he closed the page, scanned the area, and inhaled the exotic flavor of wet blackened wood. The lights would be extinguished soon once the medical examiner removed the bodies, if anything remained of the sheriff and his wife. His gaze followed the dog and FBI handler as they moved around the perimeter of the house. He hadn't set any devices in the yard. He'd noticed dogs running loose in the area and didn't want them tripping an IED and spoiling everything. His attention drifted to the other agents, standing close together in animated conversation. They would be leaving soon and he didn't plan on being on the highway when they headed home. He'd had his fun and now it was time for him to vanish in the wind with the smoke.

CHAPTER FORTY-FOUR

It was getting close to daylight by the time they arrived at the Crazy Iron Forge in Louan to speak to Roger Suffolk. The adrenalin rush from the explosion had gone leaving Jenna exhausted, but she had to act now before a suspect slipped through their fingers. When Kane killed the Beast's headlights, they rolled along the driveway and the truck became invisible in the darkness. Ahead, a light set above the forge, illuminated Suffolk's truck. Jenna hadn't noticed any CCTV cameras but instructed Kane to park in the shadows and douse the interior lights. She planned to look through the windows of Suffolk's truck for anything incriminating. Easing her way out of the door as quietly as possible, she walked around the Beast but behind her Carter cleared his throat. She spun around to look at him. "What?"

"It's the middle of the night and we're poking around a place of business." Carter had removed his helmet like the others and his hair stood up in all directions. "Don't you think it would be safer if we went to the front door and left Kane and Jo to do a quick recon of the area? I'll take Zorro with me, and he'll give me a sign if there are any explosives in the house."

Seeing the wisdom in his idea, Jenna nodded. "Okay. As far as I'm aware, Suffolk doesn't have a dog, so we'll be able to surprise him."

"Before you go." Kane moved to her side. "If this is the bomber and he built the drone, it's likely he has created some type of security around the house. He could already know we're here. He has some expensive equipment inside the forge and that light is not a deterrent." He glanced over toward Jo. "Take Jo with you, she'll pick up any change in his mannerisms or mood. I'll do the recon."

"Are you okay with that, Jo?" Jenna looked at her in the dim light.

"Yeah, let's go. We have two more suspects to visit." Jo pushed her fingers through her hair. "We'll need to be on scene tomorrow to follow up on the girl's disappearance and check out the sheriff's house. We need a couple of hours' sleep or we'll be no good to anyone."

"Okay let's go." Glad Carter had found her flashlight unbroken in the field, Jenna switched it on and led the way past the forge to the garden path. They congregated on his porch. "He's not going to be happy being woken up at this hour."

"Too bad." Carter hammered on the front door. "FBI, open up, Suffolk, we'd like a word with you." He hammered again. "FBI."

Jenna could see a glow through one of the windows, and then the porch light came on in a blinding flash of white. She blinked as the door opened an inch or two and a young woman poked her head out.

"Roger is in the shower. I'll go and tell him you're here."

The door shut and Jenna raised her eyebrows at Jo. "It didn't take him long to replace Dawn. I wonder if he knows we took her? I doubt the Louan Sheriff would keep it to himself."

"We'll ask Suffolk how old she is, seems he likes them underage." Jo had dark circles under her eyes and yawned. "Sorry, I'm beat."

Heavy footsteps came down the stairs and the door flew open. Suffolk glared at them wide-eyed. "It's late, why are you here? Someone die or something?"

"Who is the girl?" Jo squared her shoulders and lifted her chin.

"None of your business." Suffolk moved close to Jo and stood menacingly over her. "This one is seventeen, so you can back off, lady."

Jenna pulled her weapon and beside her Carter did the same. A low growl came from Zorro. The dog's lips had pulled back from his teeth forming a brilliant white line of threat. She straightened.

"Step back, Mr. Suffolk. We're not here about her. We need to ask you a few questions and they won't wait until morning."

"Get on with it." Suffolk glared at her. "But I'm never too cooperative when someone is pointing a gun at my chest."

Jenna holstered her weapon but Carter only stepped back a pace out of the light, his Glock raised in both hands. She nodded. "Where were you around nine tonight?"

"Blackwater." Suffolk stared down at her, with his eyes boring through her. "I was stuck on one side of a housefire. I couldn't get through, so had to wait until the fire department cleared out."

A tingle crawled up Jenna's spine. "What took you out there so late?"

"I work all day and make deliveries after five most times." Suffolk shrugged and his immense shoulders seemed to heave. "My last delivery was out at a ranch. The man I spoke to was Dan Springer, his ranch is south of town. I'm sure he'll verify I was there. I'd gotten caught up in traffic so I parked and waited. After an hour or so, I discovered the road was closed ahead. I walked to the local café and spent my time there and when the smoke cleared, I went back to my truck and waited for the road to reopen. I haven't been home long."

"Did you see the explosion?" Carter moved out of the shadows with his weapon holstered. "It was Sheriff Stuart's home."

"I heard them. I figure the entire town heard them." Suffolk narrowed his eyes and peered at them. "Is this why you're here? Someone saw me in town and you figure I had something to do with the explosions?"

"We're interviewing everyone on scene, yes." Jenna refused to be intimidated by him. If he believed someone had seen him in town that would work in her favor. "So, what did you see?"

"Nothing." Suffolk thought for a beat. "Three explosions close together and then two more a long time after, maybe an hour or more. When I came out the café the sky glowed red and the smoke was thick."

"So, you just sat in your truck surrounded by thick smoke and waited?" Jo raised one eyebrow in question.

"No, I waited in the café." Suffolk looked down his long nose at her. "I had my laptop with me and it's free Wi-Fi in the café. I watched some shows and played some games to pass the time."

"Did you know about Pamela Stuart's abduction?" Jo wasn't backing down. "The young girl who went missing in Blackwater yesterday?"

"Well, it's all over the news, so yeah, I heard." Suffolk sighed. "So what? Kids go missing all the time."

"Do they?" Jenna did not break eye contact. "Do you own or have you ever owned a drone?"

"No." Suffolk glanced at his bare feet. "Is that all?"

Jenna had a thought. "Just one more question. Did you do the repairs on your wife's vehicle?"

"Nope, I had it serviced at the garage in town." Suffolk leaned against the doorframe, fully in control and relaxed. "I don't have time to service vehicles."

The car servicing would be easy to check and she wondered why it hadn't been mentioned in the report, after a fatality. Jenna glanced at Carter but he didn't have a question. "Okay. Thank you for your time."

As the door shut in their face, Jenna hurried back along the pathway. She turned to Jo. "What do you think about Suffolk?"

"He's overconfident, and like before has a solid alibi." She frowned. "His job affords him the perfect excuse for moving around. It seems too much of a coincidence we have him in DC at the time of the bombings and both here."

"The problem is, if everything checks out, we're back to circumstantial evidence again." Carter walked behind Jenna. "We need more to charge him with murder one."

Jenna thought for a beat and turned to look at him. "Would it be enough to pull his phone records and see if he made a call around the time the explosives were detonated?"

"I figure that would be a waste of time." Carter bent to rub Zorro's ears. "He's using burner phones to trigger the detonations. Only a fool would use their own device and leave a record of the call."

"I agree, he's way too smart for that." Jo looked at her. "But I figure a judge would authorize a search and Kalo could work on it for us." She buttoned her jacket and shivered. "It's up to you."

"Okay." Jenna headed toward the driveway. "I'll leave it for now."

Jenna found Kane leaning against the Beast sipping coffee from a to-go cup. "Find anything?"

"Nope." Kane shook his head. "You?"

"Yeah." Jenna pulled open the door and inhaled the smell of coffee. In her absence, Kane had filled three to-go cups from the Thermos. "He was in Blackwater and had his laptop with him."

"And he's so confident, he admitted being there." Jo climbed into the back seat and reached for a cup with a sigh. "He has an underlying aggression and right now, I'd place him on the top of our list."

CHAPTER FORTY-FIVE

As they rolled into Prairie View, there wasn't one light from any of the homes. It seemed everyone was tucked up in bed. Aggravated clouds of moths surrounded the streetlights in a frenzy and as they passed below, the trees lining the side of the road cast zebra shadows across the blacktop. Exhausted and dangerously close to falling asleep, the light and dark stripes flashed like a *don't walk* sign. Jenna shook her head to dispel the hypnotic effect and as Kane pulled up outside Simon Dexter's house, she fixed her attention on the gray sedan parked in the driveway. She finished her coffee, hoping the caffeine burst would keep her awake and ran through the suspect's file on her phone. "Okay, Dexter lives alone, was on scene of the Woods' fire, has been in DC, and is a firebug. He had a hankering for Sophie but was warned off by Wood, same as Cleaves. At this time, he is only a person of interest. We don't have enough on him right now."

"He seemed nervous to me when we interviewed him." Kane looked at her. "He doesn't act confident enough to bust into people's homes."

"I agree." Carter leaned forward from the back seat. "Most folks around here have weapons in the house. The only way I figure Dexter could have gotten inside uninvited would be if he was known to the family."

"I'd like to go this one alone with Jenna." Jo was staring at her phone. "From Kane's notes, Dexter was intimidated by them, he gave up Cleaves at the get-go. It would be interesting to see how he acts with us. Maybe we'll get to see the other side of Simon Dexter."

Jenna forced her lips into a smile. "Okay, but poke me if I fall asleep on his porch waiting for him to come to the door."

She climbed out the truck and they made their way up the driveway. Jenna ran one hand over the hood of the old gray sedan and turned to Jo. "It's warm, he hasn't been home long either."

"I sure hope he's not involved with Suffolk." Jo unbuttoned her jacket and touched her weapon as if to reassure herself. "This case would make more sense, if two men were involved."

As old case files percolated through her mind, Jenna stared at her. "We've had them all, brothers, one leading the other into crime, and then there was the pedophile ring. Now we have three men, all up to the necks in underage girls. All of them would have remained under the radar if Wood hadn't made a noise about his daughter and chastised Suffolk about the treatment of his wife." Suddenly fully awake and energized, she nodded slowly. "Maybe one of them noticed Pamela Stuart on their travels, maybe members of the Louan sect, church or whatever, are in Blackwater as well. Sheriff Stuart is an honorable man, he'd never have allowed a group of men to use underage girls in this way. This would have made him a threat and they'd have needed to remove him."

"It sure makes a lot of sense." Jo smiled at her. "Although proving it will take a ton of detective work."

Jenna marched up to the front door and thumped hard on the wooden panels. She noticed a doorbell and leaned on it, hearing a constant buzzing inside the home. "FBI. Open the door, Mr. Dexter."

The door opened and a ruffled bleary-eyed man stood before them. With a receding chin, his hooked nose seemed to take up all his face. The smell of smoke was heavier on his clothes than her own. By the look of him, he'd been sleeping in them. "Mr. Simon Dexter?"

"In the flesh." Dexter's mouth curled into a yellow toothed grimace. "This is the second time the FBI have dropped by. I want to see your IDs. This is police harassment."

"I'm Special Agent Jo Wells." Jo held out her cred pack. "This is Jenna Alton."

"I know you." Dexter pointed a finger with a dirty nail at Jenna. "You're the sheriff out of Black Rock Falls. What are you doing in my county, chasing after the guy who beat you up? Nasty cut on your neck there, Sheriff."

Unperturbed, Jenna stood her ground. "Investigating a crime. Where were you tonight, Mr. Dexter?"

"Out." He scratched his belly and yawned. "You'd better come inside. I made a pot of coffee and fell asleep waiting for it." He turned around and headed down a hallway, stopped, and looked at them. "If you want to talk, I need to sit down."

Concerned by the way he'd dismissed them as a threat, when the sight of an FBI agent would normally have most people worried, Jenna shook her head. "Not this time. Come back here. It will only take a few minutes of your time and we have other folks to visit tonight."

"Go to hell." Dexter kept walking.

Surprised by his attitude, Jenna straightened. "If I step inside your house, it will be to take you in for questioning." She waited a beat. "Your choice, Mr. Dexter."

When he turned slowly and eyed her with contempt, she eased her Glock out of the shoulder holster and dropped it to her side. She noticed the flicker of doubt in his eyes at her action and she wondered if he had the same opinion of women as Suffolk.

"You'd draw down on an unarmed man?" Dexter held up his hands, shoulder high, and walked toward them.

Jenna didn't raise her weapon but stared at him, trying to judge his intentions. "I don't know if you're armed, Mr. Dexter. Just keep those hands where I can see them. All I want to do is to ask you a few questions. I'm confused by your attitude."

"There should be a law against women carrying guns." Dexter stopped a couple of yards from them his eyes blazing with suppressed anger.

"Why is that, Mr. Dexter?" Jo stepped closer to the open door. "Women have equal rights in this country and by law, you're required to obey the direction of a law enforcement officer."

"I'm here, aren't I?" He glared at Jenna. "Ask your questions and then get the hell off my property."

Jenna holstered her weapon. "Where were you tonight?"

"I was in Blackwater. I went to see the fire." Dexter shrugged. "Or is there a law about that now?"

After taking out her notepad and pen, Jenna glanced past him and took in the unkempt house. She turned her attention back to him. "What time was this?"

"Maybe ten or later, I'm not sure." Dexter shuffled his feet. "It was a housefire. It lit up the sky like a wildfire. I came home just before."

"How did you know about the fire?" Jo stiffened beside her. "You can't see it from here."

"I have a scanner." Dexter rubbed his chin. "I like watching fires. The flames are like evil spirits leaping out of hell. Chasing firetrucks is a hobby. It's exciting."

Recalling Kane's notes on the last interview with him, she frowned. "You find people dying in fires and the destruction of property exciting?"

"It so happens I do." He paused a beat as if regretting his words. "Well, not the people dying, I guess."

"I see." Jenna examined his demeanor closely. "You didn't help the Wood family escape the fire here in town, did you? Were you aware that Sophie had fled the house?"

"No." He frowned. "I liked her. She was pretty."

"And is Sheriff Stuart's granddaughter, Pamela, pretty?" Jo twirled the earbud of her com, in her fingers as if bored. "Have you made an offer for her too?"

"No, I haven't made an offer for her." He looked annoyed. "Why? Has her family complained about me as well?"

Ignoring his question, Jenna raised her eyes from her notepad. "You mentioned you have a scanner, so you'd know that Pamela is missing. Have you seen her or know her whereabouts?"

"No and no." Dexter leaned against the wall. "Can I put my hands down now?"

Jenna shook her head. "Did you see anyone you recognize at the fire?"

"Yeah, it happens I did." He smiled triumphantly sending a waft of fried onions in her direction. "I saw the blacksmith, Roger Suffolk, and John Cleaves. John is a fire chaser like me."

"Do you own a drone, or have you ever owned a drone?" Jo raised her gaze.

"A drone?" Dexter barked a laugh. "I'd love to own a drone so I could get some footage of the fires from above but right now, I don't have one."

"Okay, that's all for now." Jenna folded her notebook and pushed it into her pocket. "Thank you for your time."

The man's eyes seemed to burn into her back as she headed down the pathway. When the porch light went out and plunged them into darkness, she pulled out her flashlight and turned to Jo. "Did you get anything from him?"

"He has no respect for women and by looking at the state of him and his house, he doesn't care about himself either." Jo sucked in a breath and let it out in a yawn. "Is he the bomber? I doubt he has the brains but we'll keep him on the list of possible suspects."

They walked back to the truck and climbed inside. Carter was missing and Jenna noticed him coming around the back of the house with Zorro. "What is he doing? I hope that's not an illegal search."

"Nah, just giving Zorro a run." Kane pushed both hands through his hair and massaged his scalp. "He took off in that direction so I guess Carter followed."

Jenna rolled her eyes. "Sure he did."

"Nothing." Carter secured Zorro in the back seat and slid in beside him. "The place is clean."

"Cleaves next?" Kane examined her face. "Or do you want to speak to him in the morning?"

Determined to keep going, Jenna shook her head. "I know where Cleaves was tonight. Dexter just informed us that he was in Blackwater. They're both fire chasers and use a police scanner for information." She sighed. "I'd like to see if he knows anything about Pamela. We asked Dexter and he claims to not know she went missing and for an avid follower of a police scanner, and the media coverage, he should have known. This alone makes him suspicious."

"Then Cleaves would be using the same device." Kane pulled a woolen cap over his ears against the early morning chill. "One thing is for sure, either way he's not going to admit knowing her, is he? I think we'd be wasting our time." He looked at Jenna. "Unless you believe he might have Pamela holed up in his house?"

"I'm so tired I don't know what to think." Jenna pressed her knuckles against her sore eyes. "I don't have probable cause to break down Cleaves' door and search for her. We have no connection between them at all."

"Then why?" Carter yawned explosively.

Jenna leaned back in the seat and sighed. "I'm worried Dexter and Cleaves could be working together and figured showing up on their doorsteps tonight might slow them down some."

"I doubt it's two men and we don't know if Pamela going missing is a coincidence." Kane looked at her. "We'll need to search for a possible link between our suspects and Sheriff Stuart. Without that we have nothing."

"We'll also need evidence to connect the Blackwater bombing to the one at Louan." Carter popped a toothpick between his lips. "Right now, all the evidence from the drone is in evidence bags inside Wolfe's van and we haven't examined the crime scene yet."

Jenna nodded. "I know it's too early to make conclusions but I'm worried about Pamela. What if he has killed her already?"

"It's a possibility." Jo chewed on her fingers. "From the reports, the Blackwater deputies have the search for her well organized. They are on top of it, Jenna. We need to concentrate on the bombings."

Head fuzzy from lack of sleep, Jenna looked at Kane. "My gut tells me it's the same person."

"Yeah, I agree. Bombing is an unusual way to kill, and too much of a coincidence to be different people." Kane started the engine. "One thing for sure is that this murdering SOB is following an escalation pattern. He's getting worse."

"I have to agree." Jo clasped her hands together. "And we haven't seen his best work yet."

CHAPTER FORTY-SIX

Jenna stared at the clock beside her bed in disbelief, she'd slept through until ten. Why hadn't anyone called her? She checked her phone, no missed calls, no messages. She climbed out of bed and the consequences of the explosion hit her like a ton of bricks. Her knee ached, her hip was stiff and the cut on her neck stung. She gave her black cat Pumpkin a stroke and watched her stretch and then curl up in a ball, before limping into the bathroom. She looked at her reflection in the mirror, and gasped. Apart from washing her hands and face and cleaning her teeth, she'd fallen into bed and dropped asleep in seconds. Her hair was a tangled mess and she had bruises all over. Sighing she turned on the shower and stepped inside. It was the continuation of a very long day and all she wanted to do was crawl into a ball like the cat and sleep until Christmas.

Sometime later, she found Carter at her kitchen table and Kane cooking breakfast. "Is Jo awake?"

"Yeah, she's outside on the stoop talking to Jaime." Carter looked up at her from his laptop. "We all overslept but it was time well spent. Updates have only just started to filter in."

"Okay." Jenna poured a cup of coffee and leaned against the counter sipping the rich brew. She looked at Kane, hair wet from the shower, and in a world of his own stirring eggs. "Did you get any sleep?"

"Yeah." He gave her an appraising look. "Before you ask, my head is fine. How are you?"

Jenna pulled a face. "You really don't want to know." She turned and pushed bread into the toaster. "Thanks for cooking breakfast." She inhaled the delicious smell of sizzling bacon and sighed. "I thought we were all out of bacon."

"Apparently, Jo ordered a ton of supplies and they arrived just as we'd finished tending the horses." He shrugged. "We have enough food here for a month. The overflow is in my freezer."

"It's all part of our assignment budget." Carter stood and took the heated plates out of the microwave. "You'll get a paycheck as well."

"That's right." Jo came into the kitchen and smiled at her. "My move to Snakeskin Gully came with a ton of provisos. Trust me, I intend to use up every cent of my budget each year. I'm planning on making our field office a force to be reckoned with." She collected cups and placed them on the table with the fixings.

Breakfast had become a well-oiled ritual, everyone pitching in to help. Jenna took out the silverware and laid the table and before long they were all sitting down eating. She looked at Jo. "How's Jaime?"

"She's good." Jo sipped her coffee. "She misses me of course but it's a way of life for us and she copes well. The puppy helps as well. She loves Snakeskin Gully, the small school, and friendly people. She told me she never wants to leave."

"I always wanted a permanent home when I was a kid too." Kane looked up with a forkful of eggs raised to his mouth. "I was an army brat, moving from place to place, country to country."

"Yeah? Was your pa in the service?" Carter liberally spread butter on his toast.

Jenna shot Kane a meaningful look across the table. He never discussed his past life, not ever. Carter could have checked him out and would likely know his file verbatim.

"Two-star." Kane continued to eat.

Jenna didn't recall any mention of a two-star general in Kane's resume, when he applied for the job as deputy. She needed to change the topic of conversation fast and cleared her throat. "Time's getting on. We'll need to head out to Blackwater as soon as we've finished here. I'll find out when Wolfe plans to be there. You mentioned updates?"

"Yeah. First up, I already called Wolfe and the fire chief. They're heading out to the crime scene at noon." Carter pushed his empty plate away and looked at her. "There's been no sightings of the girl. Nothing. It's as if she placed her bag against the tree and walked away. They checked the fingerprints on her backpack, they're the same as they found at her home." He sipped his coffee. "Ah, let me see. Kalo's been hunting down connections between our suspects and social services, and both Wood and Sheriff Stuart. He's had a few hits. Wood used to live in Blackwater before he inherited the ranch out of Louan from his father."

Jenna sighed. "Yeah we knew that, it's in my report." She leaned back in her chair. "Anything else?"

"Let me finish." Carter mirrored her pose and raised one eyebrow. "Wood worked in Blackwater, that's where he met his wife. There the sheriff and Wood both had dealings with John Cleaves. Apparently, he'd been stalking an old girlfriend in DC. He was arrested in DC and received a slap on the wrist with the proviso he took counseling. He refused and fired his lawyer, saying he'd lose his job if he remained in DC for the required time. The magistrate gave him three months' jailtime."

"So, we have a tie in to the DC magistrate and lawyer." Kane was expressionless. "But not to Sheriff Stuart or Wood."

"Well, the story didn't end there." Carter stood and refilled his coffee cup and took the pot back to the table. "He verbally abused his DC lawyer, said he'd get even, and the judge added an anger management course to his sentence. It was the same lawyer who died in DC." He spooned sugar into his cup and then added cream before sitting down. "When the girlfriend moved to Blackwater, Cleaves started to follow her around and the situation replayed apart from the time in jail. This time, he took the counseling with Wood but wasn't cooperative and threatened to get even with Sheriff Stuart for arresting him."

Considering the new evidence, Jenna looked around the table. "Do we have the threat to the sheriff in a statement?"

"Nope." Carter met her gaze, his green eyes flashed with something like amusement. "Kalo hacked into the sheriff's files and found Cleaves made a one-on-one threat, so I'm afraid it's hearsay." He held up a finger. "Wait there's more."

"You sure like to drag things out, Carter." Jo refilled her cup.

"He found Dexter had no significant connection to anyone, but this is where the story gets interesting." Carter paused a beat to sip his coffee. "Roger Suffolk's best buddy was a guy named Graham Lindley. They were both raised in Blackwater. They parted ways when Lindley reported him to the sheriff for messing with underage girls. Suffolk was thrown out of school and they had a very public brawl in town. Sheriff Stuart hauled them in for fighting, charged Suffolk with property damage and assault but allowed Lindley to walk free."

"How so?" Interested, Jenna leaned forward.

"I think I know but I'll come to that in a second." Carter looked pleased with himself. "The very next day, Stuart hauled Suffolk downtown again and held him for forty-eight hours, I assume to hunt down any proof of the underage girl accusations. He was released without charge, so I figure they couldn't prove he'd committed an offense." He sighed. "Soon after, Suffolk and his family moved to Louan to be more involved with their church."

Jenna pushed her hair behind one ear. "Graham Lindley is the name of the Blackwater magistrate, but he's in his late sixties so can't be the same person. How does this tie in with the bombings in DC?"

"The magistrate in DC is his son. The friend Suffolk had a fight with way back. It was his secretary involved in the car bombing, which makes it too much of a coincidence." Carter rested his cup on the table. "They had the same name. Suffolk had a motive: his career in law was over and so was his place on the college football team."

Jenna frowned. "How old was Suffolk when this happened?"

"Eighteen." Carter shook his head. "Seems he still has a hankering for underage girls."

"If Suffolk was blamed for something his folks probably raised him to believe was okay, it would be very confusing for a teenager." Jo frowned. "But it wouldn't be enough to trigger murder."

"Oh, I don't know." Kane looked up from his plate. "My question would be, how involved was Lindley? What if he was initially involved with underage girls as well and then rolled over on Suffolk for immunity? That would sure trigger a fight between friends. It's not beyond reason to believe that a magistrate might be tempted to cover up crimes to save his son's reputation— not everyone's squeaky clean." He leaned back and stretched his arms high above his head. "If Lindley was involved but then walked, it gives Suffolk motive. His best friend ruined his life." He dropped his arms, groaned, and then rubbed one shoulder.

Unsure, Jenna looked from Kane to Carter and back. "I've always thought Sheriff Stuart was lawful, but they're close friends." She drummed her fingers on the table. "Hmm, I'd say seeing his ex-friend successful in DC, while Suffolk was doing manual work, might have given him a motive." She shot a look at Kane. "But it doesn't tie him in with the lawyer. What motive did he have for killing him and why the secretary?"

"I don't know about the lawyer, it's something we need to look into more closely." Kane raked his fingers through his hair. "The car bombing, if Lindley's secretary refused to allow Suffolk to see him, she could have become a target. We're not talking about a logical mind here, Jenna. This guy is sick."

"Both of our main suspects fit the profile, both are confident and carrying on professions." Jo fiddled with her earring. "The getting even is an excuse they find perfectly normal. An eye for an eye mentality. This is what makes people like this so dangerous: they fit right in and act normally."

CHAPTER FORTY-SEVEN

Married life for deputy Jake Rowley had become like driving down the mountain highway without brakes. The past six months had flashed by so fast it had been like a dream. The only negative was the time it took driving into the sheriff's office from his new ranch. Not that it was far away but living in town had its advantages. He had always been there to open the office for Sheriff Alton. Now with his chores, tending the horses, and the general running of things, his life had become a little chaotic. With the sheriff, working with the FBI and only having old Deputy Walters as backup, his days seemed to be getting longer. On weekends, the team often took turns in the office and monitoring the 911 calls but he couldn't expect the semi-retired Walters to carry the extra burden. It was just as well Maggie was there to lend a hand. Living close by, she'd taken to arriving early and opening the office and by the time he arrived at eight, she had a pot of fresh coffee brewing.

He'd spent the morning chasing down complaints, and then sat at Jenna's desk to sift through the pile of messages. People called the sheriff's department for the most ridiculous things. Dogs barking made the top of the list, dogs digging up people's yards a close second. He had three calls about a person complaining that their neighbor looked at them strangely. The phone on the desk rang and he picked up the receiver. "Deputy Rowley."

"This is Jan Cotterill. I called you about my missing car?"

Rowley pushed a hand through his hair. "It's in the system, Mrs. Cotterill. No one has found it yet I'm afraid."

"That's because it's here. Right back in the barn where I left it. It looks fine, no damage but it has mud on the tires and it smells real bad." Mrs. Cotterill sounded worried. *"I'm not so young anymore, and I'm scared to open the trunk. Can you send someone around to take a look?"*

Rowley rolled his eyes and took a pen out of Jenna's chipped mug on the desk. "Okay, give me the address again and I'll be right there."

He took down the details, it would be faster than looking up her file. After making a note in the daybook, he pushed on his Stetson and went to the front counter. "The woman who reported her vehicle missing has just found it in her barn. I'm going to check it out, she figures it smells."

"Maybe she left her groceries in the trunk?" Maggie smiled at him. "You check in now, like the sheriff told you. I don't want to be telling her I don't know where you are when she comes by later."

Grinning, Rowley tipped his hat. "Yes, ma'am."

The small ranch was at the mountain end of Stanton Road, on the same side of the highway as the Triple Z Bar and not half a mile from where Harvey Haralson had claimed to have found the Ford sedan in the forest. Rowley took the driveway through the trees. Ahead was the house but he noticed a cutaway through some trees leading to a corral. He pulled up outside the house but before he could call in his arrival to Maggie an elderly woman came down the front steps and headed to his SUV. She was robust with graying once black hair tied into a bun and wore rubber boots and a bright floral apron. He buzzed down his window. "Mrs. Cotterill?"

"Yes, that's me and my vehicle is in the barn. If you give me a ride. I'll show you?" She moved to the passenger door and opened it. "Turn around and go down the road to the barn."

"Sure." Rowley reached for his radio. "I'll just call in to let dispatch know I've arrived."

He made the call and then reversed the SUV to the dirt road leading to the barn. The road twisted and turned through a small wooded area, which effectively cut it from view from the house and road. Anyone could have taken the vehicle and returned it without being seen. "When did you notice the vehicle had been returned?"

"Just before I called you." Mrs. Cotterill frowned. "I was planning on hosing down the barn before the deliveries arrived. It gets dusty in there and I get asthma." She pointed. "See, it's parked right inside, not just inside the door where I usually leave it."

The smell of death filtered through Rowley's window. He turned to her. "Are the keys in the vehicle?"

"Yes, just as I left them but I didn't get inside." She looked at him. "I went straight back to the house and called you."

The delicious breakfast Sandy had provided, hotcakes, maple syrup and strips of crispy bacon, solidified in his stomach. A flood of dread washed over him at the thought of finding a dead body in the trunk of the vehicle. The Amber Alert and image of Pamela Stuart flashed through his mind. The latest bulletin had said she hadn't been found. Was it a coincidence another vehicle had gone missing in the same area as the Ford used to kidnap Sophie Wood? Had the bomber taken Mrs. Cotterill's vehicle and used it to abduct Pamela Stuart? Or was he being paranoid and someone had left a dead animal inside the trunk?

He glanced at the woman. "Wait here, I'll go and look." He climbed out from behind the wheel and pulling out surgical gloves from his pocket, headed into the barn.

The smell increased with each step and the wind moving through the trees made soft moaning sounds. Keeping to the shadows, he moved along the perimeter of the trees and pulling his weapon eased into the dim light inside the barn. He glanced around. The vehicle was parked in the open space beside two disused stables and a hayloft. Empty sacks and feed pellets littered the dusty floor but from what he could see the barn was deserted. He holstered his weapon and using his flashlight checked all around and under the sedan, aware if he was dealing with a bomber, he might trip an explosive device if he just went and opened the trunk.

Convinced the vehicle was clear, he opened the door, peering over the back seat and checking for anything inside. He found nothing. He bent, pulled the keys from the ignition, and walked around to unlock the trunk. It sprung open with a whine. Heart pounding, he peered inside, right into the sightless eyes of Pamela Stuart.

CHAPTER FORTY-EIGHT

It was a magnificent day, too beautiful to be working on a murder case. Jenna wished she could be out riding, with the sun on her back and the smell of pine trees in the air. As they headed out the gate to her ranch, her phone chimed and she peered at the caller ID. "Morning Wolfe, we're just leaving now."

"It's not about the Blackwater case, Jenna. Change of plans." Wolfe sounded his usual calm solid self. *"Rowley just called. He's found Pamela Stuart, well he believes it's her. She's in the trunk of a stolen sedan in a ranch near the Triple Z Bar. Not far from where the other vehicle was apparently dumped."*

Stomach clenching, Jenna swallowed hard. She looked at Kane. "Head for the Triple Z Bar." She turned her attention back to the call. "Okay, we're on our way. Can you send me the coordinates?"

"No need, it's the last driveway before the Triple Z. Rowley said it has a bright blue mailbox, with the name 'Cotterill' printed on the side." Wolfe cleared his throat. *"I've had deputies on scene since we left Blackwater. The crime scene is secure but we'll have to be there without delay."*

Jenna couldn't hold back a wave of remorse for the Stuart family. She swallowed the lump in her throat. "Okay." She disconnected and gathered herself. "Rowley's found a body in the trunk of a car and he believes it's Pamela Stuart. Wolfe is on the way."

"That's not what I wanted to hear this morning." Kane's eyes filled with concern. "Why didn't he call you? He's out at a crime scene with no backup."

Confident that Rowley could handle himself, Jenna squared her shoulders. "He followed procedure and called in the closest assistance, which in this case was Wolfe. Remember, Rowley runs the office while we're tied up with the FBI. He did exactly what I would have done, he called Wolfe."

"Maybe it's time to get another deputy." Jo leaned forward in her seat. "With both of you out on cases, he's often left to cope on his own. Old Deputy Walters is getting way too old to be his only backup."

With her mind on the loss of another girl under her watch, the last thing Jenna wanted to think about was breaking in a new rookie. "Yeah, I guess, but I'd like someone experienced this time rather than a rookie."

"Then you have to consider why he needed to leave his last sheriff." Carter shrugged. "You may be taking on someone else's problem."

Jenna snorted. "What, like Kane and you?" She glanced at Kane. "Both of you seemed to work out just fine."

"It's real bad news about Pamela Stuart." Kane's fists tightened on the steering wheel. "I had the crazy idea we were free of murders for a time." The nerve in his cheek twitched. "I can't figure this killer out at all."

"Dealing with a pyro psychopath is new to me too." Jo sounded tired. "He's not following any pattern I'm aware of and is taking on different characteristics as he goes along in his rampage of destruction." She sighed. "The kidnapping and raping aren't usual and I can't imagine what he'll try next or who will be his target."

"I can't imagine how the families are coping, losing so many family members." Jenna shook her head. "It was turning out to be such a normal year. I just knew something would come along and spoil a perfectly good summer and toss all our plans to the wind."

"Sorry." Jo's shoulders slumped. "I shouldn't have asked you to get involved."

Aghast, Jenna turned in her seat to look at her. "Oh, I wasn't complaining about the work, Jo. It's the psychopaths who believe this part of the world is a killer's playground." She turned back in her seat.

The forest called to Jenna as they turned onto Stanton. She opened her window and inhaled, taking in the scents of the pines and wildflowers. It was a fresh, delightful smell and cleared away the cobwebs in her troubled mind. The frequent murders had come close to destroying her joy of the forest and mountains. If not for her friend, Atohi Blackhawk, she'd have feared living in the area but he'd taught her many things about the forest and its healing powers. Now, she respected the majestic mountains and valued the trees and wildflowers. She stared out the window and had a sudden urge to run into the forest and escape. She'd been a DEA agent, dealing in drug trafficking, and although she'd seen her share of cartel murders, hunting down psychopaths who burned, raped, and murdered hadn't been part of her job description. Being the sheriff of Black Rock Falls had taken her into the depths of criminal minds so twisted they gave her nightmares.

"You okay, Jenna?" Kane glanced at her. "There's fresh coffee in the Thermos if you need one."

Jenna smiled at him. "I'm fine. I'm trying to figure out how to take this killer down. The social services link is a solid lead to concentrate on. If he's going to hit again, we need to be one step ahead of him."

"They all make mistakes sooner or later." Kane concentrated on the road. "We're getting closer, and it's only a matter of time." He turned onto a dirt driveway. "This looks like the place."

Wolfe's white van came into view and then Rowley's marked SUV. As Kane headed toward them, Jenna scanned the area. Trees gave good cover to the old red brick barn. It looked as if it had been built last century, the bricks had moss growing over damp patches on the outside, and someone had patched the roof with unmatched tiles. From what she could see, it was a typical style inside—hay loft, a couple of stables and raised areas to store grain or feed. Before she had the chance to open the door, the stench of decomposition reached her. She buzzed up the window and coughed. "Don't get too close, the truck will stink."

"The smell might work to our advantage." Kane pulled up some ways away from Wolfe's van. "Whoever returned the vehicle had to go somewhere. Maybe Duke will pick up a scent?"

Jenna pushed open her door. "It's worth a try." She climbed out, pulling a mask from her pocket, and pushed it on her face. "Have at it."

She led the way to Wolfe and Rowley and nodded at Emily and Webber, standing to one side. "What have we got? Is it Pamela Stuart?"

"It sure looks like her." Rowley's expression was grim. "Poor kid."

"I'll need a formal ID from her parents before confirming." Wolfe led her to the trunk of the sedan. "I've photographed and videoed the scene. I don't want to touch the vehicle or body here." He narrowed his gaze. "I'd rather tow it to the mortuary with the body in situ. I know it's unconventional but I have a sterile area, and I don't want to risk losing any trace evidence by removing the body here."

"Okay but we can't leave the bodies in situ at the fire scene either. I gather it's cool enough for us to get inside now?" Jenna pulled on surgical gloves as she walked.

"Yeah, it's cooling but unsafe." Wolfe grimaced. "There'll only be carbonized remains and I doubt we'll find anything of interest. A fire reaching such high temperatures destroys everything."

"So how do you want to proceed? Kane wanted to see if Duke could pick up a scent trail of the killer."

"He could try but there's something else." Wolfe's brow wrinkled. "I found residue of a substance on the body. I believe he sprayed her with a chemical, maybe he tried to destroy trace DNA evidence."

Jenna nodded. "Okay let me take a look."

She heard Jo's sharp intake of breath as they stepped forward. A body in the first stages of decomposition was never a pleasant sight. The eyes of victims remained in Jenna's memory most of all and compelled her to catch their killer. Filled with the need to cover the girl's nakedness, she gathered her professional cloak around her and examined the body, not touching but observing, seeking any clue. She could sense Kane and Carter doing the same.

"I'll wait in the truck." Jo turned away and walked back to the Beast.

Moving away from the disturbing scene, Jenna walked around the vehicle, peering inside the windows. It was clean, too clean and she'd seen a wiped down vehicle many a time. Walking back to Kane and Carter, she removed her gloves. "Okay Kane, see if Duke can find anything."

"I'll see if the killer left a scent inside the car." Kane opened the driver's door and took Duke close. "Seek."

When Duke sniffed the ground and then took off through the trees, Jenna stared after him in disbelief. She looked at Kane. "Give me the keys, he's heading in the direction of the Triple Z Bar."

She caught the keys he tossed her and she watched him dash into the woods with Carter on his heels and Zorro bounding along behind. She turned to Wolfe. "I doubt the killer is hanging around close by. Do you want us to meet you at the crime scene in Blackwater?"

"Yeah, I'll tow the sedan back to my office, get the body on ice, and leave." Wolfe shut the trunk. "I'll work on her when we get back. I'll ask Emily to contact the Blackwater Sheriff's department to contact the next of kin and they'll organize a time for her parents to do a viewing."

Jenna nodded and headed to the Beast. She opened the door and adjusted the seat; the way Kane had it set, she couldn't reach the pedals. Throwing a look at Jo, she smiled. "Duke picked up a scent, Kane and Carter are on it, and we'll meet them on the other side of the woods." With some degree of concern, she started the engine, turned the truck around. Not that she had any problem driving, but piloting Kane's pride and joy did make her a little apprehensive. By the time they headed along Stanton, she made out Kane and Carter standing in the Triple Z parking lot. She pulled up beside them and leaving the engine running, pushed the seat right back and then climbed out from behind the wheel. "How did he go?"

"He came straight here and sat down." Kane stared down at the ground. "There's nothing here, not even a tire track but at least we know how he did it. He left his vehicle here, hidden in plain sight and found himself another ride. When he'd finished with the vehicle, he dumped it close by and walked here."

Jenna waited for Kane to get the dogs settled in the back, climbed inside with the others, and fastened her seatbelt. "I didn't see any cause of death on the body. Her neck looked untouched, no visible puncture wounds or blood."

"The broken blood vessels in her eyes would make me think suffocation." Kane headed toward Blackwater. "She was wearing her shoes and they were muddy, scratches on her legs. I'd say she'd been walking through the forest."

"Something else." Carter leaned forward. "Wolfe will be all over the mark on her cheek. I figure someone had his hand over her face. With any luck she'll have picked up some DNA inside her mouth on her teeth maybe." His eyes flashed with anger. "The government trained me to kill the bad guys without thinking about it. I carried out my orders no questions asked but being a cop is a completely different ballgame. I've had to change my attitude." He dragged in a breath. "As a man, I want to take the killer down but as a cop I want to see him thrown in jail for the rest of his life."

Jenna nodded. "The reason that keeps me focused is something Kane told me. He said it was easy to kill a person but you can't give back a life if you make a mistake."

"Mistakes happen all the time." Kane glanced at her. "We've made mistakes, built up a case to find it was someone else." He looked back to the highway. "Carter has the right attitude, a lifetime behind bars is at least some compensation to the families."

Jenna hoped so because the memory of Kane's anger when he'd found out the man who'd killed his wife walked free was still fresh in her mind. He'd wanted to tear him apart with his bare hands and yet she'd seen his cool detached combat face in times of great danger. When the time came, when they had absolute proof the man was the DC bomber and the perpetrator of the horrific crimes in the surrounding counties, which Kane would she be dealing with—the cool professional or the revengeful husband?

CHAPTER FORTY-NINE

Wolfe towed the vehicle into his drive-through inspection area and once his van was unhitched, closed the doors at both ends. The removal of the body took no time at all. Pamela was small for her age and after taking the normal precautions against contamination, he lifted her out onto a gurney and took her straight to the examination room. Conducting a preliminary examination at this time was crucial as trace evidence was easily lost by delaying. He'd taken the temperature of the body at the crime scene. With Emily and Carter watching on, he checked her body. He noticed the slight bruising on her cheek and immediately swabbed her tongue, lips, and front teeth for DNA evidence. He took samples from under her fingernails, while Emily bagged the girl's sneakers and socks.

"Dad there's a ligature mark on her ankle, not a zip-tie this time. It looks wider and it's bruised her ankle." Emily pulled down the magnifying lens and turned on the bright light. "It's scraped the skin too."

Wolfe moved closer. "She was shackled. I've seen the same damage from prisoners."

"Are those burns on her thighs?" Webber frowned. "She has them on her lower torso as well."

Wolfe peered at the marks and then rolled her over. "I'll have to look closer at these but I don't believe they're burns in the true sense of the word. I've seen similar marks when clothes are torn off a victim and they present more like a rope burn." He looked at Webber.

"There's no sign of any apparent injury, my initial guess would be suffocation. We'll find out in the autopsy. The body temperature was the same as the trunk and going on rigor, she likely died twelve to twenty-four hours ago. As she was heated inside the trunk, it's difficult to determine a closer TOD."

"So, he took her somewhere overnight and killed her the following morning?" Emily looked at the corpse with compassion. "She must have been terrified."

Wolfe covered the body with a sheet and gave the signal to Webber to slide the gurney into a drawer in the wall of the mortuary. He pulled off his gloves and turned to Emily. "We have to go and pull the bodies out of the housefire now. Do either of you need a break?"

"No, I'm fine." Emily glanced at the stainless-steel wall of drawers. "She doesn't look too bad but I'll do what I can to make her look asleep for when her parents come to view her." She looked at him. "Do you want me stay back to fix her up and conduct the viewing? It will save time if we get a positive ID."

Pleased Emily was taking more responsibility, he nodded. "That would be a great help. Don't answer any questions about cause of death. Just say it's undetermined at this time."

"I know the drill, Dad." She patted him on the arm. "Go, I'll be fine."

Wolfe turned to Webber. "What about you? Need a break?"

"No, I'm good to go." Webber shook his head. "Although seeing these young women murdered doesn't get any easier."

Wolfe slapped him on the back. "Without compassion we might as well walk away. It's the drive we all need to find the answers. Remember we speak for the dead. We tell their stories and the truth will find their killers."

CHAPTER FIFTY

The house smelled of wet burned newspaper mingled with the stomach-turning odor of a recent cookout. The odor of fire still lingered in the air, and scattered swirls of smoke, filtered through Kane's mask in an acrid aftertaste. He stared at the gutted ruins of a once beautiful old ranch house. Only a few of the structural beams had survived, the explosion and fire had rendered the residence into a pile of wet ashes. He waited outside, with Jenna and Jo staring at Wolfe's meticulous gathering of evidence. With a fire, the less people inside the better until the scene had been documented, photographs and samples taken. Carter worked alongside the fire chief, Matt Thompson, sifting through ashes for parts of the explosive devices, and they walked out, gloved hands blackened to the wrists.

Kane took in the evidence bags in Carter's hand. "Find anything?"

"Yeah, I'll need to work in Wolfe's lab to piece it together." Carter handed over the evidence bags to Jenna. "I've taken scrapings from what's left of the stove. There's residue of an accelerant I'm not familiar with and I figure he used it in the cruiser bombing as well."

"Do you recognize the substance, Matt?" Jenna looked at the fire chief. "It's in your field of expertise."

"Structural damage, and fire management and cause are more my field." Thompson removed his gloves. "On the surface this looks like a gas explosion and I would say the propane tank exploding would have caused the damage and flare up. I'm not convinced this was a bombing at all. I don't see any signs of an explosive device. What Carter has found could be the remnants of cellphones or TV remotes."

"I see." Jenna didn't look convinced. "So, a difference of opinion?"

"I stick by my conclusions." Thompson shrugged.

"That's why I'm on the job. I'm an explosives expert and I find what you clowns miss." Carter snorted and turned to Jenna. "Will you make sure this evidence is under lock and key while I clean up? It might be what we need to nail this guy."

"Sure." Jenna held out her hand to Kane. "Keys. I'll get it squared away. You go inside the house. I've seen enough and Wolfe will bring us up to date later." She looked at Jo. "Coming?"

"Yeah. I've spoken to all the witnesses." Jo turned to follow her. "There's nothing more for me to do here."

Kane handed her his keys and watched Duke follow her back to his truck. He waited for a smart comeback from Thompson from Carter's insult but he said nothing. "Will you send us a copy of your report?"

"Sure." Thompson stared after Jenna. "I don't want your boss telling everyone I'm not doing my job." He stomped off toward his truck.

"I think he's a jerk. He is more of an insurance assessor than a fire chief. He misses evidence and should know a fire that intense wasn't just caused by a propane tank exploding." Carter glanced at Kane. "Did you see how he backed down when I insulted him? How many guys do that?"

Kane bit back a laugh. "Tons. He can't deal with you or me, so he figures he'll come down hard on Jenna." He grinned behind his mask. "Oh boy, has he picked the wrong person. She'll eat him for breakfast."

"Yeah, that I know." Carter clicked his fingers and Zorro ran to his side. "I'm done here. I'll clean up and we'll wait for you at the café."

Kane nodded. "Sure. Take Duke with you or he'll end up getting his paws cut on all the broken glass around here. He's over at my truck with Jenna." He headed into the building.

Taking slow steps, he scanned the area. He took in the direction of the burn marks. The intensity of the fire was in three different locations. The house had literally blown apart in three directions. He'd seen similar results from grenade attacks on buildings during his tour of duty. He stepped with care over the floor and made his way to Wolfe. "This is different from the first fire. More intense."

"It got away from the firefighters." Wolfe's gaze narrowed over his facemask. "In Louan they acted swiftly and extinguished the fire. Here it was well ablaze and they were more concerned about stopping it spreading to the other ranches. I guess it's a call they had to make. Whoever was inside couldn't have survived the blast so they made the call to let it burn." He sighed. "Which means we have zip to go on in the way of evidence. The marble tabletop is what protected the lower half of the body of one of the victims. It's female, so I assume it's the sheriff's wife. He's that curled charcoal smudge on the floor there where I've marked it."

Kane winced. "It doesn't even resemble a body."

"Nope. We'll have to sweep it up and bag what we can find. Ashes mostly." Wolfe indicated toward a body bag. "The other remains are in there. The zip-ties are intact."

"Do you need any help?" Kane dragged his attention away from the bag.

"Nope. You didn't need to see the bodies, Dave, Carter has it covered. I know working this case is hell for you." Wolfe's eyes showed compassion.

Kane shook his head slowly. "I need to be involved if I'm going to find the killer and you know I'd go rogue if Jenna pulled me off the case, plus how could we explain my absence to Jo and Carter?"

"Then I guess it's for the best." Wolfe straightened. "If you went rogue, I'll be the one hunting you down and that's never going to happen."

Relieved, Kane slapped him on the back. "Good to know. Anything else I should know?"

"Em called just before. The parents of Pamela Stuart have made a formal ID. I'll be conducting the autopsy this afternoon around four. It's going to be another long day." Wolfe sighed.

Kane could feel his reluctance. "I guess you wanted to spend time with the girls this weekend?"

"I always treasure my time with the girls but Emily was planning on going out with friends and Julie is babysitting." Wolfe shrugged. "I might get home in time to read Anna a bedtime story but then it's just me and the TV. The girls are growing up so fast, it's as if my life is stuck on fast forward."

Kane nodded. "I know how you feel." He slapped him on the back. "I'll see you at four."

He ambled out of the ruins and headed down to the café but the idea of eating didn't appeal to him. He just wanted to go home and wash the stink of fire and death away. Sometimes knowledge could be a bad thing. He'd always believed his past actions had caused the death of his wife but discovering sweet, innocent Annie had been the target of a deranged maniac was unconscionable. The anger raging inside him since seeing the image of her in the wreckage, her beautiful eyes fixed in death hadn't abated. Yeah, he'd fought to keep control and would do his duty but no one could ever know that under his professional mask, revenge was riding on his shoulder like an evil twin.

CHAPTER FIFTY-ONE

Inside his cellar, his secret cellar, well hidden under the floor of a closet, he made the final touches to the explosives he'd designed. Without his drone, he had no choice but to deliver them to the house of the magistrate personally. Abe Coleman, the new Black Rock Falls magistrate, and his wife Pearl, had moved to the area the previous year. It had been a surprise to see the man's face in the local newspaper at a charity function with his wife. They had kids, too young for his taste, a baby boy and a daughter that looked around five or six, but the wife was pretty. He connected the last wire and leaned back in his chair. He'd have his revenge on the self-righteous magistrate by watching his house and family burn. After a couple of weeks of seeing the FBI run around in circles, he would move on and find a distraction elsewhere in Montana.

He'd wait until nightfall and then steal a vehicle, not a sedan this time, but an old pickup, something easy without all the technology and alarms most had these days. The one thing about Black Rock Falls was that they had a good supply of old pickups. He placed the explosives inside a backpack he'd purchased at a garage sale in Blackwater, and carried it upstairs. It was as safe as houses, only by dialing a burner phone, would trigger the detonator. He smiled to himself. "You're good."

Inside his home office, he slid the bag under the desk and checked out his computer. He'd spent some time scanning the town using a Google app, going all over town looking at ways to cover his tracks and used the maps to view the houses. The easiest place to park, how to get inside without being noticed. Everything he needed to see was available online. He'd taken all contingencies into consideration, even taking a bait to put down a dog if necessary. He leaned back in his chair, searched for a few more houses for sale and looked at them just to have an excuse for searching the area. These days cops could find out anything from a computer even if the history was deleted, they had their ways and he was too smart to fall into a trap.

He opened his social media page and thought for a beat and then smiled as he wrote his post.

There's something special about a Saturday night. A date with a good-looking woman and spending time gazing into a log fire. I can't wait.

He'd take a long shower and then he had a few things left to do in town before he finalized his plans. He leaned back in his chair and stared at the ceiling just enjoying his thoughts. Today another cycle of his life would end and very soon, he'd enjoy the freedom of choosing what happened next. He'd find a job in a town far away and discover what entertainment satisfied his new urges. He stood and laughed, enjoying the shifting of the heavy burden from his shoulders. Something inside him had changed when he'd taken Sophie. He'd liked the girls, so soft and compliant, maybe they'd be the first of many. They'd been so easy to take and they understood the danger of non-compliance from the get-go. He wondered briefly why he felt nothing when they'd died but then he'd mourned the death of his son with outrage, not tears. He shrugged it off. Surely, it was a normal reaction not to worry about something he had no longer use for? The girls had made him feel something, power maybe but he'd enjoyed it. People would rant and rave and complain about their lost daughters but no one would suspect him, not ever, and as sure as hell no one would ever stop him.

CHAPTER FIFTY-TWO

It suddenly made sense to Jenna, why Wolfe had designed the morgue into sections divided into airlocks, with doors that needed a card to access. As they paraded into the reception area, the air was cool but not cold, clean and had the soothing aroma of lavender wafting from an infuser. The capsulated foyer, with a corridor on the left led to a similarly sanitized area comprising of three rooms. One, a non-denominational chapel for grieving relatives was something Wolfe had insisted on including. Another comfortable room he used as a waiting room or to sign documents. It had sofas set around a table, a coffee machine, and refreshments. The third room was the viewing room and every attempt was made to avoid the shock of seeing a loved one dead. The body, carefully cloaked and arranged, could be viewed through a small window or by a video feed, the latter designed to make the reality seem more remote.

Not so, through the airlock. Goosebumps rose on the exposed flesh on Jenna's arms as she entered the sterile passageway. The noise from Kane and Carter's boots sounded irreverently loud on the pristine white tiles that graced the floors and walls. There were four similar thick glass double doors and a red light over an entrance indicated an autopsy was in progress. They suited up in the alcove outside an examination room in silent dread of standing witness to the product of a deranged murderer. Jenna looked at the eyes peering over the top of the masks. This would be a day none of them would forget for a long time. "Ready?"

At the nods from her team, she scanned her card. The doors whooshed open and they moved inside in single file. Inside, the temperature had dropped and it was as if she'd stepped into a refrigerator, which was a good description of the morgue with its walls of stainless-steel drawers, and shelves. As they walked, the antiseptic tang in the air gave way to the repulsive smell of burned and rotting flesh. It hung in the air like an oily patch on a pristine lake waiting to cling to anything that passed its way.

"Right on time." Wolfe carefully removed a white sheet from the charred remains of a pair of legs. "From the DNA comparison taken from her daughter, this is all that remains of Cathy Elizabeth Stuart. Please note the zip-ties around the ankles. Buzz Stuart's body has been carbonized but I was able to extract DNA to make a match. I have ruled the deaths of Buzz Stuart and his wife as homicide, the cause of death undetermined."

"They died in the fire, surely?" Jo moved closer to the gurney and shook her head. "The poor woman, she must have been terrified."

"I wish my job were that simple, Jo." Wolfe covered the remains and indicated to Webber to replace them back inside the drawers. "There is no evidence to support a cause of death. If I assume the fire killed them, they could have been shot, stabbed, suffocated, poisoned or any number of causes. If I had bones, I would search for damage to indicate possible cause but we have nothing, so the cause remains open."

"I understand." Jo nodded.

Jenna straightened as Pamela Stuart was removed from the drawers. Her stomach gave a twist of regret for not finding this girl. The sheet rolled back but the staring eyes had closed and although pale, she could have almost been asleep. She looked at Emily. "You did a good job, Em. Although nothing would ease the pain of losing a daughter, seeing her like this would make it less traumatic."

"That was the plan." Emily stood opposite Wolfe and Webber at the head of the gurney. "They're devastated. It was more difficult than performing an autopsy but I guess it's part of the job." She looked at Jenna and her eyes filled with tears. "There was really nothing I could do to help them."

"You are helping them." Wolfe pulled down the microphone. "You're going to tell her story through the findings of an autopsy. We'll find evidence to bring her killer to justice."

A bell sounded in another room and Emily hurried out the door. Jenna stared after her. "Is there something wrong?"

"No, we took samples from under the victim's fingernails on arrival. That's the DNA sequencer I set up when we got back from the fire scene." Wolfe shrugged. "She had cells under her nails but they could have been her own."

Holding her breath waiting for Emily to come back through the door, Jenna stared into space as Wolfe described the body of Pamela Stuart, her height, weight, and age. She was small for her age but in good physical condition. The door buzzed open and Emily came in and handed an iPod to Wolfe. Jenna exhaled and waited in anticipation.

"We have foreign DNA." Wolfe handed her the tablet. "I ran a match against her own. She could have scratched her killer."

Behind her, Carter sprang into action. He was on his phone making a call. Jenna looked at him. "Can the call wait until we're finished here?"

"Nope." He looked at Wolfe. "I have Kalo standing by, can you send him the data? He'll run the DNA through all databases, it will take hours or maybe days but if this guy is in the system or has had his DNA tested to discover his family tree, we'll find him."

"You can email straight from the tablet." Wolfe looked at Jenna. "Are you ready to proceed?"

Jenna watched Carter head for the hallway and nodded. "Yeah, thanks."

"In my preliminary examination, I noted hemorrhages in the eyes and a mark on her cheek consistent with an imprint of a man's hand. She, as you can see, has superficial injuries. Scratches and marks on her thighs consistent with the removal of her clothes by force. She has deep contusions embedded with soil on her knees. There is evidence of tape residue on her wrists and face but the residue has debris in it so it was removed before she died. The search for her, discovered a school backpack but no fibers or remnants of her clothes or tape have been discovered at this time. The X-rays taken before you arrived show no indication of blunt force trauma, or strangulation."

"Someone disturbed him." Kane stood arms folded across his chest. "She made a noise and he smothered her to keep her quiet. He must have been somewhere secluded, a safe place for him. The injuries to her knees are significant, they go with the torn clothing. He forced her to her knees and raped her in the forest, didn't he, the lowlife?"

"If you'll permit me to continue, I'll examine her." Wolfe's eyebrows raised. "Maybe you need to take a break?"

"Yeah." Kane's eyes flashed with rage and he headed for the door.

Dismayed, Jenna stared after him. She could hear his boots pacing on the tile outside the door. She forced her mind to concentrate on the autopsy. "Do you have a time of death?"

"The heat of the trunk confuses the body temperature reading." Emily looked at her. "From the state of rigor, she was dead inside the trunk at least overnight. Which would mean he kept her alive for at least the first night she went missing. We estimate the time of death to be sometime on Friday morning."

"There is indication of forced sexual activity." Wolfe's eyes held a deep sorrow. "You have your hands full with this murderer."

"I wonder exactly what happened to him to trigger another violence spree." Jo shook her head. "If this is the DC bomber, to him it's history repeating itself but, before, the clean way he killed made it almost impersonal. More of a payback. This time, the raping and torture of his victims, means someone else is involved. Someone was taken from him of great value and revenge is the only motive I have for this twist in his MO."

Mind reeling with the implications, Jenna's mind wandered during the rest of the autopsy. The findings would arrive neatly in a report but what Jo had said concerned her. Both of their main suspects had very personal reasons as motives but had the killing of Sheriff Stuart been the end of the vendetta? She allowed the evidence to filter through her mind. What did social workers, sheriffs, lawyers, and magistrates have in common? She turned to Jo and gripped her by the arms. "I have it! I've been thinking this guy must have done time, got out of jail, and wanted revenge on the people who put him there but apart from Cleaves spending three months in jail, the social worker part of the puzzle doesn't add up. Okay, they might assist an ex-con but where are they most active? Child protection."

"So, you think one of our suspects was placed in the system and they went batshit crazy and decided to killed everyone involved?" Jo looked astonished. "That should be easy enough to hunt down but why go off on a killing rampage now? This doesn't look like the work of an eighteen-year-old?"

Excited, Jenna shrugged. "I don't know, maybe dealing with the Woods triggered an old memory or something. We need to get back to the office and find out if any of our suspects were in foster care." She whirled around and looked at Wolfe. "Is that okay?"

"Yeah." Wolfe's eyes sparkled over the top of his mask. "Go get 'em, Jenna."

CHAPTER FIFTY-THREE

Julie Wolfe checked the time. She didn't want to be late at the Colemans' house. Now she had her own vehicle, a rather tattered but sound SUV her father and Kane had practically built from scratch, and a shiny new driver's license, she could do odd jobs at the weekend. Her sister Anna had a friend at school, Lucy Coleman, and Julie had met her mother a few times. When Lucy's mother asked if she could babysit Lucy and her baby brother, Peter, for three hours on Saturday night, she'd jumped at the chance. The Colemans wanted to celebrate their wedding anniversary at the new tavern in town. Her father had agreed, as Mr. Coleman was the local magistrate, although she expected him to run a background check on the entire family. She went to look in on Anna. With her dad and Emily at the morgue playing with dead people, Anna would be happy with the housekeeper, Mrs. Mills, who'd become almost like a grandma since they'd arrived in Black Rock Falls. She headed into the family room and smiled, recognizing the songs to a popular movie. Mrs. Mills and Anna were engrossed staring at the screen. Julie raised her voice. "I'll see you later. Tell Dad I should be home by ten and if not, I'll call."

She headed for the front door, swinging her car keys. The new freedom was a curse as well as an advantage. In the last week or so, she'd taken on all Emily's driving chores, and her phone was filled with messages to stop by stores to buy groceries or pick up or drop off dry cleaning. It was as if she'd suddenly become an adult and although it kind of felt good, she wasn't quite sure if she wanted to give up her childhood just yet. Would her dad still throw hoops with her now or was his catchphrase of "Where are you going?" becoming the new normal in her life?

The workouts in the gym her dad and Uncle Dave had built in their downtime, had made her aware of the dangers of living in Black Rock Falls. Her dad had trained them like a drill sergeant, even little Anna had been given instructions on how to run away from a threat. Then Uncle Dave had had a long talk with them, telling them that bad people look just like everyone else, and all the ways a bad person might try to lure young women into bad situations. She understood more than they gave her credit for, most kids of sixteen knew the way of things and she'd heard Emily discussing cases with her dad and Uncle Dave. Unlike some, she didn't spend all her time gazing at her phone or on social media. She had plans and they included becoming a pediatrician, which meant good grades and hopefully a scholarship to a good medical college. She'd promised her mom she'd work hard at school, and she never broke her word.

The drive to the Colemans would take twenty-five minutes. They lived in one of the ranches recently built out of Glacial Heights. It was a secluded area for the more affluent people in town and not far from the new ski-resort. She drove a little slower than necessary, not risking the possibility of having an accident the first time she'd traveled this far alone. It was dusk and the forest loomed on one side of the road, hiding the trails in deep shadows. This far from town the streetlights were non-existent and the idea of getting a flat or being stranded alone sent shivers up her spine. She pushed the thought away; her car was mechanically sound and her dad, Uncle Dave, or Jake Rowley were not far away if she needed help. By the time she arrived at the Colman's ranch, she'd gained more confidence and negotiated the treelined driveway with precision. Small lights led the way to the front of the house, a huge redbrick, with a riot of flowers in garden beds.

She parked beside the magistrate's silver SUV and climbed out. A cool breeze brushed her legs and rustled the leaves on the trees. Somewhere in the distance, she heard the shriek of an owl and the flapping of wings. Looking over one shoulder into the darkening night, she shook off the uncomfortable feeling of being watched, collected her bag, and headed for the steps. The idea to bring her laptop to complete her school assignments had been Emily's. Once the kids went to sleep, she'd have a nice peaceful place to study. She didn't have time to ring the doorbell before the door flew open and Lucy stood in the doorway, dressed in PJs with a broad grin on her face. She smiled at the little girl. "Hello, Lucy."

"Come in, Mommy's getting dressed." Lucy hurried along the passageway. "She said to wait in the family room and she'd be down soon."

A wonderful aroma of fresh baked cookies wafted on the air. The house was modern and a polished floor she could see her face in ran the length of the hallway. The family room was huge with a fireplace big enough to roast a pig. Overstuffed leather sofas sat around a coffee table and a flat screen above the mantel was the biggest she'd ever seen. An elk's head stared at her from another wall and on a bookcase, pictures of the family, wedding photos, fun holiday times and baby photos all in silver frames. A box of toys sat in one corner, piled up high and spilling onto the carpet. She looked at Lucy. "What would you like to do tonight?"

"Well, Mommy said I have to be in bed by seven-thirty so could you read me a story?" Lucy looked at her expectantly. "Daddy doesn't like me watching TV before bedtime but I like bedtime stories."

Relieved she would be easy to care for, Julie nodded. "I'd like that fine."

When Mrs. Coleman came into the room, bringing with her the scent of perfume, she smiled at her. "Is there anything special I have to do for John tonight?"

"No, he'll sleep right through now." Mrs. Coleman patted her hair. "Just check on him every hour or so, Lucy will go straight to sleep. She has a routine and falls asleep without a fuss. You have my number and my husband's but if anything bad should happen, call 911 first and then us but I'm sure with a medical examiner for a father, you know the drill."

Wondering what could possibly go wrong for her to call 911, Julie nodded. "I have all the sheriff's department's numbers if necessary but is there a problem I should be aware of?"

"No, not at all." Mr. Coleman came into the room. "It's a precaution is all. The children will be asleep, you can watch TV, help yourself to whatever you need."

"I baked cookies and they're still cooling on the counter." Mrs. Coleman smiled. "We'll be about two to three hours is all." She turned to kiss Lucy on the cheek. "Off to bed with you."

"Julie is going to read me a story." Lucy blinked up at her parents.

"Just the one." Mrs. Coleman smiled at Julie. "Then she'll go straight to sleep." She followed her husband to the front door.

Julie stood for a moment, watching the Colemans drive away. She closed the door and stared out the window. It was almost full dark now and the trees seemed to close in around her. All alone, with two children to care for and for some reason the gnawing feeling of someone watching her just wouldn't go away.

CHAPTER FIFTY-FOUR

Exhausted, Jenna rested one hip on the edge of the table and stared at the notations on the whiteboard. No matter which way she looked at the circumstantial evidence, she couldn't find enough to put forward a solid case against a suspect. She took the pen and swiped a line through two names on the board and then turned and looked at her team. "Taking all the evidence, I think we can remove, Dexter and Haralson from the suspects list. We already discounted Peter Huntley, the other person who had a problem with Wood, earlier on, so I figure we need to concentrate on Cleaves and Suffolk."

"With the suggested link between social services, cops, magistrates, and lawyers, I'd keep Peter Huntley on the list." Kane collected the scattered statements and tapped them into a neat pile. "He might appear to be living quietly here in town but we don't know what's going on inside his head and we don't know if he was in DC at the time of the bombings. In fact, we don't know anything about him."

"My head is spinning." Jo rubbed her temples. "Instead of going around in circles, and going over these files again, could we just make a list of the main points we have on each suspect?"

"That would help, with all of us working on different suspects it's hard to keep track." Carter looked at Jenna. "Do we have contact info on Peter Huntley?"

Jenna nodded. "Yeah, it's in his file along with everything Phelps from the social services told us about him."

"I'll ask Kalo to run a background check on him. He might be the sleeper." Carter stood up and went outside the room to make the call.

Jenna stared at the whiteboard. It had notations everywhere. She moved to one end and placed the names, Suffolk, Cleaves and Huntley on the top of the board and separated them with vertical lines. "Okay this is what we have so far:"

Roger Suffolk.

Spousal abuse.

Prefers underage girls.

Was in DC time of the bombings.

Was in Blackwater and Louan time of bombings.

Has experience with explosives.

Had a fight with Wood.

Wife died in accident caused by brake failure.

Unremorseful.

Jenna turned to look at them. "Then we have the secretary of DC magistrate Graham Lindley died in the car bombing. Lindley was the friend who reported him for chasing underage girls and caused his family to leave Blackwater." She sighed. "So, what's missing? Suffolk had no other dealings with Sheriff Stuart."

"Did we look?" Kane lifted his gaze from his tablet. "His wife wrecked her car in Blackwater. That would've come under Sheriff Stuart's jurisdiction." He scanned the files. "Yeah, Stuart handled the case and he had a question mark on the brake failure. He hauled Suffolk in for questioning. From the case file Kalo sent, Suffolk's lawyer wanted an expert opinion and it was placed into the hands of a Louan brake specialist and later went on to a car insurance assessor. He passed the claim."

"Wonderful." Jenna snorted. "All members of Suffolk's sect, no doubt. He did mention he thought her death was divine intervention."

"Most likely they belong to his sect for it to be blatantly swept under the carpet." Kane shook his head. "It's quite clear from Sheriff Stuart's notes he made a lot of noise in an effort to find justice for Suffolk's wife."

"Then we come along and poke at the wasps' nest and likely caused Stuart's death. Suffolk knew we were checking out his wife's death from our questioning. His church grapevine would have informed him we've been all over asking questions. Suffolk wouldn't have wanted Stuart joining forces with us and reopening his wife's the case, so he removed the problem." Jo looked from one to the other. "Suffolk fits for the local bombings and he didn't like us poking around but apart from the fight way back with Graham Lindley we don't have any physical evidence to link him to the DC bombings."

"Not yet." Carter stood in the doorway. "Kalo is chasing down links now. Still no DNA match. It could take days or never."

Jenna added to Suffolk's list:

Investigated by Sheriff Stuart after wife's death and the underage girls' accusation.

She chewed on the pen scanning the notes. "Okay, next we have John Cleaves:"

Fined for stealing C-4 from workplace.

Fined for starting fires.

C-4 found in house is the same batch as DC bombings.

On scene at Luan and Blackwater bombings.

Had a dispute with Wood over Sophie.

Arrested in DC for stalking his girlfriend.

Jailed for 3 months in DC. Had a problem with his counsel and magistrate.

The lawyer representing him, died in the bombings.

Was in DC at the time of bombings.

Had a run-in with the Blackwater sheriff for stalking his girlfriend again but walked when he agreed to counseling.

Likes underage girls.

She turned to the team. "Anything I've forgotten?"

"Nope." Kane was scanning his files.

Jenna looked at him. "Okay next, Peter Huntley:"

Involved with social services due to unemployment.

Children removed by Connie Wood and placed in care.

Children put up for adoption.

Huntley contacts Sam Cross who represents him pro bono and gets the children back with parents.

"I can find no other charges against him but I would say he'd be very resentful toward the Woods." She shrugged. "He's been a model citizen since moving to Black Rock Falls. Unless we can find anything to implicate him, he's way down on my list of suspects."

"Okay. We all know this isn't finished, we've established a link between social services and the sheriff's department in all of the suspects." Jo stood, placed her hands on her lower back, and leaned back with a groan. "Looking at the main points who would you place on a list for possible targets?"

Trying to make her brain focus, Jenna stared at the lists, going down each one. She turned around. "A magistrate?"

"Yeah, my thoughts exactly." Kane scratched his cheek. "The problem is which one in which county? There are two here in Black Rock Falls, two in each of Louan and Blackwater and at this point we're just guessing."

"The suspects seemed to have brushed shoulders with at least three of them at one time or another." Carter moved his toothpick across his lips. "We can put them on alert, inform the local law enforcement of a possible threat?"

Thinking of her own depleted department, Jenna nodded. She pulled out her phone and went to her contacts list. "I'll call our local magistrates and give them the heads up. I don't have the resources to have an around the clock surveillance on their homes." She looked at Kane. "You contact the deputy sheriff at Blackwater and Carter, you've got Louan." She made the first call to Rowley. "Hi Jake, we've been looking at the case files and believe a magistrate might be the next target. It's likely to be one from Louan or Blackwater but I'm contacting ours just in case they see anything suspicious around their homes. If you get a call, contact me immediately."

"Well, you don't have to worry about Abe Coleman. He's just sat down at a table at the tavern near us." Rowley paused a beat. *"I heard that Daryl Chatsworth is off on a fishing trip this weekend."*

Relieved she had two of the magistrates accounted for, she sighed. "That's great. If you could give Coleman the heads up before he leaves, it will put my mind at rest."

"Yes, ma'am."

CHAPTER FIFTY-FIVE

It was full dark when Julie heard a noise. She picked up her phone like a security blanket and listened. Had Lucy slipped out of bed and crept downstairs? No, the house was so quiet she could hear herself breathe, and it wasn't soft footsteps on the stair carpet she could hear, the crunch on gravel was coming from outside. Heart pounding, she closed her laptop and switched off the kitchen lights. Without hesitation, she called her dad's phone. It went to voicemail. He was still busy in the lab. Fingers trembling, she dropped her voice to a whisper and left a message. "Someone is outside the house. I'm calling 911."

Glass shattered in the panel beside the front door and seconds later the door flew open with such force it slammed against the wall. Heavy boots clattered on the polished floor toward her. Someone was checking the rooms. Terrified for her safety and the two sleeping children upstairs, panic gripped her. She had a split second to react. Out of the confusion, the drill she'd performed with her dad a million times fell into place. She closed her phone and pressed her emergency tracker pendant. The alert would go to not only her dad's phone but to Uncle Dave and Jenna's phones as well. A predator might check her phone to see if she'd dialed 911 and kill her and the tracker was immediate contact to help and unrecognizable. She had no time to hide, a man carrying a Glock in one hand with a backpack slung over one arm charged into the room, bringing with him the smell of sweat and cigarettes. She willed the children to remain asleep. If he didn't know they were in the house they'd be safe.

"I saw the light go out." The room flooded with light and a tall man with broad shoulders, dressed in black and wearing a balaclava, pointed his weapon at her head. "Where is everyone?"

Petrified, Julie's throat closed, she tried to speak but her heart pounded so hard, she just stared at him until the press of the cold metal of the gun's muzzle at her temple freed her tongue. She hardly recognized her squeaky voice. "They went out to visit a friend." She looked into his dark eyes. Feeding information to anyone listening to her one-way communication tracker was paramount. "Why are you pointing a gun at my head?"

"Give me your phone." He took it from her, checked the last dialed number, and smiled before dropping it on the table. "So not so smart huh?" He walked around her flicking at her hair. "You're too old to be one of the brats, too young to be the wife. Just who are you, pretty girl?"

Scrambling for anything but the truth, she flicked her eyes toward him again. "I'm Abe's cousin, I came here for school."

"When will they be home?" He looked around the kitchen.

Trembling, Julie sucked in a deep breath. If this was the bomber, he'd want all the family in the house to kill them and she needed time for her dad to get there and save her. "Late, they said around midnight."

"Perfect." The man dropped his backpack on the table, pulled out zip-ties and smiled at her. "Turn around. Hands behind your back."

The zip-ties cut deep into Julie's flesh and when he pushed her into a chair the horror of who was standing before her dropped into place with a tsunami of fear. This had to be the bomber she'd heard her dad discussing with Emily. Teeth chattering and frozen with indecision, she stared hopelessly as he pulled two small devices from the backpack and slapped them underneath the kitchen table, one at each end. She looked at him. "What are you sticking under the kitchen table?"

"They're a surprise for when your cousin comes home." His voice sounded almost conversational. "They come home, carry the kids up to bed, and then come back down for a nightcap, maybe a snack before bedtime. They follow a pattern like most folks. You on the other hand are a bonus I wasn't expecting." He waved his gun at her. "You're coming with me."

She had no choice, fighting an armed man was out of the question. If she acted calm, he might not hurt her. "Where are we going?"

"Not out for pizza, that's for sure." He dragged her to her feet and shoved her toward the door. "Make one sound and I'll cave in your skull. I won't kill you but as long as you're breathing, we'll get along fine."

As he propelled her toward the door, she crunched over broken glass and stumbled down the steps. He urged her along the driveway and as they rounded the first bend an old SUV with its nose parked into the trees came into view. "Does that old white SUV belong to you? It's older than my ride."

"I told you to shut your mouth." He opened the trunk and tossed in his bag.

She looked over one shoulder at him and the interior light shone on eyes devoid of emotion. "Get inside or I'll kill you right here and enjoy watching you die." His words cut through her like a voice from a grave.

Images of what might happen to her flashed through her mind. Every muscle twitched and her limbs refused to cooperate. The next moment he'd lifted her and hurled her inside. Once her knees had hit the cargo space, pain shot through the back of her head. Lights flashed in her eyes and she vomited bile. She heard him curse and another blow glanced off her ear. She fell forward onto a carpet smelling of dog, her vision blurred, and everything around her spun into a world of black.

CHAPTER FIFTY-SIX

The wail of sirens filled the room and Jenna's heart missed a beat. It was the sound none of them ever wanted to hear; one of Wolfe's daughters was in danger. She grasped the phone in trembling fingers and met Kane's gaze across the table. "Julie."

"I'll track her, you listen. Wolfe will be trying to contact you on the landline." Kane stared at his screen. "She's at Glacial Falls."

Jenna twisted the tracker ring on her finger, willing her tired mind to act faster. She turned to Jo and Carter, who were looking dumbfounded. "We all have trackers, they're—"

When Julie's voice came through loud and clear detailing the situation, she passed her phone to Jo. "Write everything down, she says." She turned to Carter. "If this is the bomber, there's a chance he'll be heading for the forest."

"I'll go get the chopper." Carter stood and pushed on his Stetson. "It's refueled and ready to go but I'll need your cruiser to get there fast."

Jenna threw him the keys. "We'll meet you on Stanton Road at the turn off to the ski-resort."

Carter nodded and ran out the door. Jenna headed for her office and waited. No call from Wolfe. She called him and his phone went to a message, so she called the landline, knowing a light would flash in the laboratory. She waited for a time before he picked up. She didn't give him time to speak. "Where's Julie? She triggered her tracker."

"She what? She's babysitting at Abe Coleman's house." She could hear Wolfe running to his office and throwing open a drawer. She

could hear the same muffled ringtone that came through her own phone. *"Oh, Jesus, I hadn't realized it was so late."*

"Kane is tracking her, Carter has gone to get the chopper, and Jo is listening in. We have everything covered." Jenna took a deep breath. "Where did she go?"

When Wolfe rattled off the address, Jenna made a note. So, there are young kids there as well, how many?"

"Two." Wolfe had dropped into a professional zone. *"We need to get there now."*

Jenna nodded. "We're on our way. I'll handle the kids. Go and meet the chopper on Stanton at the ski-resort turn off. Carter will need you to track Julie."

"Copy." Wolfe disconnected.

Jenna ran back to the others and collided with Kane coming out the door. "What's happened?"

"He's set explosives and we've just sent our expert to collect a chopper." Kane grabbed her by the arms. "He's on the move. The vehicle is moving at speed toward the mountains."

Jo came out the room, her face pale. "She's not saying anything, I think he's knocked her out. She's in the back of an old white SUV. That was the last I heard apart from a door slamming. The vehicle is still moving north."

Indecision swept over Jenna. She had two major problems: saving Julie and getting the Coleman kids to safety. The weariness had vanished in a surge of adrenalin. She gave herself a mental shake and looked at Jo. "Where will he take her?"

"Going on the other two, I figure he has a place in the mountains." Jo looked at Jenna. "What's the good of the chopper, we can't land anywhere in the forest?"

"It's an FBI chopper, it can drop us down on a harness if necessary and there's a spot to land in a parking lot on a plateau not far from the

Whispering Caves. There's an old trail down the mountainside we can use." Jenna turned to Kane. "We need to get over to Glacial Heights to get the kids out the house before he detonates the explosives."

"We should have by midnight, that's when he expects the family to arrive home." Jo's eyes flashed with concern. "He'll probably secure Julie somewhere and return to detonate and watch the explosion."

With a plan of action forming inside her head, Jenna grabbed her duty belt from a hook on the wall and abandoned her shoulder holster. "I figure we'll need everything at our disposal. This guy is very unpredictable and we don't know what he has in his arsenal. We'll suit up for a riot. Jo keep listening, Kane come with me, I'll grab rifles and ammo from my office."

"We'll need Duke." Kane turned and headed back into the communications room returning seconds later with the bloodhound at his heels. "Zorro has turned into a statue. We'll have to leave him behind." He tossed Jenna her jacket and headed for the door pulling on his own. "We'll suit up at the house."

Jenna's mind was running like a freight train. "We'll need Rowley to take the kids to safety and contact their parents. They must be in town somewhere."

"I'll call him, you grab the supplies. There are four survival backpacks in the closet in your office, we'll need them if we're going into the forest." Kane pulled out his phone and made the call.

Loaded for bear, they sprinted out the door and climbed into the Beast. Jenna didn't have to say a word to Kane, she added the address to the GPS and he took off spinning his wheels. Siren wailing and blue and red lights flashing, they headed through town. The Beast weaved through the Saturday night traffic. The town seemed to be packed to overflowing. Tourists standing in groups on the sidewalk watched in morbid interest as they flashed by. Jenna stared at them, hoping the white-water rapids or the camping and hiking had drawn them here, and not the hope they'd witness another serial killer wreaking havoc.

They hit Stanton doing ninety and a cold shiver went through Jenna as she stared into the forest. Her stomach cramped with anxiety. Sweet, fun-loving Julie could be trapped somewhere in the deep shadows with a murdering rapist. The Beast accelerated and the trees became a wall of darkness, streetlights flashed by blinking like a don't walk sign. The vehicles they passed became flashes and as each minute went by, Jenna's anxiety grew for the girl she regarded as a little sister. It seemed to be taking hours to get to the house but in truth it had been minutes since they left the office. She stared at the GPS on the screen. "Can't you go any faster?"

"Not if you're planning on surviving." Kane slid between a truck and an eighteen-wheeler and then took off at breakneck speed and overtook a line of traffic. "It's not far now."

Pulling her mind back to the task she turned to look at Jo. "Anything from Julie? Can you hear anything at all? She's wearing a pendant and you should be able to hear her speaking."

"It was very loud at first but she hasn't said anything else. She's alive, I can hear her breathing, steady and even, and the sound of an engine. They're still moving but slower this time." Jo checked the tracker app on her phone. "They've headed into the forest toward the mountain."

"She's unconscious." Kane glanced at her. "Or she'd be whispering. Those trackers can pick up a pin dropping and she knows it. If he takes her into the caves, we won't be able to hear her. The mountains cut off all communication signals." He left Stanton and drifted the Beast around the corner into Glacial Heights. "Give me directions, Jenna."

Jenna stared at the screen. "Next left and then it's the third house along."

"You suit up." Kane glanced at her as they hit the driveway. "I'll go in and get the kids."

Aghast, Jenna stared at him. "Oh sure, send a six-five man wearing black into a kids' bedroom at night. Somehow, I think you're going to have a problem. I'll go. I've met Lucy, she came to Anna's birthday party. You suit up and go see what explosive he fixed to the kitchen table. He doesn't know we're here. You should be okay."

"Should be huh?" Kane flicked her a glance. "I'm not messing with anything that madman created. I figure we both go and get the kids and hightail it out of here. I've met Lucy as well. She'll recognize me and you can't carry both at the same time. Julie is getting farther away by the second and she is more important than this damn house. Rowley is right behind us. He was in town having dinner opposite the magistrate and his wife. He'll be here soon. I told him not to allow them to come to the house." He pulled up some distance from the front door.

They all tumbled out the door and pulled on liquid Kevlar vests and helmets. Jenna looked at Jo. "Wait here. Keep listening to Julie."

"Okay." Jo pulled on a helmet. "Go get the kids."

As she ran toward the house with Kane, Jenna could make out Julie's SUV parked outside and the front door standing wide open. She moved her flashlight over the front steps and all around the door. "I can't see any trip wires."

"Me either." Kane moved ahead of her and took the stairs two at a time. "How do we do this without scaring the kids?"

Turning on lights as she went, Jenna looked at him. "Keep your voice low and reassuring." She opened a door with the name "John" in alphabet block figures and as the light from the door flooded the room, she made out a little boy fast asleep. She turned on the bedside lamp, sat down and gave him a little shake. "Hey John, I'm Sheriff Alton, I'm going to take you to your mom and dad." She picked the little boy up blankets, teddy bear and all and handed him to Kane. "This is Deputy Kane. He's going to take you downstairs and we'll take you and Lucy straight to Mommy and Daddy, okay?"

The little boy said nothing and just burst into tears. Kane looked helpless and made shushing noises as he carried him downstairs. Jenna went to the room marked "Lucy". She turned on the light and the little girl sat up in bed and stared at her open-mouthed. "Hi Lucy, it's Jenna, remember me, from Anna Wolfe's party? You came to my ranch?"

"Yes." Lucy stared behind her. "Has something happened to Mommy?"

Jenna shook her head. "No, your parents are fine and on their way. There's a problem with the house and you need to leave."

"Okay." Lucy jumped from the bed, pulled on her dressing gown, slipped on her slippers, picked up a fluffy duck, and looked up at her. "I'm ready."

By the time Jenna had gotten downstairs, she could hear a siren in the distance. Jo was sitting holding John in the back seat and Kane was behind the wheel of Emily's SUV and rolling down the driveway. She pushed the little girl into the Beast, climbed behind the wheel and followed him. When Julie's vehicle was outside the gate, Kane jumped out. She gave him an exasperated look. "You wanted to save that old wreck?"

"Rowley isn't here yet, we had time." Kane leaned into the window and looked at her. "It's not an old wreck. It just needs a paint job is all. I'm planning on getting to Julie before he hurts her and she'll need her ride. I found her sweater inside, Duke can use it to find her, if he has her holed up anywhere." His eyes flashed with anger. "This guy has done enough damage, ruined enough lives. Whatever happens next, I'm going to take him down."

CHAPTER FIFTY-SEVEN

Trying to keep her mind three paces ahead of the speed things were happening wasn't easy. Time was ticking by and they needed to get to Julie. Jenna ran crime scene tape across the driveway and had tied it off as Rowley arrived with Sandy and the Colemans close behind. They carried the children to their parents and she turned to Rowley. "Escort Mr. Coleman and his family to his parents' home in Blackwater. Get the Blackwater deputies to stay with them until I give them the all clear. We believe the bomber is heading to the Whispering Caves with Julie."

"Yes, ma'am." Rowley frowned. "It's pitch-black out there. Do you want me to call Atohi, he knows the forest better than anyone I know?"

Right now, Jenna would take all the help she could get. "Sure, I would welcome his help. Give him the details. I don't want him walking into a trap." She stared at the house. "Call the bomb squad from Helena, they'll have to come by chopper. Tell them our specialist is on another case."

"Copy that." Rowley stepped away to make the call and then walked back to her. "Atohi and his grandfather were heading back to the res, they are about five minutes from the plateau. They'll take the trail down and meet you at the caves." He headed to speak to Mr. Coleman.

Jenna climbed into Kane's truck. "Let's go."

"Where is Julie now?" Kane set off along Stanton at breakneck speed.

"Moving at about three miles per hour toward the Whispering Caves." Jo gave Jenna an anxious look. "He must have been using them all along. How did Rowley miss the signs?"

Jenna turned in her seat to look at her. "It's a huge area of catacombs, there are other ways in and out but not many of them are known." Her phone chimed—it was Wolfe.

"I'm on Stanton, next to the ski-resort turnoff, I have my flashers on. I can hear a chopper. There's room for him to land on the road but I need you here now." Wolfe sounded amazingly calm. *"We must board fast before a vehicle comes down the highway."*

Jenna could see his lights ahead. "We're two minutes away."

They screeched to a stop behind him, Kane took the Beast off road and parked on the edge of the forest. They jumped out, and grabbed Duke and their backpacks. Wolfe was standing beside his SUV, dressed in his Kevlar vest, helmet and carrying a backpack and medical kit. A chopper appeared from above the trees, its light searching the road. Kane ran out waving his arms. Wolfe leaned inside his SUV, turned off his flashers and slammed the door. As the chopper landed the bright lights of an eighteen-wheeler appeared on the highway coming fast. Air horns screamed in the distance as they rushed to get on board. Deafened by the whoop, whoop, of the chopper's blades and engine, Jenna could see Kane's lips moving but his instructions carried away on the wind. Without warning, her feet left the floor as he lifted her and hurled her inside the chopper. Duke slid past her and rolled into the seats followed by backpacks and a medical kit. Jenna scrambled deeper into the cabin as Jo landed sprawling behind her. Terror gripped her as the oncoming eighteen-wheeler's lights illuminated the cabin, it was right on top of them. Frantic, she stared at the open door for Kane and Wolfe. The chopper shot straight up and then banked to one side sending her sliding toward the open door on her knees. She hooked one arm around a seat and grabbed Duke's harness. On her other side, Jo was hauling herself into a seat and strapping in.

The next moment Kane's head popped into sight. Without effort, he grasped a loop suspended from inside the door of the cab and slid inside. The chopper's engine roared as they lifted high above the trees. An instant later, Wolfe's head appeared. He was riding on the skids, his gaze on the eighteen-wheeler passing below them. When Carter hovered above the forest, Kane braced himself legs apart and hauled Wolfe inside. The door slid shut behind them and both men looked at her with raised eyebrows as if surprised to see her hanging on for dear life spread-eagled on the floor, with one hand white knuckled on Duke's harness. She quickly realized that being in mortal danger in a chopper hundreds of feet in the air was just another day for them. Shaken, Jenna released Duke and crawled to a seat. She stowed her backpack, strapped in, and then attached her headphones. The entire heart stopping pickup had taken less than two minutes.

Jenna looked at the others. Jo appeared to be fine, Kane was securing Duke, and Wolfe was checking his supplies.

"Where to and what's the game plan?" Carter's voice came through the headphones. He glanced over his shoulder to Jenna.

Jenna gripped the seat as they banked sharply to the left. "No plan yet. Head toward the mountains, Wolfe will have a bearing for you in a second."

Wolfe had sat in the seat beside Carter and rattled off coordinates from his phone. "We'll need to drop into the forest and follow them by foot." He made a feral noise deep in his throat. "The signal just vanished. The last coordinates are close to the mountain."

"He's taken her inside the caves." Kane frowned. "If we propel down, he'll hear the chopper and might do something stupid plus we don't know how to find our way to the Whispering Caves in the dark. It's not on any GPS maps. We'll need to use the mountain trail."

Jenna looked at him. The urgent need to get to Julie burning inside her. "It will be too late. If he has her in the cave we need to be down there now."

"Wait." Kane was texting. He looked at Jenna and then back down at his phone. "Atohi and his grandfather are descending the trail from the plateau, they have flashlights and will send up light beams, when they hear the chopper, we'll propel down to them. It's faster than negotiating the forest at night."

"The harnesses, ropes, and gloves are stowed behind you on the left." Carter rose higher. "Get ready, coming up to coordinates in three minutes."

"Copy that." Kane grabbed the harnesses and handed them around. "What about Duke?"

"I'll take him with me." Carter was concentrating on the instruments. "He'll be able to guide me down the trail. Get ready, I see lights."

"Okay. Kane first and then Jenna, Jo next, and I'll follow last." Wolfe stood and checked Jo and then Jenna's harness. He looked at Jenna. "No arguments."

"I'll be right beside you, Jenna." Kane gave her a nod as if sensing her apprehension. "You remember how to do this right?" He attached his bag to the rope and leaned out watching it drop toward the target.

Trying to stop her bottom lip trembling, Jenna pulled on her gloves. "Yeah, it's been a while but I'm good to go."

Fear made her legs tremble as she removed her headset and said a silent prayer. Kane had set up two ropes but she hadn't repelled from a chopper since training and never in the dead of night onto the side of a mountain. It was dangerous for them and even more so for Carter. The drop would be a long one because if Carter took the chopper closer to the mountain and hit a rocky outcrop, they'd all be dead. Her heart was in her mouth as she attached her backpack to the clip on the rope. On Wolfe's hand signal, she lowered it out the door being careful not to tangle her rope in the skids. Kane moved without hesitation, and watching him brought back the confidence she needed. He sat with his legs hanging out the door and on Wolfe's command, turned one-eighty degrees and dropped effortlessly onto the skids facing the door. He looked at her and jumped backward into darkness. The rope moved swiftly through the rappel ring and then Wolfe tapped her on the shoulder.

Fear had her by the throat as she eased her way to the door. The wind buffeted her and the mountain loomed out of the night caught in the chopper's lights. Paralyzed with fear, she stared into the darkness and then Julie's face flashed into her mind. She turned and dropped, her feet slipping on the skids. She took a deep breath, tensed her leg muscles, and propelled herself away from the chopper. The next instant the rope was moving through her hands, a latent memory rekindled as she dropped and braked a few times until lights came into view. She heard Kane's voice yelling at her to slow down. A few feet later and someone had her legs and she fell into Atohi's strong arms. With her legs threatening to collapse under her, she grabbed his arm to steady herself. "Thanks." She nodded at his grandfather, Nootau.

In seconds, the ropes were flying back up to the chopper and then Jo arrived as cool as a cucumber and Wolfe dropped down beside them. The ropes went back up and the chopper vanished from sight above the trees. Jenna watched him go. "How will he know where to land?"

"We had friends with us, they'll be flashing their headlights." Atohi smiled at her. "Don't worry. Mingan will lead your friend down the trail and then return to guard the chopper. There is no time to waste. Come this way." He led the way down a narrow trail.

They'd not walked for more than a few minutes when an explosion rocked the mountain. The ground beneath Jenna's feet trembled as if the mountain was shaking itself awake. She grasped at branches to steady herself as pebbles rained down on them and rushed past them bouncing up and striking her legs. "Oh, Jesus, I hope that wasn't the chopper."

"That came from below and to the right." Kane used his flashlight to scan the area. "See over there, it's a dust cloud."

"That is the main entrance to the Whispering Caves." Nootau shook his head. "The man heard the chopper. He's aware we're after him and must know his way around the caves. Only the elders know the safe ways out of the catacombs." He frowned. "And not one of them would kidnap a young woman and bring them here." He shook his head. "Although explorers from the early days made maps. They believed they'd find gold, the fools."

"How far is the next entrance?" Kane turned to look at him.

"Maybe a mile or so but it's difficult to navigate." Nootau frowned. "The mountain will be angry at being disturbed, the last time man set dynamite into the rock, the falls changed direction and washed away an entire village."

Jenna straightened her weary back and looked at her team. "Keep moving, we're only surmising he's blown up the entrance. I want to see for myself."

"My daughter is in there and I don't know if she's dead or alive." Wolfe loomed up behind them, a shaft of moonlight crossing a face chiseled with undisguised rage. "I hope he's left a hole big enough for me to crawl through because I want him to know I'm coming for him."

CHAPTER FIFTY-EIGHT

Wishing she could stop time, Jenna ran beside Kane as they followed Atohi through the forest. They reached the cave entrance and she stopped to stare in dismay. Her flashlight revealed a pile of rocks blocking the entrance, and above a landslide clung by a few bushes waiting to bury it forever. She looked at Kane. "Now what?"

As Kane and Wolfe scanned the area with their flashlights, Jenna sipped from a bottle of water. She turned to Jo. "This isn't looking good. This could be a distraction. He could be hauling her miles away and will escape free and clear."

"No, he's in there and must have been carrying Julie." Atohi was crouched on the trail heading in the other direction. "He came this way, along an animal track from the firebreak. There are no footprints leading away. He must be inside the caves."

Dust was still settling over the pile of rocks. Jenna glanced over the area. "We'll need people at the other exit."

"My grandfather can take your deputies." Atohi moved to her side.

"Good idea." Jo looked at her through the gloom. "I'm convinced he trapped himself inside on purpose. I figure he plans to hole up in there until we leave." She turned to Atohi. "Did you come across anything at all in the caves? I'd say he has supplies hidden inside there somewhere and knows another way out."

"No, we saw nothing to say he'd been there apart from a piece of twine, used as a guide." Atohi rubbed the back of his neck. "He could have hidden supplies anywhere inside. The caves are vast and go off in many directions. We went to the passageway that led to the waterfall, as we believed the girl fell from there." He thought for a beat. "There was a cavern with an old mattress but it looked as if bears had used it as a restroom. We didn't think he'd keep a woman there."

"Jenna." Kane was standing on one edge of the rockslide beside Wolfe. "We've made a hole through into the cave."

She hurried to his side and aimed her flashlight into the dark recess. The drop inside was at least six to eight feet. She shone the beam all around. The passageway was empty for at least fifteen yards ahead. Standing back, she examined the surrounding rocks. Unstable was an understatement. Where Kane and Wolfe had pried the massive boulder from the pile, dirt and pebbles spilled down from above, like sand through an hourglass. She stared at the men, both had masks of determination. "Neither of you will fit in there. I'll go." She unbuckled her duty belt and handed it to Wolfe.

"Jenna." Kane gripped her arms and stared at her, his expression like granite. "This man has no respect for women. It makes no difference if we're dealing with Suffolk or Cleaves, both have the same beliefs and both are dangerous unpredictable men. You won't be able to reason with him. Give us time to clear away more boulders and we'll all go."

Shaking her head, Jenna lifted her chin. "No! We're all out of time and even I can see moving any more of those rocks will cause a landslide. I'm going after Julie and either help me climb inside that hole or I'll ask Atohi."

"I'm going too." Jo moved up beside her. "Both of us are quite capable of taking on one man." She removed her backpack and checked her weapon. "I know how to deal with a psychopath, let me do my job."

"There will be no communication once you go inside, your phones are useless." The nerve in Kane's cheek ticked. "We won't know what's happening or be able to provide backup. You'll be on your own."

Swallowing the apprehension growing inside her, Jenna nodded. "Yeah, I know." She looked at him. "I agree with Jo, he'll be holed up inside and figures we can't get to him. We'll be able to surprise him."

She heard a bark and Duke came bounding out of the dark with Carter close behind. "Good to see you made it down the mountain."

"You had any doubt?' Carter gave her an exasperated look. "I heard the explosion." He aimed his flashlight at the rockfall. "That's going to come down. If you're planning on crawling in that hole, you haven't got much time. One drop of rain or if the wind picks up, you'll be stuck inside and it will take days to dig you out, maybe we'll never get to you." He scanned the rockface. "We need a crew out here to shore this up." He pulled out his phone. "I'll see what I can arrange."

"Thanks." Jenna moved slowly to the hole, and dropped her bag and then her duty belt inside. Her flashlight went next and she breathed a sigh of relief when it spun across the sandy rock floor and filled the gloom with light. She turned to Kane for assistance and Nootau tossed her a ball of twine. She fumbled it and then looked at him enquiringly. "What's this for?"

"Tie one end to your belt and give the ball to Kane to feed out as you go." Nootau smiled his teeth flashing white in the darkness. "Now you have a communication and tracking device. Keep turning left, the right will take you to the falls and certain death."

"Thank you." Jenna attached the twine to the back of her belt and handed the ball to Kane. "Two tugs, means, we're okay. Three means we've found him." She met his gaze. "Will you help me climb inside?"

When he lifted her and lowered her into the hole, she dropped her voice for his ears only. "I promise, I'll find Julie and bring him out to face justice, Dave… for Annie."

Jenna watched his eyes as he lowered her inside the cave; he was wearing his combat face but the slight nod he gave her said more than any words he could have uttered. His strong grasp slipped away and she dropped, landing in a squat and looked all around listening for any sound. The caves had a damp, feral smell and cobwebs hung like dusty lace drapes from the roof. She straightened, collected her flashlight and backpack, before giving Kane a wave. Jo's backpack came through the hole and then Jo dropped in beside her. Sand and pebbles peppered their helmets like buckshot.

"Wait." Kane's voice sounded so far away. "Wolfe has one of Julie's sweaters with him, take Duke, he'll lead you to her."

Within seconds an evidence bag dropped through the hole and Duke was lowered down, swinging in his harness, his eyes wide. Jenna ran to lift him down. "Good boy." She untied the rope, opened the bag, and offered it to Duke. "Seek." He walked around and then sat and looked at her. Dismayed, she turned to Jo. "He can't find a trail."

"The bomber probably carried her inside but will have to put her down eventually." Jo stared into the darkness and her eyes widened. "What was that?"

A breeze rushed through the cave moaning like an evil spirit and every hair on Jenna's body stood to attention. She hated dark places and, after listening to Atohi's amazing stories, was convinced spirits roamed the catacombs. Gathering her courage, she turned to Jo. "It's just the wind. The caves make strange noises but the only monster we need to worry about is the bomber."

Drawing her weapon, she looked at Jo's determined face. "Let's go."

CHAPTER FIFTY-NINE

The deeper they moved inside the catacombs, the more surreal it became. Critters scampered away from them and the eerie wind spun around them like a thousand voices. Disoriented, Jenna touched the twine trailing out behind her, a small comfort but would it be long enough? As they approached the next bend, Duke stopped dead, sniffed the floor, and gave a little triumphant yelp. Jenna attached his leash and grabbed Jo's arm. They turned off their flashlights and it was as if she'd gone blind. She bent close to Duke and whispered in his ear. "Stay."

Heart pounding, Jenna led the way, her back to the wall and inching one step at a time around the bend. The blackness surrounding them was so dark she couldn't see a hand before her face and she moved each foot forward with caution feeling her way. The air was rancid and thick with a stink like sewerage. This must be the place Rowley had described. Moving with care, she edged around a damp wall, and ahead a slight glow reflected on the rock wall. She leaned into Jo. "Not a sound."

Edging her way to the corner, she peered around and her heart raced. A lantern hung from a hook in the roof spilling a circle of light. Directly below it, Julie sat on an old mattress, with one ankle secured in a manacle to a loop in the floor. Her head hung down and she looked battered. Her long blonde hair was tangled and matted with leaves. Not far from her, a man paced, his boots crunching on the gravel. He was muttering to himself and punching a fist into one hand. The next moment he stopped and turned slowly, looking in her direction. Jenna moved back into the shadows, sure he couldn't see her. She took a good look at him. It wasn't Roger Suffolk, he wasn't big enough, and Cleaves wasn't quite so tall. Who was he?

When he bent and slapped Julie around the face, Jenna wanted to act but she froze on the spot when he pulled a Glock from his waistband and held it to Julie's head. Beside her, she could hear Jo breathing and almost feel the anger rising in her friend but revealing themselves now would get Julie killed, and the chances of taking the monster alive would be limited.

"You told me you were Coleman's cousin." The man bent and grabbed Julie's chin and stared at her. "But your driver's license says Julia Wolfe." He let out a string of profanities. "You're Shane Wolfe's daughter, aren't you?"

Julie nodded. "Yeah, you sure picked the wrong person to mess with. My dad will tear off your arms and feed you to the bears for kidnapping me." She looked at him and smiled. "He's relentless, he'll never give up, he'll hunt you down and Uncle Dave will help him. You'll never hurt anyone ever again. They're already coming for you." She grinned at him through bloody teeth. "I'm not scared of you."

"You should be." He lashed out again. "I'm going to enjoy killing you."

"Go right ahead." Julie spat blood. "It will only make it slower and more painful for you in the end."

"You're no use to me. There's no fun in playing with you." The man let out a howl of frustration, pulled out a flashlight, and headed down the passageway.

Jenna bent, picked up a pebble, and tossed it at Julie. When she turned and looked at her, Jenna could see the fear in her eyes but she hadn't expected her to burst into tears. Men who raped fed on vulnerability. Jenna moved a little into the light and shook her head wiping at her eyes. She mouthed the words, "Stay strong and fight," and then melted back into the shadows.

There was no strategic position to take the advantage. Julie sat in a small cavern, with a passageway that appeared to break into two. How far the man had walked into the darkness on the left Jenna had no idea. It would be easy if she could grab Julie and run back to the entrance but she had no way of removing the manacle without the key. Moving would be suicide... unless... She squeezed Jo's arm. "Can you make it into the right passageway if I cover you?" Jo was invisible beside her in the dark. "We'll see him if he heads back this way by his flashlight."

"Nootau did say the passages to the right lead to the falls and death." Jo peered around her. "I guess if I stay hidden at the entrance, it will be okay. We sure as hell can't take him down from here." She took off straight across the cavern and disappeared down the right passageway. A few seconds later she poked her head out and gave Jenna a wave.

The sight of Jo had given Julie courage. She pulled the long chain tethering her onto the mattress in a coil and was on her feet. Terrified for the girl's safety, Jenna could see Julie was planning to attack. A dangerous move with an armed man. The notion of shooting him came into Jenna's mind and she dismissed it. The walls were granite and if she missed, a ricochet could kill in such a small area. She got Julie's attention again and made hand gestures to indicate she kept the monster talking. When she nodded, Jenna sagged back against the wall.

A light bobbed in the darkness and the crunch, crunch, crunch of boots on gravel came closer. The man appeared, holding himself straighter and walking with confidence. Jenna's heart sank. He'd come up with a plan and one he liked by the smile poking through his balaclava. As he entered the cavern, he removed the balaclava and Jenna stared in disbelief. The man grinning at Julie was the fire chief, Matt Thompson.

Head going into overdrive, Jenna gaped at him, his horrendous plan hitting her like a sledgehammer. If he needed an excuse to rape and murder Julie, he'd just given himself one. She could identify him now. As he moved toward Julie, Jenna stepped from the shadows.

"How did you get in here?" Matt's eyes flicked all around as he pulled the Glock out of his waistband and aimed it at her.

Jenna laughed at him to throw him off guard. "You can't do anything right, can you, Matt? You took the wrong girl. You messed up. You've been messing up all your life, haven't you?"

"You shut your mouth." Matt held the weapon steady. "You know nothing about me."

Jenna snorted. "Really? Then how come I'm here waiting for you to show, huh?"

"You think you can take me down?" Thompson's eyes had gone cold, as if another person had stepped in to take control.

Jenna pulled her weapon and aimed it at him. "I'm not alone. Unlike you, I'm not stupid. We have you surrounded."

The next instant, Julie lashed out with her foot, taking out Thompson's knee. He staggered forward and she kicked him again. On his knees with one hand still gripping the handle of the Glock, Jenna sprinted out and kicked the gun from his hand.

With a battle cry, Jo barreled into him from behind and they sprawled to the ground. Thompson pushed up taking Jo with him on his back. Jenna shoved the Glock away and was heading toward him with her weapon aimed at his head.

"I'll kill you all and burn everyone you love." Thompson tossed Jo off like she weighed nothing and was back up on his knees.

"Oh no you don't." Julie rushed in, wrapped the chain around his neck, and pulled. "How do you like being chained up like a dog?"

Thompson roared and rolled, trying to grab Julie's legs. She danced away as far as the chain allowed. Jenna raised her voice. "It's over. Make one more move toward Julie and I'll have great pleasure in sending you to hell."

"I am hell." Thompson gave her a sadistic smile. "Go ahead, pull the trigger."

Jenna shook her head. "I'd rather let Wolfe have some time alone with you. Arms behind your back."

"I don't take orders from women." Thompson grabbed at the chain around his neck and coughed. "You'll have to shoot me."

Jenna handed her Glock to Julie. "Don't hesitate, if he overpowers us, shoot to kill."

She read him his rights and with Jo's help, they cuffed Thompson and searched his pockets. They found two cellphones and the key to the shackle. Jenna took back her weapon and released Julie. "Your dad is waiting for you outside and we have deputies on their way to take him in." She tugged three times on the rope and received a tug in reply.

"You won't be triggering any explosions from these." Jo removed the batteries from the phones and pocketed them.

"Stupid woman. You should have put a bullet in me. Handcuffs won't prevent me from killing you." Thompson, jumped to his feet and swung his head making the chain cut through the air.

The chain whirred as it gained momentum in its deadly sweep of the cavern. Jenna thrust Julie into the passageway. Now she'd have to break her word to Kane and take Thompson down. Death was too good for what this man had done, families needed justice through the courts, and Kane needed to face the man who'd killed his wife. Jenna pulled her weapon and aimed for his head. With the chain whizzing by, it was her only choice, but would make the shot fatal. "Stand down."

A flash of brown came out of the darkness and with the chain flashing above his head, Duke hurled himself at the monster, sunk his teeth into the front of his pants, and didn't let go. Thompson howled like a wolf and dropped to his knees unable to dislodge Duke's grip. Duke growled and shook his head, his sharp canines digging deeper into vulnerable flesh. Without a second thought, Jenna holstered her weapon, rushed in, and slipped the manacle around his ankle. The metal lock closed with a satisfying click.

"You've got nothing on me. I'm going to hunt you down and make you pay." Thompson's words came out in a growl of pain. "I know where you live."

Jenna rolled back on her knees ignoring him. Her prisoner wasn't going anywhere until backup arrived. "Okay, Duke, you can let go now. It's time to go home."

CHAPTER SIXTY

The time it took for help to arrive seemed like hours and Jenna sighed with relief when Kane and Wolfe emerged from the tunnels with Nootau. They'd left at once and made the mile or so journey through the forest in short time, but negotiating the catacombs had slowed them down some. During Jenna's wait, Thompson's words had played on her mind. Did they have enough evidence to link him to the bombings?

After they'd made the trek up the mountain, Carter flew straight to Black Rock Falls Hospital and landed on the helipad. Once Wolfe had carried Julie inside, Carter headed to town. With Rowley and the Louan deputies blocking Main, he put the chopper down outside the sheriff's department. Inside, Jo formally charged Matt Thompson with the kidnapping of Julie Wolfe. It was a charge that would stick and hold him in the cells. With the threat safely locked away, Jenna sat with Jo in her office sipping coffee to wait for Carter and Kane to arrive. She yawned and looked at the clock. "I'm getting tired now."

"Me too. I'll be glad when we can hand over to the Louan deputies and get some sleep." Jo peered at her over the rim of her cup. "It was pretty tense in the caves when the guys arrived. I understand Wolfe's anger when he saw the state of Julie but the way Kane changed when he confronted Thompson was almost like seeing a psychopath with a victim. Although he didn't touch him, I could almost cut the tension. It must be his sniper training, I guess. They can fall into a zone and block out emotion."

Wishing she could confide in her about Kane's secret hell, she averted her gaze and nodded. "Yeah, he does that, I call it his combat face. With Wolfe, I figure he kept it together well, although I could see he wanted to tear the man apart." She turned to stare at her computer screen and quickly changed the topic of conversation. "We don't have enough solid evidence to charge Thompson with the bombings." She frowned. "By changing his MO each time, with a good lawyer, he'll do a plea bargain and be out in a few years."

Voices came in the hallway and Jenna stared at the door. Kane and Carter strolled in waving an evidence bag. She looked at them. "Okay, please tell me you have some evidence to nail this guy?"

"Oh yeah." Kane laid the evidence bags on the desk. "Two explosive devices. Don't worry, they're safe—but Thompson made a mistake. We found a fingerprint on the tape and it's a match. The trademark soldering is identical to all the other devices."

"Wait, there's more." Carter tossed a toothpick in his mouth and did a dramatic pause. "Kalo called, Thompson is a match for the DNA found under Pamela's nails. It was on the database. Thompson had given a sample of his DNA to formally identify his son, who was killed in a housefire last year."

Jenna nodded. "How come I didn't know about that?"

"Thompson lived in Blackwater and the housefire was in Helena." Kane filled two cups with coffee added the fixings and handed one to Carter. "Kalo hunted down links between Thompson and the three main points of our conclusions, social workers, magistrates and cops."

"Yeah." Carter stirred his coffee. "Thompson was tossed from foster home to foster home and ended up abused. Years later, he put in numerous complaints about the system and one complaint made it to court but he had a lousy lawyer and the magistrate dismissed the case. When he couldn't get justice, the bombings occurred."

Jenna nodded. "So, I assume the people killed in DC were the ones involved in the case?"

"Yeah, he targeted the social worker and lawyer, but why he killed the magistrate's secretary is still a mystery." Kane dropped into a chair and sighed wearily. "Then comes the circumstances around the Blackwater bombings." He stared at the ceiling. "We were that close." He held his forefinger and thumb an inch apart. "Thompson must have been satisfied with his revenge in DC and settled down in Blackwater, married and had a son. His wife died in a car wreck, he took up drinking and someone reported him to child protection. It was Connie Wood, who took his two-year-old son away and put him in foster care. He ran off with him on a visitation day and Sheriff Stuart arrested him for abduction. After the arrest Connie Wood stood up in court and labeled him an unfit father and the boy was placed in another home in Helena. The magistrate responsible was Abe Coleman."

Rubbing her temples Jenna peered at him. "Oh Lord, and then his son died in a housefire at his foster parents. That would have been the second trigger that caused all the recent bombings."

"Yeah." Carter gave her a long look. "Then what happened, Jo?"

"It was the profile I surmised at the get-go. The first bombings were all about him, his revenge on the system but the second wave of bombings specifically targeted the family unit because he'd lost his son. His son's death would have triggered the dormant psychopath and he wanted revenge." Jo shook her head. "The problem was, as he went along escalating, he was starting to enjoy himself. It was probably the first time he'd felt anything for a long time." She sighed. "Raping Connie Wood was his way of getting even and knowing he would kill her children was his revenge."

"I'd like to speak to the prisoner." Kane finished his coffee and stared at her. "He hasn't lawyered up yet, has he?"

"No." Jenna took in his relaxed demeanor but he couldn't hide the rage in his eyes. She looked at Carter. "Would you mind updating the files while we're gone? The Louan team are dropping by to take care of the prisoner overnight and they'll be here soon."

"Sure." Carter pulled out his phone. "Kalo sent me all the details."

"I'll re-write the charge sheet." Jo smiled at her. "We got him, guys."

Jenna followed Kane down to the cells. "Dave, don't do anything stupid." They stopped in the hallway to lock up their weapons. "I know you want revenge, but he'll pay for his crimes."

"I just want to look into his eyes, Jenna." Kane met her gaze. "I have to do this and put Annie's ghost to rest."

Swallowing the lump in her throat, Jenna nodded. When they reached the cell door, she swiped her card and as Kane walked inside, she operated the recording app on her phone. "Mr. Thompson, Deputy Kane would like to speak with you. You have been advised of your rights."

"I know my rights." Thompson sat on the bunk, passive and unthreatening.

"We have evidence against you for the DC bombings and the local ones, fingerprints, DNA from Pamela Stuart." Kane stood hands by his sides, relaxed. "I understand revenge and figure that was your motive for killing people. Being abused as a kid always leaves scars. Seeing your son taken away and then dying in a fire must have been devastating."

"I made them pay." Thompson lifted his gaze to Kane. "They deserved to die."

"You believed that innocent children just like your son deserved to die?" Kane inclined his head.

"No, they died to revenge my son." Thomson glared at Kane. "An eye for an eye."

"And what about the people in the truck you bombed?" Kane hadn't moved a muscle. "Why did you bomb their vehicle?"

"He was collateral damage." Thompson shrugged. "She was the target. That bitch refused to give me an appointment to see the magistrate. I'd sit there all damn day and he'd slip out the backdoor."

"That was pretty slick, getting a bomb into an agent's vehicle." Kane shook his head. "Now that took skill."

"It was easy." Thompson stood, placed his hands on his hips and smiled. "I waited for her to leave her desk and slipped a device inside her purse. She carried a nice big purse and then I followed her. As soon as she slipped into the truck, boom."

"So, for following orders, because it wasn't her decision to give you an appointment," Kane's expression hardened and he clenched and unclenched his fists, "you wiped out an entire family?"

"Can't you see why I hated happy families?" Thompson looked at him and smiled. "Those people needed to be stopped. First, the people in DC destroyed my life by not listening to what happened to me in foster care and then when I'd gotten my life back together, another group of so called, do-gooders took my son and destroyed my family. Why should they be happy when they were responsible for the death of my son?"

"So, you burned them all?" Kane's eyes flashed in anger.

"Yeah and I'd do it again in a heartbeat. They all deserved to die but the secretary, she just pissed me off. I didn't destroy her family, just her and her husband. So what?"

"Yeah, you destroyed her family." Kane stood rigid. Every muscle had tightened like a coiled snake. "She was pregnant."

The words hit Jenna like a sledgehammer. She let out a gasp and stopped the recording, that was privileged information. She had to get Kane out of the cell now. "Kane, I think that's enough."

"Not yet." Kane stepped closer but didn't touch Thompson. He just stared at him. "You'll be charged for killing a federal officer and officers of the court in DC. They'll want the death penalty and when that day comes, look out into the audience because I'll be there watching the show. No lethal injection for you, you'll swing or fry." He turned slowly and nodded to Jenna to open the door. "Let's go."

As they left the cells and the main door clicked shut behind them Kane sagged against the wall and closed his eyes. Jenna put her arms around him and hugged him. "I'm so sorry."

When he buried his face in her neck, she could feel dampness on her skin. She held him until he straightened and looked down at her. Not able to express the words to give him the comfort he needed, she patted his arm. "Will you be okay?"

"Yeah." Kane pushed a hand through his hair and cleared his throat. "I could almost feel Annie with me, as if she was standing beside me, confronting her killer." He looked at her, his eyes tragic. "She's at peace now. I can feel it in here." He touched his heart.

"You caught her killer and now her work here is done." Jenna leaned in and hugged him again. "She'd be so proud of you."

"The nightmare is over, Jenna. The image of her that haunted me has gone. From now on she'll only be a beautiful memory." Kane stepped back and looked into her eyes. "Let's finish up here and go home."

EPILOGUE

Three months later

As August arrived spreading more color across the landscape, Jenna leaned back on the new porch swing and watched Kane moving along the fence line with Rowley making repairs. The Thompson case had taken a long time to wind up. The amount of evidence they presented had been more than any case she'd handled before and the hours had been long and tedious. One of the most chilling pieces of evidence they'd found during this time were the cryptic posts Thompson had made on social media. Each one coincided with the bombings and gave a frightening insight to his disturbed mind. They'd searched his house and found a cellar, the entrance hidden inside a closet with all the evidence they needed to prove without doubt, he was making explosive devices. For now, Thompson waited in federal prison, without bail until his case came to trial but with all the evidence against him and the confession she had taped, the chances of him walking free was more than a million to one.

Roger Suffolk remained a free man with no charges laid against him. Dawn Richardson had been placed with a foster family out of Snakeskin Gully, and no amount of persuasion would make her return to Louan to stand witness against Suffolk. With no other women coming forward with a complaint, he had no charges to answer. After extensive investigation into Mrs. Suffolk's car wreck, the case stalled when they discovered the vehicle had been crushed by the insurance company. All they had as evidence was the previous examinations of the vehicle, which cleared Suffolk of any wrongdoing.

It had been great working with Jo and Carter again and watching them fly away had tugged at her heartstrings. It seemed they'd all become close and now they made up part of her extended "family". She looked forward to visiting Snakeskin Gully in her downtime to meet Jo's daughter, Jaime and spend a relaxing weekend with friends but she had to admit, the FBI held no allure for her. She preferred her life as the sheriff of Black Rock Falls.

At last, life had gone back to normal and three months without a case had Jenna scratching her head. It was like waiting for the other shoe to drop and the anticipation grew with each passing month. She patted Duke on the head and rubbed Pumpkin's ears. How easy it was to make animals feel safe. The pain Kane had carried deep inside for so long had faded and she believed he'd finally turned the corner. He laughed more and had an easy going way about him. It was as if she was seeing the man before the car bombing emerging from a cocoon of sadness.

They'd spent alternate weekends working on the ranches. Jake and Sandy Rowley's ranch needed a lot of work and she'd pitch in with Kane to help them. With nothing much happening at the office, she looked forward to getting her hands dirty. She'd also spent some time looking over applications for another deputy. She had funding for two more but with Rowley's old house sitting empty, she could take her pick from a ton of experienced men or women from around the state. She put the notion on the back burner as the front gate alarm buzzed. She headed to the front door, in the screen she made out Sandy waving at the camera and opened the gate to let her in.

As Sandy came up the driveway, she sounded her horn and Rowley and Kane picked up their gear and headed toward her. She jumped out the truck and suddenly the three of them went crazy, jumping around and laughing. The next instant, Duke leapt to his feet and headed toward them barking like he'd gone mad and ran in big circles around them. Bemused, Jenna stared at them and looked at Pumpkin. "Hmm maybe there's a special on peach pies at Aunt Betty's?"

They all climbed into the truck and headed for the house. Jenna stood to meet them as they tumbled out all grinning like Cheshire cats. "What's happened? Did you win the lottery or something?"

"Better." Sandy grinned from ear to ear. "I've just talked the guys into building me a nursery."

A LETTER FROM D.K. HOOD

Dear Reader,

I am delighted you chose my novel, and joined me once again in the exciting world of Jenna Alton and Dave Kane in *Promises in the Dark*.

If you'd like to keep up to date with all my latest releases, just sign up at the website link below. Your details will never be shared and you can unsubscribe at any point.

www.bookouture.com/dk-hood

Writing this story has been a thrilling adventure for me. Delving into the lives of ex-Secret Agents and serial killers was a dream come true. I enjoyed researching every aspect of the crime scenes.

If you enjoyed my story, I would be very grateful if you could leave a review and recommend my book to your friends and family.

I would love to hear from you – so please get in touch on my Facebook page or Twitter or through my website.

Thank you so much for your support.
D.K. Hood

 @DKHood_Author

 dkhoodauthor

 www.dkhood.com

 dkhood-author.blogspot.com.au

ACKNOWLEDGMENTS

Many thanks for the tremendous support from the team at Bookouture, to the wonderful readers who took the time to post great reviews of my books, and to those amazing people who hosted me on their blogs.